# Curiouser

*a novel*

Christina Coryell

Books by Christina Coryell:


<u>The Camdyn Series</u>
A Reason to Run
A Reason to Be Alone
A Reason to Forget
For No Reason
Unwrapped


<u>Girls of Wonder Lane</u>
Simply Mad
Crowned
Curiouser


Facebook: www.facebook.com/AuthorChristinaCoryell
Twitter: @c_tinacoryell
www.christinacoryell.com

# Curiouser

To Mom and Dad,

For teaching me about
hard work and kindness,
and for all of your love and support

# Chapter One

## Alexis

Four years have passed since I woke up on the other side of the mirror. That morning I stared at my reflection, feeling beautiful and accomplished and ready to conquer the world. By the time I glimpsed my own countenance the next morning, everything had been ruined.

It would seem that one would sense a huge switch like that before it occurred, but that didn't happen for me. I dipped a toe into Wonderland, and suddenly things shifted. Everything made sense, while nothing made sense. Toxic formulas invited me to taste, mocking "Eat Me" or "Drink Me" as though they could alter reality. And I did what they suggested, making myself more noticeable or invisible, until the white rabbit appeared and I found myself careening after him, headlong into a hole.

Things were definitely not as they appeared, and the aftereffects of the descent clouded my brain. I grew convinced that I was larger than life and my arms and legs were poking precariously through the windows of the house, yet I was so insignificant that an ocean of tears could sweep me away.

Trapped on the wrong side of the mirror, I could see the girl before she stepped inside, innocent and trusting. The desire to warn her overcame me, but it was too late.

There was no return, and it was too late.

So I've learned to make the best of the nonsense in my own way, while I'm dwelling on the other side of the mirror. There are glimpses of beauty here, after all. Sometimes I see wonder on this side, like when I take a moment to glance behind me at the sleepy little darling in my backseat. Such beauty doesn't belong in chaos, which is why I decided to try to break free. If I manage to get myself far enough away from where I first entered the rabbit hole, perhaps we can find ourselves on the proper side of the mirror after a time. We can start fresh, forging new identities with brand new reflections, only slightly altered by their pasts.

But then my eyes drift to the rearview mirror and the vision of the red pickup truck pulling a trailer, its driver peering straight ahead toward my car, mocking me with his uninterested stare. This is no beginning for him, but simply a frivolous lark of an adventure. Why shouldn't he tail us the entire way to Louisville, forcing himself into our lives and stranding my forward motion to a permanent halt? Jake McAuliffe doesn't care which side of the mirror he's on—he works both with ease, proffering his smile on unsuspecting new Alices, using that dimple in his left cheek to his full advantage.

And so I force my focus back to the road ahead of me, determined to do whatever it takes to begin again, fully aware that my past is barely beyond my taillights.

The road ahead of me stretches on with barely any traffic in sight, so I glance back at my dozing daughter, her hair the shade of brown sugar twisting in soft curls under her chin. Bailey Nicole Jennings is three and a half, and although part of me feels that I've always known my daughter somewhere deep in my soul, I also wake up most mornings feeling like I might have been lost in a dream and she doesn't really exist. She is the sole individual I can credit for keeping me sane some days, but she has also been the reason for most of my downward spirals. Not that I regret her presence in my back seat—far from it. The only thing causing me consternation at the moment is the red pickup behind me, and that's only because I'm allowing the man inside to steal my peace.

Folks in my neck of the woods were plenty shocked when my little beauty was born and I decided to name her Jennings, completely ignoring her father. Shouldn't I have ignored him, though, when he opted to do the same to me?

I shake myself out of that mental torture, knowing to dwell on it now when he is so clearly in my sights will only drive me half insane. My focus on making this trip should reach no farther than the occupants of my own vehicle, making a future for myself and my daughter. What Jake feels he has to prove in following us is beyond the scope of my imagination at present, and I'd like to keep him out of my line of thinking at least until we reach our destination.

Bailey takes the opportunity to release a slight sigh as she shifts in her car seat. She's nearly the age I was at the first memory that I can readily recall, which almost sends me into a panic when I realize that simple fact. My wish for my daughter is to give her a life she deserves and love her enough for two parents, but when I think that she might soon be at the stage where she will remember our day-to-day happenings, it causes me more fear than I'd like to admit.

My earliest memory always draws me back to five years old, my parents' little house, so much red, and that fateful day when I lost a bit of my innocence.

Nick and Crystal Jennings were blessed in the early days of their marriage with two healthy pregnancies that resulted in two very different daughters. Mom says that I was an easy baby, never giving her any trouble, sleeping on a schedule, seemingly pleased at the mere thought of being alive. From the moment she came wailing and screaming into the world, however, it was a well-established fact that Heather would be the daughter who craved attention. There was never any serious consideration given to what our roles would be within the family unit, because we simply were who we were. It didn't seem profitable for me to thwart nature's design, so I learned to blend into the shadows whenever Heather wanted her spotlight.

Dad was a preacher in Jackson, Tennessee in my early years. Mom supported him by loving everyone imaginable, giving selflessly of her time and resources, and trying to raise two daughters in their parents' footsteps. I was an easy sell to the idea; Heather, on the other hand...

She was four when she confronted me on the validity of our parents' convictions, and although it was par for the course with my younger sister and would be for the remainder of time, my five-year-old brain found her rebellious spirit distressing and unnerving.

"Those cookies are for tonight's meeting," Mom told us both as we stood there in the kitchen, me wearing a romper with strings tied at the shoulders, while Heather was attired in the requisite pink leotard with a purple tutu. I simply nodded my understanding, while Heather's head remained stationary, not acknowledging that she heard. The twinkle in her eye was unmistakable, because I had seen it before.

The instant Mom left the room, Heather climbed onto a chair and placed her chubby little fist on the counter.

"Mama said no." It was a superfluous statement, because Heather heard our mother just as clearly as I had, but I felt the need to reiterate the simple fact.

"So?" Her sticky fingers reached out for a cookie, plucking it up into her palm, greedily pressing her lips together.

"God can see you, Heather," I whispered, glancing back at where our mother had just disappeared into the hallway.

"Uh-uh." She shook her head at me, the ringlets that formed at the bottom of her dark hair bouncing with the movement. "Didn't last time."

She was always slightly ornery at best, but she didn't usually try to justify her actions.

"How do you know?"

"He didn't stop me."

"You're supposed to stop your own self," I informed her, taking my role seriously. *Look out for your sister,* my parents always told me. Goodness knows I tried.

"They just tells you that to get you to do stuff," Heather informed me as she climbed down, pinching off a piece of that cookie to shove between her lips. My conflicted young mind watched as she swung her arms back and forth on the way out of the room. When she paused at the doorway to stuff the rest of the cookie into her mouth, she gave me a rude, smirking grin, showing me the cookie mess through her teeth.

She strolled into the hallway as though she had done nothing wrong, and for the first time in my short life I wondered if she might be right. She had blatantly done something she was told not to do, and there was no adverse reaction. There likely wouldn't be one, either, unless I decided to go against my nature and react like a tattle-tale.

Her words bothered me more than I liked to admit. Though they were spoken out of petulance, they rattled something deep inside that I hadn't bothered to try to that point. They affected me so much, in fact, that I decided to attempt to prove her right later that evening.

We had a modest ranch-style home, with three small bedrooms and one bathroom. The bathroom situation would not prove to be a nuisance until later in life, when Heather decided she had to look her best at everyone else's expense. On that particular day, though, I sat fully clothed on the lid of the toilet, staring at the green and black-marbled Formica countertop. It was clean, of course, just like everything always was, with no water spots or toothpaste remnants. Cleanliness was next to Godliness—another mantra from my mother that Heather didn't subscribe to, but seemed to be written somewhere on my conscience.

Directly underneath that countertop, in the first drawer next to the toilet, dwelled a box that held untold treasures. I had seen them when my mother readied herself for special occasions... bright colors, plush brushes, and tubes filled with richly-hued creams. We were not to touch, and even Heather had been sensible enough to obey that command. But if I was going to test it, I was going to test it in a big way, full-out and brash as though I were preparing for my own funeral.

Rising from the toilet, I stood before the drawer, wrapping my small fingers around the brass handle. With one gentle tug it moved toward me, the yellow box adorned with a painting of blue hydrangeas coming into view. My hands closed around the box as I drew it out of the space, placing it atop the counter so gently it didn't even make a whisper of noise. As I pulled the top of the box up, the hinge creaked and the lid sprung in the air a couple inches before I pushed it fully open.

The choices were endless, and I knew the rules: *Never touch the things Mommy keeps in this box. Understand, Heather? Off limits.* She never felt the necessity to ask if I understood, because of course I did. She never had to tell me anything twice.

Still, it was I who stood there staring at the makeup in the box, waiting for something to stop me from reaching into that treasure trove. Other than my little internal whisper of my mother's voice, nothing was coming through. Grasping a black tube with a shock of red under the clear cap, I drew it toward me, staring at its contents. Lipstick. There was no hiding lipstick, was there?

The cap slid off rather easily into my palm, and I pressed the waxy paste to my bottom lip, drawing a line with the deep crimson. There was no lightning, or Formica splitting in two, or the mirror bubbling as a physical confirmation of my wrongdoing. It was simply wrong, what I was doing.

Determined to take it as far as necessary, I pushed harder, grinding the lipstick against my mouth until my entire pout was blood red. When I was finally satisfied, I placed the clear cap back on the tube and shoved the lipstick into its place in the box, returning it to the drawer. One swift push back into place and the bathroom was returned to its previous state, no sign of anything having taken place in that room besides the rather obvious stain on my face.

I'd done it, hadn't I? For a moment, I was as carefree about the consequences of my actions as Heather. She would have felt triumphant, I'm certain—disobeying never seemed to have an adverse reaction on my little sister, even when it led to punishment. There was no triumph in my gaze, though, as I stared at my reflection. The girl staring back at me smacked of sorrow, shame, and remorse.

Hastily grabbing a tissue from the box on the counter, I began brushing at the red, trying to make it disappear. With each swipe it spread across my face, uglier and more distorted than it had been a moment before.

Minute after minute passed while I tried desperately to erase my guilt, pronouncing it more boldly on my face all the while. Instead of a little pucker of color, my entire chin looked burned and bruised, the area under my nose turning the shade of a ripe strawberry. I moved to retrieve a washcloth from the linen hutch to my left, then shoved it under the faucet, running warm water until it was soaked through. After wringing most of the water free, I lifted that cloth to my face, rubbing at the red splotches until I felt my skin tingling from the pressure and the force.

Finally, the lipstick appeared to be on the cloth instead of my skin, which was mottled with red spots that appeared almost rash-like. I wasn't one naturally given to blushing, but it appeared that I was overly embarrassed, or that someone had slapped my cheeks. The initial results of my deed had been erased, but the consequences remained on my delicate skin.

Dropping the washcloth into the trash, I placed a couple crumpled tissues over it to hide the evidence. With a short pause at the door to listen for footsteps, I eased myself into the hall and pretended to itch my nose so my hand would be in front of the proof, should someone happen to see me. When no one seemed to notice my reemergence, I headed straight for my bedroom, closing the door to the outside as I flung myself under my bed until the evidence passed, if it ever would.

Hiding there under the bed, one thing was certain to me with more clarity than anything up to that point in my young life:

He saw. In my heart, I felt it deeply. Heather was wrong, He saw everything, and I hated trying to hide the red.

# Chapter Two

## Alexis

My eyes lift to the side mirror, where I notice the red pickup behind me again. Red, like the memory that was just flooding my mind. My heart was ready to be completely removed from Jake, separated by the miles and a state line. Not that he ever had a piece of my heart, or even a sliver for that matter. Bailey does, though, and I despise the fact that he can have so much influence over our lives.

It's been only the last six months or so that he began taking an interest in Bailey, and despite the fact that I longed to block his involvement, my sense of propriety told me it wasn't right. At first I only allowed him an hour or two with her at a time, but once he had proven trustworthy, I allowed him to watch her on Saturdays while I was working.

It was my own fault, I suppose. The call came about the interview in Louisville, and instead of trusting my gut instincts and leaving Bailey with my parents, I allowed him to convince me. It wasn't difficult, to be honest…the man could be smooth enough to convince a nun to give up her vows on her deathbed.

Had I been on the phone with him, the outcome likely would have been different. Telephone Jake is cocky to the point of seeming smarmy, that flirtatious tone in his voice grating over my nerves like the tines of a rake scraping a leaf pile on a concrete slab. Not that he's flirted with me in years—he basically loathes the fact that I exist, and the feeling's largely mutual.

There's something charming about the face-to-face Jake, though. His words drip with earnestness, his countenance growing expressive, the tone of his voice becoming gentle. He's practiced in getting his way, and those easy good looks don't hurt his cause.

He dropped Bailey off that particular day, and when I told him about the interview he casually offered to watch her for the weekend.

"I'd like to be able to spend some time with her, especially if you're thinking about moving." He said that with such a sincere look on his face, I actually found myself considering his words. It would be wrong for me to withhold Bailey's father from her when he was honestly making an effort for a change, right?

My lips began agreeing before I fully convinced my head, and once the words were out, it was too late to take them back.

When I answered the door that Sunday after returning to Jackson, he looked slightly worse for wear, but Bailey was in one piece and seemed happy. It was only after he left that the words began tumbling out.

"Jay take me to see Cam. I sleeped in her bed."

And just like that, a million mental images flooded my mind, looking nearly identical with the exception of the minor details. Jake and some half-naked woman letting *my daughter* sleep between them on the bed. Jake and some half-naked woman letting *my daughter* sleep to the left of them on the bed...to the right of them on the bed...above them, below them...my heart constricting in my throat. Jake and some half-naked woman not sleeping while *my daughter* was on the bed.

Outbursts of temper were never something I chose to exhibit. Even in my lowest moments, I portrayed a composed resolve that I managed to practice to flawless execution. Perhaps it was because I was accustomed to seeing various forms of hysterics from my own sibling, or maybe simply because I knew what was expected. In either case, I was the steady one.

That trait came in handy in that moment, while I was inwardly seething but didn't want to frighten my innocent little girl. Even though I remained composed on the outside, inside I was tossing furniture and vowing to kill the man. How could he ask to let him spend time with her when all he wanted to do was take her to the house of one of his random conquests? Most likely someone he met at the bar the weekend before, and Bailey simply got in the way.

"You slept in the bed with Cam?" I calmly attempted to clarify, my knuckles turning white where I clenched my fingers into fists.

"Uh-huh." She bent her head to the ground, rolling herself into an awkward variation of a somersault. "I weared her clothes."

*My daughter slept with a bar fly wearing one of her slinky nightgowns.*

"What did this Cam look like?" I asked, fighting the emotion in my voice.

"She pretty, like an angel. And she sing to me, but sad and cried. Jay hugged her and kissed her face."

My mind mentally processed her story. *Jake took my daughter to see his lover of the week. Broke up with her, and she cried. He likely took Bailey to soften the blow, but figured he might as well have one more night. Put my little beauty to bed...*

So I didn't feel guilty at all when I received the call that I got the job in Louisville. Bailey wouldn't be able to see Jake anymore? Thank God, and good riddance. I didn't say a word to him about Cam, the sleeping arrangements, Bailey's tales... Instead, I pretended like nothing was wrong and simply told him we were moving to Kentucky. He didn't argue, and didn't beg me to let him see Bailey. I thought we were in the clear.

But life would have the last laugh on me, which is increasingly obvious as I gaze into my rearview mirror once again.

My mom loved reading us bedtime stories. I remembered that from an early age, and while I don't recall specific instances before learning to read on my own, I know that they occurred.

Sometimes when I read a book to Bailey I find that it's vaguely familiar, like déjà vu. Other times a story will instantly trigger memories of something Heather said, usually betraying her smart mouth. Most of her comments were followed by a scowl or scolding from our mother, but those things rolled off Heather's back without so much as a second glance.

I had one such reemergence of a memory just a couple weeks ago, as I was reading *Alice's Adventures in Wonderland* to Bailey. We were laughing together at the nonsense, while I made funny voices to try to coerce her into giggles. It suddenly hit me that my mother had read the exact same book to me, making funny voices, grinning at my own laughter. The story of Alice fascinated me— having a grand adventure simply by being curious and living in a dreamland fueled by imagination.

"I can picture you as Alice, sweetheart," Mom said to me with a smile. "You have the calm demeanor to try to restore order to a nonsensical world."

Heather's coarse laugh sounded through her nose as she threw her seven-year-old head back. "She couldn't be Alice. She's the boring old sister trying to make everybody be boring."

"I'm not boring," I protested, hugging my fluffy white stuffed dog close to my chest.

"Yep." She lowered herself to the floor, making a point of fanning her hair about her face as she spread her body out on the carpet. "You wouldn't chase a rabbit down a hole. You wouldn't even get up. You'd be afraid to break the dumb rules."

"That's not nice, Heather. Apologize to your sister."

She let out an exaggerated sigh as she sat up, her annoyance clear in her glare as she tilted her head in my direction. "I'm sorry you're boring, Alex."

"My name's not Alex," I countered.

"Alex in Boringland."

"That's enough, Heather. Go to your room."

Heather waited until she was almost to the door to turn and stick her tongue out at me, when she knew Mom wouldn't see her. Heather didn't always fight with me, but if she wasn't the focus of our games she could only go a few hours at best without goading me about something or other.

Mom left her finger between the pages while she closed the book, a visual acknowledgement that we didn't have to be finished. I appreciated her signal to me that Heather didn't run every aspect of my life.

"Do you think I'm boring?" I squeaked out in a whisper.

"No. You're kind, and caring, and a good girl. The world needs more of all those things."

"I'd follow the rabbit, because I'd want to help him."

"Of course you would."

"And I like to have fun."

She stretched her arm around my shoulders and pulled me against her before she uttered another word. "I know that, and Heather knows too. Don't let her upset you."

I tried not to. Really, I did.

When I woke up the next morning, though, I found a giant sign on my bedroom door that read BORINGLAND, and she refused to stop calling me Alex. Mom said to let her be and she'd forget it in a day or two.

Yet here I am, twenty-five years old, still letting it be. Still waiting for her to stop calling me Alex.

# Chapter Three

## Jake

There are times when an open highway feels less like an escape and more like a torment. Moments when the freedom it affords looks like a prison. Had it not been for my focus on the taillights of that old white Mitsubishi for the last hundred miles, I might have driven myself half mad thinking about the different directions this road could lead.

Truth be told, the only direction I wanted to travel was back. Back in time, back the other way, back home.

I suppose there's a thought process a man goes through when he's burned every bridge that held his life together in the first place. And mine are scorched, singed, and still smoldering. The only one remaining is the rickety rope bridge between my red pickup and that white car, and with one false move it might snap in two.

Alexis tried to sever it before we ever left Jackson. "You really don't need to come along," she insisted. "There are people who can help me move."

But I'd made a promise, and I never break my promises.

*… like I told you before, heartbreaker: I always keep my…*

"Promises," I state to the empty cab of the truck as I clench my fist around the steering wheel. "You can't get any of it back, either. Everything…gone, just like that."

The white Mitsubishi taps its brakes, so I slow a little behind the car, putting a few extra yards between us. She's not exactly thrilled to have me accompanying her on this journey; I can see it in her eyes every time she glances up in the rearview, but I'm not about to give her the satisfaction of acknowledging that fact.

She can keep seething at me from a distance, and I'll just pretend everything's fine.

Trying to force my attention away from the situation, I tap the scan button on the radio dial, searching for a new station to fill the silence. Somehow winding up on static, I hit the button again.

*Your cheating heart...*

My palm slams into the button, silencing Hank before he gets out a full sentence. Not that he would make me feel guilty even if I heard it. After all, I haven't done anything.

In my case, though, not doing anything is more than enough. At least if I'd done something, I'd be driving around with a memory instead of simply feeling like a tool. A memory worth having, at least, and not the one that keeps jogging through my mind. Blonde curls, toned legs, those tennis shoes pounding out a rhythm on the pavement in front of my truck while I let out a low whistle. That memory isn't doing me any favors.

*How do I look my best friend in the eye every day, knowing I want what he has? Knowing I want his wife?*

Squinting my eyes, I force a shake of my head to steer clear of the things I said. To try to forget the way those blue eyes searched mine as I told her I never break my promises, even though I wanted to. A hundred times I wanted to. I wanted her.

It should have been harder to say, shouldn't it? It should have stuck in my throat, where I'd have to force out the words almost against my will. Instead, it slid out effortlessly and uninhibited. Not like the words I said to him. Those edged out in reluctance and severed the strongest bonds of friendship I've ever created.

Recalling the conversation almost makes me sick. The sound of betrayal. The absolute self-loathing I felt at that moment.

Was it really only two days ago?

"Whatever it is that's happened, it'll be okay," Parker told me over the phone. "You've been through tougher before, I'm sure. I've seen you go through some pretty rough times, Jake."

"This one's different. I don't have a choice."

"You always have a choice, so don't run out on your friends. Camdyn and I will—"

"I can't stop thinking about her."

I hadn't prepared to use those words. There was going to be a generalized reason I was leaving, some well wishes. But when he began trying to convince me not to leave, they immediately separated us like a giant wall.

"About who?"

I couldn't...didn't have the nerve to speak her name.

"Who?" Parker asked again, more forcefully this time. "Not Cam."

"I swear to you, I haven't touched her."

"Haven't touched her? You feel the need to tell me that? That I could even think she would..." His voice trailed off, thick with emotion. "Did you tell her this? Did you tell my...*my wife*...that you're in love with her? Did you?"

"No, man. No."

"Don't. She's dealing with enough crap right now. Don't you dare add to her troubles, you hear me?"

Something popped in the background—a door being slammed, something being thrown—I couldn't be certain.

"Answer me, Jake!"

"I heard you, okay? I heard you."

"This is my fault, all of it. None of this would have happened if I was there." His sigh was loud on the other end of the line. "What kind of husband am I? I can't protect her from anything."

"You should be home with her," I agreed. "She needs you."

"Shut up. I can't believe you have the nerve to try to tell me what *my* wife needs. In fact, don't even think about her."

"I can't control my—"

"Get it under control then." Something else clanged in the background, and then I heard the sound of two boards banging together, along with a string of expletives. "You're a lousy friend." More expletives, causing me to cringe because Parker never swore.

"That ever cross your mind? Maybe I shouldn't be lusting after my best friend's wife?"

"Of course it crossed my mind. That's why I've never touched her."

"Because if she was anybody else's wife, what difference would it make? Just shoot first and ask questions later? You don't know the guy, so what if you take his wife?"

"That's what you think of me?"

The sound of boards slamming together sounded again in the background. "It's not what I think, it's what I know. We're friends, remember? I know you're a little fuzzy on the rules of that sort of relationship, but it entails having the other guy's back. I didn't drop my end of the bargain."

I knew we were friends, too, because his accusation stung way more than it would have coming from anyone else.

"I'm still your friend, Parker."

The noise on the other end of the line grew eerily quiet.

"Be a good role model for your daughter, then. And have a little self-control. I'd have told you that a long time ago if I wasn't a lousy friend, too."

The white Mitsubishi veers to the exit ramp, and I follow without a lot of thought. Alexis gave me the address in Louisville in case we got separated, but I have no intention of that happening. If not for that car leading me blindly the whole way there, I probably wouldn't make it to the destination at all, simply because my heart's not in it.

Bailey's...

Well, she's a definite puzzle to me. There's a protective instinct when she's with me, and I definitely care about what happens to her. She's sort of cute, with her garbled words and the way she's just figuring out how the world works. The fact that she has a dimple in her cheek like me is pretty cool, but I mostly enjoy that for the annoyance factor it provides when it comes to Alexis.

The thing that bothers me the most is the fact that I never feel like her dad. I feel like a sperm donor, pretty much confirming what Alexis has insinuated countless times, which also sets me on edge. Maybe that makes it harder for me to bond with Bailey—the fact that I know Alexis is her mother.

I should feel like her dad, right?

As she pulls into a McDonald's parking lot, I sound my annoyance through a groan inside the cab of my truck. Getting this trip over with sooner rather than later is preferable. "Bailey needs to eat," I can almost hear her saying. Most likely true, but even I know not to take a three-year-old into McDonald's if you're in a hurry. That's practically a no-brainer.

It takes me a minute to park the truck with the trailer attached, and by the time I'm finished, the girls are already inside. Pulling open the glass door, I see the two of them standing near the counter. Dressed in a sports jersey and a baseball cap, if I saw Alexis from the back I might think she was a guy for a split second. Bailey is latched to her mom's leg, brown curls slightly mashed against one side of her head like she was laying on them in the car. I step up just in front of Alexis and drag out my wallet.

"Hi Jay."

"Hey Bailey." Turning, I offer her a smile. "What's up? You take a nap in the car?"

"I felled asleep."

With nothing else to offer, I nod and glance at her mom. She never fights with me, but that's only because something holds her back. Every time she looks at me, it's plain to see she wants to tear me apart.

"What do you want, Bailey?" I ask. "Something to eat?"

"We can pay for our own food," Alexis pipes up.

"Bailey can pay for her own food?"

She hesitates, probably thinking she didn't word her statement exactly right, but I pushed her buttons and she doesn't want to argue with me. Instead, she'll clam up like she always does, her eyes burning a hole in my skull. Just once I wish she'd haul off and punch me and get it over with so we could act like civilized people for a change.

What she really meant to say was that she didn't want to owe me anything, not even the couple bucks it takes to buy a cheeseburger. I received her message loud and clear.

"She likes hamburgers with nothing on them."

I can tell Alexis would rather attempt walking on broken glass than give me that information. Part of me wants to shake her and tell her to knock it off, but it's her game and I'm going to let her play it as long as she wants.

"Can I take your order, sir?" the teenage girl behind the counter asks. When I turn to look at her, she immediately clamps her gaze on her register.

"The little lady wants a hamburger meal with a milk, and she doesn't want anything on the hamburger." The cashier's so wide-eyed, I try to put her at ease by smiling. "Sorry for being difficult, but what a lady wants, a lady gets, right?"

Her cheeks turn pink, and she focuses on the register again. "Yes, sir."

"Alexis?"

She doesn't answer immediately, so I turn my head to where she's standing behind me, wearing that look I've seen too many times to count.

"I'm not really hungry."

Sure, she's hungry. She'd rather starve than let me pay for her food, though, so we begin another round of the game.

"I'll have a Big Mac and a large coffee," I tell the cashier, retrieving a ten dollar bill from my wallet.

"Will that be for here or to go?"

"Here." The fact that I happen to say the word at the same time Alexis says "to go" causes the cashier's eyes to dart back and forth between us. "Here, please. Thanks a lot."

Bailey's already noticed the play area and is pulling her mom's arm trying to head in that direction. Since the choices are to head toward the slides or stand next to me, Alexis and Bailey quickly disappear.

She only lets Bailey play for about ten minutes before she takes her to wash her hands so she can eat her burger. My Big Mac is long gone, so there's really nothing for the two of us adults to do but sit here awkwardly not talking to one another while Bailey eats. The fact that she's a slow eater makes it even more excruciating.

Finally, she says she's finished and Alexis breathes a sigh of relief.

"Let's go to the restroom, sweetie," she says to Bailey.

"Don't need to." She fumbles with the legs of the toy she received in her kids' meal, moving them back and forth.

"I need to, so you have to come with me."

"Go ahead, I'll watch her," I offer. There's no mistaking that look on her face, and I have zero doubt that she wants to tell me no. How can she, though, when it seems so ridiculous? What possible explanation could she throw out for not letting me watch my own daughter while she goes to the restroom?

Rising from her chair, she refuses to look at me as she heads away. Bailey doesn't look at me, either, being too invested in that toy she's holding.

"Your daughter's really well-behaved," I hear a voice behind me. "You and your wife must be really proud of her."

Turning, my eyes lock on a woman who looks to be in her mid- to late-forties, stylishly dressed and holding her phone in her hands.

"She's not my wife, but thank you."

"Her's Alex," Bailey says, which causes the stranger to smile at her.

"Your kids seem to be having fun," I casually mention, hearing the ear-piercing screams coming from my right and attributing them to her offspring, since she's the only other person in the area.

"Oh, they're my grandkids."

"Really? You don't look old enough to have grandkids."

"Come on, Bailey, time to go," Alexis interrupts, following what must be the shortest restroom visit ever recorded. Someone should alert Guinness about it.

Bailey doesn't move. Not a flinch or a twitch or anything to acknowledge that she heard a voice.

"Bailey, listen to your mom," I say. She lifts her head and peers at me under those long, dark eyelashes, but she doesn't argue. Her tiny tennis shoes hit the floor as she rises to her feet.

As I gather the trash and take it to the receptacle, the girls head toward the door. By the time they reach the car, I've managed to catch up with them, and I tell Bailey "see you later" as her mom straps her into her car seat.

"If we get separated, I'll see you there," Alexis tells me without bothering to glance in my direction, still focusing on Bailey.

"No worries. I'll be right on your tail the whole way, Alex."

She springs back from the car, those dark eyes drilling into me. I thought I'd seen all her icy glares and flat dirty looks, but this one takes the cake. Somehow I've warranted such an imposing stare-down that I'm almost convinced her eyes really could pierce me. Surely she'll let me have it now—scream, pummel me, call me an imbecile…something.

But no, the glossy mask slides back on as she steps around the side of the car without a word and shuts herself into the driver's seat. Still immersing herself neck-deep in whatever game she's playing.

Without question, though, something I did just upped the ante.

# Chapter Four

## Alexis

The nerve of that man! The unmitigated, unadulterated gall of that man!

Weaving his manipulative, impulsive, irresponsible tentacles into every situation. Flirting with that still-in-high school McDonald's cashier, and that woman who was old enough to be his mother. I swear, the man would likely flirt with a rock if he thought he could make its eyes trail after him when he walked away.

To live in a world where rocks had eyes. Maybe then his kind couldn't hide under them. Maybe then I could actually go to the restroom and leave him in the company of my daughter, instead of simply walking a few steps away and spying on them because I don't trust him.

And even Bailey, blindly obeying him just to show me up. "Bailey, listen to your mom." Naturally he'd say that in front of other people to make me look weak and pathetic, and she'd choose that instant to get up like she probably planned to do in the first place. Purely a coincidence that she did it after he spoke, but I'm sure it looked like...

And where does he get off calling me Alex? Twisting the knife a little after he'd already sliced through me with that whole Bailey obeying him bit.

Ugh, I hate him.

No, not really, because my dad taught me years ago not to hate. So I guess I just dislike him. Really, really can't stand him. Maybe loathe him even.

Plus, I'm not too happy about the fact that my stomach is growling right about now.

And I abhor the fact that I still need to pee.

⁂

"Will Gump and Nan come?"

Bailey's quiet voice is enough to make me turn down the volume on the rock song streaming through the car speakers. Usually music has a way of calming me down, but the sight of that man in the truck behind me is demanding some loud, screaming guitars and pounding drum beats.

"Do you mean to our new house in Louisville? Sure, they'll come sometime. Probably not right away, but we'll come back to see them."

"I want Gump."

"I want Gump too, baby, but we'll be alright."

Bailey and my dad have been in love with each other since the first time their gazes locked together. Maybe even before that, really. One of the nurses placed Bailey in his arms in the hospital room, and he stared down at her little red face as though dumbfounded. He traced the side of her small hand with his index finger, and she clamped onto it as though she'd been waiting nine whole months to find it. I'm pretty sure she seized a piece of his heart that day, too, which was evident as I watched him cry with my baby in his arms.

His reaction naturally led to crying for me as well, which was unfortunate as my mom hadn't taken her pictures yet and I was already swollen and puffy. Add a blotchy, red face to the mix, and the whole lot of us looked half crazy.

It's a beautiful memory.

The first time Bailey attempted to name my dad, he was pulling her around the yard in a wagon. She was eighteen months old, or maybe twenty, and she was giggling loudly enough as he jostled her around the yard that I'm sure even the distant neighbors could hear. He paused a few minutes later to catch his breath, and she was most definitely unpleased with his action. She balled her hand into a fist, puckered her lips, and yelled, "Gump!"

He was Grandpa. That's the only name I had ever used in front of Bailey, other than Dad of course, but her version of Grandpa burst forth as Gump. He loved it so much, for the next week he asked Mom every night if we were having shrimp for dinner.

Mom got so tired of him asking, she made him shrimp four nights in a row. He probably hasn't eaten shrimp since.

"And Hoppy?"

Lifting my eyes to stare at Bailey in the rearview mirror, I fight to avoid sighing.

"Sweetie, Hoppy is in one of the boxes in the trailer behind Jake's truck. Remember? I told you that earlier."

Three times, at least. Hoppy is Bailey's best friend in the whole wide world. I've heard this statement more times than I can count. The fact that he's a stuffed rabbit with one ear longer than the other and one of his button eyes cracked in two is irrelevant to my daughter. He's real, he matters, and I'm a horrible person.

Should I have remembered to put Hoppy in the car next to Bailey? Maybe even buckle him in as though he were real? Probably. Putting him in a dark, scary box isn't earning me any mom points, but I haven't been raking those in recently anyway. Par for the course.

"Hoppy crying in Jay's truck."

"Hoppy's not crying, sweetheart. His little button eyes don't have any tear ducts."

"He sad. Jay don't love him."

*Hmm, seems to me that should make Hoppy want to dance on the face of the moon.*

I begin laughing out loud at my little inside joke, and Bailey doesn't appreciate it.

"Not funny Mommy."

"I'm sorry, baby. I'm not laughing at you."

"Hoppy's not funny."

"Hoppy's not funny? Are you kidding me? Don't you remember what he did last night?" Bailey tilts her head as she stares into the rearview mirror, meeting my eyes. "He picked up that stick you brought in from outside, and he used it like a cane. What was that song he was singing and dancing to?"

"Ummm…" She pinches her lips tightly together and her eyes dart upward, as though she's trying to stare into her memory.

"'Stayin' Alive?'"

"Yeah, ah, ah, ah, alive!"

We giggle together as she grins and attempts to dance in her car seat, which limits her motions to a few wiggles and squeals.

"See?" I say when she calms down. "Hoppy's probably back there in that trailer teaching all the other animals to dance. Maybe they're practicing an entire show that they'll perform once we get to our new house."

She seems okay with that explanation, because she reaches her fist up to rub her arm against her nose and lets out a sigh.

"Hoppy *is* funny," she decides, turning her attention out the window.

And just like that, a few of my mom points return to me. Very few, but I'll take them just the same.

We stop about thirty miles this side of Louisville to pick up a U-Haul van. My parents know a woman who was preparing to buy some new furniture, so they worked out a deal with her to sell me her old couch and loveseat. She had her new items moved in the day before, so the movers loaded up the van and left it sitting overnight at her house.

Jake doesn't appear to be overly thrilled with our pit stop. I was prepared to drive the van to the house and then come back to get my car, but he insisted that he drive the van. Instead of staring back at his annoyed face in the red pickup, now I'm enjoying the varied scenery of an annoyed face in a U-Haul van. The sheer delight is nearly overwhelming.

Pulling off I-65 to make the final turns toward our destination, I slow as a car merges between my car and that van. Despite the fact that I want to separate myself from his vehicle, he's forced me to be indebted to him today. Losing him in traffic would undoubtedly mean waiting while he tooled around trying to find the place, and knowing Jake he would drive around the block a few extra times just to make sure I have to wait on him.

Three times I flip the turn signal and wait for Jake to signal behind me, with the roads getting progressively smaller, until my tires roll onto the sleepy little street that is Wonder Lane. I hadn't given it much thought before, but the fact that Alex is moving to Wonder Lane would send Heather into a fit of hysterical laughter. The added fact that Wonder Lane seems as boring as Heather would insinuate makes the self-inflicted wound hurt a little more acutely.

I really should learn not to let her take up residence in my mind uninvited.

# Chapter Five

## Jake

Wonder Lane. Never has a street been more inappropriately named than this snooze-inducing place. Houses that blend together, looking similar yet slightly different, most impeccably groomed but out-of-date. Alexis pulls up in front of one near the cul-de-sac, an old-fashioned white-sided number with black shutters. Looks like the most boring house on the boring street.

Probably shouldn't have expected less.

She parks her car against the curb on the street, so I back the van into the driveway. Bailey is out in the yard almost immediately, poking around with curiosity while Alexis unlocks the front door. My mind had been telling me all the way here that I'd unload the trailer and find a quiet place to be alone, or possibly a loud place where I couldn't think. When she stopped to pick up this van, though, my evening pretty much went up in flames. Instead of finding a place to crash, I'll be unloading the furniture, going back for the trailer, making a second trip...

I stretch to the dash of the van, grabbing my wallet to shove it in my pocket. A couple of the neighbors seem to have noticed us and are watching with curiosity, so I attempt to offer them my most charming smile. Alexis will waste no time in letting them know what she thinks of me, so I might as well get a leg up on the competition.

"Bailey!" Alexis calls as she steps across the driveway, most likely getting ready to scold her for touching the dirt.

There seems to be no reason for me to beat around the bush, so I throw open the back door of the van to see what sort of mess I've gotten myself into. Two pieces of living room furniture that look like something my granny would have found too feminine, and an overwhelming scent of potpourri.

"Oh," Alexis mumbles as she steps up behind me. For the first time today, she has morphed away from angry into something else. I can't quite put my finger on it, but it smacks of disappointment or disgust.

"Can you help me, or am I solo?" I ask. She just stands there looking stunned, and I glance at Bailey, who's digging her fingers deeper in the newly discovered dirt. "With the couch? Can you help me with the couch?"

"It's not what I…"

The stammering is a new touch. She might not ever tell me what she's really thinking, but she never seems to search for her words. They're always right on the tip of her tongue.

"Can you help me with the couch or not? Because wrestling it alone isn't going to be the bright spot of my day."

"Yes," she answers, puffing up a bit. "It's just…it smells so horrible. And it's hideous."

"Really? I hadn't noticed."

She's totally right, of course. The couch flat stinks, almost like someone gave it a bath in that stuff my granny used to spray on her pantyhose to keep her skirt from sticking. I'm envisioning this woman fearing that her couch might not be fresh, so she douses it in some type of flowery cleaner. It's a bit overwhelming to the senses.

I lean over the side of the couch to make certain there's nothing to prevent us from picking it up easily. "I'll put you on the back side." That feels like the gentlemanly thing to do, so she won't have to walk backwards down the ramp. I look in her direction to see why she's hesitating, and can't help but notice that her face has gone a couple shades of red.

That's another thing about Alexis that perplexes me to no end. How can she be such a wild, party-it-up kind of girl and still act so completely naïve and awkward about everything? I guarantee I happened to mention the words "back" and "side" while I was bent over that couch, and my words caught her looking at my tail end. She probably thinks I said that on purpose, some kind of innuendo to insinuate that I knew she was staring at me.

Most definitely not the case. I mean, it might be something worth attempting with anyone else but Alexis, but I'm not interested in barking up that tree again. Ever.

"The back of the couch," I clarify forcefully, watching that mask of indifference slip back over her face again. "You gonna be able to handle it?"

"I can pick up the couch," she states without emotion as she moves deeper into the van. Part of me doubts that she can, because she doesn't seem very sturdy. Granted, her size could be fooling me a bit due to her tendency to wear those big, baggy sports jerseys. And I should have a pretty good grasp on what her actual size is because of...well, obvious past reasons, but my memory of all that is a little hazy.

"Count of three?" I suggest, reaching for the bottom of the couch. "One, two, three."

My end of the couch rises into the air, but hers only comes up about five inches before it bumps back down, jolting me in the process as it jerks against my hands.

"I thought you could do this," I complain.

"I can."

"Without ripping my arms off?"

There's the angry Alexis I've come to know.

Her side of the couch comes up before I'm ready, so I stoop to jerk mine up as well, hurriedly stepping down the ramp and heading for the front door. We don't even manage to get halfway across the yard before she yells out the word "stop" and the couch legs disappear into the six-inch grass.

"I just..." She glances at Bailey in what appears to be an attempt to keep her eyes away from me. "I can't put that inside. It smells like the weird perfumed body powder under my Great Aunt Betty's bathroom sink."

Folding my arms across my chest, I regard her silently for a moment as I try not to grin. This would probably be a great opportunity to tease her or insert a sarcastic comment, but my thoughts are jerked away from the subject at hand as I pause to sneeze. My eyes start watering from the force of the action, so I rub the back of my hand across them defensively.

"Maybe it will air out if you leave it outside a while," I suggest. She seems okay with that idea and heads back into the van to assist with the love seat. Our second attempt goes much smoother, partly because the couch is smaller and partly because we've already performed this drill once. As she lowers her end of the love seat to the ground, I do the same with mine, backing away and pressing my palms against my eyes.

"Are you okay?" she asks, and I try to refocus my eyes as I sniff.

"I'm pretty sure your friend has a cat."

"Just because she smells like my great aunt does not mean she has a cat."

That statement makes me laugh as I fight another sneeze. "I have no idea what your great aunt and cats have to do with one another, but my allergies are alerting me to the whole cat thing pretty loud and clear."

My eyes have a bit of trouble focusing on her through the mist of the allergic haze, but she actually looks concerned.

"Is there something I can do?"

"Nah, I have some Benadryl back in the truck with my stuff. I'll be fine. So, you're good with the couch here?"

She glances up the street as she wrinkles her nose. "Do you think it'll be safe?"

I follow her gaze up the road and see absolutely nothing to make me concerned about her possessions, especially the flowered monstrosities sitting on her front lawn.

"I doubt you have anything to worry about. I'd say you live in one of the quietest neighborhoods available."

"Yeah, I wanted a good neighborhood for Bailey."

My first instinct is to say something nice to her about that, because it seems pretty cool that she's placing Bailey's safety at the top of her list. The words get stuck in my throat, though, because a couple rogue sneezes force their way out instead. While I'm shaking off sneeze number three, Alexis pushes a tissue into my hands.

"Thanks," I say, nodding at her. "And thanks for keeping my kid safe."

Her dark eyes cloud over as she glances at Bailey tracing pictures in the dirt, and just like that my attempt at having a normal conversation with her is over.

By the time I return the van, pump myself full of Benadryl, and make my way back to Wonder Lane with the truck and trailer, it's getting pretty late. Alexis asks me to leave the trailer and wait until the next day, so I park it in her driveway and find myself sitting unmoving in the cab of my truck. Without the trailer hitched behind me and those taillights in front of me, it would be really easy to keep traveling. The road could take me to a million different places where no one knows my name. Starting over is really tempting.

Not as tempting as turning my truck around and heading back to Tennessee.

About two miles from Wonder Lane, I find a little mom and pop motel. I ask them about rooms for the week, and the older gentleman behind the desk keeps me conversing about the weather, fishing, and dozens of other things that feel like a nuisance at the moment. He seems like a nice enough guy, offering me a beer while we're having our talk. He doesn't seem to notice that I nurse it for at least thirty minutes and still have to take it to my room with me.

The motel's not such a bad little stopping point. I've been in way worse for way longer, so I'm not complaining. It looks clean, and there's no weird smell. My mind goes back to Alexis and her comments about her aunt. I can't help but laugh to myself, imagining those horrible pieces of furniture as the focal point of their little house.

As I'm shaking my head at the thought, I cross to the bathroom and tip the neck of my beer toward the sink, watching as the amber liquid flows down the drain. How many beers have I poured out when the nights wound down? Hundreds? Thousands?

My eyes drift toward the mirror, and I study what I see there. A little pink tonight due to the unfortunate encounter with the cat couch, but sky blue, merging into darker blue at the edges. Remarkably like my dad's, with the exception of the brown specks embedded here and there to add a hint of something else. God's private joke to remind him that I'm my mother's son, Dad always said. Because she's full of it, and a little of that spilled over into me.

Focusing back on the bottle, I tip it once more to make sure it's empty and then place it in the trash can. Nobody back home would believe for a second that I've never had a beer. "I've seen him drinking almost every weekend," they'd probably say. It would be almost true, because they've seen me with bottles of nearly everything. And those bottles have touched my lips, but the liquids inside never go any further.

It might be the only secret I have left.

Something draws me from a dead sleep, and I lay in the stillness, trying to figure out why I'm suddenly so alert. Then I hear a whimper in the next room, and I know she's back. She should have known to wait until morning, but she never learns. It seems like she should be able to figure out, if my thirteen-year-old brain can grasp it.

She'll tell me tomorrow that she had nowhere to go. Whoever the guy is will have kicked her out, and so she's back. I won't remind her that she's married to Dad, and whether or not he deserves her or she deserves him, it's a fact they both need to acknowledge.

I move to the door and quietly pull it open, just enough so I can peer into the room and make sure they're both upright. Mom's sprawled across the floor with the mark of Dad's handprint on her cheek. Dad has his head in one hand, sitting on the worn-out recliner, a fifth of whiskey against his knee.

They're both thinking they deserve it. I'm not sure how I know this, but it's clear as day. He thinks she has every right to run around on him because he can't manage to face the day without liquor running through his veins, and she thinks he has every right to hit her because she can't remain faithful to him.

They'll be the talk of the town tomorrow, because things spread quickly in this trailer park. If they woke me from a dead sleep, they surely alerted the neighbors as well.

Not that they aren't the talk of the park normally, on any given day. Mom's forty-two and Dad's thirty-one, which makes for some fascinating gossip, since he was barely eighteen when I was born. If a comment can be made, I've heard it and then some.

I watch them for a while, to make sure he keeps breathing and she eventually stands up. Both of them do, so I doze off.

When I come alert again, I'm sitting on the front step of the trailer, a rickety makeshift wooden contraption that might fold up right under me. Abby James rides her bike up in front of my place, pausing to glance back at her friends. Three of them wait where she left them, standing in a row, like she's on a dare of some sort. She probably is, so I wait for the taunting.

"What gives, Jacob? Where'd your dad go?"

"He's at work, just like he always is."

"My dad said your dad got fired from the plant, and he ain't got no work to do. He's sitting down at the bar drinkin'."

Abby's no better off than me, really, except I haven't heard about her parents trying to kill each other. Her clothes aren't finer than mine, and she's doesn't have good grades at school. She might be kind of cute if she weren't so nasty, but her attitude makes that impossible to see.

"If your dad knows everything, why're you asking me?"

"'Cause your dad done said your mom's taking you away with her, to live with her relatives in South Carolina."

It bothers me that she knows my business, but I'm not going to deny the facts.

"True enough. We're going to find better."

"Ain't gonna be no better, just different. Anyway, you'll be back here soon enough."

She tilts her head at me when she says that, just enough to make me think she might miss me when I'm gone.

"Why do you say that?"

"'Cause she won't want you long, either. Don't nobody want you, Jake McAuliffe."

She has the nerve to smile at me before she rides off to her friends, and as they stare at me and giggle behind their hands, I make a vow to myself right then and there:

Someday I'll make you want me, each of you. I'll start with Abby and then I'll go down the line, wiping the smug grins off each of your faces.

Long fingers wrap around my shoulder, accompanied by my mom's voice. "Jake?"

Bolting upright, my breath comes out in a panic as I focus on the small motel room. I force myself to try to focus on the walls of the room as I wipe the sweat from my forehead. It's been forever since I had a dream about my mother, or even allowed myself to think about her. She hadn't really wanted me, just like Abby said. When granny got sick, I was right back with my dad.

But I did make Abby want me, along with every single one of her friends. And lots of other girls, just to prove a point.

The only one I couldn't make want me was Camdyn, and that was because I refused to hurt Parker.

Otherwise, maybe I could have... Maybe.

# Chapter Six

## Alexis

There's a company in Louisville that will come to your house and take anything you don't want, and as soon as Jake drove off in his truck, I contacted them about the couches. I'm not entirely certain why I did it. There's the fact that they look like they belong on the set of *Golden Girls*, and the added bonus that they smell like they've been doused with every bottle of perfume those fragrance testers at the mall have in stock.

Truth be told, though, I would feel slightly guilty about having them in here, knowing that they would mean Jake could never come inside the house due to the cat allergy. It might present me with an unexpected blessing, although I would despise myself a little.

But they really were ugly.

By the time I manage to unload the trailer, it's eleven o'clock. It might have been easier to wait until Jake comes back tomorrow, but I'm indebted to him enough already and I don't like the feeling. Besides, I don't have a wealth of belongings. Those couches were to be my main furniture.

The mattress for my bed was the hardest thing to get inside, mostly because it was awkward, but I did it. I'm a lot stronger than Jake gives me credit for, or really anybody else for that matter.

Since there's nothing left for Jake to do, I'm hoping he'll show up tomorrow and tell us goodbye. There's nothing for him here, and he doesn't really care about Bailey. Not enough to follow her across state lines, at least.

The boxes are still sitting around the house unopened, except for the one with Hoppy. Bailey insisted that he be released from the box the minute I started unloading. She cared more about that rabbit than sheets for her bed or locating her toothbrush. Not that finding her bedding mattered in the least. She's currently curled up against me on my own bed, because she's scared to stay in a house without Gump.

I could pretend that her feeling of security coming from my dad doesn't bother me, but I won't. My parents have been the absolute best gift God ever gave me, right up until I had Bailey, but they're too parental. They totally overshadow me with their proud gazes, loving statements, and the ability to say "no" just by lifting their eyebrows. They're such perfectly wonderful parents that I pale in comparison, and not by a small margin either.

Sometimes I feel like those kids in that movie where their dad shrank them. Things are going on around me, and I'm leaping up and down, waving my arms, screaming. "I'm here! I'm here! Can't you hear me?"

No one ever does.

Maybe that's why it bothered me so much earlier when she jumped as soon as Jake gave the order.

Or maybe it's just because I've always been invisible, and it's finally getting on my last nerve.

"Jay go home?" Bailey asks, picking at the fuzz on her blanket.

Did Jake go home? That's a loaded question if I've ever heard one. I'd imagine Jake is probably at some seedy bar at the moment, trying to figure out which prey he'll go after.

"Sure," I say noncommittally, not loving the idea of lying to my daughter. "Hey, did you ask Hoppy what he thinks of the house?"

"Didn't ask him," she answers. Her melancholy threatens to spill over to me, and I definitely don't need both of us sitting here acting mushy about missing Gump.

"Well, let's ask him." I gently remove Hoppy from her hands and hold him at attention in front of her, his feet resting against her abdomen. "So, Hoppy, what do you think of our new home?"

Clearing my throat, I attempt to prepare my best rabbit voice. I've perfected it in the past few months: a little throaty, deeper than my own, with a hint of a lisp. It's most likely the opposite of how a real rabbit would sound, but it works for us.

"Well, in actuality Miss Bailey of the Jennings, I was a tad bit on the worried side, but let me tell you...this house is THE BOMB."

Hoppy's hands travel in opposite directions, as though there is an explosion happening as we speak, and Bailey giggles.

"Why?"

*Why? Hmm...why?*

"Because...you live on the coolest street in the entire cool world. As soon as I saw the name, I got cold shivers all up and down my back." He shakes for effect, and she smiles up at me. "Wonder Lane. It sounds just like that book your mom's been reading to you. Tomorrow I'm going to do some poking around to see if I can find the rabbit hole. I just know there's going to be a load of ridiculous, wonderful things here."

"Can I go in the hole with you?"

"Do you think I could even imagine going in without you? What would be the fun in that?"

She stretches her arms out to take him and pulls him against her, rubbing his worn-out face on her cheek.

"Thank you Hoppy."

Settling beside her, I allow the warmth of her arm to press against mine as I stare up at the ceiling. It's beyond bizarre, I know, because I *am* Hoppy, but...

Just once, I wish it was *thank you Mommy*.

Bailey drifts to sleep without much effort, and I lie awake staring at the blank wall and wondering if this will ever feel like home. It should feel like a beginning, but instead it reminds me that nothing is as I expected. That empty space couldn't be more appalling if it was a giant billboard that said, "Welcome to your second choice."

Is it even a second choice? It feels like a fifteenth, or a four hundred fifty-seventh.

Easing myself off the mattress, I mindlessly begin unpacking some of my belongings, looking past the few dishes I own to concentrate on the quieter-to-unpack options—clothes, shoes, towels. As I pull one of my shirts out and smooth it across my leg, a familiar black book catches my eye.

Hundreds of memories compete for my attention, mostly good and the majority benign. Faces I haven't considered in a while, standing near my locker, laughing about their weekends or something that was just said.

They all start to fade as one moves into focus. Cody Hewitt, sitting right in front of a seventeen-year-old version of myself. His dark, wavy hair is always too long in the back, and he has that spot to the right that curls toward his ear. I'm glad it curls like that, because otherwise I wouldn't know that he has that one solitary freckle on his neck.

He turns around when the teacher isn't looking, mouthing the words "help me" as he offers a crooked grin. His teeth are perfectly straight, with the exception of one of the bottom incisors that sits slightly higher than the others.

Just like every other time he's ever focused those hazel eyes on me, I can physically feel the blood traveling through my veins. I'm pretty sure he's the most attractive male to ever walk the planet. I've believed that to be the case since the seventh grade. The only two people I have ever admitted that to are Heather and my best friend Sadie, and neither one of them was in agreement.

It's not my fault they have bad taste.

Somehow Cody and I always end up in math classes together. It's quite a puzzle, because he doesn't seem to be great in math. In every single class we've shared, he's parked himself directly in front of me, and without exception he winds up turning around to beg for my assistance. Heather says he follows me around because he's secretly infatuated with me, and he doesn't even know it himself.

I doubt that's the case.

Cody can consistently catch even the most imperfect spirals on the football field. I'm pretty sure I'm the only one on the sidelines who notices every move of the average-build tight end. Every other cheerleader on the squad wants to be noticed by our quarterback, as though confirming the cliché to be a fact of nature. Brad Travis knows they're looking at him, and he gives them all their slivers of his attention, one at a time.

Heather joined the cheerleading squad because she wants to be the center of all the attention, both on the field and off, but I joined just to be near Cody. Four years I've performed chants and dances and high kicks and tried to get the crowd going all so I could stand next to the sidelines and see him a little clearer.

Cody Hewitt is the main reason I love football.

He's the reason for a lot of things, really.

Looking at the front of that yearbook and then glancing at my beautiful daughter, it fully hits me: It's his fault I'm here almost as much as it is my own.

A quick glance at my phone tells me that it's one o'clock in the morning. There are plenty of things I could blame for my sleeplessness: different surroundings, anxiousness about my new job, unease about Bailey's situation here, or even that gas station burrito I had a few hours ago. They're all smokescreens, though, because the fact is I unleashed a few ghosts when I was staring at that yearbook.

It does me no favors to think about the girl I was then, all wide-eyed innocence and blind trust. When I think about the time wasted, down on my knees, elbows resting on my bed as I pleaded for Cody... Daydreamed about Cody. Made sure beyond a shadow of a doubt that God knew I wanted nothing but Cody.

My dad's sermons probably went in one of Heather's ears and out the other, but I listened with my whole heart because I knew about the red and I was determined to stay away from it if at all possible. Lying equaled red. Unkindness equaled red. Disobeying our parents and putting on makeup in the girls' bathroom at school equaled red, as I tried to tell Heather countless times.

When I was in the eighth grade, Dad stood in front of the church and said something that changed my entire outlook. I'd spent my entire life to that point avoiding doing wrong because I didn't want to feel the condemnation, but there was more. Dad said if you delighted yourself in the ways of the Lord, He would give you the desires of your heart. Translation in my fourteen-year-old mind: Do what God wants, and Cody will want to be my boyfriend. Fall in love with me. Marry me even.

That's what I began praying about my situation, as earnestly as possible for a junior high girl. "Guard my heart and keep me on the right path. Help me be the girl You've designed me to be. Please watch over Cody and keep him on the right path, too, so he can someday be mine. And if it could happen tomorrow, that would be spectacular."

Every day I would admire him, from afar on the bad days and from close up on the good days. He would talk to me, tease me, sit with me at lunch, and I'd feel certain that it was going to happen any second. And every night I would make sure I reiterated my request to God, just in case He got busy in the last twenty-four hours and lost track.

Freshman year I saw Cody holding hands with Mindy Thomas after third hour English, and I flung open my locker, pretending to be looking for something while they strolled past me. It was the first time I had ever been tardy, and Mr. Samuels didn't even look crossways at me when I entered fourth hour Algebra ten minutes late. Cody did, though. He turned around in his seat and asked me if I was alright. What was I supposed to say? You just ripped out my heart and stomped on it? I told him I wasn't feeling well, and he told me he was sorry. He asked if there was something he could do. My heart wanted to say *break up with Mindy*, but my brain knew better than to mouth the words.

The fling with Mindy was short-lived, for which I was glad and felt slightly vindicated. Cody was never going to be happy with anyone but me; I was certain of that fact. He still didn't have the instructions from God, though, because that January I walked around the side of the bus just in time to see him locking lips with Jen Mitchell—the rudest, most condescending girl in our entire class. They were an item until the end of the school year, and then parted ways in the summer.

Sophomore year Cody showed up the first day attached at the hip to a girl named Constance Martinez. She moved into town over the summer, and luckily for him they were in the same neck of the woods. Constance was rather sweet, slim and small-statured with a mess of black hair and a slight Hispanic accent. She had no trouble making friends in our small town, and was genuinely liked by everyone.

She was the first girl I ever loathed.

Junior year Constance moved back to Arizona, and Cody moved on to Emily, Nicole, Amber, Chelsea... My only saving grace was the fact that each girl only had his arm for about a week, and then he was back with me, sitting at my table for lunch, asking me for help with math, talking to me about the plays he made in the football game the week before.

By our senior year, I think everyone knew Cody and I were destined to be together. Everyone except Cody, that is. He never once had a serious girlfriend that year, and we spent every single available free moment together at school. He even started driving me home in the evenings, sometimes coming inside and chatting pleasantly with my mom before we worked on homework together. I was so crazy mad in love with him, most days I could hardly see straight. That year was the best and worst of my life, being so near Cody I could almost drink him in, yet not being fully able to claim him as my own.

Late that March, the class voted on yearbook superlatives. It wouldn't have been a stretch for me to imagine being voted Most Studious, Teacher's Pet, or a laundry list of other things, but my name somehow ended up in the most unlikely of places: Class Sweetheart.

Class Sweetheart. Me, Alexis Jennings, the girl who had not been out on one date in her entire life. The girl who had been pining away with unrequited love from the moment raging hormones entered her body. The girl who was holding on desperately to the hope that she would one day have the desires of her heart, even though the last sands of the hourglass were starting to slip through one by one as that last year of school came to a close.

And next to my name, printed in black ink: Cody Hewitt.

He laughed it off as a joke, of course. Everyone did, stating that they placed our names together because we were like two peas in a pod. Best friends destined to be immortalized in a humorous way for all time, right there in the pages of our yearbooks.

I laughed it off, too, because I had no choice. We had been friends for such a long time, I couldn't blurt the fact that I was in love with him and expect him to accept it without a genuine relationship meltdown. It would be completely dishonest of me to be his friend while I felt that way, wouldn't it?

It was funny right up to the day that we posed for our picture. We probably sat there together for half an hour as the photographer attempted to get a good frame, one or the other of us cracking a joke or accidentally blinking when she snapped the shot. The poor woman was trying every trick possible, and the two of us were awkward enough about the situation that we simply couldn't just sit there and smile for the camera.

"Well, you're the sweethearts, so why don't you just kiss her on the cheek or something?" the photographer finally suggested.

Cody cleared his throat. I remember because my own heart felt like it had risen to my throat, and I wondered if his was having the same reaction. He shifted toward me a little, and he could have just leaned in and pretended to kiss my cheek, but he didn't. Instead, he reached out and placed the tips of his fingers against my chin and then stopped, holding his hand there as if frozen. My curiosity was getting the better of me, so I turned just enough so I could look at his face.

I force a deep breath into my lungs as I drag my thoughts back to the present, shaking loose the grip of my memories. The yearbook sits open on my lap, and I gaze down at it, running my index finger across the page that I've looked at thousands of times over the years.

Class Sweethearts.

Cody Hewitt and Alexis Jennings.

And there, beneath my finger, the perfect moment Cody Hewitt noticed me captured for all eternity.

"Whaddya want, Alex?"

"Good, you're awake," I announce to the phone. I must be feeling nostalgic, because the sound of another human voice just made me want to choke up in the most illogical way.

"'Course I'm awake. It's Saturday night. D'ya think I'd be home or somethin'?" Heather's voice comes across the line rather slurred and drowsy, so I know she's been out painting the town.

She also seems to slip into a countrified drawl when she's been drinking, which is showcasing itself in all its glory.

"Please tell me you're not driving."

"That'd be stupid." She laughs, and I can hear the music playing loudly in the background. "Sadie Lou's drivin' me 'round. We're havin' a girls' night."

"Sounds like fun."

"Whatever. You'd never go on a girls' night. You make it to Louisville okay? Jake follow you the whole way?"

Rising from my position on the floor, I walk to the living room window, lifting the blinds to look out at the sleepy street. "Yeah, he followed me the whole way. He had the trailer on, though, so it didn't offer him many options."

"Sure 'nough he had options. Like you need trouble to follow you out of town."

"Just a temporary nuisance. He'll be gone tomorrow."

I can hear that the engine of the car comes to a stop, and the absence of that noise is accompanied by Heather's groan. "Sadie's makin' me get some coffee."

That thought brings me a little relief, even though Heather's still grumbling on the other end of the line.

"Let me talk to Sadie," I tell her, waiting as she hands the phone off.

"Hey Alexis. Your trip go okay?" Sadie's voice drops to a more authoritative tone. "Just get in there and get a coffee, Heather. I'll wait for you." Letting out a sigh, her voice softens once more. "Seriously, how do you do this? I had to ask my mom to babysit Jonah so I could babysit Heather. Doesn't it make you crazy?"

"Yes, I have to, and yes." The sound of her laugh warms me a little. "Thank you for keeping an eye on her."

"You owe me. How's Bailey taking it?"

"Not so good."

"Poor baby. She'll get used to it, though. Kids are resilient. How are you taking it? Be honest."

"I'm awake after one o'clock in the morning." Admitting that feels like a shortcoming somehow, and I don't want any pity. "I've forgotten what that felt like, before Bailey slept through the night."

"It stinks today, sweetie, but you're doing the right thing."

My eyes dart to the hallway, and I think about Bailey sleeping on that mattress on the floor.

"Am I?" Tears threaten to spill over, and I bite the inside of my cheek to try to force them back. "I'm not so sure right now."

"I feel like we've had this exact same conversation before, only backwards. You told me I was stronger than I thought. You stood next to me while I took the first steps."

"And I'd do it again in a heartbeat," I'm quick to assure her.

"I know. That's the kind of person you are, and that's exactly why you're going to rock this new start. You'll go to your job Monday, and things are going to feel normal in no time."

"I'm sure you're right."

Hesitation keeps me from saying more, and I hear Heather mouthing Sadie in the background as she returns to the car.

"Don't let him get to you," Sadie tells me softly, as though she's hiding our conversation from my sister.

My heart clenches, because I can't figure out how she knows I'm thinking about Cody. Am I that completely, pathetically obvious after all these years?

"How did you know he was getting to me?" The question comes out so tentatively, I'm not really sure I said it out loud. She begins laughing, though, which cements my embarrassment at having uttered the words.

"You've been with the man all day. How could he not be getting to you, at least a little?"

Jake. She's talking about Jake, of course.

"Yeah, he's a trip."

There's a very small part of me that wishes she meant Cody, because then she could tell me to get a life or knock it off or give me an abrupt proverbial kick in the pants. But she doesn't, and I hold it inside, right where it belongs.

Not everything's about Cody, after all.
Not really.

# Chapter Seven

## Jake

"The wages of sin are death, make no mistake."

Probably one of the rudest wake-up calls I've ever received, courtesy of what sounds like an older woman in the room next to me, probably a longtime smoker by the sound of her voice. A televangelist's rant is permeating through the walls, turned up way too loud to be considered polite for our close proximity. The only reason I've been able to pinpoint her voice against his is because she feels the need to keep interjecting "amens" to punctuate his words.

The guy on the TV launches into one of those over-the-top prayers. I'm not really a praying guy myself, but I consider offering up a plea to make the two of them shut up. When he tidies up the end of his prayer and begins asking for donations, I groan and submit myself to the beginning of the new day.

Welcome to Louisville.

Empty. The trailer is completely empty, and the two disgustingly ugly couches have disappeared. Placing my hand against the side of the trailer, I stare inside in disbelief, feeling all of two inches tall. After I assured Alexis that her neighborhood seemed safe, and her belongings wouldn't be taken...something like this is bound to crush her, right?

Part of me wants to drive away and pretend I don't know, but it feels like the cowardly option. Instead, I head to the front door, hesitating on the porch for a minute, trying to decide how I'm going to break the news.

There's no doorbell. That realization strikes me as odd, because don't all houses have doorbells nowadays? Instead of dwelling on it, I knock on the door and shove my hands in my pockets, rocking back on the heels of my tennis shoes.

*Hey, Alexis, someone stole your aunt's putrid couch. Sorry about that.*

*Oh, someone stole your junk? That stinks. Guess you chose the wrong neighborhood after all, huh?*

*Look, you're the one who chose Louisville. I'm just along for the ride.*

Exhaling louder than normal, I glance back at my truck in the driveway. This is why I don't get involved. I'm lousy at comfort and sympathy and all that stuff. I tried to push past it to help Camdyn and be a shoulder for her to cry on, and all that got me was some screwed up feelings and the loss of a great friend.

The door creaks as it opens, and I jerk my head back around to see two brown eyes peering up at me through the crack.

"Bailey, is that you hiding behind the door?"

"It's Bailey," she announces, moving the door enough that I can see her Cinderella nightgown and bare feet. "Did you knock?"

"I did knock. Is that proper procedure?"

"Proppy what?"

"Never open the door, Bailey!" Alexis orders as she rushes up behind her, all wild and unkempt. "Do you understand me? What if it was someone you didn't know?"

"It's Jay," Bailey tells her with a shrug. Her nonchalance in the face of her mom's panic makes me want to chuckle, but I control myself.

"Don't open the door ever again. Tell me that you understand." Bailey doesn't answer immediately, so Alexis grabs her by the shoulders and turns her so they're face to face. "You hear me, Bailey?"

"Okay."

Alexis closes her eyes momentarily as she shakes her head, and I take the opportunity to let my eyes sweep over her. She must have fallen asleep with her hair in a ponytail, because it looks like it traveled during the night to where it's currently resting just above her left ear. Her fitted T-shirt bearing the word "Indians" and her tight running shorts are accentuating her curves just enough that I can't resist letting my gaze linger on them a hint too long. She opens her eyes just as I drag mine back up to her face, which immediately gets her flustered.

"I just got out of bed," she explains, her fingers reaching down to tug on the legs of her shorts, failing in her attempts to make them longer. Giving up, she crosses her arms against her abdomen in a protective gesture.

It dawns on me that the constant baggy clothes might just be a fashion statement she reserves for my benefit. But why? Is she that determined to make sure I'm not attracted to her? The prickly cactus of a personality would probably do the trick on its own, but I can't deny as I stand here looking at her that she's a pretty stellar package. Outwardly, anyway…if it were possible to ignore the fact that she's dull as dishwater and always has a scowl on her face.

"Mommy snores."

Alexis throws Bailey a defensive glance, which allows me the opportunity to examine her one more time. For the life of me, I don't remember having seen those stunning legs before. Not that I remember much about our…incident, but I'd gladly get that memory back to see what attracted me to Alexis in the first place. Heck, I'd like to go back to that memory and tell my younger, screwed up self to run like the wind.

"I don't," Alexis insists, shaking her head as she speaks. "I don't snore."

"Our daughter has a fantastic vocabulary." I can't be bothered to hide my smile as she pins me with that icy gaze she's fond of throwing around. "For a three-year-old, I mean."

"She's almost four."

That look she's giving me is almost screaming, "You should know that." And yeah, maybe I should. I probably would in the back of my mind, if I did the math and thought it made one iota of difference in her speech abilities. Truthfully, I don't know whether she speaks well or not, I was just trying to needle Alexis. Looks like I managed to find success in that department.

"When Mommy sleeps, she does this…"

I look down at Bailey just in time to see her roll her head back, drop her mouth open, and let her tongue hang out like she's catching flies. The temptation proves too great, and I laugh as Bailey straightens up and grins at me.

"Okay, Bailey. Why don't you go find Hoppy." Alexis shoos her back inside as she attempts to halfway hide herself behind the door.

"Don't be too hard on her about the door. No harm came out of it."

She glances back to make sure Bailey is out of hearing range before she turns her gaze toward me. "With all due respect, you have no idea about keeping her safe."

"No idea? Are you kidding me?"

"You're not exactly…"

Whatever she's getting ready to say will only make my blood boil, and I'm not up for hearing any insults this morning. My mind is preparing to tell her so when I realize the boxes from the trailer are inside the house.

"Who helped you unpack?" My words sound harsh and accusing, but since I'm all but certain she was about to call me a deadbeat, I'm not sure I care.

"I did it myself."

"And Aunt Betty's couches? Don't try to tell me you moved those yourself."

"I got rid of them."

My hand seems to reach up to my baseball cap on its own accord, needing some sort of diversion to fight the exasperation building inside. Lifting it and settling it onto my head a couple times does nothing to tamp down my frustration, but it affords me a few additional seconds so I don't overreact.

"The furniture we had to go out of our way to pick up yesterday," I finally say, linking both of my hands over the cap against the back of my head. "The furniture in the van that I had to drive thirty senseless miles last night to return? That furniture?"

She appears ready to lash out at me, or maybe she can't decide between being confrontational and trying to keep my eyes off her clothing. Either way, she restricts herself to releasing a sigh as she drops her head.

"This isn't the life I want for Bailey," is all she says, quiet enough that I can barely hear her from two feet away. "You've made whatever point you're trying to prove, so feel free to go. Nobody asked you to be here."

"Yeah, you did. The minute you took my kid out of state, you played my hand."

"If you truly think that, I'm sorry, but we're fine on our own. Bailey's going to be fine."

*Better off with no father than with you.* That's what I hear, loud and clear. *'Cause nobody wants you. Nobody.*

"No," I tell her as I shake my head, refusing to allow the words to penetrate. "No, I'm not playing into that game. She's my daughter too, so unless you want me to fight you for some sort of custody agreement, I want the opportunity to see her."

"Why are you here?" she asks, tears filling her eyes. "You can stand here all day giving me pretty speeches, but we both know you don't care. And as much as it bothers you to hear it, we also know she's better off if you're not involved."

"Really?" Her words cut just deep enough that I can feel some emotion roiling inside, and it flat ticks me off. Shoving the door back, I step into the house, watching her height increase about an inch as she tries to assume a defensive stance.

"This is my house, Jake. You have absolutely no right to step foot inside it unless you're invited."

Glancing at the door, I slam it closed with my palm and hesitate for a second before turning toward her, trying to contain my temper. Leaving my hand against the door at shoulder height, I stare at the wall so I don't have to witness the condescension she's throwing my way.

"Right here." My voice sounds surprisingly measured, so I only take a quick breath before I continue. "You need a lock right here, and on the back door too. A door security guard that you can only unlock from the inside, but that's too high for Bailey to reach. I'll pick a couple up and come back to install them. Not today, though. I'll wait until you can get off your self-righteous pedestal long enough to act like a civilized person for five minutes, in case it takes me that long."

My hand slides down the wood until it locates the doorknob, and I tug the door open as I step back onto the porch. The trailer immediately catches my eye again, and I'm hit with the realization that I'll be the one who has to take it to the rental place. Groaning inwardly, I retreat into my truck, pulling out onto the street so I can back to the trailer. While I'm lowering the tongue coupler socket onto the trailer hitch ball, I glance up to see Alexis standing against the door frame, watching me with her arms across her chest.

It's a pretty low blow to stand there taunting me in those tight shorts, daring me to be attracted to her, just so she can prove she doesn't want me either. She did want me once, though, and there's proof enough.

"I've got to tell you, it's pretty interesting to hear you say that she's better off if I'm not involved," I throw at her, moving toward the cab of the truck. "Seems to me you should have said that to twenty five-year-old Jake, but you didn't. In fact, you weren't satisfied to not have me involved. You needed proof, and then some kind of acceptance, and then you smeared me in three counties to the point that I couldn't find a job. So if this isn't what you wanted, Alex, maybe next time you should be a little clearer."

The instant I shut myself inside the confines of my truck, I rest my head against the seat and force a calming breath, the word *hate* rolling through my mind. It kind of throws me for a loop, because normally things tend to bounce off of me and I don't take them to heart, but there it is anyway.

*I hate...*
*I hate...*
Alexis? No, it's way too harsh, and I don't hate Alexis.
I hate the way she makes me feel, though.
Completely worthless.

# Chapter Eight

## Alexis

New starts should feel like embarking on adventures, or turning over new leaves. Ad lib a thousand clichés that should describe my first Monday in Louisville, and I'm certain none of them would include sitting in my car in the high school parking lot, alternately sobbing and trying to reapply my mascara. How am I supposed to teach algebra to a bunch of hormonal teenagers when I myself am behaving like one? They're going to smell my incompetence and descend on me like a pack of gray wolves.

Not that I don't have an excuse to feel a little out of sorts. I woke up in a foul mood, a carryover from yesterday and my dealings with Jake. He showed up around dinner time, and when I opened the door, he simply held the locks in front of my face. He wouldn't even look at me. Once I moved out of his way, he went to work installing the lock on the front door, and then he moved to the back door. Only a few minutes and he was finished, marching back out to his truck without having uttered a single word.

He'd made his point, and I felt like a colossal jerk. There's definitely no love lost between the two of us, but he *is* a human being. Besides, I do feel a little guilty about what went down when I was pregnant, even though none of it was really my doing.

My feelings about Jake got lost in the shuffle, though, as Bailey and I began preparing for our day. She was excited that we were each starting at our new schools, which was how I decided to present the daycare/preschool to her in hopes that she would be more accepting. I dressed her in the brand new outfit that Nan bought her before we left. She looked at herself in the mirror for quite a while, admiring the black leggings and pale pink dress with the large bow near her waist. She was totally ready, except for the fact that she wasn't.

I know I should have seen it coming. She's been at home with my mother every other time I was at work, with the exception of the few days I let her spend time with Jake. The idea of going to school is fantastic and sounds very grown up, until you're the three-year-old standing at the door, staring at the curious, unfamiliar faces. They're already friends, and they're playing together, and the young woman with the lovely smile and the voice that's practically made for speaking to children is engaging you in a friendly conversation, but…

She's not Nan.

Commence uncontrollable hysterics and clinging to my leg, the likes of which I've never before experienced. The poor young woman trying to peel her off me, who I discovered is named Traci, kept looking up at me from her kneeling position, trying to offer me encouragement with her eyes. No doubt she had encountered scenes like ours before, but I wasn't accustomed to my daughter being unreasonable. A little persnickety at times, perhaps occasionally intent upon embarrassing me, but never anything like the vicious little fiend clawing at the leg of my black pants. The black pants that looked freshly pressed and stylish when I left the house, but had since been covered with slobber and some iridescent mucous-green streaks that I tried not to think about less they turn my stomach.

She never stopped, and I had zero options. We weren't back home in Tennessee, and I couldn't call Nan to the rescue. I couldn't phone Gump and beg him to help me. Instead, Traci held my beautiful little girl in a tight grip using both her arms as I attempted to make a break from the building, the sound of her screams assaulting me as I ran through the hallway.

"Mommy! Mommmmmmmy!"

So here I am, desperately trying to suck it up. Trying to tell myself that I look acceptable in my crisp evergreen button down shirt, tucked into my pants over my cream-colored camisole. Trying to convince that puffy red face in the mirror that I don't look like I've been crying, even as I watch the moisture rise in my eyes again. Trying to convince myself that I'm not a total fraud—that I have something worthwhile to offer high school students.

Trying to make myself believe I'm an adult.

Someday I'll look back at this day and chuckle. Ten years from now, I'll put my arm around the new young teacher and offer a conciliatory smile. "On my first day, I cried in the car and then spent ten minutes in the bathroom trying to scrub snot off my pants." She'll give me a defeated grin, and I'll tell her to hang in there.

Today is not that day. Today my wet pant leg is making swishing noises against my flats as I walk toward my classroom. Today my right eye is red not because I was crying earlier, but because I made a valiant attempt to replace my mascara in the bathroom and managed to stab myself with the wand. Today my face is completely void of makeup, and I look like I should be facing the desk, not sitting behind it.

I'm toast.

Drawing in the deepest breath possible, I expel it slowly as I cross the threshold into room eight. My desk sits cattycorner near the back of the room, and I glance toward the empty space at the front, seeing a scrawny podium. Nothing about it seems welcoming to me, and at the moment it feels like the one and only thing I have some control over. Placing my purse on one of the student desks, I grip the side of my desk with both hands, dragging it a few inches. The metallic scraping sound against the tile is offensive at best, but it does nothing to staunch my determination. If anything, it propels me to finish faster.

Twice more I tug against the desk, moving it a couple inches at a time, until a touch against my shoulder causes me to jump what feels like a foot.

"What do you think you're doing?" the male voice barks at me. Turning, I allow my gaze to fall on the man who's invaded my privacy. Tall, slender, and unintimidating, with short silver hair capping a youthful face. "You can't move the furniture, but I'm sure you know that."

There are times for being unreasonable, and this most likely isn't one of them, but after the morning I've had, my brain simply can't take any more.

"Why? Why can't I move the furniture? It's my classroom."

His eyes flash with what appears to be recognition. "So sorry, are you Alexis?"

Straightening in an attempt to look a little more presentable, I wipe my hands on my thighs as he extends one of his.

"Alexis Jennings. I'm teaching algebra and I obviously woke up on the wrong side of the bed. Sorry about that."

"No need to apologize," he says, taking my outstretched hand. "Roger Jennings, Business Ed. I should have known you weren't a student by the way that you're dressed, especially since people get my age wrong all the time."

"They think you're fifteen?"

He grins as he lifts the far side of the desk, so I follow suit and begin backing the piece of furniture toward the front of the room.

"Hardly." He smiles as he places the desk onto the floor again. "Something more along the senior citizen route, usually. Anything else you want to adjust while we're at it? Replace a window? Maybe knock out the far wall?"

"I think I'm good."

"Let me know if you change your mind. I'm next door."

"It seems a little unfortunate that we wound up next to one another. Mr. Jennings and Ms. Jennings. They're going to assume..."

"That you're my daughter, most likely. So, this is your first position?"

Hiding the slightly disgusted expression on my face proves impossible. "Is it obvious? Am I that green?"

"No, we were told that it's your first teaching assignment. This is my fourth year."

"And how old are you?" I shrug my shoulders as he narrows his eyes a bit. "Curiosity is getting the better of me."

"I don't think you're supposed to ask me that, but since we're practically related..." He pauses to give me a wink, almost as though he's trying to assure me he's joking. "I'm twenty-seven. And you?"

"Twenty-five. We're practically twins."

"Practically. If anyone gives you trouble, send them to your brother next door." He begins to walk toward the hallway, so I retrieve my purse and place it atop my desk, slightly renewed in my spirit.

"Thank you, Mr. Jennings!" I call after him.

"Roger," he insists as he walks away.

My first class consists of twenty-two students who spill into my room chatting and laughing about their weekends. Not one of them seems to notice me or realize that the room looks different as they find their seats. That fact is intimidating and relieving at once, because getting their attention might be difficult, but at least they're not staring too curiously at me. Not yet, anyway.

Leaning against the desk, I watch them silently for a moment. The room is set up a lot like I remember my own high school, with five rows of desks. My gaze drifts to the second row, third seat from the front. That would have been my seat, back in the day. A mountain of a guy with a desperate need of a haircut sits there now, tapping his pencil against the desk like he's practicing a drum cadence.

Directly in front of him, that seat would have belonged to Cody. The kid sitting in it has his head down, glancing at something on his lap, and I can almost picture Cody in his place. They have the same dark hair, same build. Wrong hands, though. Cody's hands had long, tapered fingers, as though designed to capture and cradle the football. This kid's hands are short and stocky. And waving. They're waving.

My mind snaps to attention with a start, realizing the entire class is now focused on me as I stare absently at some random kid's hands like I'm struck dumb. The heat creeping into my neck might not be noticeable any other time, but since I'm flying makeup-free at the moment, I fear it might be showing on my face.

"Good morning," I eke out, rising from my spot and pressing my hands together tightly in front of me. "My name is Alexis Jennings. No, I am not related to Mr. Jennings next door. I just moved into the Louisville area this weekend, and although I'm very sorry about the untimely passing of Mr. Alberts, we're going to learn a lot together during the remainder of the year."

"Do you really think it was untimely?" the long-haired drummer pipes up. "Dude was, like, a hundred."

Of course the kid in *my* seat would be the one hassling me.

"Do you think Mr. Alberts would call it untimely?" I toss at him, doing my best to pin him with an authoritative stare. Whether or not it's working is a mystery, because I feel a little like a Chihuahua barking at a Rottweiler.

"I doubt he planned to kick over in the teachers' lounge."

His statement rattles me even more, because no one bothered to tell me he passed away here at school. Dragging in a huge breath, I manage to choke on it and have to cough so many times I'm afraid the poor girl in the front row thinks I'm about to follow in the previous teacher's footsteps. She's actually perched on the edge of her seat, about to run for the nurse.

Turning, I grab my bottle of water from the desk and take a slow sip, uttering an internal prayer before I return my attention to the class.

"Well, this has been a pleasant introduction, but I'd like to start over, if we may. If you all will pull out your books, that would definitely be a step in the right direction."

The mountainous drummer drops his book onto his desktop with a thud, causing half the class to jump in surprise.

"You, sir," I begin, not averting my eyes from his face. "Your name is?"

"Andy."

"Andy...do you have any idea what you've just done?" Lifting myself to sit on the edge of my desk, I clasp my hands together in my lap, keeping my voice low. "The algebra book you have on your desk is the most fragile of all the books. It's not a book to be tossed about as though it's nothing. You should take great care of it, Andy. Do you understand why it's so delicate?"

His eyes widen as he glances around at his classmates. "Wh...why?"

"Because it's full of problems, that's why. I'm counting on you to solve every one of them by the year's end."

He rolls his eyes, but a few of the other students snicker, which is enough of an ice breaker to allow me a second to breathe. Dragging out my paperwork, I grab a pen and twist off the cap, placing it on the opposite end.

"Shall we get to know everyone?" I suggest.

"How old are you?" the girl in row four, seat three asks. Doesn't even bother to shoot her hand into the air. Not a good start.

"Only questions properly asked by waiting for permission will be answered in my classroom," I inform her, pausing while her hand raises into the air. "Yes?"

"How old are you?"

I am an adult, and they will not defeat me. My day might have started with crying in the parking lot, but it will not end that way.

"Perhaps you could create an equation about it? The way I dress times the way I look, divided by the number of years I would have gone to college…"

She wrinkles her nose as she shakes her head. Andy raises his hand, waving it like a flag and making grunting noises, because naturally I won't notice his bulky form gyrating in front of me unless he accompanies his motion with sound.

"Yes, Andy?"

"Are you one of those genius kids who went to college when you were thirteen?"

Maybe Mr. Alberts didn't expire from natural causes after all. Maybe it was the unwavering persistence of Sir Andy Second Row Third Seat.

"Do you hear that?" I whisper, leaning forward slightly. Almost as one body, the students in front of me tilt closer.

"What is it?" the bespectacled girl directly in front of me wants to know.

"Crying. I knew it. Andy, your book is in bad shape. Pop it open and see if you can solve one of its problems."

"Aw, man."

The girl with the glasses smiles at me, and just like that, my heart gets a slight hint of convincing that things might be okay after all.

I should have never let my guard down. If Heather were here, she'd say I've managed to fall through the rabbit hole for real this time.

All I can say is that I believe I know what Alice must have felt like when she met the caterpillar, upon being told she was a wretched size. It's akin to "you don't belong here", or "you don't quite fit in", and I've been hearing that all day.

My first period class was beyond relentless. Even after I gave them quite a lecture on the rudeness of asking an adult's age, and especially a woman's, they wouldn't let up. I suppose it would have been easier to simply tell them I was twenty-five and have it over with, but I stood my ground on the sheer principle of the matter.

I must admit, I nearly lost it when Andy tried to arrive at the answer in the roundabout fashion of asking me whether it would be legal for us to date, *you know, if I wasn't his teacher and if we were off school premises.*

Was sending him to the principal's office an overreaction? Perhaps, but it was the only way I saw to end the conversation in that moment.

After second period, I managed to sneak to the faculty restroom to try to apply my mascara again only to be caught by the librarian, who scolded me for hiding out and threatened to call my mother. My mother! She ushered me out of the room and smacked me on the rear like I was the field goal kicker and it was fourth down at the fifteen yard line.

Part of me wanted to turn around and give her a piece of my mind, but then I thought it might be funnier if she realized who I was later. At a faculty meeting, maybe. Or in front of the superintendent, perhaps.

At the end of third period, I made the mistake of looking at my phone. When I saw that the daycare called about fifteen minutes before, my heart started palpitating and my brain flew through a million different scenarios at the speed of light. Bailey ran away. Bailey cried so hard she passed out. Bailey has disowned me forever.

My hand shook around the phone as I listened to the ringing on the other end, standing in the corner of my new classroom and trying to obtain what little privacy I could by the practice of turning my back to the room. When a voice finally connected, I'm certain I sounded frantic, half-hissing into the phone with a panicked whisper that I didn't want my new students to overhear.

"Oh, Bailey's mom," the woman at the daycare stated. "We didn't want to bother you, but she's wearing a diaper."

"Uh huh." My attempt at being quiet seemed to be thwarted by the fact that the class was suddenly hawk-eye focused on me.

"We don't allow children into the preschool program here unless they're potty trained."

"Oh, she is." Closing my eyes, I cringed at my partial untruth. "Sometimes it's just precautionary, you know... We mostly have it covered, but since she's in a new place today, I wanted to make sure."

"There won't be any diaper changing in this program."

"It's not a diaper."

"She urinated in it, ma'am. It's a diaper."

"It's not a diaper," I insisted, my voice getting slightly louder than I anticipated. "It's... structurally sound paper underpants."

My new fourth period students erupted into laughter behind me, but the potty policewoman was not so easily amused.

"Fine. She soiled her paper underpants. Please don't let it happen again."

"Absolutely not. We're one-hundred percent full-out using the potty from this point forward."

I can still hear the ringing of their laughter in my ears as I stand at the entrance to the cafeteria. There is no earthly way I'm going to be able to ensure Bailey's completely potty trained by tomorrow. She's progressing, but not to the point where I can put her in regular underwear. The entire morning's roster of students thinks I'm completely insane. And, to top it all off, I forgot my lunch and I'm currently trying to figure out whether or not to actually eat the square pizza on this lime green tray.

But I'm not crying. I'm not in the bathroom, and I'm not crying.

Scanning the room, my eyes settle on a table near the back corner, one solitary young lady sitting there with her eyes on her food. Immediately my mind whooshes back to my own high school cafeteria, freshman year, and I see Sadie in front of me.

She's sitting there alone, pushing her fork into the pile of rice on her plate, smashing it one way and then the other. I'm fairly certain she doesn't see me approaching, because she doesn't flinch when I move next to her. When I place my tray across from hers, her gaze lifts slowly, measuring the space between us in what appears to be an attempt to judge the safety of my presence.

I don't say anything as I sit down, and she peers at me from underneath a fringe of black bangs. Her hair wasn't black last year. If my mind serves me correctly, I think it was a mahogany shade. The roots of her hair would probably give me the proof I need, but I try not to stare.

"Anybody sitting here?" I ask, trying to keep my voice friendly. Rather than answer straight away, she glances from one end of the table to the other, as though she wants to point out the fact that I should be more observant. I've never been good at starting conversations, so I refuse her silent assessment and go on being awkwardly myself. "I hope you don't mind the company."

"Where's your friends?"

Sitting at the second table, same as always, but I'm not about to tell her that.

"It's just me. Please don't make me eat alone, Sadie Lou."

The mention of her childhood nickname causes her to look me full in the face, and I can see the smeared edge of her black eyeliner where she's been rubbing it with her finger.

"Whatever you're doing, don't."

"I'm eating lunch."

"You know what I mean. Don't pretend you can't see people looking over here."

"I hadn't noticed," I tell her, sinking my fork into my rice and capturing a sticky, tasteless blob in my mouth.

"Dang it, Alexis, you're going to ruin your reputation. I don't mind sitting by myself."

"Of course you mind, and how exactly would I ruin my reputation? It's not..." Leaning closer, I peer over my shoulder before returning my eyes to her. "It's not contagious, right?"

It's been ages since I heard Sadie laugh out loud, and I'm fairly certain the entire student body turned to stare at the both of us in unison.

"You know what? You're just naïve enough I can't tell if you're being serious or if you're making a joke," she says with a grin. "I suppose I've been next to you in health class, though, and you got pretty good grades."

"Well, I won't sample your milk, just in case." We share a genuine smile before we go back to picking at our food. "I don't see what the big deal is, anyway. Every single person in this school has something secret they're shoving under the rug. In your case, you just have the misfortune of wearing it like a billboard."

"Except you. What secret are you shoving under the rug, little miss perfect?"

Glancing back at my usual table, I see Cody leaning over to Mindy, whispering something into her ear.

"Let's just say I've been having to keep some unpleasant thoughts captive today. The past several days, really."

"Hardly the same thing," she argues, shaking her head. I can tell I'm chipping away at her, though, because the side of her mouth tips upward. "I'll pretend you're right, just for lunch. I've got no worries."

Shrugging, I stab a piece of pineapple with my fork. "I don't know if I would go that far. I saw the red pen on your English essay this morning."

"Shakespeare," she mutters, rolling her eyes. "Completely Greek to me."

"Early Modern English," I correct. "The outdated words and complex sentence structures make people think it's Middle or even Old English, but I haven't heard anybody think it's Greek before."

She gives up on her food and places her elbows on the table, settling her chin on her fists. "Do you ever *not* pay attention in class?"

"Sure." My nonchalance causes her to raise her eyebrows.

"Other than when Cody's talking to you?"

"Hmm, that I don't know how to answer. He's awfully distracting." She laughs again as I try to get a sticky piece of rice to detach from my fork. "Do you remember the time our moms took us to the creek and you caught that frog? You stuck it in my hair and it got hung up in my braid. A couple of the most horrifying moments of my life."

"Yeah, I remember."

"I don't know when we stopped hanging out, but we should rectify that situation."

That's a complete falsehood, and we're both absolutely aware of that fact as we glance at our plates, trying to ignore the obvious. Sadie hasn't been around anyone really since she started a friendship with her neighbor and his older brother last year. I'm not one to take part in gossip, but I've heard things whispered about what they're smoking, drinking, taking, doing. Some of it might be exaggeration, but circumstances indicate that other pieces definitely aren't.

Since she doesn't offer any conversation, I continue on with my awkward prattle. "You should come over tonight. We could work on Shakespeare together."

"I don't know…"

"My mom will probably make chicken for dinner. And I promise not to copy your assignment."

"You're such a dork."

"Don't hold that against me! You've known that since we were in elementary school."

"It's not that I don't want to, but… You know it's not a good idea for me to come to your house."

"Are you worried about its structural integrity? Sure, you've gained a little weight lately, but I seriously doubt the floor will cave in. My dad walks on it all the time, and he's probably got at least thirty pounds on you."

"Alexis, I'm sure your dad doesn't want a fifteen-year-old pregnant girl sitting at your dining room table."

"Because he's a preacher," I finish for her, tilting my head to the side.

"Of course because he's a preacher," she whispers, her eyes traveling over my shoulder to stare at the cafeteria behind us.

"I get it." Pushing my tray to the left, I lean against the table, folding my arms in front of me. "You don't need to worry. I'll tell him to cool it."

"Right," she counters with a fake, rather sad laugh, shaking her head.

"He'll listen to me. I know he can come on pretty strong with the love and compassion and all that, but he can hold himself back. I can't promise he won't sneak in at least one hug, but…"

"Very funny."

"You know, you can sit at the grown-up table." Twisting my head to the side, I'm immediately pulled out of my memory by the sight of my classroom neighbor Roger, who offers a lopsided grin.

"Thank you," I reply with a hint of sarcasm, but I gratefully follow him so I don't have the misfortune of making yet another mistake.

"Halfway home, huh?"

His comment stops me in my tracks, because there's no way he could know I'm thinking about my own high school.

"Pardon me?"

He smiles as he sits down at a table and motions to the spot next to him, where I drop my tray unceremoniously. "Just an expression. The day's midway to being over, so we're halfway home."

"Oh, sure." A forced smile graces my face, but I can't seem to make it convincing.

My mind's not really here, anyway. It's back at my parents' kitchen table, sitting in front of a plate of spaghetti, watching my dad crack jokes with a very pregnant Sadie Lou. I hadn't been able to rein him in that night. He showered Sadie with the biggest boatload of acceptance she had seen, and she was a fixture at our home from that point forward. God knew she needed us, and that I'd need her later.

"Halfway home," I whisper to myself, staring at that lunchroom pizza, my thoughts held captive somewhere between Kentucky and Tennessee.

# Chapter Nine

## Jake

Roxanne's voice filters through my dream and causes me to toss in my bed, clamping my eyes shut against the light coming in around the edges of the curtains.

"Hey sugar," she croons, making me wish I could block her out. Even after two weeks here, I can't get used to having the woman wake me up every morning. Tossing back the comforter, I stretch my fists in opposite directions and try to work the kinks out of my back. Something has me in knots, and I have a feeling it's a combination of the blonde who haunts my dreams, Alexis, this lumpy bed, and....

"I missed you, baby."

Blech.

Pausing at the door to the bathroom, I lean against the frame, blinking back a momentary feeling of dizziness caused by rising from bed too quickly. The instant it passes, I turn to gaze at myself in the mirror, lifting a hand to rub it across two days' worth of stubble on my cheek. That guy in the mirror looks about as excited as I feel.

*"You got out of her car, Miguel. After telling me you were working late, I watched her drop you off in front of your office."*

Releasing a sigh of exasperation, I step around the door and into the bedroom, banging my fist loudly against the wall a couple times.

"Roxanne!" My voice sounds sleep-drowsy and hoarse, so I bang again. "There are people trying to coexist with you."

She coughs, and for a second I can smell her cigarette smoke coming through the wall, permeating my clothes, seeping into my skin. That seems ludicrous, so I decide it must be my imagination.

"It's time for my programs." There's a pause while she coughs again, a little more forcefully this time. "Only time we gotta keep the noise down is at night, when normal people sleep. You need a friend, honey. When I get off the phone with Bud, you come on over here and watch the programs with me."

That sounds a little bit like hell on earth.

Sinking onto the bed, I drop my head into my hands and try to block out the sound of her Latin American soap opera. There's no temptation to rest on my laurels and postpone finding a job, because sitting here all day listening to Roxanne is not appealing to me in any way, shape, or form.

Truth be told, she hits a little too close to home. In another city, in another state, in another motel, she could be my mother. A random, aging barfly, chain smoking in the motel room where she's taken up residence, looking for the next guy. Of course his name is Bud. It's just generic enough that it can serve as a nickname for every single guy she meets. Can't remember which man she's supposed to be with that night? Just refer to them all as Bud, and she has it covered.

It's rather amusing that Roxanne spends a little part of each day listening to those televangelists. They're basically running the same scenario she's running on guys at night. Step one, convince them they're not good enough on their own. Step two, let them know you have the answer. Step three, steal their cash. Strangely enough, she shouts out her "amens" to the television next door and has no idea she's being taken for a sucker.

And the fact that I've just gone down that path in my mind confirms that my reality has turned into some sort of sideshow.

Fourth stop today, and I can't seem to make any headway. Downturned economy punctuates every spiel, and I get it, but it's growing old. Nobody's hiring for construction jobs, and that's where I have experience. Sure, I've been bartending for a week at an Italian chain restaurant, but that's nights, and...

Nah, I'm not going to complain about it. I had a great job that I loved, working with my best friend, and I'm the only reason that gig's gone.

This place is a little more highbrow than the others I've visited, and part of me doesn't even want to bother stepping inside. The doors are glass, though, and once the receptionist glances up and sees me, I feel like I have no choice.

"Hey," I offer as I step through the door, only realizing it's not a proper greeting after the word has left my lips. Smoothing my hand across the abdomen of my white Henley, I absently grab the bottom hem of the blue flannel shirt covering it. My jaw clenches in frustration as I wonder why this awkwardness didn't plague me back in Tennessee. I distinctly remember having no problem commanding a room, or even appearing cool under pressure.

Kentucky is not wearing so well on me.

"May I help you, sir?"

*Find the words, McAuliffe. Career search... Qualified candidate... Experienced in...stuff.*

A disgusted-sounding laugh escapes, just quietly enough to make the receptionist tilt her head as she stares at me, eyes growing a little larger while waiting for my response.

"I need a job. It feels like I've been all over this city, and no one's hiring. I'm sure this place isn't going to be any different, but what the heck, right?" *Man.* "I'm sorry. It's been... I'm not having a great day, but that's no excuse to be rude. I apologize."

Apology evidently not accepted, because rather than replying, her eyes dart around me as she avoids me altogether.

"Regina, did my two-thirty ever show up?"

The sound of a male voice draws my attention to my right, and I cringe at the thought that someone else might have heard my little outburst.

"No, sir. No sign of him."

"Hmph." The man steps up beside me, crossing his arms over his chest. His weathered no-nonsense face seems even more work-hardened due to the fact that he's wearing a deep gray T-shirt with the company logo on the front. "People are undependable anymore. Flat undependable. And lazy. Back in my day, you showed up early for a job interview." He pauses and looks in my direction. "Like this guy. He's early. What's your name, son?" I decide not to waste any time before taking part in the offered handshake.

"Jake McAuliffe, but I'm not on your schedule."

"Then you're earlier than I thought. Come on."

He turns the corner into a room marked only by a wooden desk and half a dozen hard hats scattered on pegs on the wall and sitting on bookshelves. A couple are yellow, but most are white, with one scuffed version that looks about twenty years old. His leather chair groans as he sits in it, but he doesn't seem to notice as he grabs a cheap pair of drug store glasses from his desk.

"Jake, you said?" His words are straight to the point as he places the glasses on his face and glances at the papers on his desk. "The guy who needs a job bad enough to burst in here and verbally vomit all over my receptionist?"

Ouch.

"It was uncalled for, no question. Frustration is starting to wear on me."

"Well, at least you want to work. This generation seems to be lacking in that characteristic." He grabs a business card from the top drawer of his desk and flips it across toward me. "Bob Phillips. I'm looking for a site manager. You have to have experience in general framing and electrical or you're of no use to me."

"Sure, I do. Have experience, I mean."

"You get fired from your last job?"

If the questions were any more rapid-fire, I'd swear I was at a shooting range.

"No, sir. I recently moved here from Tennessee."

"And you didn't have a job lined up before you moved? That isn't very good planning."

Part of me wants to drop the business card on the desk and thank him for his time, but this is the closest thing to a real interview I've had in this town.

"I didn't give it a lot of thought. My ex moved here with my daughter, and I followed them here."

He leans back in his chair and folds his arms across his chest as he regards me over the frames of his glasses. "That speaks to your moral aptitude. The fact that you're devoted to your family indicates that you'd apply yourself at your job."

Maybe I could get this guy to write a letter to Alexis. *Jake is not a deadbeat.* She'd probably demand that it be notarized and witnessed by a judge.

"Well, I have another appointment in just a minute, but see Regina at the front desk and have her give you an application. Just fill it out and make sure you list your references, and I'll be in touch."

"Thank you."

For a brief moment my outlook actually looks a little brighter, until I sit down to begin filling out that application. Address…I don't know? Room eleven, right next to Roxanne? Listing my job experience doesn't make me feel special, either, since I have that big break during the time when I couldn't find a job thanks to Alexis. But those things are trumped when I get to the section marked references. There's absolutely no getting around it.

I have to list Cole Parker. His words from our last conversation ring through my mind.

*Lousy friend. Have a little self-control.*

So I hand my application to Regina with a forced smile, knowing full well the only job I'll have at the end of the week will be recommending wines that complement fettucine alfredo.

The sun banks off the top of that white-sided house in such a way that it almost blinds me when I turn my truck into the driveway. I could try to blame the fact that I almost sideswiped that Mitsubishi on the glare, but it's more likely a result of my slight distraction. The fact that I haven't set foot on this property since the day after we arrived is likely not going to sit well with Alexis, and definitely won't aid in proving to her that I want a relationship with Bailey.

Because I do.

I think I should, anyway.

It's just warm enough that I ease out of my jacket while I'm walking to the door, pausing to glance through the window at the front of the house. Some fairly loud music is filtering out to me, and Bailey's hopping up and down, shaking her head. She's also wearing one of the weirdest outfits I've ever seen. Pink checked shirt over green pants, complete with suspenders. She's also got a ridiculous-looking pointy felt hat on her head with a yellow flower sewn in the middle.

Shaking my head, I prepare to knock on the door, but stop short when Alexis comes into my line of view. Her movement holds me captive as she sways in front of Bailey, huge smile lighting her face. No doubt she'd be attractive if I didn't know her, in those pencil-thin black jeans and the draped purple top that barely covers her midsection as she raises her arms. She might be beautiful, but her dancing is kind of odd, especially the thing she's doing with her arms. It's almost... Ah, air guitar. Makes sense now.

Her eyes flit to the window and she spots me. Immediately the party is over, and she turns rigid. Heaven forbid I figure out that she's a human being.

The sound of the music disappears seconds before she opens the door, face slightly flushed and fire in her eyes. One of these days I'd like to see her in a crowd to determine whether she's always ticked off at the world, or if she reserves that emotion for me.

"Jake."

That's it, just my name, and she offers nothing else. No way am I letting her get to me today, though.

"Alex."

If she ordered me to march twenty paces and then shot me in the back when I got to nineteen, it wouldn't surprise me one bit.

"I thought you would have gone home by now," she says as Bailey takes up residence by her mom's leg.

Pretending I don't get her meaning, I glance at my watch. "Nah, it's still early, and I only live a couple miles away." She'd like it if I turned tail and headed to Tennessee, but it's not an option. Turning my attention to Bailey, I raise my eyebrows. "Nice outfit, kiddo."

She wiggles her pointy-toed shoe coverings at me, which is useful because I hadn't noticed them up to this point. It gives the entire getup a whole new "wow" factor.

"I'm a gnome," she announces proudly.

That actually explains a lot. Sort of.

"She had her Halloween party at preschool yesterday and she really likes her costume," Alexis explains.

"Well, I really like it too," I add, dropping to one knee to be closer to Bailey's height. "You're probably the cutest gnome I've ever seen."

"Prob'ly," she agrees, wrinkling up her nose.

"What are you doing here, Jake?"

There's no beating around the bush with this one. I'm telling you—if I turned my back for a second, the woman would impale me. Letting out a heavy sigh, I rise to my feet so I can face her.

"Just here to see my kid."

"And you have."

"For an extended period of time."

"We'll have to work something out lat—"

"Right now works for me, unless you're practicing for a dance recital."

Her cheeks flush immediately, which makes her look even prettier, so I force my gaze onto Bailey.

"Hey, I'm sorry I missed the whole Halloween thing yesterday, but I brought you a surprise."

"A prize?" Bailey rubs her hands together and shakes her entire body, which nearly makes me bust out laughing. The kid sure has a ton of personality. As an added bonus, her excitement must hit a nerve with Alexis, because she stands back and allows me to enter the house.

As soon as my feet hit the old hardwood in the entryway, Bailey is bouncing up and down with excitement. "Here. It's in the pocket of my jacket."

I've never really witnessed a kid opening a present before, but the way Bailey's tearing at my jacket, I'm a little worried that she might rip it apart. Within a few seconds, though, she whips out a handful of crumpled paper, gazing forlornly at her find.

"Paper," she states with clear disappointment, tossing it behind her.

"Other pocket," I mumble as I bend to retrieve the mess, feeling a split second of panic as Alexis reaches the bunch of napkins before I have a chance.

"'Layla,'" she states as she narrows her eyes. "'502-356...'" Shaking her head, she adjusts one paper to her other hand as she reviews the next one. "'Thanks for the laughs. Tessa. 812—'"

"I'm a bartender," I insert.

"Of course you are." She never skips a beat. "'I'm in town for two more days. Call me, day or night. Emmie.'"

"Found it!" Bailey exclaims, brandishing her giant package of M&M's like a WWE wrestler showcasing the Big Gold Belt. If it weren't for the fact that Alexis still has those napkins, I would find it hilarious.

"'Pasta primavera? So-so. Pinot Grigio? Pretty good. Bartender? Scrumptious. Result? Still hungry. I'll be at Risky's until 2. Alexis.'" She balls the napkins together in her first. "What a charming person to share a name with."

Can I really be held responsible for the fact that a couple of women left me their numbers? It's not as though I was singling them out for the specific purpose of picking them up. The job requires a certain amount of friendly attention if one wants to make a living from tips. Since that's my only option at the moment, I do what I have to do.

She crosses to the bar that separates the kitchen from the living room and drops the napkins onto the counter. At that specific moment she recognizes the business card among them that she hadn't seen seconds ago, and her eyes lift to bore into me, the hard glint there expressing her anger in volumes. As quickly as it appears, it slides off her face, a general indifference taking over as she smooths each napkin separately on the countertop.

The back of that business card is just lewd enough, I'm grateful she didn't read it out loud.

I draw my attention to Bailey, still dancing around with her giant bag of candy. This would be a perfect moment for Alexis to scream at me. It wouldn't exactly be justified, but she could call me a lowlife or player or something. The fact that she clams up again like normal is almost enough to tick me off, because it means she doesn't expect anything else of me. She thinks I'm a scumbag.

"Maybe I can take Bailey to the park," I suggest, simply wanting to put some distance between us.

"No."

"What?" My head snaps in her direction, where she's taken her eyes off me and is beginning to unload the dishwasher. Even though she isn't watching, I take two steps toward the counter and gather those papers in my fist, dropping them into the trash can at the end of the counter. That's what I would have done with them anyway, when I remembered that I stuffed them into my pocket in the first place.

"You're welcome to talk to her here while I'm cleaning the kitchen."

Man, sometimes I want to give her a piece of my mind. How am I supposed to respond to that? Thank you, Your Majesty?

I know exactly what I *want* to say.

*Hey, Alexis, remember when you had Bailey and I was court-ordered to take a paternity test because you wanted child support? I remember because your entire family dragged my name through the mud.*

*Can't really forget it because there's a gaping hole in my employment record at that time. And then after all that, you decided you didn't want a dime of my money and just cut me loose.*

But somehow I manage to keep my mouth shut. Instead, I focus on playing with Bailey for the next hour and a half, completely ignoring her mom. I don't even bother to tell her goodbye when I leave the house. The way she hangs in the fringes and waits for me to leave, she'll probably attack Bailey with a disinfectant the minute I'm gone just to get the taint of me off her.

Pretty sure that's a lost cause, since my blood's running through her veins.

The truck offers me a bit of sanctuary as I shut myself inside. Paying attention to my kid shouldn't be this hard, should it? Granted, it would have been a little easier if Alexis hadn't been lurking about like a mother lioness waiting to pounce on me if I stepped out of line. Even so, nothing in me feels parental and I have no idea how to relate to a little girl. But I should still get some kind of life bonus points simply for participation.

My cell rings on the dash of the truck, and I glance at it to see the number. I can't think of anyone who would bother to call me, and the fact that it's a number I don't recognize is almost enough to convince me not to answer. Curiosity wins out, though, so I give a halfhearted "hello" as I draw it up to my ear.

"Jake McAuliffe?"

"One and the same." The voice on the other end sounds vaguely familiar, but I can't place it.

"Bob Phillips. Can you be in first thing Monday to talk particulars? I'd like to have you start right away."

The phone nearly falls from my hand as my heart lurches in my chest and I try to sit a little straighter. "You mean I got the job?"

"As long as you're committed to the hard work. That Parker fella you listed as a reference had nothing but great things to say about you. He told me I'd be crazy if I didn't hire you."

Some response is probably necessary but I'm finding myself rendered speechless. Why would Parker do that? It makes no sense.

"You still there, son?"

A quick shake of my head brings me back to the conversation at hand.

"Yes, of course. I'll definitely be there Monday morning. Thank you."

"Just don't let me down," he says as he hangs up.

Turning to peer over my shoulder, I back my truck up until I'm on Wonder Lane, ready to head out of the sleepy little subdivision. Before I can make my way down the street, though, I pause briefly to allow the warring thoughts inside my head a moment to percolate.

If there was ever a doubt in my mind up to this point, Cole Parker is most definitely a bigger man than me. And he was right about one thing: He has this whole "friend" business figured out in ways that I definitely don't. No wonder Camdyn...

And the fact that I couldn't just leave well enough alone will probably haunt me for a really long time.

# Chapter Ten

## Alexis

We haven't seen Jake since the day after we arrived in Louisville, so what are the odds that he would choose the exact moment we were having a dance party to knock on the door? And not just any dance party—a potty party. The fact that I convinced the directors that she was having a hard time adjusting due to the fact that she was accustomed to being with my mother was almost a miracle in itself, but Bailey officially went three days without any accidents at preschool. After seven days of condescending scowls when I picked her up after school, it felt like an accomplishment worth celebrating. So we were having a blast rocking out to the music, and then there he was.

Talk about a buzz kill.

Giving her that giant bag of M&Ms that would be more suitable for a bowl on a receptionist's desk was bad enough, but those notes in his pocket... It was almost like he wanted to rub it in my face that he had women throwing themselves at him.

*Look, Alexis. See all these women who want to be with me? You were nothing special.*

Not going to lie—in the deepest recesses of my mind, one of my strongest desires is to erase every trace of memory I have of Jake McAuliffe. Not that I have very many particularly vivid memories, but each smidge of something in my subconscious makes me feel like a subpar version of myself.

Oh, who am I kidding? I actually feel like a subpar version of myself most of the time.

Still, when I turned around to throw an empty popcorn bag in the trash and saw those names and phone numbers sitting there on top of my garbage, something tightened in my chest. From the absolute depths of my being, I wish Jake was a fine, upstanding, respectable guy. The past is the past and what happened is what happened, but despite my aversions to the truth, Jake is Bailey's father. There's no reasonable scenario where I wake up twenty years from now and he hasn't impacted my daughter's life.

Naturally, I'd prefer it if he wasn't the kind of guy who had so many offers, he carried them around by the pocketful and dumped them in the trash like they were nothing.

My eyes dart over to the living room, where he's kneeling next to a game Bailey set out as they spin a wheel to see who can earn the most jewelry. He's actually being more good-natured about it than I imagined, even if things between us are chillier than a brisk hike around the peak of Everest. I'm well aware that's partially my fault, too, but what does he expect? I can't allow him to leave the house with Bailey after the incident with Cam and the bed and Bailey wearing her clothes.

My face heats up just thinking about it.

Taking my anger out on a spot on the counter, I dig the sponge in, rubbing with all the force in my arm. It doesn't budge easily, and I glance into the living room again, inspecting Jake's profile. It seems ridiculous to think about it at this point, but I've never really taken a long, hard look at him. Oh, I don't mean we've never made eye contact or anything like that, but anything further than that...

The night we met, I wasn't exactly at my best, and I don't remember much about him. After that, things were weird enough between us that I couldn't bring myself to full-out stare at him. Now, it seems like every time I meet his eyes he's either making fun of me or trying to tick me off, and I don't look at him long for fear that I might lose my temper and punch him in the nose.

But I get it. If I was a random woman in a random restaurant and he was a random bartender and he was flirting with me...

Well, I'm still not idiotic enough to call him scrumptious, or to write my name on a napkin for that matter.

I flick my eyes down to that spot on the counter to make sure I'm in the right place before I glance at him again, absently shifting the sponge from my right hand to my left. He's not an exceptionally big guy—maybe three inches taller than me at most —and he has the appearance of being fit without really trying. Or to elaborate, he fills out his T-shirt nicely and is trim, but I seriously doubt there's any hidden six-pack under there or anything.

Images of a dark room flick through my mind like an old video reel trying to come into focus. The smells of cologne and pungent alcohol. Lips moving their way down my neck.

Sharply inhaling, I twist and throw the sponge at the sink, shaking my head. That's how my Jake memories usually show up— unwanted and intrusive, when I least expect them. Kind of like Jake shows up himself, come to think of it.

And it looks like my spot on the counter is actually an imperfection in the coloring, so I've been wasting my time. Kind of like dealing with Jake.

A still, small voice inside pleads with me to be nice, because he is currently wearing two pink beaded necklaces while he sits on the floor with my daughter, and I think I see a gaudy yellow earring dangling from his ear. He has nice ears. Not in a weird way or anything, they just fit the size of his head.

His nose is perfectly symmetrical right down the center of his face, too. And that little cleft in his chin that gets covered up if he has even a hint of a five o'clock shadow—don't even get me started. Not to mention that dimple in his cheek that he graciously passed on to Bailey.

It would really be nice if there was something wrong with him, that's all. If he weren't always so, "Hey, ladies, look at me. Aren't I handsome?"

The flirting wouldn't be quite as annoying if it didn't work.

He glances my way just enough to catch me staring at him, so I drop my eyes to pick at the non-existent spot on the counter again. The two of them don't hesitate as they continue playing their game, and as soon as his eyes leave me I try to hide a small smile. I totally saw it. His eyebrows rest a little low on his forehead, causing him to look like he's always squinting those blue eyes of his under that light golden brown hair. That's his flaw. His eyebrows are too low.

Somehow that decision makes me feel a little better as I finish cleaning the kitchen, rubbing down the inside of the cabinets, polishing silverware that is so cheap I could probably snap it in two. Anything to occupy my time so I can keep an eye on the two of them without looking like an anxious mother hen.

He makes it an hour and a half before he gives out. Two rounds of that jewelry princess game, a few minutes of Bailey bossing him around on the particulars of being a horse, and then about three seconds of pretending to be said horse before she gives up and decides she wants to do something else.

"Jay color," she orders as she hands him a crayon, but he rises to his feet instead and says he has to leave. Rather than protest, she just shrugs and sits back down to her animal coloring book. His footsteps sound as he heads to the door, but I choose to look the other way so we don't have to go through an awkward conversation. Or an argument. Or a pseudo-argument because I won't allow it to become a full-blown argument.

The instant he's gone, I move to the garbage and pull those napkins out, studying them one by one, growing more disgusted by the second at the kind of life he leads. Jerking open the drawer behind me, I grab the disposable lighter, holding the first napkin out as I create a flame that licks up the paper and moves toward my fingers. Right before it burns me, I toss it in the sink.

The act was just therapeutic enough that I repeat my motions, feeling the heat rise from another napkin as the flame moves across the swooping letters in the name until it dissolves into ash. Again I click the button to ignite the paper, and once more, until all that's left is that business card. The idiotic legal assistant actually has her name and business address on this one. I should call her boss.

One deep breath and I light the business card in the sink, watching it curl up as it smokes. An ear-piercing beep sounds overhead, and the lighter drops to the floor as I jerk backwards.

Another beep and another, while I frantically search for something to stand on so I can silence the alarm above me. Without much furniture, I'm drawing a blank.

"Moooommmy!"

Bailey stands in the hallway with her hands over her ears, her frightened eyes wide as she penetrates me with her stare. I try to comfort her, but she won't have it as that beep keeps sounding.

"Moooommmmmmy! Stop it!"

Unable to find anything to stand on, I grab the broom and hurry back to the kitchen, jabbing it up at the smoke detector to try to make the noise stop. Before I can get it under control, I manage to dent the sheetrock above me in two different places. And then the beeping starts again just a few seconds later.

Pulling up the window in the kitchen, I grab a towel and wave it above my head a few times until the beeping comes to a halt. As I hang my head, I can't help but hear Bailey murmuring beside me. Turning, I take in the presence of my sweet girl, hands pressed over her ears and tears running down her face.

"I'm so sorry," I whisper, opening my arms. Rather than move toward me, she stands in place, shaking her head. "Bailey, it's okay, it was just a loud noise. Nothing happened."

Still, she won't move toward me, so I sink to my knees to look her in the eyes, placing my hand on the silky fabric of the gnome costume against her shoulder. Her bottom lip pushes out, but she remains rooted to her spot. My attempt to draw her in my direction using my hand falls short, so I tilt my head as I look into her eyes.

With a little huff, her lip sticks out even further.

"I peed my pants."

# Chapter Eleven

## Alexis

There's something about holiday dinners and the Jennings household that combine to create an exclusive club of sorts. And since Mom and Dad have been involved in ministry over the years, we've entertained a lot of people at our table. Sometimes they were elderly widows, or families whose daughters or sons had recently gotten married, and once even a Korean family who wanted to see American traditions firsthand. They were always well-fed and even better-loved.

Either you're a Jennings dinner veteran, or you're not.

As an honorary family member, Sadie Lou is most definitely a Jennings dinner veteran. She's also the only person who can look at me across a table without saying a word and manage to make me feel self-conscious, defensive, anxious, and accepted in a mere matter of seconds.

"Jonah, how is third grade treating you?" I ask, averting my gaze from Sadie's green eyes. Her son shrugs as he stares at his mashed potatoes.

"Okay. Multiplying is hard."

"You should know better than to diss math when you're talking to Alex," Heather announces to the entire table, not bothering to look up from her plate. I can't for the life of me remember her boyfriend's name. Jesse? Jerry? Johnny? I allow my eyes to linger on his face for a second, until he catches me staring and meets my gaze.

Jeremy.

I don't know why I even bother. He'll be gone by next weekend anyway. Heather has an unspoken three-week rule. Week one is window shopping. This is where she meets said guy, gives him the once-over, and decides whether he is worth a further inspection. Week two is the equivalent of going to one of those used car sites to determine whether the automobile has any fatal flaws. Prior wrecks, bad transmissions, bent frames. In Heather's case, I would guess it's something like body odor, bad breath, or maybe the inability to pay for her dinner.

Week three is the test drive, and I'll spare myself the ickiness of thinking too deeply about that.

Jeremy stares at me a little too closely before he glances back at Heather, and instinctively I know what he's thinking. If I wore a little more makeup and a little less clothing, and a fairly constant smirking grin on my face, I might look a lot like my younger sister.

"I listen to people diss math every day," I offer to Jonah, along with a smile. "In fact, there's one boy in my first hour class who thinks he has to take a dig at me at least once a morning. But you'll be glad you figured out multiplication one day when you're at McDonald's and wondering how many cheeseburgers you can get with five dollars."

"Or you can just calculate it on your phone the way Steve Jobs intended," Heather adds, giving me a grin so I'll know she's teasing.

"True." I stop picking up green beans with my fork just long enough to make sure I have Jonah's attention. "But…you'll never *be* the next Steve Jobs with that kind of attitude."

Jonah shrugs, because he's nine and probably just wants the whole lot of us to leave him alone. I'm supposed to be an adult and sometimes I feel the same way, so I know where he's coming from.

"What does Miss Bailey think of her new house?" Sadie wonders as she drags a slice of turkey through the brown gravy on her plate.

"It's not like Gump's," Bailey tells her, picking up a green bean with her fingers. "Jay made big locks to keep out bad peoples."

"Bad peoples?" Mom asks, eyes wide as she glances in my direction. She can't be forced to bring the glass any closer to her lips than where it stopped a couple inches away, probably because I haven't countered Bailey's words yet.

"Jake installed new locks so Bailey couldn't open the door when I wasn't in the room, that's all. No bad people."

"Jake spends a lot of time with you two, then?" Dad might have posed his question lightly, but it holds a depth that I don't miss. He wants to know how far I've come to forgiving Jake, as though it's just a cut and dry option. I love my dad immensely, but sometimes that bleeding heart compassion doesn't translate to the real world.

"He's been over three times since Halloween. Always on Saturdays, and usually for just over an hour."

"Does he live near you then?" Mom wonders, finally allowing the glass to her lips.

"He says he does, but I have no idea."

"Well, where does he work?" Dad wants to know. "Has he been able to find a job up there?"

"He told me he's a bartender."

Heather clears her throat, and I can't help but glance in her direction. Her eyebrows rise a bit as she tilts her head at me, and I know if we were in private she would make a joke about that statement. Jake practically living in a bar, he spends so much time there, or something or other.

"I think it's real nice you let the boy in Bailey's life," Mrs. Hathaway states. She's so quiet, I'd nearly forgotten she was at the table, down at the end just between Sadie and my dad. She offers me a timid smile, her delicate white hair framing her face in a bob with the ends flipped under. The soft-spoken octogenarian was one of the few people who actually stood by Dad's side three years ago when…

But it's Thanksgiving, and best not to think about those things while I'm supposed to be counting my blessings.

"It's nice to have all of us together today, isn't it?" Mom's voice has suddenly taken on a token of whimsy, and it almost makes me a little nostalgic. Thanksgiving was so happy and joyful, back when our only troubles were wondering who to invite to dinner.

Back when my parents didn't worry about paying their mortgage, or trying to find work.

And deep inside, I know it's all my fault.

"I guess Jake couldn't accept our invitation?" Mom pushes on, and I can actually feel my neck growing crimson under her attentive stare. Unable to flat-out lie to my mother, I simply shake my head. He couldn't accept the invitation, because I didn't extend it to him. Bailey and I were driving five hours back home for Thanksgiving, after all. Why would I want to include the one person who would impede any chance of happiness?

"I wonder how he'll be spending his holiday," Mom adds. That statement actually causes Heather to kick me under the table. I definitely don't have extrasensory perception, but somehow I'm still reading Heather's mind. *He'll be drunk in a few hours—a bleached-blonde with a skintight skirt stretched over her thighs hanging off his neck. Or if he's working, he'll be getting said blonde drunk. Letting her give him tips.*

Oh, who am I kidding? I can't really say any of that with certainty. She could be a brunette, or a redhead.

"Bailey, I think your house sounds great," Sadie interjects, effectively saving the day. I don't want to spend our entire Thanksgiving dinner talking about Jake, after all. "In fact, I can't wait until Jonah and I get some time to come up and see you there."

"You come to my house?" Bailey asks excitedly. "And Gump and Nan?"

"Just as soon as we can," Dad says, reaching out to tap Bailey on the nose. "Sometimes old Gump can't get off work so easily."

That's another thing bringing down my Thanksgiving happiness. I know that Dad's going to be heading off to work tomorrow, and we won't be able to spend the day decorating for Christmas like we used to. His job managing a pizza chain restaurant in Jackson doesn't leave a lot of time for recreational activities, and he hasn't been there long enough to build up much vacation time.

Mom is in the same boat, although she does have the weekends unplanned, since the doctor's office where she works as a receptionist is only open Monday through Friday.

"You Black Friday shopping with me and Sadie Lou?" Heather asks, completely ignoring the hurt look Jeremy gives her. Face it, buddy—it's week three. You're practically out the door already. Poor sap.

"I don't know..." Averting my eyes from Heather is pretty simple, but Sadie drills me with that stare. "You know I don't go in for that Black Friday stuff, and I really don't care for the crowds. Besides, the Louisville Jennings clan is kind of limited on funds this year."

The last part is intended as a joke, and I even offer a self-deprecating grin just to prove the intent, but Mom visibly deflates. She's never been overly fond of the idea of her baby (of course I mean Bailey) moving out of state. Add to that the fact that she decided to get a job after she wasn't tasked with the job of watching Bailey during the day, and she feels a little like I ripped out her heart.

She's never told me that, just to be clear—merely an observation.

"She's going," Heather announces, proving she doesn't care about my feelings or my opinion.

"I can't keep Bailey out that late."

The instant the words leave my mouth, I know they are uttered completely in vain. Complaining about being tied to child care when I have a room full of people dying to watch my child is probably not my best strategy.

"Bailey can stay with me," Dad says, exactly as expected. "She needs a little Gump time."

"Guuuuump!" Bailey exclaims comically, reducing everyone to laughter.

And so my night is planned without me having a say, sort of like everything else in my life.

"Aw, come on party pooper! We haven't even hit the good sales yet."

I'm past the point of arguing, so I lean across the hood of the car and place my head on my arms, feigning exhaustion.

"She's being dramatic," Heather assesses, dragging me backwards by the belt loop at the back of my jeans. "You not having fun at all? Kentucky make you a fuddy-duddy already, Alex?"

"Fuddy-duddy," I repeat, expelling all the air in my lungs at my sister as I turn to give her a stern glare. "We just hiked three-hundred miles in the cold and the dark to go to Wal-Mart. Wal-Mart, Heather."

"Three-hundred miles," she scoffs. "The cold air is going to her brain. Anyhow, it would have been worth it if I could've got that computer."

Sadie laughs as she leans against the car beside me. When she slouches, we're almost the same height. Otherwise, she stands about six inches taller than me. Maybe that's why she always manages to be slightly intimidating—I'm fairly certain she could crush me if she wished.

"But was it worth standing in line so you could get all those Vin Diesel movies? Really?"

"Yes," Heather answers succinctly, "and the footie pajamas. I needed those, ya know."

"I can't imagine you sleeping in footie pajamas," Sadie tells her.

"Who said anything about sleeping in them? I'll wear them while I'm watching the Vin Diesel movies."

I unlock the door to my car, and Sadie responds by moving a couple steps away.

"You're escaping, aren't you?" she asks, giving me a knowing look.

I attempt a small smile, but my heart's not in it. Not in anything lately, really. Things would be better while visiting home, I thought, but it's not turning out that way.

"You can bring Heather home, can't you Sadie?" The look I'm sending her is supposed to be gently pleading, but I sense that it's coming across more like hopeless desperation. "Maybe it's the trip back home, but I'm completely wiped out."

"It wasn't Kentucky. You always have been a fuddy-duddy, Alex," Heather says.

"Just hush, will you?" Sadie offers a sympathetic, thin smile.

"She knows I'm teasin'." Heather takes a step toward me and leans over to press a kiss to my cheek just for show. "I love ya, Alex."

"Knock it off," I tell her with a grin. It's difficult to remain annoyed with Heather, because... Well, she's Heather. Ornery as they come, but still my little sister, and I've got this weird instinct to protect her even when she's ridiculous.

"We'll hang out tomorrow," Sadie tells me as I slide into the car seat. A nod of my head is all I give in response before I close myself inside, breathing in the cold November air.

I don't make it home. Instead of turning down the familiar road, my car makes its way down an alternate path, onto a sleepy dirt road, and eventually to a little clearing to the right of the dirt that stands on top of a hill overlooking houses and fields below.

Louisville greeted me several weeks ago like a stranger, welcoming me slowly and with trepidation. Jackson welcomes me back like a bad dream that I can't escape, taunting me with memories that won't be forgotten. The white Mitsubishi doesn't belong here in this clearing any more than my mind should be entrenched in reminiscing, but I can't seem to back away.

A familiar country song's refrain streams from the radio, thanks to a local station I found on the way back. The haunting melody of love lost causes me to close my eyes as I bring my hands up to rub them across my face, attempting to clear the cobwebs from my mind.

Cody Hewitt.

The last time I was here was with Cody Hewitt, and as I stare out the windshield at the scattered houselights below, melancholy threatens to overtake me.

"I'm not used to seeing this side of you," Cody told me, glancing over from where he sat to my left on the tailgate of his old rusted-out Ford.

"The fun side? The relaxed side? The late-at-night side?" I allowed myself to let out a laugh as I pondered his words.

"Naw, I just meant that I'm usually in front of you turning toward the left, not the right. But you look the same from either side, really."

I dragged my palms down the thighs of my jeans as inconspicuously as possible. The night was warm for April, but not warm enough that I should be feeling the moisture gather on my palms. Definitely not warm enough that I should feel the tiny beads of sweat threatening to show up at my hairline. My hands went up to push back my hair, testing to make sure my nervousness wasn't obvious by swiping at my brow. No perspiration yet, thank goodness, but I made sure I kept my hair away from my face just in case.

We'd been working on the morning's trigonometry assignment at my parents' kitchen table, just like we had been every evening that week. Cody was really not great at math. There were some months that he barely pulled out a good enough grade to keep him on the football team, but he kept taking math anyway, semester after semester. He was such a go-getter on the football field, I imagined that he just wanted to teach math who was boss, or maybe prove that he could get a grasp on it.

Heather insisted that he took math just so he could ask for my help.

The song coming from the cab of the pickup truck shifted, and I heard the first few lyrics of "Every Mile a Memory," the Dierks Bentley tune that played countless times that year. It was impossible for me not to notice, because it was fitting that I'd be thinking about remembering everything around me, when we were so close to graduating. When Cody was so close to being gone.

"So, um, that photo thing today was a little awkward, huh?"

Of course he meant the yearbook photo that we took earlier in the afternoon, after which he couldn't stop giving me odd looks. I'd tried to ignore his strange behavior, but as soon as he finished his homework he asked if he could take me for ice cream. My heart lurched inside my chest as though it wanted to break free and run at him, but I managed to appear nonchalant as I asked my mom if it was okay.

Sitting on the back of Cody's truck that night, I was determined not to let him see my emotion.

"I guess." Accompanying my delayed answer with a shrug of my shoulders, I placed the palms of my hands at the edge of the tailgate and leaned forward slightly, looking at the trees down below us.

"It would be nice if you could do what you want without changing things, you know? But I guess we're almost to graduation anyway. Not much to lose anymore."

His words came to me almost like gibberish, and I tried to brush them off rather than read anything into them.

"The irrepressible Mr. Cody Hewitt," I teased, forcing myself not to look in his direction. "I figured you did what you wanted all the time."

"Heck no." He leaned his head back, staring up at the mess of leaves above us. It was impossible to see the stars with all those trees so close. "Been wanting you for a long time, and I've never done anything about that."

My breath suddenly felt like it was pinging around in my throat, not making it in and out of its normal volition. My thoughts were jumbled inside my head, too—so much so that I couldn't force a coherent word out of my lips. How long had I been waiting for Cody to want me?

So many years, it felt like forever.

*God, thank you.*

His finger slid down my arm, and my skin went from almost too warm to instantly chilled as I fought goosebumps.

"Look at me," he whispered.

I'd spent so many hours, days, months, trying to pretend that I didn't care for Cody. The thought of having it out in the open was slightly terrifying.

Still, I turned to meet his gaze, those hazel eyes slowly caressing my face as they drifted over me. The truck shifted beneath me as he moved closer, inching toward me until our thighs were touching on the tailgate.

"Why didn't you say anything?"

The question had come out of my mouth without much thought, and as soon as it slipped forth, I wished I had sucked it back in. What did it matter now why he hadn't said anything? He had finally come around, and I should have been grateful.

"You've always been too good for me," he said, a smile breaking onto his face. "Even so, I could see it in your eyes today, that you feel the same way I do."

Nodding, I swallowed as I sensed him moving toward me. His eyes drifted closed, and I knew he was going to kiss me before his mouth hesitantly touched mine. The first thing I noticed was that his lips were warm, making me feel numb all the way down to my toes. All I desired was to wrap my arms around his neck and melt against him the way I'd imagined a million times. Unable to make myself move, though, I simply sat there allowing him to kiss me.

After so many years, I'd grown accustomed to the patience required every day, but Cody must not have felt the same. In no time at all, the kiss that had begun tentatively grew eager, and he pressed up against me, attempting to draw me closer while at the same time holding me at arm's length. An agitated sigh escaped his lips, but that didn't stop the kiss. He deepened it instead, and although I thoroughly relished my very first such experience—that I had been saving exclusively for Cody from the time I was thirteen years old—part of me thought he might swallow me whole.

But I let him continue to kiss me, wrapping my fingers around the top of his arm where his T-shirt sleeve met his skin. Content to be touching Cody while his fingers pressed against my back, not bothering to pause to breathe.

I have no idea how long Cody kissed me, but I know it was long enough that my mouth felt bruised and I could feel myself almost gasping for breath when he pulled away. I'd seen these moments on movies, and I mentally ran through what would happen next. Maybe he'd drop his forehead against mine, or cup my cheek with his hand. *I love you, Alexis.* Because of course he did. We were meant to be together.

Instead, he let out a deep breath, as though he'd just sprinted and was trying to get a second wind. And then he started talking about his brother's new car.

I drop my forehead to my hands at the top of the steering wheel, wishing I could somehow make the memory a little less hollow. Make it hurt a little less fiercely. Shouldn't it be less numbing after all these years?

But I can't seem to stop the replay from continuing in my mind. How he had started talking nonchalantly about unimportant things…a graduation party, his dog's propensity to leave the fence, a sports banquet for the football team. It wasn't until he casually mentioned the prom the following weekend that my entire world came crashing down.

*Oh, he couldn't take me—I knew that, didn't I? Because he had already asked Vivian a couple months before and she had a dress and everything. It wouldn't be fair to her to cancel, really. And besides, it wouldn't end well between the two of us. Not that I was irrational or crazy or what-have-you, but just because…*

"Well, darn it, Alexis, it's prom, you know? I have expectations about how the night's going to end."

And I remember exactly the way it felt when my heart sank to the pit below my chest, farther than I had ever felt it reach before in my life. The moment Cody rejected me, not because he didn't have feelings for me, or because I somehow didn't measure up to his expectations.

I was too good for him.

No, not too good for him—too "good" for him.

From the minute I'd been able to consciously do so, I'd been saving every single "first" I would ever have for Cody, praying he'd do the same for me. And even though I knew some of those things had long since passed on his part, I'd still kept my end of the bargain.

But at that moment, on the tailgate of his pickup, I was quite sure he would find the entire situation funny. Alexis Jennings—eighteen years old, just weeks away from graduation, experiencing her first kiss with a guy who...

Well, who had expectations, and not with me. Goody-two-shoes Alexis, who never did anything wrong and surely wouldn't give him what he wanted.

Of course Dierks chooses this moment to come across the radio speakers once again, how could he not? While I'm sitting in the same spot where every dream I ever had almost came true, but ultimately came crashing down around me in shambles.

"Every Mile a Memory," this hollowed out spot on the side of the gravel road perfectly content for me to sit here thinking about Cody. Perfectly content to allow me to pour out my tears on the steering wheel of my car on Thanksgiving night, thinking about all the ways my life has turned out wrong.

# Chapter Twelve

## Alexis

There are some things that you have to become acclimated to in the mornings—bright light from the sun, the loud noise of your alarm, having a child pounce on you before you're fully awake, a cold bathroom before you step into the shower.

And then there's the cheerfulness of Gump. Er, Dad. I've never been able to acclimate to that, no matter how I've tried.

This morning he's decided that he's a canary. Or maybe a screech owl. In either case, he's singing along to the radio like he deserves an audition on reality television.

Of course Bailey thinks he's the absolute end-all. I'm almost regretting the fact that we came home, because taking her back to Louisville is going to be such a nightmare now that she's had her Gump fix.

True, I probably wouldn't be quite as irritable this morning if I hadn't been out until one in the morning, and if my eyes weren't sore and puffy from the ridiculous crying. Still, when Dad sings "Stop! In the Name of Love" at the top of his lungs it's difficult for me not to ask him to stop in the name of everything holy. It is seven o'clock in the morning, after all.

"How about pumpkin pie for breakfast?" he asks, leaning down to where Bailey sits at the table. When she raises her eyebrows, he gives her a sly grin. "Nan will never know."

"Nan's right behind you," Mom corrects. She's wearing a pair of red flannel pajamas with tiny pink stripes down the leg, but somehow the woman looks put together. And her hair looks brushed.

*Probably because she brushed it, Alexis.*

Self-consciously straightening the hasty bun I fixed on top of my head with my own mess of uncombed hair, I wordlessly reach for the pumpkin pie. No one even seems to notice until I press the button on the can of whipped topping, when the hiss-spraying sound emits and suddenly all eyes swivel to my plate.

Yes, I'm eating half a can of whipped topping, people. Get over it.

"Was the shopping that bad?" Mom asks with a tinkling laugh, looking ten years younger than her actual age. Her caramel waves reach just past her shoulders, and they fall exactly like those big curls the girls used to go for back in the 1940's and 1950's. Combine that with her trim figure and her poise, and she's very old Hollywood glamour. If she ever tried to be glamorous, that is.

"Don't ask," I mumble as I slip a giant spoonful of whipped cream into my mouth. Bailey smiles at me, so I give her a goofy grin before I lick the corner of my lips to be sure I'm not a mess.

"It's a full two-spooner, Crystal," Dad says in a nasal-sounding voice, following that by making a siren noise with his mouth. Bailey claps at that one, clearly thrilled that my father is making fun of me. I can't help but smile myself as he stares at me, nerdy-handsome with his dark goatee that has a couple smatterings of gray. He's always had glasses since I can remember, and has been thin as a rail, although he has a teensy bit of a paunch around his waist now. Probably from eating pizza constantly at work.

Mom steps up beside him, and he places an arm around her waist, where they stare at me like a couple of Stepford parents. Their coloring is such that they could be siblings themselves—same hair, brown eyes. If it weren't for the fact that I look similar to them, I'm fairly certain I would be that odd kid that doesn't fit in.

No, that would be Heather. Heather is the shooting star trying to resist being put into a box.

Rather than think about it too closely, I shove a bite of the pie into my mouth. It's creamy and cold from the refrigerator, and covered with entirely too much whipped topping. Perhaps I was a little too overzealous there.

"Are you girls going to put up the tree today?" Mom wonders, gazing lovingly at Bailey.

The pie turns to a rock in my stomach. As though I wanted to come to Tennessee to sit in my parents' house alone putting up their tree while they're at work. We're alone enough in Kentucky as it is.

She must sense my sour response, because she pulls away from Dad to pour herself a cup of coffee. "Maybe Sadie could come over," she suggests.

Sure, maybe Sadie can come over here and strip me bare of pretense. The girl is like an emotional bullwhip.

"Yeah, Mom, we'll wrestle with your tree," I agree, hoping she'll leave Sadie out of it. I'm feeling vulnerable enough as it is. "You think we can do that, Bailey?"

"Wrestle?" Bailey wrinkles her nose, looking to Nan for confirmation that I'm crazy. Silly me, I thought we had made a little progress in the last month or so. But no, here she is still looking to Nan and Gump as her parents and I'm just the placeholder until she gets back to them.

Or maybe I'm just oversensitive and in a bad mood.

Before any more of the tree trimming plans can be dissected, Dad begins singing "Jingle Bells," and I go back to my pie as though a four-hundred calorie dessert is going to solve all my emotional hiccups.

Just as I expected, Bailey gave up on the tree about ten minutes after I pulled it from the box. Plumping branches and strategically placing them on the metal pole isn't exactly her forte. Once I get to the actual decorating process, she might be full in, but that's going to take a while.

Black Friday. Bleak Friday is more like it, although it wouldn't be obvious from the sounds in the living room. Bailey's watching some old Bugs Bunny cartoons my parents had in the closet, and the Road Runner's *meep* greets me as I pluck another branch from the box and give it a shake to remove the dust.

When Dad left this morning, he told me I could bring Bailey by to get some pizza at lunch if I wanted. I shrugged it off and said we might be by if we finished the tree, but the truth is, I don't want to visit Dad at work. Don't really feel like I could without feeling like I completely, utterly failed him, and this bleak Friday is bad enough as it is.

Reaching into the box, I pull out the top of the tree, my eyes focusing on the folded paper at the bottom. Gold lettering accompanies a picture of a red poinsettia, the word "rejoice" written at the top. Dragging it up from its current position, I flip it over to look at the back. In bold black letters, there's the name of the church that was home away from home for so many years. Directly underneath: Nick Jennings, Pastor.

Had it been sitting there last year, too? Did we not notice it, or did someone see it and prefer to leave it there for the nostalgia?

The morning slice of pie threatens to revolt in my stomach, so I sit on the couch and take a deep breath. Bailey is still engrossed in Wile E. Coyote and has no concern for what her mother is doing. Probably best, because my throat instantly chokes up as I fight back tears.

They hadn't known I was there. Had they known they never would have said a word. Well, not to my face, anyway. They would have waited until I had turned my back like proper gossips. Dad wasn't aware of my presence, either. I had entered by way of the back door by his office, bringing him some papers that he left at home.

"…can't have that kind of thing here, and you know it," I heard as I started to come around the corner. Pulling up short, I pressed my back against the wall. The voice wasn't immediately recognizable, but I narrowed it down to one of three women who pulled rank among the parishioners.

"You can't expect me to—"

"There should have been a wedding by now, Pastor. It's not right her being here without...well, it's not right."

Dad's heavy sigh, audible from such a distance and from my hidden spot, pierced my heart.

"I've already told you, there will be no wedding."

"She must do what's right."

"It's not that simple."

Male ramblings mingled with the angry female voices, one rising above the others. "She doesn't know who the father is?"

"Of course she does. You're talking about my daughter!"

"And because she is *your* daughter, she directly reflects on all of us. I for one won't have people thinking—"

"That you're able to love someone who is a part of this family? That you have compassion?"

"This isn't about us, this is about her. We can't have her promiscuity influencing the rest of our young women. I have a daughter of my own, Pastor."

"Then you of all people should—"

"What will she do with the baby?"

"What will she..." Dad's mumbles faded out of my earshot, until his voice rose again. "...my grandchild!"

"And I'm aware of that, but that doesn't mean—"

"We've already had a board meeting about this, Pastor."

Their words continued as I threw the papers on my dad's desk and escaped out the back door, standing on the concrete slab just beyond the building with my hand against my abdomen, feeling the fluttery kicks of the baby inside me. Bailey. I hadn't even known she was a girl at the time.

And Dad didn't say a word about it. From that point forward, I never stepped foot inside those doors. Every week I had an excuse, and somehow Dad clung to his position there until Bailey was eighteen months old. Tried so hard to love them even after they pretended I didn't exist. After they discovered Jake's identity and trashed him from one end of town to the other, mercilessly and with no regard for our family in the process.

Or for his. Does he even have a family?

"Knock, knock."

Sadie's familiar voice pulls me back from the edge of that emotional precipice. Tossing the folded bulletin back into the box, I hastily rise, my T-shirt catching underneath my elbow and drifting over my belly button. I jerk it back down as fast as possible, camouflaging the extra three pounds that I've never been able to dispose of since Bailey's arrival.

I wouldn't dare mention that to Sadie. She gained a solid thirty when she had Jonah and is still hanging onto it, so I'm pretty sure she would tell me to cry her a river. Or worse.

"Ooh, you're still in the building the tree stage. Maybe I'll come back later." Sadie drops her purse onto the couch and swings Bailey up in the air, sending her into a fit of giggles. "Sweet Bailey Nicole. You've missed me, haven't you darling? Or was it only my Jonah? Do you still love him?"

"No!" Bailey screams before Sadie flips her upside down, sneaking her fingers across Bailey's stomach as she squeals.

"Girlie, you know you want to marry him." She places Bailey back on the couch and leans down to drop a kiss on her forehead, which Bailey promptly wipes away just to get a rise from Sadie. The Looney Tunes music begins again, though, and Sadie can't compete as Bailey cranes her neck to see the television.

"Bailey thinks I'm boring," Sadie decides, taking a couple steps toward me. She's clothed her form today in a Christmas sweater that boasts a brown bear wearing a green holly vest and waving a candy cane in the air. Logic informs me that it's a jolly holiday joke, but I'm just unsure enough about it that I'm afraid to laugh.

"Three-year-olds are always correct," I inform her with as dry a voice as I can muster.

"How can she think I'm boring when I'm wearing this delightfully tacky Christmas sweater?" She grabs the bottom of her garment and spins slowly in a circle so I get the full effect. "Jonah dared me to wear it."

"The kid clearly hates you. Where is he anyway?"

"Still with my mom. They left out this morning right after I woke up, since I was with Heather until the crack of dawn. Thanks for leaving me alone with her, by the way. I feel like I've sprinted a couple of marathons." Without saying a word about my shorter-than-her stature, Sadie plucks the small bundle of fake branches from my hands and settles it at the top of the tree with ease. "Speaking of sprinting, what was the deal with you last night? And yesterday at dinner, for that matter. You still letting him get to you?"

My mind immediately flashes to sitting in the Mitsubishi on that gravel road crying last night.

"I know it makes me a loser, but I really can't help myself sometimes." Giving up on the tree, I sink to the loveseat and inspect my fingers. "It's not that I want to think about him, but he'll just suddenly be there, firmly planted in my mind like there's an extension of my brain that lives in the past."

"Totally understandable." Sadie sits next to me, the odd packed-in-storage smell of her Christmas sweater assaulting my senses. "If I were in your shoes I'd probably feel the same way. It doesn't make you a loser."

"Okay, that only convinces me that you don't see the severity of the problem. And will you please remove that sweater? I can't have a normal conversation with you."

She gives me a look that indicates she isn't exactly pleased, but she unzips the front of her Christmas bear cardigan and pulls at the sleeves. The fact that she is wearing a hot pink tank top with a crown in the center declaring herself a princess doesn't exactly make matters much easier.

"There you go, cranky. Let's have a normal conversation, if we can figure out what that means."

Just like that, Sadie has me laughing. It's one of the reasons I love her—she makes me feel less Alexis. Or, I'll just say that I've learned not to take myself so seriously in her presence, and it's a good thing.

"Why should I bother thinking about someone who so obviously has been a jerk to me? It's detrimental to my sanity."

Rather than agreeing forthright, she lifts a ball of Christmas lights from the nearby box and begins unwinding a strand. "I get where you're coming from, because it would be driving me crazy, too. I mean, sure, there's a definite past there that's not exactly rosy, but the man is quite... Well, I'll just say it. He's a yummy specimen. And every time you see him it has to stick in your craw. Is he Prince Charming? Of course not, but it's like one of those horrible rock stars when you see them on television. You know deep inside that they're total creeps, but they're so pretty you can't look away."

A giggle slips out in spite of myself, because clearly she's lost her marbles.

"First of all, I had no idea you thought he was good looking at all, let alone yummy. Second, if I was running into him at the supermarket or something I would understand the constant brain possession, but I haven't seen the man in ages."

Sadie stops unwinding and gives me a stern glare. "I thought you said he stops by."

"What? No, I haven't seen him in four years."

Completely giving up on the lights, Sadie turns toward me on the loveseat. "Who are you talking about?"

"Cody." As if that wasn't obvious. Who else would I be talking about?

"Ew, Alexis," she huffs as though I've thoroughly offended her. "I thought you were talking about Jake."

Jake? Sure, because Jake is better than Cody? Because letting my mind dwell on Jake would be a better occupation of my time?

"Sweet sister Susie, Alexis."

No mistaking the fact that Sadie's disdain is palpable. Sweet sister Susie is the little phrase we made up back when she first started hanging out here, when she was accustomed to swearing under her breath. In order to help her break herself of the habit, we made up a bunch of little ridiculous phrases. Sweet sister Susie is one of the more serious versions.

"I don't know what's worse—the fact that you think that I would be better off thinking about a man who's trying to destroy my life, or the fact that you are attracted to said man." My eyes drift to Bailey out of instinct, but she's currently watching Elmer try to get that wascally wabbit and isn't paying a lick of attention to us.

Normally in this house I'd get a pat on the shoulder and someone would tell me it will work itself out. Sadie Lou isn't my genteel mother, though. She's not about to "bless my heart" and give me soft words of wisdom. No, Sadie firmly grips both of my arms and forces me to face her.

"There's nothing great about your thoughts dwelling on Jake, but at least that makes sense. He's there in your life, for better or for worse. Cody represents nothing but washed up memories that shouldn't be let out of their grave, Alex."

"You just called me Alex."

"That's all you got out of what I just said? That I called you Alex? You've got your head so far down that rabbit hole you can't see the light of day."

She knows I don't particularly enjoy being called Alex, or to have anyone mention the fanciful stories by Lewis Carroll when they're discussing my habits. Not one bit.

I should probably be angry with Cody right now for invading my mind in the first place. Or Jake, for even contributing to this conversation at all. Maybe even Heather for telling my friend about calling me Alex way back in the day. But the only person in front of me is Sadie, her hands on my shoulders as I sit facing her larger frame, while her green eyes sternly focus on me.

"Is this what happens when you hang out with Heather? The two of you sit around gossiping about me and making fun of me?"

"Do you hear yourself? Stop being such a martyr."

Pulling away from Sadie's grip, I reach for my own mess of Christmas lights, trying to place myself away from her. Lately I'm always on the verge of losing my temper, and I know in this case it's not exactly warranted.

"I'm not trying to be a martyr, you know. I'm just attempting to live with the hand life dealt me."

"Sure, by dwelling on Cody," she mutters, shaking her head. "Seems like that's the exact opposite of dealing with the hand you've been given. I'm pretty sure your hand has been forced on that particular issue more than once, honey. Learn your lesson and run the other way." Releasing her final tangle, she leans down to plug the lights into the wall, letting out a sigh when the strand only sparkles to the halfway point before going dark. A string of "sam hills" and "hecks" comes out of her mouth, her propensity for uttering ridiculous things in her path to not swearing almost sounding like it belongs on that Bugs Bunny cartoon Bailey's watching. That thought strikes me as funny, and I can't help but allow the corner of my mouth to tilt up as I glance at my friend.

"Are you laughing at my jiggly arms, toothpick?" She places one hand on her hip and gives me that sideways-smirking glare that she loves to whip out. "It's your fault I'm half undressed, forcing me to remove my lovely sweater. I was halfway to getting hives from that itchy thing, and now my plans are ruined."

The use of the term "toothpick" hits me where I live, because I really am rather self-conscious about my abdomen's lack of flatness, as stupid as that sounds. The fact that Sadie views me as a skinny little twit makes me feel almost guilty about worrying over those three pounds.

Almost.

"Move to Louisville," I blurt, crossing my arms over my stomach. "You're the only person who can make me take myself less seriously. Come on, Sadie, I need you."

"Oh, honey." She lets out a sigh as she moves herself back to the loveseat, where I sit down beside her as she takes my hand. "You know I want to support you, but I can't pull Jonah out of school here. He has friends, real ones, the kind that stick for good. And things are going pretty well for me at work, now that I'm the office manager. Besides, Brent—"

"I forgot you have a man now."

"Not really." She laughs as she lifts her eyebrows. "I don't technically have him yet, although we're heading in that direction, I hope. But surely you've made friends at work, right? What about the other teachers?"

I would laugh out loud if her question didn't make me want to cry. So far I've been the subject of only awkward conversations at school, without making any real, meaningful connections.

"The only teacher who wants to be my friend is Mr. Jennings. His classroom is right next to mine, and although he's close to my age, he dresses like Mr. Rogers."

"Sounds like a neighborly fellow."

"Right?" A self-deprecating smile plants itself on my face. "Honestly, I've never felt more alone in my life. Not even when I was walking around here with people whispering behind my back."

Sadie squeezes my hand as she stares at the floor, probably contemplating a response. "But you're not alone, really. I know you probably don't want to think about it, but he followed you all the way to Kentucky. Maybe you should...you know...befriend him or whatever."

"Jake?" I whisper, letting my eyes slide over to Bailey, who's currently stuffing a cheese poof into her mouth as she stares at the flashes on the screen. "Surely you can't be serious? How exactly would a friendship like that work? *Hello, womanizing and untrustworthy gentleman. Would you care to come into my home so we can open up and share our feelings?* Be realistic!"

"Well, at least you'd have something to look at."

That statement cannot go unpunished, and I pinch her wrist where she's holding my hand.

"Ouch!" she complains, pulling her hand back. "I'm just saying. If nothing else, you could take a few pictures to document your experience, so I can inspect them for you."

"You're terrible, you know that? Terrible. I can't believe I'm confiding in you at all."

"I'm mostly teasing. Mostly, because there is a hint of truth in there somewhere, as inappropriate as it seems." She presses her shoulder against mine, likely a joking gesture, although I'm aware of the fact that she could shove me halfway across the room if she wanted. "Do you remember the day I had Jonah? Sixteen years old, and I was terrified. My mom was there, just as nervous as me. Even though I hoped Keith would come through, I didn't expect him to be there. And that was probably a good thing, because he would have been stoned and caused a scene."

Nodding seems the only option, so I do so, wondering where she's going with her trip down memory lane.

"That was my catastrophic, 'everything crashes down on me at once' day, you know. Oh, those first few days when I realized I was pregnant weren't exactly a bed of roses either, but they were different than delivery day. Waiting for Jonah to arrive, and sitting there thinking about how I was so much less than what he needed. Wondering how I was going to keep going to school, and how I'd be able to take care of my son. And then, everything was okay."

"Because you saw his face," I offer, attempting to complete her thoughts.

"No, before that even. Everything was okay because I saw *your* face. You were a friend to me when I had none. You showed up, and you brought God with you, and you've been hanging around ever since, telling me I'm stronger than I feel and encouraging me to keep going."

"You are strong, you know."

"No stronger than you. And if God showed up for me, no way He's not going to show up for you."

She's trying really hard at this pep talk, so I give her a tentative smile so she knows I got her message. But I don't believe a word of it. It's been a long three years, and no one's showing up for me anytime soon.

That's why I tried to start over in the first place, but I can't even successfully run away.

# Chapter Thirteen

## Jake

I'm not normally one for wasting water in the shower, but today I can't seem to motivate myself. And it's not laziness or exhaustion, but more a sense that I have nothing pressing to do. The weekdays aren't so bad, because my new job keeps me plenty busy. I'm sure the weekends would be fine too if I could just find a way to snap myself out of this funk I've been in lately.

The phone starts ringing as soon as I move out of the bathroom, so as I towel-dry my hair with my right hand, I snatch the phone with my left.

"Yeah."

"Jake?"

The tentative, pleasant tone of the voice on the other end of the line nearly causes me to drop the phone. It's enough to make me instantly uncomfortable to the point that I quickly draw the towel around my waist. As though she can see me through the phone. So dumb.

"Jake, you there?"

I should have checked the caller ID so I would have been prepared. Or maybe forget processing the meaning of her call before she actually gets her words out. That might be wise.

"Yeah, I'm here. What's up? Is Bailey okay?"

That last bit slips out before I can stop it, and I don't know where it came from or why my pulse rate suddenly shot up. If something's wrong with Bailey, she wouldn't have that nonchalant tone to her voice.

"Oh, she's great. Listen, do you have plans today? I mean, are you alone?"

Any other woman I'd think she was coming on to me, but not Alexis. She's probably just asking if I'm currently in the midst of my harem. The fact that I honestly care whether or not she thinks that almost makes me madder than the fact that she thinks it in the first place.

"Always alone," I tell her, knowing full well she won't believe me. But it's the sad, pathetic truth.

"Oh." She hesitates just long enough to make me wonder if I'm supposed to ask if she's alone, but I know that's ridiculous. Bailey's there. At least I think she is.

"Is there some reason you want me to be alone, or are you just checking up on me?"

"No." That word came out a little more forcefully, so I wait patiently for her explanation. "No, I just wanted your...opinion on something, I suppose."

Didn't see that coming.

"You want my opinion on something?"

"Yeah, um, the roof has a leak."

A chuckle escapes as I toss the towel on the bed and turn to jerk a T-shirt off its hanger. All of my clothes currently smell weird—the scent of fresh spring flowers, according to Felicia. She and Cliff invited me over on Thanksgiving when they found out I had nowhere to go. It seemed a little strange at the time, spending a holiday with random people I don't know who happen to own the motel where I'm staying. But she asked if she could help me by doing my laundry, and I'm not going to look a gift horse in the mouth.

Still, my clothes have never touched fabric softener before, and it's taking a lot of getting used to.

"I'll be right over to look at it," I say, feeling more on even footing now that I know it's just a home repair issue. *That* I can handle.

"Are you sure?"

"Just let me put my pants on and I'll be over."

She hangs up just like that. Yeah, the conversation was mostly over, and I should have withheld the bit about my pants. But I'm not really sorry.

Alexis is waiting in the driveway when I pull up. Bailey's whirling around her on her tricycle, furiously pumping the pedals like she's in a race for her life. The second the noise of the truck door slamming meets her ears, she hops off the tricycle and sends it toppling over as she begins jumping up and down.

The sight of it stops me in my tracks, because I've grown accustomed to a sort of indifference at the sight of me. Elation is definitely new.

"Jay! We's putting up Christmas lights."

Well, they've placed a strand of lights sort of wobbly-like around the front window. In some stratosphere, I suppose that counts.

"Hey, Bailey. What are you talking about, Christmas lights? It's not getting close to Christmas, is it?"

"Yep! And I'm gonna get you a present."

"Me?" She's made it to my side by this time, so I lower myself to one knee so we can see eye-to-eye. "What are you going to get me?"

"A prize." Her hand closes over mine against my knee, chilly and soft, and I'm certain my eyes grow wider than I intend. She definitely doesn't usually touch me.

"I like surprises." There seems to be a rather large lump in my throat, but I try to swallow around it. "So, how about you? What should I get you for Christmas?"

She screws up her face like she's giving it some intense thought. Man, she looks like her mom. No doubt she'll be a stunner when she's older.

"Promise not to ask Mommy?" she finally whispers. Naturally that causes my eyes to dart to Alexis, who is busying herself with the task of righting the tricycle so she isn't eavesdropping. Or more precisely, so it looks like she isn't eavesdropping. I know she always hears everything we say.

"That's not a very nice thing to ask someone to promise. Why do you want me to promise that?"

"'Cause she'll say no."

Those big brown eyes blink up at me through those thick lashes, and I swear the kid must be a magician. She's touching a nerve and almost making me emotional.

"Just tell me and maybe we can give it some thought."

Rather than answer, she turns around to give her mom a good, long look. Satisfied that she isn't peeking, she turns back to me and whispers, "I want a puppy."

*Sure, kiddo. Because if I follow through and buy you a puppy, your mom will hate me even more.*

"Well, did you ask the big man, see what he said?"

"God?" *God, as if He cares whether you have a dog or not.* She bats her eyelashes a couple times, like she's trying to look like an innocent little waif.

"No, I meant Santa Claus. The big man, you know?"

"I hope the leak doesn't turn out to be too much trouble," Alexis interrupts, appearing by my side almost instantaneously. "I could call the landlord, but I want to make sure it warrants a call first. I mean, I don't want to interrupt his Saturday if I don't have to."

But she's perfectly content to interrupt my Saturday. Not that I had plans, and it's best just to push that thought out of my mind.

"You have problems with your landlord not wanting to fix things?"

"Benny? Not at all." She squints as she looks up at me, bringing her hand up to shield her eyes from the sun. "It's just...when he comes out to check things he always brings his friend Bob. They start telling me jokes and stories, and before I know it they're showing Bailey how to use their tools and hours have passed. Bailey absolutely loves it, but I always feel like I'm wasting their time, if it's something small I could fix myself."

"They has skunks in a box!"

I can't help but laugh as I turn my attention back to Bailey. "Skunks in a box?"

"Not exactly, but they did tell a story about skunks," Alexis explains.

"And they wanna nail boards to my head."

"No," Alexis says, shaking her head. "Put a board on top of her head so she'll stop growing like a weed."

"I think I get the picture, so hopefully I can help you out. Where's the leak?"

Bailey takes my hand in hers and begins pulling me toward the house, and I'm not sure exactly how to respond. She never, ever holds my hand. It's not making me uncomfortable, really…merely nervous. I'm pretty certain Alexis isn't going to like her being familiar with me, but I don't have the nerve to turn around and see if I'm right.

It only takes a minute for me to determine that the problem needs to be located via the roof, and thankfully the landlord has a ladder hanging along the wall in the garage. Without saying much, I haul it out to the side of the house and begin climbing.

Before I've managed to diagnose the exact problem, I hear a woman's voice ask Alexis if she lives here, so I glance in their direction to find a black BMW parked on the street with a beautiful brunette making her way across the yard. There's no mistaking the protective stance Alexis takes as she moves between the young woman and Bailey, looking up at me in the process.

Something inside tells me to leave her alone, because she won't want me interfering, but there's a stronger instinct winning out that's forcing me to get up and try to protect Alexis. I guess my head's confused, because I'm supposed to be guarding Bailey, right?

In either case, I find myself turning backwards so I can climb down the ladder, trying to detect the concern Alexis has with each step I take toward them. Honestly, I'm not seeing it. But the newcomer is prettier than she seemed from the rooftop, and those jeans are fitting her just right.

Maybe Alexis is jealous?

No, that's crazy.

"This is my neighbor, Harley Laine," Alexis announces as I cross the yard. "She needs some repairs on her house."

"Hey!" *Hey, that's all you got? You're an idiot.* Clearing my throat, I try to drag up some remains of the suave I normally possess. "Nice to meet you. I've done my share of pretty much everything you can imagine construction-wise, so I'm your guy. Oh, Jake McAuliffe." My hand thrusts itself out almost of its own accord, and I wish I could kick myself. The old me would have had her in his truck by now.

"Jake," she repeats, rewarding me with a smile. Nice smile, but it makes her seem young and innocent. Not really the vibe I was hoping for.

"So, what is it that needs fixing?" I ask, trying to shrug off my awkwardness.

"A ton of things, really, but for now I've just got a couple holes in the wall that I need repaired. To be honest, I don't know much about that kind of thing, but could I have my boyfriend talk to you?"

If someone told me this is a movie and the slow motion button was pressed, I would believe it. I swear, when she said the word boyfriend, it halted in the air between us and then whooshed over me like I could have reached out and swatted it away.

The crazy thing is, though, I'm actually a little relieved.

"Sure, have your boyfriend call me. That's fine. You want my number?"

Harley nods, so I step over to my truck and jerk open the passenger door. Next week I'm supposed to have my own business cards, but for right now I've got nothing but one that has been sitting on the console of my pickup for a couple years. It's faded and slightly creased, with the picture of River Rock Bed and Breakfast on the front.

Instantly I'm back in Tennessee, sitting at the table at the bed and breakfast, a huge mess of biscuits and gravy on my plate. Cole and Artie are talking about the work we'll be doing later in the day, and Rosalie's behind them scrubbing dishes and telling me to mind my manners. She likes to mother me. I suppose she does that to everyone, but I'm not really interested in being mothered. Not that I don't appreciate the breakfast, because I do.

And then she walks into the room, cheeks flushed from a run, blonde curls pulled into a half bun/half ponytail. It's impossible to keep my eyes off her, and Cole has the exact same problem. She turns in our direction with that almost timid grin, and the blood heats in my veins, because I wish she'd look at me the way she looks at him.

I shake my head to try to get Camdyn out of there, flipping the card over to scribble my number across the back. Tennessee's gone. I'm in Kentucky, and the sooner I get that settled in my brain, the better off I'll be.

Only a few strides stand between me and the ladies currently in my presence, so I take them and attempt to regain a little of the charm I was missing earlier. "Call me sometime. Or have your boyfriend call me, if you want."

"Thanks." Harley taps the card against her hand before she turns to head for her car. Back in Tennessee, that conversation would have gone differently. Pre-Camdyn, anyway. The woman threw me off my game, and I can't seem to turn things around.

"Nice wheels!" I yell across the street. She waves before she climbs into the car, revving the engine and continuing toward the cul-de-sac. My eyes drift back to Alexis, who is leveling me with that narrow gaze. Maybe she's the one causing my funk here in Kentucky, always glaring at me and trying to make me feel less than worthy.

"I didn't know *she* lived on Wonder Lane," she mutters, folding her arms across her chest and following the red glow of Harley's taillights down the road.

"You know her?"

"She's a reporter. Did you not see that news story last month where she was crying with the homeless people?"

It doesn't ring a bell, but I'm not nearly as interested in that as I am in this sudden mood Alexis is in. The easy conversation we were having earlier while she was trying to convince me to fix her leak is gone, replaced instead with a sullen, almost angry defensiveness.

She's totally jealous.

Of what, I'm not sure. Maybe it's Harley's long legs, or maybe it's the fact that I gave her my number, but she's clearly jealous.

And the conscious acknowledgement of that fact freaks me out, so I point to the roof and take my leave, preferring not to give it any thought.

Called my dad tonight.

Feeling responsible for my dad's actions is probably not a worthwhile pursuit, and I'm almost certain no one expects it of me, but it's like a sickness I can't cure. One of the things that made it easier for me to pull up and leave was the fact that he nearly cut off his leg with that darn chainsaw after the tree fell on him. It's tempting to call it a freak accident, but I can't. And if I couldn't take care of him living a mile away, it's probably a losing battle to begin with. Unless I move in with him, and the last time I tried that...

He sounded okay, all things considered. As good as he can sound, anyway. Said he'd been talking with Cole's friend Tony, the one who's an assistant pastor or something. He used to be in AA and wants to help him. He's giving it some thought, which tells me he definitely won't follow through.

But he asked me how the job hunt was going, so I was able to give him some good news there. He also asked me how Brandy was, and I told him she was great and that she was growing up really fast. I didn't have the heart to tell him her name is Bailey, not Brandy, especially after he told me my mom was in prison. As if I didn't know she was in prison. She's been there four years.

Jerking the sheet around my shoulders, I shift myself on the bed again, trying to find a comfortable position. It's not going to happen, because the problem isn't the bed, but internal. I can't get comfortable with the ghosts no matter how hard I try.

They've been tapping on the back of my subconscious ever since I hung up the phone with Dad. *Tap, tap. How did he sound? Tap, tap. Send someone to check on him. Tap, tap. He mentioned her. That's not good.*

He always thought she saved him, the older woman swooping in to love him when no one else did. His own dad disappeared when he was just a kid, and the family always assumed the worst since he hadn't fared well when he came back from Vietnam. Dad's mom had a series of seizures soon after that affected her ability to care for herself, and she was taken to an assisted living facility. So Dad grew up in foster care, bouncing from one home to another, usually causing trouble.

Mom started off giving him rides to work after school, but pretty soon he dropped out and moved in with her. Then they found out about me, and Granny insisted that they get married. I'm not sure what sort of pull my grandma had over my mom, but they were legally husband and wife after that. Still are, although it's sort of a joke by now.

He lived and breathed for her, though. I was too young to know how it started—the drinking, I mean—but I know it had to do with her. I've seen the repercussions of her visits and his behavior directly after, so it's not much of a leap. She ran around on him with other guys, and he would numb himself until she showed up. Of course she never stayed long. Sometimes a few months at a time, but other times only days.

The night I try not to think about wasn't one of those instances. That night began with a simple phone call. She didn't know who to turn to, and so she dialed his number. The one contact she could make, and she had to screw with my dad. They were bringing her up as an accomplice in a murder trial in Alabama. She hadn't done anything, she insisted, but she knew they weren't ever going to release her.

If she wasn't going to be coming back, how could he numb himself to that?

That was when I was living with Dad. I came home from my shift at work around four thirty in the afternoon and found him face down on the table with a bottle of pills beside him. Had I been much later, they might not have been able to pump his stomach.

He stayed in the hospital that night, but I couldn't face it. It seemed like too much to take. One of the nurses at the hospital managed to get the information out about my mom, and she looked it up for me. Mom wasn't just present at a murder scene. She had been implicated for helping plan the crime, and they had documents to prove it. Jealous lover, from the appearance of things. I've never looked for the gritty details, even to this day.

That's the only night I can remember where I wasn't worried about my dad. He was at the hospital and I knew there were nurses taking care of him, so I could have a night off.

It was dark by the time I walked back into the trailer. My work clothes probably didn't smell good ordinarily, but that night they reeked of the hospital. Not that it had a particular smell, but the memory of everything I had seen earlier was clinging to me. In the shower, I attempted to scrub it all away. When that wasn't good enough, I doused myself in cologne to try to cover the remnants that lingered.

A night alone in the trailer wasn't appealing, either. I had no idea where I would go, but I had to get out, so I dressed in my best clothes and ran my hands along the sides of my hair as I looked in the mirror. I didn't see myself looking back at me. I saw my dad, twenty years earlier, with the exception of those traitor eyes that pointed back at my mom.

The entire course of my life might have changed if I had simply walked out that door, but I didn't. As I made my way in that direction, my eyes fell on the table and the cap for the pill bottle. The paramedics had taken the bottle with my dad so they would know what he'd taken, but the cap remained. Next to that cap was a bottle of whiskey, the liquid still reaching the halfway mark, sitting there like it was waiting for him to return and finish it off.

I wouldn't let him have the chance to finish that bottle. Grabbing it by the neck, I carried it to the sink and began to tilt it when something inside me clenched. Why should everyone be numb except me? I deserved the opportunity to forget about everything, just for one night.

So I drank its entire contents, and I went to Jackson, and I met Alexis. And I remember almost none of it.

# Chapter Fourteen

## Alexis

The Mitsubishi is dead.

December twenty-third, and we were supposed to be on the road an hour ago, but the poor old normally-dependable car is dead.

I want Gump.

Three hours late, but we are securely fastened in the pickup and headed south on I-65. Bailey is cradling Hoppy and telling him a story in the car seat between us.

*Call him*, my brain kept saying, but my heart forced it to shut its ugly mouth. The last time I called him, he flirted with my beautiful news reporter neighbor in my driveway. The man has no shame.

But then, out of the blue, he appeared in front of the house. Just dropping by to say hi to Bailey, he said. Has a couple days off work. I guess bars aren't open for Christmas around here?

"We need a car," Bailey told him. He scrunched up his nose like he agreed before he even knew the story, which was irritating. My car is virtually an antique, I understand that, but I don't get tips from seedy women at bars, so I have to keep a tight rein on my finances.

He quickly realized she wasn't teasing, and after he looked at it for a few minutes, he said he thought it needed a new starter.

*"Thank you very much, I'll begin checking on that immediately."*

That's what I should have said, but it didn't happen. Instead, every single simmering emotion my body possessed bubbled over to the surface, and I started crying. Sobbing, actually. *We were supposed to leave for Jackson this morning,* I blubbered. *I just want to go home.*

And now I am going home.

In Jake's truck.

Which means I'll have to come back in Jake's truck.

With Jake.

"Do you, uh, want to come in?"

*Please say no. Please say no. Please say no.*

"No, I'll pass."

My heart has never breathed such a huge sigh of relief.

Jake steps out of the truck and reaches into the bed to grab the box of gifts, small though it is, and our overnight bag. I occupy myself removing Bailey from her restraints, and when my sleepy girl realizes where we are, she lets out a scream.

The sound of his baby's voice is all it takes, and my dad emerges from the front door, holding his arms out so she can step inside. I'd like to run up to my dad and squeeze him, too, but I'm paralyzed by fright. Jake has never met my family. Even though they've never said so, I'm sure they have been ashamed of me at times and convinced that I'm not so bright. Introducing them to Jake would be like proving that I'm a total dunce.

*Sweet sister Susie, will he try to flirt with my mother?*

"Did you bring a friend with you?" Dad asks Bailey.

*Say no, Bailey. Just pull him in the house.*

"Jay," she admits with a shrug, like it's no big deal for us to be dragging him around. Or vice versa.

"Oh, this is Jake?" Dad rises and takes Bailey's hand, stepping toward the truck like a man on a mission. Jake glances at me before he stiffens, placing the strap for the bag over his shoulder and holding the box in front of him like a shield. "Nice to meet you, son. Will you join us for dinner?"

"Huh?" Jake was clearly not prepared for this turn of events, nor am I. Dad appears to be undeterred.

"Sorry, I guess I should introduce myself. Nick Jennings."

Jake shifts the box to his side so he can take my dad's proffered hand, and my breath has refused to move for so long, I'm slightly afraid I might be turning blue.

"Crystal made a pot roast, potatoes, carrots... You will stay for dinner, right? She stashed an apple pie in the cupboard, but if you care to join us I'm sure she can be convinced to break it out."

"Um, I..." Jake looks to me for a reaction, but what am I supposed to say that doesn't make me look like a total nut? "Sure, I've never been one to pass up pie."

My life is over.

"Jake, honey, do you live around here?"

Crisp cranberry cupcakes, my mother just called Jake honey. Where is Sadie Lou when I need her? Or Heather, for that matter?

"I mean your folks, of course. I know you're living up in Kentucky now."

"Yes, ma'am, my dad lives about thirty miles southwest of here. My mom lives in Alabama."

"So, how did you meet Alexis?"

Mom has no idea what she's doing. Jake clears his throat as he picks apart the apples in that pie. I guarantee it's not as appealing now as he thought a little while ago.

"A friend of mine introduced us," he says simply. "We share some mutual friends."

This is news to me, as I'm quite certain we don't run in the same circles.

"How are you liking it up in Louisville?" Dad continues the conversation, stuffing his mouth full of pie like this is the most normal meeting in the world.

"Well, I guess I'm still getting used to it, sir," Jake tells him. He's throwing around the *sirs* and *ma'ams* like he's straight out of a 1950's time warp. It's plumb weird.

"You live relatively close to Alexis?"

"Yes, but I'm in a temporary situation now. I didn't want to find somewhere permanent to live before I had a steady job locked down. But I have a really good employment situation now, so I'll likely be looking for something soon."

*Ugh, please don't ask him about working at a bar.*

"And what kind of employment do you have there?" Dad asks, completely ignoring my unspoken pleas.

"I've got a supervisor position at a large construction company."

"Since when?" I blurt, unable to hide the surprise from my face.

"Couple months ago."

Mom gives me a questioning and accusatory glance. It's uncanny the way she can pull both those things off at once. I'm sure she's wondering how we could have ridden in the same truck for hours and I have no idea what the man does for a living. Well, we weren't exactly sharing pleasant conversation on the way down here.

"And what are you doing for Christmas?"

"Oh." Jake lifts his napkin from his lap, setting his fist next to his plate. "I hadn't really given it any thought. Didn't even expect to come back until Alex started crying. I don't do well with outward signs of female emotion."

I give myself a mental kick in the rear and shake my head, a disgusted smile gracing my face.

"I don't mean anything bad by that," Jake quickly adds. "Her car wouldn't run, and she was just upset about that, I guess. And it is almost Christmas, so it would be hard to get it repaired. It's no problem."

"It's very kind of you to change your plans for them," Mom informs him.

Jake's a saint. I'm officially going to have to extend the distance I run away to Mars, or maybe even Venus.

"You should stay for Christmas," Dad says. I nearly choke on my pie. One centimeter to the left in my windpipe, and I'm pretty sure I would need the Heimlich.

"Oh, I couldn't impose on you." Jake shifts uncomfortably in his chair, and I'm glad this conversation isn't only bothering me.

"It's no imposition. You are my little Pumpkin's dad, after all. We would love to have you."

His face turns a muted shade of pink, almost as though he's embarrassed. Nothing in the world could possibly embarrass Jake, so I'm sure it's my imagination.

"That's a nice offer, and I thank you, but I should really go check on my dad."

"But maybe you can come back tomorrow?" Dad presses. "A couple of the steps on the back deck are a little wobbly."

"Dad!"

"Sorry, I just thought since he's an expert..."

Jake actually laughs as he shakes his head. "Sure, Mr. Jennings. I'll come back around tomorrow and take a look at your steps."

Apparently that signals the end of the conversation, because Jake rises from the table and my dad decides to stand beside him. He claps Jake on the back like he's a respectable person, and not the jerk who impregnated me and then wouldn't speak to me for months. It's almost grotesque.

"Thanks for dinner, Mrs. Jennings."

"You're welcome, and feel free to call me Crystal."

Jake smiles as he tilts Bailey's chin up with his finger and winks at her. "See ya tomorrow, Bailey."

"Bye, Jay."

He and Dad disappear around the corner, and I can't help but stare stupefied at my mother.

"He seems like a nice young man."

"Well, he isn't," I whisper, checking to make sure Bailey can't hear me. "Stop treating him like he's normal."

"Alexis." There it is. That voice that used to stop me in my tracks as a kid. Subtle, soul-crushing disappointment. "I figured Bailey would be calling him by something other than his given name by now."

"He doesn't deserve it," I state, knowing I'm going to get a look but not particularly caring.

"Well, I like him."

*You like everybody*, I want to say, but I don't dare. I'm not really one for sassing my mother, even at the age of twenty-five.

Spending so much time with Jake today made repressed memories of *that night* come flooding back to my mind. I haven't allowed myself to think about it for ages, because it makes me feel stupid and dirty and damaged, but that goes with the territory when it comes to Jake, I suppose.

I can't figure out what he meant about a friend introducing us, because that didn't happen.

Senior year of college, spring break, and I was hanging out on the front porch with Sadie and Heather. It was chilly enough that I was sporting a long sleeve T-shirt, but Heather had on tight black shorts and was painting her toenails bright pink.

"You'll never guess who I saw at the gas station this morning," Heather stated.

"Who?" I wondered with very little interest. Most of Heather's "guess who's" didn't interest me.

"Cody Hewitt."

Instantly I sat up a little straighter on the porch swing. Sure, Cody had broken my heart a few years before, but that didn't change my feelings for him. I doubted I would ever truly stop loving Cody.

"Don't you even want to know what he said to me?" Heather added, giving me a little smirk.

Frankly, I was afraid she would tell me he asked her out. That would be a very Heather thing to inject into the situation.

"Sure, what did he say?"

"He said he's going to be at a party tonight at the Tanner place and he really wants to see you. Said he doesn't want to leave town without seeing you."

"You're pulling my chain."

"Nope. Scout's honor. He said he would be hurt if you didn't show up."

"Sadie?"

My friend recognized my plea without having to express anything further.

"No, Alexis. I'm not going to be party to that. That jerk broke your heart."

"But he was just a kid," I explained, desperate for some way to cover his mistakes. "Things are different now."

"I'll go with ya." Heather shrugged her shoulders as though it was nothing, and my heart stuck in my chest.

That should have been enough to tell me to let sleeping dogs lie. If Heather was offering to do something with me, it probably wasn't a good idea.

I order my brain to stop thinking about it as I turn in the bed and wrap my arm around Bailey. The gentle sound of her breathing calms my mind momentarily, and I inhale the scent of her strawberry body wash. Mom had given her a bath while I sat on the couch with my hands wrapped around a mug of cocoa, trying not to listen to the haunting words of "O Come, O Come Emmanuel" on the radio. That song always makes me feel churned up inside.

After her bath, I sat at the end of the bed and combed her silky, baby-fine hair as she stared in the mirror against the wall. The same mirror that has been in this bedroom for as long as I can remember. I gazed at myself in it when I was Bailey's age, most likely. I watched myself in it *that* night, too—entirely too much makeup on, my hair curled into bouncy waves around my face, white tank top that I fought the urge to pull up against my neck, and those jeans of Heather's that seemed to be painted onto my thighs.

And then Heather started getting a migraine, at first just the bright lights of the bathroom bothering her, but soon she was on the bed with a pillow pulled over her head and her fists against her ears to block out the noise. I should stay and make sure she was okay, right? Mom and Dad were at some sort of revival meeting a couple counties over. She needed me.

Only she insisted she didn't. It was my one chance with Cody, she said. I shouldn't screw it up on account of her.

But how did I even know if Cody had changed his mind? What if things were still the same as they were before?

I'll never forget the way Heather's groaning voice sounded under that pillow.

"Oh, for heaven's sake, Alex. You're such a darn prude. Just give the man what he wants, and you'll get what you want. It ain't that complicated."

# Chapter Fifteen

## Alexis

Heather takes a big swig of her bottled water before she props her feet on Lionel, the bottom of her fuzzy boots resting against his jeans. Can't say that I would particularly be pleased with her action, but he doesn't seem to mind.

I'm not sure what week Lionel is on. Since she had what's-his-name at Thanksgiving, I'm fairly certain his longevity can't be over a month. Heather's not normally a two-timer, at least as far as I know. Judging by his level of interest, I'd say he's still at week two, and she hasn't given him all the goods. Either that or he's just that into her.

"Lionel, have you seen that huge Christmas tree in the window at Heather's work?"

Full disclosure—I have no idea whether there's a huge Christmas tree at the drug store. There usually is, so I'm just making an educated guess.

"Nah," he says, glancing at Heather. "Where do you work, babe?"

Definitely week two.

"Jay's here," Bailey announces, taking her attention away from the Grinch on TV long enough to look out the living room window. Sure enough, his truck is in the driveway and he's walking across the yard with Dad, headed to the back of the house for the farce of looking at the steps. Nothing's wrong with them. Why Dad felt he needed an excuse to get Jake back over here is beyond me.

Heather hops up from the couch and peers out the window, practically stepping on Lionel. He looks slightly annoyed, but uses the opportunity to take a glimpse of her backside. I don't know where she locates all these winners, but this guy's a doozy.

"Holy whiskers, Alex, he's fine. I'm a little jealous." Heather turns herself toward me, raising her eyebrows suggestively. She realizes a little too late that she's still perched next to the man of the month. "Oh, no offense, Lionel."

It's been purely a strategic decision never to allow Heather and Jake in the same room up to this point. Sadie's met him twice when I was dropping off Bailey, simply because I didn't want to go alone. Taking Jake's blatant flirtation is bad enough on a normal day, but I don't want to see it employed on my sister. Or vice versa.

"Time to go," Lionel announces, rising from the couch. "We're supposed to be at my grandma's, remember?"

"Shoot," Heather whispers, craning her neck to try to see around the kitchen island to the back door. "I always miss the fun."

Pretty sure Heather never misses the fun, actually.

The two of them make a noisy exit as Heather yells through the house to Dad that she's leaving, but he ignores her. Mom throws her a hasty "see you" from the kitchen, and then they're gone. Part of me wishes I could have escaped with them, as uncomfortable as it would have been.

<br>

Jake's wearing a forest green button-down shirt rolled up to his elbows and a pair of Levi's that fits him like a glove, and I'm pretty sure that's not the standard outfit for fixing the steps. It's probably the best I've seen him look, and I can't help but be a little miffed. Is he trying to butter my parents up for something? What could he possibly want from them?

Thankfully, Dad's having a more leisurely conversation with him tonight. Do you like sports? How about that new superhero movie? You much of a fisherman? And Jake's taking it all in stride, which is again forcing me to ask myself why he's here. The whole thing is so strange.

As soon as we're finished with dinner, Dad states that they're going to a Christmas Eve service at church, and asks if Jake would like to join them. He politely declines, but I can tell by the look on his face exactly what he thinks of church, even if he doesn't say it out loud. I make my own lame excuse about needing to wrap gifts, and Mom and Dad think they're doing me a favor by agreeing to take Bailey with them. Dad winks at me to confirm that fact, like we're in on some big secret.

Distaste for church might be the first thing Jake and I have in common.

"But we ran out of wrapping paper," Mom blurts as they prepare to head out the door.

"I'll run to the drug store and get some," I tell her, not wanting her to expose my half-truth.

"But you don't have a car."

My arguments seem to be rapidly slipping away, and the fact is I don't care one iota about wrapping paper. I'll use black garbage bags if I have to.

"Don't worry Mrs. J. I'll drive her to the drug store. It's the least I can do to thank you for the great meal."

I swear, it's like he's that Eddie Haskell kid on *Leave It to Beaver*. Why can't my parents see through this slick act?

"Thanks, Jake," Mom says, all sweetness as she gives him a smile and picks Bailey up to carry her out the door.

I can't bring myself to look at him, so I head to the hallway and grab my coat off a peg on the wall. When I return to the living room, he's standing by the door, studying his surroundings. Studying my life.

"Ready," I announce, thinking how ridiculous we'll look, him appearing like he's on a hot date and me wearing yoga pants and a big black puffer coat. That pretty much tells the entire story of our relationship, though, so it's fitting.

Part of me is slightly afraid that he might try to open the door for me, so I make sure I beat him to the truck and make it a nonissue. His politeness is not wearing well on me, since keeping up a certain level of disdain for him is essential in maintaining the status quo.

"You don't like church," he states as he closes his door and starts the engine. "It's just funny, seeing how your dad used to be a pastor and everything."

"Church doesn't like me." That sounds ugly and abrupt, and way too personal to be sharing with Jake. "How do you know that about my dad?"

"Told me earlier while we were outside."

Sure, because suddenly they're best friends.

My nerves direct me to force my gaze out the passenger window, ignoring the fact that we're alone. We haven't been alone in a long time. Never would have been alone if it hadn't been for Cody.

I should have never gone to that party without Heather.

And why haven't I ever gotten angry enough about the whole situation? Cody turned out to be nothing but a lying, backstabbing jerk. Smoothly making his way up to me at the party, looking mostly like the same old Cody, but with a new manly air about him. Dancing with me, holding me close, and pouring me drinks. Putting his lips against my neck by my ear and telling me that he'd be right back. *Just wait for me, Alexis. Wait for me.* As if I hadn't been doing that for as long as I could remember anyway.

But then there he was outside, getting into his truck with Mindy, driving away into the night. And I was left standing there alone, the unfamiliar booze in my system kicking into overdrive and clouding my senses. Perfect timing for Jake to step up to me, looking handsome and exciting, two drinks in his hand. Naturally I took one and let him call me gorgeous.

"You think the drug store will still be open?"

For a second I feel unbelievably self-conscious, as though Jake can see my memories playing out in the cab of the truck. But then I tell myself that he's not a mind reader and force a deep breath into my lungs.

"Heather said they'd be open until nine."

That's as far as the conversation goes before the silence envelops us again, so he flips the radio on, which settles on some Christmas cheer. Probably hard-pressed to find anything else playing on Christmas Eve.

The heater vents are pointed in such a direction that they're blowing the scent of his cologne toward me, and the smell suddenly fills my mind with all sorts of pictures I don't want to see. Kissing on the couch in the corner of a stranger's living room. Stumbling against the wall in the hallway upstairs. Jake's truck keys poking into my hip through the pocket of his jeans as he pressed against me on the bed. Waking up with sudden nausea, and finding the bathroom in the unfamiliar house just in time. The knowledge that someone was asleep in the bathtub next to where I was retching. Someone I didn't recognize. Trying to retrace my steps to the correct bedroom, and only knowing I was in the correct place because I recognized Heather's jeans on the floor. The entirety of Jake's form from behind where he was sprawled on top of the comforter. My head pounding in a way that probably rivaled Heather's migraine from earlier in the evening.

All I could think to do was get out of there as fast as possible and try to forget it ever happened. I didn't realize I had my tank top on backwards until I reached my car. I had been too busy using Jake's cell phone to call my own, so I could try to figure out who he was after I left. Wasn't it weird that I didn't know his name? I was certain Heather couldn't even boast that mistake.

But I definitely couldn't go home. That's why I wound up in Sadie's driveway at five o'clock in the morning, and she found me at a little past nine, passed out over the steering wheel of my car, completely unaware that I had altered my life for the rest of eternity.

"This the right place?"

Jake's voice startles me, and I flinch a little as I glance over at him. I'm sure he has no recollection of our time together. He was drunk enough to pass out, and I'm just one in a string of endless women.

"Yeah, that's it."

I bolt from the truck as soon as he puts it in park, wanting to put as much distance between us as possible. Once I get inside the store, though, I just need a minute to avoid him. The Christmas aisle is near the middle, but I move around the perimeter of the store, peeking toward the door to make sure he's not following me. The instant I see his head pop through the entrance, I spin into the closest aisle, stepping into a Tennessee Titans shirt stretched across a firm chest. My hand jerks away from the poor guy's pectoral muscle as I take a step backwards.

"I'm so sorry," I mutter, bringing my eyes up to his face. Probably a mistake, because he's got one of those megawatt smiles that melts girls' brains. And a beautiful woman on his arm. And a ring on his finger. *Why are you even looking at that?* "Just searching for wrapping paper…and there it is, right in front of my face. Sorry again."

"Find it?" Jake asks as he steps around the opposite corner, halting next to me as though the sight of Santa wrapping paper is an affront to him. Except he's not looking at Santa wrapping paper. He's staring at the man wall I stumbled into.

"Jake," the guy says, surprise evident in his voice. I glance between them, sensing there is something bigger happening than Christmas wrapping.

"Parker," Jake acknowledges with an uncomfortable nod. "How's it going, man?"

"Why didn't you tell us you were back in town?" He steps forward and takes Jake's hand, pulling him into one of those odd man-hugs that's kind of one arm, half the back, like they can't commit all the way. As though taking a full, open hug would be too touchy-feely.

"It was a spur of the moment thing," Jake explains, glancing at me. "Sorry, I have no manners. This is Alexis. And this is Cole Parker and his wife, Camdyn."

"Bailey's mom," Camdyn says, reaching for my hand. "It's really nice to meet you. You have such a beautiful daughter. She's not with you?"

"She's with my parents," I tell her, trying to assess her statement, unable to come up with one good reason why a pretty blonde-haired stranger knows my kid.

"Jake and I are good friends," Cole adds. "I still can't believe you moved to Louisville. Did you get the job?"

"Yeah, I got it. Thanks for that, by the way."

If they're such good friends, his presence sure makes Jake uncomfortable. For the guy who just sat through a second dinner with my parents without any hesitation, I'd say that takes something pretty big.

"I'm glad things are going good for you," Cole says to Jake. "Your dad okay?"

"Sure, he's good. We probably better hurry, right Alexis? She's got a lot of stuff to do tonight."

"Hey, come over to Aunt Rosalie's tomorrow for lunch, won't you?" Cole places a hand on Jake's shoulder, probably so he can't escape. "Bring your dad if you want. Alexis and Bailey too. You know she'd be glad to have you."

"I just can't...Alexis has her parents and everything..."

"We understand," Camdyn insists, wrapping her arm through Cole's. "Don't be a stranger, though."

I don't even care what kind of ridiculous Santa wrapping paper is in my hand—I simply grab the closest thing with the intention of walking toward the front. My attempt at a polite goodbye is probably less than stellar, and in any other circumstance I would never grab Jake by the arm and drag him anywhere, but he seems incapable of proper movement while we're in the presence of the people who are supposedly his friends.

He doesn't wait with me at the register. Instead, he marches himself right back out to the truck and revs the engine, like he might abandon me inside the place. For a second I'm actually worried that he will, because he's Jake and that would be a very Jake-like thing to do. When I finish paying the ridiculous five dollars for the wrapping paper, though, he's still sitting there, tapping his fingers against the steering wheel like he's typing a book in there.

"Your friends seem nice," I say as I step into the truck. He puts the truck in reverse and backs out of his parking space.

"Yep."

"You didn't seem especially happy to see them."

He waits to answer me as he looks down the street to make sure there's no oncoming traffic. "Didn't expect to see anyone I knew, that's all."

I guess I can understand him reacting like that after seeing someone he knows…if he's got a felony arrest warrant outstanding or something. Maybe that's why he followed me out of town?

It's a preposterous thought, and I don't consider it anymore as we drive back to my parents' house, complete silence in the cab of the truck with the exception of the Christmas music. "I'll Be Home for Christmas" seems an inopportune selection, but he doesn't move a muscle to change it, so either it doesn't bother him or he's got too much on his mind. The way his jaw keeps flexing, I'd go with the latter.

Breathing a sigh of relief, I grab the handle on the door as we pull into the driveway. Ridding myself of Jake immediately is the ideal choice, and then not seeing him until the day he takes us home.

Maybe I can convince Dad to take us home. Put Jake out of his misery.

"Do you mind if I come in and use the restroom?" Jake asks. "I've still got a bit of a drive."

*No.* "Sure."

Ugh, how do I reconcile having a chip on my shoulder with the fact that the man drove us all the way down here? It's proving to be quite a conundrum.

He follows me into the living room, and I flip on the light as he heads into the hallway. While he shuts the door and closes himself inside, I put my coat on the peg, withdrawing the drug store receipt from the pocket and crumpling it in my hand. As though erasing the evidence can erase the whole night.

The clicking noise alerts me to his exit of the bathroom, and when I turn and see the agitation evident in his body posture, my heart immediately catches.

"Jake," I begin, watching as he stops to turn his head toward me. "What was that back there? Are you in some kind of trouble?"

"Trouble?"

"Don't try to tell me you weren't acting a little strange."

His eyes narrow as he shakes his head almost imperceptibly. "Mind your own business."

His tone causes my breath to catch in my throat. Sarcastic needling I'm accustomed to, but open antagonism is new. I don't like it, and I really don't enjoy the fact that it worries me even more.

"Mind my own business? If you want to be in Bailey's life, then your actions *are* my business."

"You're dead wrong about that," he says, turning fully toward me as though he's preparing himself for a fight. "Last I checked, it took two people to get us into this situation. You can act holier than thou all you want, but I know all about you. Your reputation precedes you."

"Oh, that's cute, you talking about *my* reputation. Give me a break."

"Because you're so snowy white, are you? You didn't look so innocent the night I met you. And why do you think I came over to you in the first place? 'There's your ticket,' my buddy told me. 'Heaven Jennings. She's always up for a good time.' Talk about a sick joke."

"Heaven…" I blurt, understanding slowly sliding over my subconscious. Lifting my hands, I place them atop one another over my mouth so he can't see the sick shock registering on my face. "You thought I was Heather."

The entire area of my abdomen seems to constrict and tie itself in knots, and if I wasn't so blindsided by the realization, I might be sick. Of course he thought I was Heather. For that split second in time, *I* thought I was Heather. I acted like Heather and paraded around like Heather, and I got what was coming to Heather.

"Who the heck is Heather?"

Who is Heather? The one who never has consequences, even though she drowns herself in red.

"My sister. The female version of you."

*Even Jake—flirty Jake who would take any woman who looked his way—he didn't want you. He only wanted Heather.*

That was it, wasn't it? When he realized he really had Alexis, he wasn't interested. I know I should feel disgusted and angry, but part of me can't see any further than the little crack in my heart. How could I have traded my future to someone who thought I was Heather?

He paces toward the far side of the room, lifting a hand to the back of his neck. "I guess the joke was on me. This sure hasn't been heaven."

His slightly smug, arrogant countenance pushes past that little crack and causes me to teeter on the verge of furious as he paces around my living room as though he owns the place. Somehow, though, the recesses of my mind are only longing to lash out at Heather for convincing me to be like her.

Nearly trembling, I fold my arms across my chest as I watch him cross the room yet again. "You're seriously complaining about me? As though I'm the one who has the terrible habits, taking our daughter around and doing God knows what with God knows who." My thoughts go back to the story Bailey told me about Jake—the one that cemented my decision to leave in the first place. "When Bailey came back that day telling me about Cam…"

He stops walking, those blue eyes drilling into me, and suddenly everything makes sense.

"You've been with your friend's wife." The words come out in a hushed rush as I shake my head.

He crosses the room, coming within a foot of me before he squeezes his fist into a solid ball and grips it at his waist. "If you were a man, I would hit you for less."

"That's what all that was about at the drug store, wasn't it? You've been with your friend's wife. Does he know?"

"I haven't touched her, and I don't intend to, so shut up."

I don't even see Jake anymore. Instead, I see the male version of Heather, telling me I'm boring, to be quiet, that I never have any fun. Telling me that he's better than me.

"Must be the only woman in the county you haven't touched," I mutter before I can stop myself.

He widens his stance and sticks his finger out so that he's almost touching my chest, eyes blazing. "You have a lot of nerve considering the way we met. Why do you think I argued the fact that I was Bailey's dad? No telling how many guys you—"

"None, because you're the only guy I've ever..."

The words die on my lips, yet hang in the air as though they refuse to die in the atmosphere. We simply stand here staring at each other, both simmering, neither one knowing how to follow that statement. Part of me hopes he'll just turn away and walk out the door, but he doesn't. He pins me with those dirt-tinged blue eyes, and I almost wish he'd try to touch me. I'd love to punch him, just once.

"So that was the first time you..." He follows that unfinished statement with a coarse laugh, rolling his eyes.

"Did you follow us to get away from that woman? Tell me the truth. You don't care about Bailey at all."

He backs away from me, placing his hands behind his head like he's preparing to be searched. It occurs to me that I'm holding my breath, so I force myself to exhale.

"Yes, I care about Bailey." He sounds more exhausted than insincere. "I care about Bailey, okay? I try really hard to want to be part of her life, but it's just..."

Dread fills me as I wait for him to complete his thought.

"What?"

"You." He directs his gaze at me once more, and instead of anger, I see something entirely new. "Do you have any idea what it's like to be hated?" Grabbing the door knob, he twists it and jerks the door wide enough that I feel the chill of the outside air. "I do, and it's getting really old."

He begins to pull the door closed, but before he can walk out into the night, I drop my head. Swallowing past the hesitation that has risen in my throat, I shove my hair behind my ear.

"I don't hate you, Jake. I hate myself."

# Chapter Sixteen

## Jake

Merry Christmas.

That's the only phrase running through my mind as I close the front door of the Jennings place, feeling the ache as sharply as if she stabbed me in the back.

I can't even walk to my truck. Wouldn't know what to do once I got there. Am I supposed to go home and sit with my dad, ringing in the holiday with a glass of eggnog and a shot of whiskey? Not interested in the least.

So I park myself on the porch swing and sit here until my nose starts to sting. My fingers are ice cold, too, and I'm considering getting up simply for the warmth of the truck when the front door creaks open. I choose not to look, just in case she's got anything else to throw at me.

But apparently she doesn't. Instead, she hands me a pair of wool gloves and sits down beside me, wrapping an afghan over her shoulders. It looks like something my granny would have draped across her sofa back in the day.

"Sorry," I whisper, stretching one glove over my fingers. The meaning of my sorry is lost in that little word, though. For losing my temper with her, sure, but also for everything else. For seeing me at my worst. For taking advantage of her at her worst.

"Me too." She relaxes her back against the swing, gazing out into the dark night. "You didn't force me to do anything. The truth is, I was prepared to do whatever I had to that night."

Meeting her eye is impossible, because after that conversation in the house, I feel flat sick about everything. It had been easy to deal with Alexis when I thought...well, certain things about her. But now that I know that she's not who I thought, it makes me an even bigger jerk.

"Cody Hewitt," she continues, ignoring the fact that I'm uncomfortable. "He was the guy I went to the party to meet. I thought I was in love with him. I mean, I was. Or am, or was. Not so sure of anything anymore. But he left me there and took off with another girl. Do you know him?"

"No, sorry." It feels like there's something else I should say, but it's too hard to think up any other words right now.

"Yeah, well, maybe it's not such a bad thing. Had it been Cody, and this had happened, what if he didn't want me? That would have been pretty brutal, if I was in love with the guy." She looks at me, which I can see from the corner of my eye, but I don't meet her gaze. "I guess I shouldn't be so crass. Obviously you have feelings too."

Do I? Not the right kind, it seems.

"And I shouldn't have jumped to conclusions about your friend Cam. When Bailey came home talking about being in her bed and wearing her clothes, I naturally assumed the worst."

So that's where that came from.

"My dad broke his leg."

"Oh. That stinks."

"No, I mean he had a tree fall on his leg that day, and then he tried to cut the tree that fell on him with his chainsaw. When I found him he was covered in blood, and I panicked. Camdyn kept Bailey while I took him to the hospital, that's all."

"Why didn't you just call my parents?"

"Because your family hates me. They trashed me all over town, before Bailey was born. At least I thought so, until yesterday. I'm having a hard time figuring them out."

"It wasn't them," she tells me, drawing her knees up and hugging them against her chest. "Some people from the church. I don't know why I'm telling you all this. Feel free to tell me to stop."

Something about that statement gives me the courage to look at her. Really see her, from her deep brown eyes to the tiny scar she has on her left cheek, and all I see is Bailey. Everything beautiful about Bailey comes from Alexis. Someday this will be the face of my daughter.

"My dad tried to kill himself." Her eyes widen as she returns my gaze. "I came home from work and found him there at the table. After watching what they did to him at the hospital, I came home and drank all the whiskey I could find. That was the night I met you."

"Why?" She looks nothing but innocent as she continues to stare at me. "I shouldn't ask that, I apologize."

"He'd just found out my mom was arrested. She and her boyfriend killed a man. Well, she didn't do the killing, but she helped with the planning. And something just…" I drag my gaze out to my truck, taking a deep breath. "He's not really good at handling things. When she left, he started drinking and he hasn't stopped."

"When did she leave?"

"Twenty some-odd years ago. I don't know why I'm unloading this on you. Nobody knows about my mom. 'She lives in Alabama,' I always say. Which is technically true, but it's not of her own will." I start to rub my hand across my cheek, but realizing I have the gloves on, I cross my arms tightly. "So, this guy you were looking for, you been in contact with him since then?"

"No, because then there was Bailey, and deep inside I know he's all wrong. Lesson learned a little too late." She smiles as she looks into the distance, and somehow I know the smile's not for me. "The thing is, I do have some good memories. Mostly from math class, and some others. We were friends, the two of us. Good friends. I'm a math teacher, did I ever tell you that?"

The rapid fire randomness of her words makes me chuckle. "No, I didn't know."

"High school algebra. Mr. Alberts passed away, in the faculty lounge as it turned out. That's why they needed a new teacher in the middle of the year like that."

I can't help but smile, and she nudges me with her elbow.

"There's nothing funny about that," she complains.

"No, I was just thinking about having you as a math teacher. I don't know how those poor guys in your class pay attention to what they're doing."

"You can't do that," she tells me, twisting on the swing bench so she's facing me, her arm propped on the back and her head resting against it. "I'm immune to your flirting."

"I so wasn't flirting."

"You flirt all the time, with everyone."

"Talking is not flirting, Alex. And just because I happen to make an observation about your looks doesn't mean I'm coming onto you. It's just an observation."

"I don't like that."

"What?"

"Being called Alex."

"I can tell. I don't like being told I'm flirting."

"But you are."

"Then I'll just keep calling you Alex, whether you like it or not."

"Whatever," she states with a heavy sigh. Her obvious annoyance is slightly funny, but I don't allow myself to smile and give it away. "Are you going to sit out here all night?"

"Don't know. I haven't given it a lot of thought."

"Are you staying with your dad?"

"I feel like I'm playing twenty questions." It seems easier to deflect than be genuine, mainly because I'm still feeling a little raw from our exchange of words inside. I thought for sure she was going to punch me this time. And I probably deserved it.

"You don't have to answer," she says, shifting to put her feet back on the ground.

"I stayed at a hotel in Jackson last night. I went to see my dad, but I didn't want to stay there. Just too weird, you know?"

"Why is it weird?" She settles back against the swing like she changed her mind about getting up, sweeping her eyes over to me. She has expressive eyes. Part of me thinks she could converse without even moving her lips.

"Moved out after he… The night we…" For whatever reason I can't form a complete thought that makes sense, so I clear my throat and try again. "I couldn't take care of him anymore. I'd been doing it for so long, and I just realized that he had to want to take care of himself. So I moved out and haven't stayed there since. He seems okay. Not exactly okay, but well enough for Dad. He's never really okay."

She shivers a little, and I slide off my gloves to hand them back to her.

"Sorry I've kept you out here," I tell her. "You should go inside."

Accepting the gloves, she stands and I feel the porch swing shift beneath me with the loss of her weight. Rising, I move toward the steps and glance out at my pickup while she opens the front door.

"You coming in?"

The words surprise me, so I turn to see if she meant them. She's not smiling, but those eyes aren't telling me to get lost. They're telling me she's the type to take in strays.

In this house, with these people, I probably am a little like a feral cat.

"Why not?" I accompany my words with a shrug and follow her back into the living room, shedding my coat and placing it over the back of a recliner. She drapes the afghan over the back of the couch, just like my granny would have. Totally called that one.

"Hot cocoa?"

She doesn't wait for me to answer before she walks into the kitchen, so I take the opportunity to step over to the fireplace mantle and look at the family photos. Bailey's face is everywhere, of course, but there are a couple other photos of the four-member family pre-Bailey. The first one looks pretty dated, with the two little girls dressed in matching blue dresses and with black ribbons tying their hair away from their faces. They look mostly the same, with the exception of the fact that the shorter one seems like she thinks she has somewhere better to be.

The other photo tells a slightly different story. Maybe the girls are high school age? Alexis has a smile plastered on her face with her hand on her dad's shoulder. She also has her sister's elbow propped on her shoulder, and the evil twin isn't smiling. More like dripping with condescension, like she rules the roost.

The sound of Alexis banging something draws my attention to the kitchen, so I pull myself away from the photos and round the corner to find her pouring milk into a blue saucepan that has some of the decoration faded in spots. When she follows that up by pulling a rather large knife out of the block on the kitchen island, I hesitate by the cabinets and cross my arms over my chest. As she reaches onto an eye-level shelf and grabs a paper-wrapped hunk of chocolate, she catches me watching her.

"I don't like the kind from a box," she explains.

Part of me wonders if I should tell her that I wouldn't know the difference. I can't recollect ever having hot chocolate, from a box or otherwise. Except maybe once, but I wasn't really paying attention to it.

Instead I just stand here leaning against the cabinets while she chops the chocolate with her knife.

"So, do you want to talk about your friends at the drug store?" she asks, low enough that I barely hear her over the rhythm of her knife hitting the cutting board.

The invite back inside was to get me to come clean about my dirt, I guess? She wants to make sure I won't taint Bailey?

"I didn't expect to see them," I offer, hoping that will be enough to satisfy her curiosity.

"That doesn't explain why you got uncomfortable."

She's relentless. Normally I would blow her off, but with me still feeling a little more regret than normal about the whole drunk episode, I'm having a hard time getting upset about it.

"Let's just say I didn't leave town on a high note."

Scooping the chopped chocolate up in her hands, she drops it into the pot and grabs a metal whisk from a drawer. The only person I've ever watched cook before was my granny, and she wouldn't have had chocolate. I think she did make me brownies once, but most of the time it was potatoes or eggs or fried spam. An occasional grilled cheese sandwich.

Alexis doesn't remind me at all of my granny, just to be clear.

"You didn't actually *do* anything, though."

Her words come out like a statement tinged with a hint of a question. Like she wants to think that it's true, but she's not quite sure.

"Other than running my mouth, no."

"So, is she your ex or something?"

I should have known better than to open this can of worms.

"Nope. She moved here last spring."

"Did you guys fight over her?"

If I was lying on a couch, I'd swear I was talking to a shrink. Glancing into the living room, I ponder my options. Say I just walk away...is that rude? Will she follow me?

"Don't answer that. I know I'm being nosy."

Her focus never moves from the stove, so I resign myself to pulling a chair away from the kitchen table and straddling it, placing my arms on the back.

"No, we didn't fight over her. She met him first, and that was that. Until it wasn't, and I told him, and he asked me not to tell her. But I told her too, because I'm just that stupid. So there's your whole idiotic story." A raw, irrational laugh comes from somewhere inside, completely unintentional and surprising. "And what's worse? The woman somehow threw me off. I've not been out seriously with anyone since I met her. It's like I forgot how to be me."

It dawns on me a little too late that I probably shouldn't be talking to Alexis about my dates or lack thereof, but she just keeps stirring away like we're talking about the weather.

"So you told Cole that you had feelings for his wife?" she finally clarifies. Since she glances my way, I nod rather than admitting it out loud. "Either he values your friendship, or he's a really forgiving guy, because he didn't seem angry with you."

"That makes it worse, right?"

"For him or for you?" She turns to her right and grabs a couple mugs that swing on hooks by the coffeepot. "Are you still in love with her?"

Always with that word. Why do people naturally assume that you're in love with someone? Love is what my dad has for my mom. It's not attractive or particularly healthy.

"No, I'm not in love with her. She was intriguing when I met her, and then she and Parker were together and he was different somehow. I suppose I just wanted…" My words break off as a new thought burns its way into my head. Alexis pays it no heed as she holds the steaming mug out to me, then lifts herself onto the kitchen counter to sit in front of me. Something tells me she wouldn't do that if her parents were home.

"You just wanted to be happy like him?"

Couch or none, I'm pretty sure she's psychoanalyzing me.

"It's sick, isn't it? I wish I would have figured that out a couple months ago. Could have saved myself a lot of trouble."

"You wouldn't have followed us to Louisville."

I squint as I look up at her, because staring openly at her while admitting to being a jerk isn't appealing.

"Do I have to say that out loud?" I ask, and she shakes her head. Oddly relieved, I bring the mug up and take a sip of the brown liquid, searing every taste bud on the end of my tongue. An expletive flies out before I have a chance to drag it back in.

"Might be hot," she manages a few seconds too late.

"Might be," I agree as she smiles. She has an unbelievable smile—the kind that would make a man do almost anything to see it again. Since I'm usually not able to put that on her face, I should probably give up the idea.

"Listen, can I ask you a serious question?"

Just like that, the smile is gone and I'm a little wary of this conversation. Weren't we just being serious?

"Shoot."

"My mom thinks it's weird that Bailey calls you by your name. What do you think about that?"

"She calls me J."

"Because she has problems saying Jake."

"Oh." I pause to think about it while I bring the hot chocolate up again, carefully taking a tiny sample. "I thought we just had a nickname thing going, but it's fine. I mean, what else would she call me?"

She takes a really long, exaggerated sip of her hot chocolate, and doesn't even bother to bring the mug down. No way is she flat drinking that stuff. If so, she'd be scalding her throat. She just doesn't want to say the "d" word, and I don't either.

"Jake's cool, so don't worry about it. And tell your mom that I'm okay with it, too."

"Thanks," she whispers, finally pulling the mug down from her face. Drink faker. I've done it so many times with beer bottles, I know it when I see it.

A muffled sound comes from the living room, and then the sound of the door clicking. Alexis slides down from the countertop and stands in front of me with her hands wrapped around the mug.

"All clear?" Mr. Jennings asks as he pokes his head around the corner, Bailey asleep against his shoulder. I assume he's talking about the present wrapping, but since Alexis deposited the wrapping paper on the couch when we got back, it's pretty clear there was no wrapping happening here.

"Sure, Dad. Did she tucker out?" Alexis steps toward her father and pushes Bailey's hair away from her face.

"Yep. The hymn singing put her out like a light."

Yikes. That would put me out like a light, too.

Sensing a family moment, I begin moving in the direction of the living room, stopping short when Mrs. Jennings steps in front of me.

"It's late, honey. Why don't you just stay the night?"

Mrs. Jennings kind of weirds me out, if I'm being honest. She reminds me of that Ashley's wife from *Gone with the Wind*, the quiet one who Scarlett was always walking over. My granny practically wore out that VHS tape while I lived with her, and I can probably quote whole scenes from that movie. The fact that I can't remember the wife's name at the moment is a little strange.

"No, I can't impose on you, especially not on Christmas."

"It's no imposition. You can sleep on the couch or in Heather's old room."

I force my attention away from her as I try to stall for a minute. Would it be preferable to stay in a real house instead of a hotel room for a change? For sure. I've been in a cramped hotel room for months. And Mrs. J will probably make an awesome breakfast in the morning. But there's no way Alexis will be cool with the arrangement.

A hand takes my arm just above the elbow, and I look over to see Alexis standing beside me.

"Can I talk to you for a second?"

So she's going to tell me flat out to go home. Not that I didn't expect it, but I didn't think she'd have the nerve to do it in front of her parents.

I follow her down the hall until she steps into a bedroom and closes the door behind her. Awaiting the inevitable, I shove my hands into my pockets and rock back onto my heels slightly.

"Listen, we're not friends, okay?"

Man, she's brutal.

"Yeah, not friends. Got it."

"I mean, the hot chocolate and the talking...it doesn't change anything."

"Okay." Why she seems intent to emasculate me at the moment is beyond my understanding, so I just try not to smile as she continues to look perfectly serious.

"Thanks. I just didn't want you to get the wrong impression. Spending the night here, I mean. You shouldn't be alone at Christmas, so I'm okay with it, but that doesn't mean that you and I—"

"Definitely not," I agree, nodding my head. "I'm screwed up, and you're you."

She tilts her head to the side as she gives me a half-hearted glare. If she wasn't being rude in her passive-aggressive way, I might think it was cute.

Stepping past her, I grab the doorknob and move into the hall, turning around to give her a parting half-grin.

"Glad we got that straightened out, Alex."

# Chapter Seventeen

## Alexis

There's something disconcerting about being the last person awake on Christmas morning. To pry one dry eye open, blinking into the partial darkness because it's just a wee bit too early, only to find the place beside me that Bailey occupied now vacant.

Of course that slight annoyance at finding her missing turns into a more searing grumble when I remember that Jake's here. As if the universe isn't stacked against me enough as it is, apparently it's necessary to give Jake constant refreshers in the course of "Alexis isn't a great mom." First the incident at McDonald's when Bailey wouldn't listen to me, then the time she opened the door without my knowledge. Now she's randomly strolling about the house while I'm in bed.

Yep, that's me. Mother of the year.

Part of me wants to rush out into the living room to confirm my worst suspicions, but instead I calmly march myself to the bathroom and give the doorknob a tug, finding that it's locked. Leaning against the wall, I calmly wait about thirty seconds until the guilty party steps through the door. The scent of his cologne seems to walk out in front of him, and immediately my eyes fly up to that face that I've studied more in the past day than in the sum of the past three years.

Jake nods when he sees me, and I brush past him as quickly as possible. Locking myself in the bathroom might seem safe, but not when I manage to trap the scent of the man inside the confined space with me. The warm, woodsy-spicy hints of his cologne make me feel flustered, sleazy, and desirable. I mean, makes Jake seem desirable.

Sweet sister Susie, I mean undesirable! Undesirable.

One glance in the mirror solidifies the whole undesirable thing with such an emphatic exclamation point that I can practically see it on my forehead. I really need to learn not to fall asleep with my hair in a makeshift bun. The right side is still in a haphazard updo, but the left is twisted and tangled above my eye like it's an ivy vine that tried to sprout and make its way up the headboard during the night. Pathetic. And with some beautiful dark circles under my eyes to boot.

Completely unfair, because it's hard to sleep when you know there's a half-crazy man in your house. Sure, I feel slightly more comfortable with him now that I know a bit more about his past, but he's still Jake. I'll never be comfortable with Jake.

The man definitely knows how to put *me* in an uncomfortable position, though. I'd prefer to comb my hair and look a little more presentable, but he's already seen me. There's a fine line between looking normal and trying too hard. No way do I want him to think I'm prettying myself up for his benefit. But I really don't want him to sit there thinking about how gross I am, either.

I doubt that I've ever had such a ridiculous conversation with myself.

Deciding on a less-is-more approach, I brush my teeth and smooth my hair into a new ponytail that looks purposeful rather than random.

Mom is the first person I see when I come around the corner, sitting on the loveseat alone. Dad is looking cozy on the recliner with Bailey on his lap, and Heather is looking a little too cozy sitting next to Jake on the couch. Well, her person is looking cozy anyway. Her outfit is more Friday night dance party, apart from the snow boots. Why is she wearing snow boots if there's no snow outside?

No sign of the guy from yesterday, so either he's toast or she didn't invite him. Interesting turn of events either way.

"Bailey, did you wake Gump and Nan?" I ask, crossing the room to place a kiss on her forehead.

She opens her eyes wide as she stares up at me, her own hair looking a bit like mine did a moment ago. "Nope. Gump woke Bailey up and said sssshhhhhh."

"Told you to be quiet? Why would he do that?"

She holds her finger to her lips and makes the hissing noise again. "Don't bother Mommy."

"Dad! She's my daughter, she's not bothering me. Good grief."

"You looked tired," he says matter-of-factly.

*Thanks, Dad. Next time just announce the fact that I look horrible and save us some trouble.*

"And Heather was here," Mom adds. "She was eager to get the show on the road."

Eager to get herself pressed up next to Jake is more like it. Totally disgusting and weird. I know technically Jake and I have never really been together in a normal couple sense, but she should have a little class. I'd be satisfied with very little. I'm talking the end of her pinky finger, if nothing else. That would be enough to make her wear a real shirt for Christmas morning instead of a tight white sweater with the shoulders cut out and a plunging V-neck.

"Just wanted to be with the fam, that's all." Heather's explanation might seem valid to anyone unfamiliar with her normal actions, but I see right through her charade.

Thinking about Heather's actions is an exercise in futility, though, and I don't have much chance to ponder it before Bailey insists that she be allowed to open some presents. In a flash, she has two Barbies unwrapped and is begging my dad to release them from their boxes. Jake speaks up and asks Bailey if he can open the boxes, so she carries them to him with a shrug and goes back to her other presents. He slides the pocketknife from his jeans so easily, it almost looks like a national extension of his arm movement. As he slices through the tape at the side of the box, I can't help but notice that he moves further from Heather on the couch. It's most likely an attempt to keep her away from the knife, but it makes me feel slightly better about the situation.

In fact, there's a slow burn in the pit of my stomach that's trying to force me to go over to the couch and sit between them. The only thing stopping me is the fact that I would look ridiculous and jealous. And the fact that I haven't taken a shower yet today. Do I really want to put my faded blue plaid pajamas up against Heather's Victoria's Secret sweater and faux leather pants? It would feel almost like one of those before-and-after comparisons on a makeover show.

I don't feel like being a "before" today.

Jake brings his eyes up from the box he's working on to glance in my direction, catching me staring. This is when he would normally give me one of those cocky smiles and put his dimple to good use, but instead he looks back down at his hands.

I've broken Jake's spirit. I'm a horrible person.

But it's not my fault that we ran into his friends last night and he started acting so weird. And I'm certainly not to blame for the fact that he was so confrontational afterwards. How could we not have words with the way he was acting? Sure, I feel a little guilty about jumping to conclusions, but I tried to make up for it by inviting him to come back inside. Had I known my mother was going to convince him to spend the night, I might have made sure he was gone long before they got home.

Nothing excuses the way I acted after, though. "We're not friends." As though he thought we were, really. I mean, I might as well have placed a giant sign around my neck that said, "I'm a first-class snot."

He focuses his blue eyes on me again, causing me to realize with a start that I haven't taken my eyes off him. Wouldn't that be a perfect way to spend Christmas morning? Making moony eyes at Jake while he sits next to Heather in her revealing top? What a depressing yuletide prospect.

Worrying about Jake could cause me to miss out on the joy of watching Bailey experience Christmas morning, so I force myself to focus on my little sweetheart. Her baby-fine curls swing while she dances around in front of my dad. They've given her some sort of fake guitar toy with a bunch of light-up buttons, and suddenly she's Jimi Hendrix. Paler, shorter, and three years old, but she's mastering that plastic instrument like a rock legend.

It's not unlike any other Christmas, other than the fact that Jake is here. Strangely enough, though, instead of feeling like there's an unwanted presence, it actually feels like there's something missing.

Bailey finally settles herself on the couch, lazily brushing the mane of her new purple pony with her eyes partially closed. Not even lunch time yet, and she's almost down for the count. As she goes through the grooming motions, I pick up her sippy cup of milk that is slightly warm by this point, standing up to take it to the kitchen. The minute my bare feet touch the cold kitchen tile, I halt in my tracks. Heather's standing on one side of the counter spinning the bottle of coffee creamer between her hands, and Jake's across from her nursing a cup of Dad's decaf. There's no reason for me to feel awkward in my own parents' house, but instead of walking over to the sink, I shrink back just out of sight.

"You know what gets me?" Jake asks softly enough that I actually find myself leaning closer to the wall. "She's such a great mom. How do you all do that? Is it just ingrained in your DNA or something?"

"What, like all women?"

"Definitely not all women. No, I mean in the Jennings DNA."

Heather lets out an unladylike snort, and I can tell from the sound that she's actually moved farther away, which seems contradictory.

"No, you wound up with the good Jennings. Alex has always been like a mini-me of Mom. Smart without trying, doesn't bother dressing up because she already looks great, just naturally nice. And whatever she tries, you know before she makes the first step that she's going to nail it. Seriously, sometimes I think she's got a direct line to God. They're in cahoots."

"In cahoots?" He sounds more than a little skeptical, and I can't blame him. Heather's being ridiculous.

"You know, I seriously doubt she's ever done anything wrong in her life, other than get messed up with you. And maybe listen to me a few times."

"Yeah, we're pretty much polar opposites in that regard," Jake tells her.

"You mean you wouldn't listen to me?" Heather giggles, and it's all I can do not to peek my head around the corner. "Seriously, though. If I find out you're not on the up and up with her or with Bailey…I know people."

Pressing my shoulder against the wall, I wait for his answer to come, but instead I hear Heather's voice again.

"So, you and Alex, are you…?"

My mouth nearly drops open at Heather's audacity. The only thing that could make it worse would be if Jake laughed. Which of course he does, quickly and quietly.

"No, it's not like that."

"Oh. I just figured since you came down here together, maybe something was going on."

"No," he says again, making me cringe even more. "She's way too good for me."

Heat moves across my neck and threatens to overtake my face as those words ricochet around me. *Too good.* Just like I'd been too good for Cody. Too good for everything, but somehow I still don't measure up. Really wish God would explain that little oddity that I've somehow inherited.

"Darn right, you're not good enough for her," Heather agrees. Something about her voice causes me to try to breathe more silently. "I'm not as forgiving as Mom and Dad."

Jake's sigh is so heavy I can hear it around the corner. "Trust me, if I could undo what happened so I wouldn't be *that* guy, I would."

"As long as you don't keep on being *that* guy. Bailey's kind of important to me too, you know."

"Don't worry, Alexis keeps me on a tight leash."

They both laugh at his little joke, and I know I should stop eavesdropping and take the cup to the sink, but I can't make myself move.

"She thinks she has to hold the world together." Heather's voice feels closer, so she must have stepped in my direction. "It's been like that as long as I can remember. Even when we were little girls, she was watching over me, trying to keep me from screwing up. Just don't give her anything else, okay?"

A knot forms in my stomach while I ponder her words. Exactly what does she think Jake's going to give me? The mere thought makes me shudder.

"Anything else?" he asks, likely trying to dissect her statement the same way I am.

"Yeah," she continues, dangerously close to me. "Don't give her anything else she has to hold together. It's not fair."

Bailey's sippy cup slips from my fingers and settles on the living room carpet, and while I'm bent retrieving it, Heather emerges from the kitchen and nearly steps on my fingers. Jerking my hand back, I stand to face her, slightly shorter than her frame thanks to those boots she's wearing. Why she needs snow boots on such a mild day is still a mystery to me. Why she needs snow boots with a three-inch wedge heel is a question for another day.

"Milk got warm," I tell her, raising the sippy cup by dangling its handle from my index finger. She wrinkles her nose as she stares at me, her warm cinnamon-swirl eyes trapped by a layer of black liner that makes them look harder than they are. Heather and I really could be two sides of a coin, only I'm not really sure which extreme should be left face-up.

The thought causes irrational tears to fill my eyes, and rather than ask what's wrong, my little sister leans down and wraps her arms around my neck.

"I hate warm milk," she mutters.

A breathy laugh escapes before I can catch it, and she laughs along with me as she squeezes my shoulders once more before pulling away. One tear has managed to escape from the corner of her eye, leaving a little mascara smudge, so I use my thumb to wipe it away. She smiles, and I know exactly what she's thinking. *There goes Alex, wiping away the imperfection, cleaning things up. She never could stand a mess.*

She's right, I suppose.

"He's really handsome," she whispers almost inaudibly, mischievously glancing in the direction of the kitchen. "Maybe you should make him your pet project."

"Silly Heather. I don't have time to take care of a pet."

"We getting a dog?" Bailey bounces up from her spot on the couch, grabbing my pajama-clad leg as she jumps up and down. "Please, Mommy. Puh-leeeze!"

"Maybe when things calm down."

"But Jay 'posed to get me a puppy." She sticks her bottom lip out in a pout worthy of an Oscar nomination. If Gump was in the room, he'd be a goner.

"What was Jake supposed to do?" He steps around the corner with his eyebrows raised, correcting the only flaw I've managed to notice. Well, outside flaw at least. Inside he's probably marked with a roadmap of scars and bruises.

"Puppy," Heather tells him, extracting herself from our little huddle and sitting on the couch as she pulls out her phone.

"Sorry kiddo, but a puppy seems like something you and your mom need to agree on, doesn't it?" Jake tries to confirm as he stands next to me. He gave her a stuffed dog for Christmas, so at least he made an effort. It's gray and white and very fluffy, but immobile.

"Jake, honey, do you want to invite your dad for Christmas dinner?" Mom has a way of making an entrance, that's for sure. *Hey, everyone, would you like to be uncomfortable?*

"Thank you, Mrs. J, but I don't think he'd come. Probably need to get going myself so I can visit with him a bit."

"Oh, don't leave before dinner!" If Mom can't make a case for food, the world will have turned upside down. The smells wafting into the room from the kitchen should be impetus enough to convince someone not to leave.

"Maybe Jake can take some food to his dad," I suggest. Harmless enough, and it solves both of their problems.

"Maybe you can go with him," Mom says, directing her sweet, innocent-eyed plea in my direction. It would be better played on Jake, because he's new enough that he would probably want to please her. No way do I want to go meet Jake's father.

I look at Jake and begin to shake my head, but he quickly averts his eyes and drops them to Bailey, who's given up on the puppy and is sitting at my feet with her pony toy.

Our conversation from last night trips clumsily back through my mind. His dad tried to kill himself. Jake found him at the table. Drinks all the time, and he's not okay, but okay enough. Still, Jake's too uncomfortable to stay there. Uncomfortable enough to sleep here. To spend Christmas morning with people he barely knows.

The feel of it bubbling up terrifies me, and I desperately wish that I could do something to stop it. Maybe take a breather and stuff it back into its little hole, force it to hibernate a little longer. But I know it's too late the instant my throat begins to close off.

"Would you like me to come with you?"

*Of course he wouldn't, Alexis. How insulting.*

The stupidity of my words causes me to close my eyes for a second, wishing I could get them back and forget that I'd uttered them in the first place. Jake and I are not friends. Even though it had been rude to tell him that last night, that doesn't make it less true today.

Opening my eyes, I find him staring directly at my face, watching my reaction. Since Mom's standing beside us, I offer a tentative smile, hoping I don't look too senseless. Jake's head barely inches up and down, but I see the motion.

"Yes." He continues to watch me with those distinctive eyes of his, but doesn't return my smile. "Yeah, I would."

Jake doesn't have much to say as he drives his pickup down a two-lane road southwest of Jackson. I can't say that I blame him. My own mind is teeming with so many thoughts I can't possibly corral them in order to make sense of them, so instead I focus on the plate of food wrapped in cellophane on my lap. Turkey, stuffing, sweet potatoes, green beans, my mom's famous cranberry sauce.

It's what my parents have done practically every holiday since I can remember. Taking Christmas to the less fortunate. This year they adopted Jake and acted like he was part of the family. Now they're extending their kindness to his dad through me. I'm a broken, fragile vessel of a messenger, but I guess I'll do in a pinch.

My brain is still trying to decipher the reason he wanted me to accompany him when he pulls into a driveway with dried weeds growing tall against a row of about ten mailboxes. Why is it that trailer parks always have aesthetically pleasing names that seem more fitting on lakeside cabin retreats? Sweet Pines. It sounds more like an RV park, or a convalescent home.

A bulldog on a chain barks as we pass the first trailer, the large window in the front covered with a patterned blanket. The pattern is largely indiscernible thanks to being obscured by a satellite dish sticking out of the ground like a yard ornament. The second residence has a brand new Chevy pickup sitting out front, and six concrete blocks forming the steps to the trailer. A boy of about six or seven sits on a bike next to the place, wearing a light jacket.

This is where Jake grew up.

The thought makes me picture Jake as that skinny boy, the weight of the world on his shoulders. It makes me just sad enough that I clear my throat to remove the traces of emotion.

The truck stops at trailer number three, an old black Toyota the only outside decoration marking the place. Otherwise there's nothing distinctive about the trailer featuring white at the top and a light walnut brown on the bottom.

Jake doesn't say anything as he quiets the engine, so I follow his lead, hiding behind the plate of food and preparing myself to be uncomfortable.

Why should I be afraid? I face high schoolers every day, and they haven't eaten me alive yet.

The off-white door sports a swath of dirt or mud at the bottom, and I can picture it as the place where Jake's dad taps his boots against the door before he walks inside. After a swift knock, Jake grabs the doorknob and twists, pulling the door open carefully. The way he peers into the trailer isn't lost on me. He must get nervous every time he crosses the threshold.

"Hey," he offers quietly, holding the door so I can climb up the wooden steps behind him. "Merry Christmas, Dad."

"Jacob." He attempts to rise from his recliner, but doesn't manage it on the first try. The way he's favoring his right leg in his pursuit makes me think he must still have some issues with his injuries. I expect Jake to tell him not to get up, but instead he slips an arm around his dad and assists him to his feet.

"We brought you a Christmas feast," Jake says, making sure his dad is steady. The similarities and contrasts between them are striking. Same blue in their eyes, although the elder's seem a little murky. Similar build, almost identical in height, and same hair color. Jake will probably look a lot like his dad in thirty to thirty-five years, except maybe without the sagging skin under his eyes. And it's hard to picture Jake with the slight extra girth around his midsection.

I'm not sure what I should do, so I hold the plate in front of me with a grin pasted on my face, trying to look friendly. *Oh, look, the Christmas freak is here. Can't stop smiling.*

"I had me a sandwich a little bit ago."

"You don't want to eat a sandwich on Christmas when we brought you turkey and stuffing, do ya?" Jake finally looks in my direction, stepping aside so his dad will focus on me. "Dad, I want you to meet someone. This is Bailey's mom, Alexis."

"Little stinky britches?"

It's pretty difficult to keep the smile pasted on your face with a welcome like that.

Jake chuckles before he manages to control himself and give me an apologetic tilt of his head. "The night Dad hurt his leg, when we were in the truck taking Bailey to Camdyn's house, she sort of—"

"She tooted her horn like an eighteen-wheeler," Jake's dad interrupts.

Jake can't seem to stop himself from laughing again, but he moves forward to take the plate from my hands as a smile lights his face. Without the safety hedge of the food to hide behind, I hesitantly step forward and offer my hand.

"Nice to meet you, Mr. McAuliffe."

"A fancy gal with manners to boot," he says before he accepts my hand, squeezing it awkwardly and gingerly and then dropping his arm back to his side. "Name's Danny."

My hands retreat to the pockets of my jeans in a defensive move, and I can't help but look down at my Converse sneakers. Granted, I did take a shower and comb my hair before we made the trip over here, but I'm pretty sure nobody's ever called me fancy before.

"Here, Dad." Jake places his hand on his dad's shoulder and points to the small two-person table in the kitchen area, where he's arranged the plate with a fork beside it.

"Your girlfriend want something?" Danny asks as he sits in front of the food.

"No thank you," I manage, barely more than a whisper. Jake pulls out the chair across from his dad and motions to it, so I reluctantly cross the tiny space and sit at the beat up old table. The metal trim around the edges makes me wonder if it once sat in a diner.

"Dad does automotive repair at a little shop just down the road," Jake offers as he stands by the sink, using the counter to lean upon.

"Oil changes," Danny tells me as he shoves a forkful of mashed potatoes into his mouth. "Can change the oil on near about anything, from a big rig to a tractor."

"A tractor, like a John Deere?"

"Is it a tractor?"

He continues focusing on his food, and I suppose his question was rhetorical, because he dismisses me like I have nothing more to say. It's not much of a stretch, because I actually don't.

"Alexis is a math teacher," Jake adds, gazing at me as though he expects me to bring more to the conversation. Normally I'd be happy to acquiesce, but this is brutally awkward.

"Math, huh?" Danny pulls apart a yeast roll with his fingers and nods his head. "Never had much use for schooling myself. Didn't even finish it."

Jake gives me a half-hearted closed-lipped grin, and I let my eyes drift down toward my lap.

"Dad prefers getting his hands dirty to learning about things," he tries to explain.

"And then Jacob just thinks he has to tear everything apart," Danny says, bringing his right hand up to rub his cheek. "Remember when you took apart the alternator?"

Jake raises his eyebrows as his dad returns to eating, and then he looks me straight in the eye. "I liked to figure out how things worked. Easiest way to do that is to take them apart, right? So I went through a phase where I would come home from school and deconstruct things. First it was easy things, like flashlights, clocks, and the radio. But one day I took part of Dad's engine out of his truck, and he wasn't very appreciative."

"Fool truck never run right after you messed with it," Danny says.

"It ran fine."

"It was a mess."

"That had nothing to do with me."

There's no Christmas tree here. The realization hits me as I allow my eyes to drift over the mobile home, and the thought makes me wonder what Danny was doing before we got here. The TV wasn't on, and neither was the radio. He'd simply been sitting in his chair alone.

"So, did you take things apart right here at the kitchen table?" I ask Jake, hoping to keep the conversation light.

"No, in my bedroom. Granny gave me a set of screwdrivers and wrenches for my birthday when I was fourteen. I still have them."

"But he still can't change his own oil," Danny tells me.

"I can," Jake counters. "I can change my own oil."

"I'll believe it when I see it." Maybe he's worried about his fork cutting through the paper plate and the cranberries going all over his table, but Danny resorts to picking up the turkey and eating it with his fingers. I try not to watch him and instead focus on the wood grain of the cabinets behind Jake.

"You want to see the tools Granny gave me?"

It takes me a minute to realize that Jake's talking to me. As weird as his question is, I'm fairly certain he's just looking for any excuse to talk about something other than his dad. Perusing screwdrivers seems weird, but if it makes him feel better, how can I refuse?

"Sure, I guess."

Instead of giving me instructions to follow him, he jerks his head in the direction of the living room. Rising from the padded folding chair, I cross the room until I'm standing next to Jake, where he places his hand on the small of my back and gently presses as he walks beside me. The feel of his hand against me immediately heightens my senses, and I try not to let the evidence show on my face. Of course my body wants to betray me by reacting to Jake, as though somehow it remembers things about him that I don't.

Ugh, I don't want to think about it.

The little bedroom to the right of the living room holds a twin size bed with a worn and faded brown patchwork quilt next to one solitary table stacked neatly with boxes and papers. Jake kneels next to the bed and reaches underneath to pull out an old-fashioned red metal tool box.

"This is the coolest gift I ever got," he breathes almost reverently as he opens the clasp to lift the lid. I lean in closer, taking a peek at the contents of the box. A few screwdrivers with black handles, five or six wrenches of different sizes, a small hammer with a crack in the green plastic on the grip, and a yellow measuring tape.

"That," I whisper, having a hard time wrapping my mind around his words. "That's your favorite gift?"

"Yep," he says with no regard for my awkwardness, taking out the smallest screwdriver and giving it a once-over. "First thing Granny asked me to fix was the smoke detector. It kept malfunctioning and scaring her to death."

"I can relate. That happened to me not too long ago." *Burning your napkins. Best keep that to myself.*

"I'd never tried to fix anything until she gave me the tools, and then I was fixing everything I could think of. She got real excited when I fixed the hinges on the front door." The smile on his lips causes the skin around his eyes to crinkle slightly as he stares at a blank spot on the wall. "Every Sunday, it would be this big joke about what I would fix. She'd head out to church wearing one of her dresses with the flower prints and a headscarf, telling me to keep out of trouble before she closed the door."

"She didn't take you to church with her?" Without thinking, I sit down on the bed, which causes his tools to clank into one another as the box slips in my direction. The bed is definitely not in the best shape.

"No, church doesn't really like me."

I recognize my own words from last night coming back to me, so I keep quiet as I glance around the sparse room.

"Anyway, I tightened the legs on the kitchen table, fixed the loose cabinet handles. I even cleaned up some of the wires on the breaker box. Granny was fit to be tied over that one. 'You could've killed your fool self,' she told me." He sits on the other side of the tool box, leaning forward to place his elbows on his knees as he rolls the screwdriver between his palms. "I know that probably seems stupid to you, but for a kid who was always restless, being able to fix things calmed my jitters."

"I don't think it's stupid." My fingers twine together in my lap as I stare at the little pile of tools next to me. "It helps explain why you do construction, doesn't it? Building and fixing things."

"Never thought about it like that." He grins as he turns to look at my face. "I really did mess up that alternator. Taking it apart wasn't so bad, but it was a booger to put back together. I had to use my money we made chopping wood to buy him a new one. He's never quite forgiven me for not being the engine man he is."

"Thus the crack about the oil changes." I can't help but return his smile as he shakes his head.

"You ought to do that more often, you know."

"Get my oil changed? I usually go around five-thousand miles between, but I seriously don't think that had any bearing on the problem with my starter."

"Your car is old as the hills. I doubt the timing of your oil changes makes much difference. I was talking about smiling."

"Oh," I mutter, pushing my hair behind my ear. The bed creaks beneath me, which makes me think about the last time Jake and I sat on a bed together. I'm fairly certain I'm not blushing, but I can't promise the color hasn't drained from my face.

"This isn't me flirting, so don't go all weird on me."

I force myself to meet his eyes just in time to see his gaze sweep over every inch of my face before he locks in again, those blue eyes unwavering. Just a slightly darker blue than the hydrangeas that bloom in front of Mom and Dad's every year.

"More smiling, no flirting. Understood."

"You're making a joke, but I'm totally serious. Hasn't anybody ever told you what a great smile you have?"

"All the time," I say with a shrug before I let the corner of my mouth tip up. "Not really."

"It could stop a man in his tracks. And you can believe I wouldn't just be telling you that, because we're definitely not friends."

Guilt over my words last night immediately floods my senses, along with the knowledge that I need to apologize. Should I allow myself to be friends with Jake, though? If I'm going to see him until Bailey's eighteen, things are bound to get a little uncomfortable.

My gaze darts to him just in time to watch him lift the tape measure from the tool box. He pulls the tape out a few inches and holds it toward me, twisting it slightly so he can measure the length of my arm. I narrow my eyes slightly, but he just nods as he double-checks the number under his thumb.

"Yeah, that's what I thought," he says with a hint of mischief. "Definitely can't be friends."

# Chapter Eighteen

## Jake

Back home, if we ever worked on Saturday mornings, Parker made sure to call me at least thirty minutes before our scheduled start time. I didn't have a problem waking up with my alarm, but he was always worried about me barely getting a couple hours of sleep.

Staying up late on Friday nights had been something I'd done for as long as I could remember. When I was a teenager, Dad would spend Friday nights at the bar, and I would sit at home trying to sleep. Emphasis on the word *trying*, because I never could convince my brain to relax before I knew he was safely in his bed. Sometimes he'd stumble in and land face down on his pillow with his shoes still on. Other times he'd walk in the front door and sit in the recliner, where he'd immediately pass out and start snoring. A couple times, random strangers had dropped him off at the trailer.

Those occurrences were the worst, because while Dad was sleeping it off in the morning, I had to get myself over to the bar so I could drive his truck back home. Since Dad was never a stickler for rules, I'd been driving from the time I was big enough for my feet to reach the pedals. It was the publicity of the thing that I didn't like.

*There goes Jake walking down the road. His old man must have been on a bender.*

It was four miles to the bar, and no one ever stopped to pick me up. Just shook their heads while they cut a wide swath around me as I tightrope-walked the white line. The ones who weren't intent on making me miserable, anyway. Every once in a while a car driven by one of the neighborhood jerks would swerve a little too close and I'd have to hop into the ditch.

Once I was on my own, it felt normal to be out every Friday night until the party died down. Parker was always afraid I was hung over the next morning, and I didn't tell him differently. It was important that I controlled my own situation, and I couldn't do that if I was buzzing or wasted.

He'd probably laugh if he knew my new habit involved waking up at the crack of dawn without any reason. Might not believe me if I told him I usually fell asleep watching *Almost Midnight with Jamie Price*, either. If I manage to escape before mid-morning, though, I avoid the uncomfortable sounds of Roxanne sweet-talking Bud. Just judging from the parking lot and what vehicles are in front of my neighbor's room on a weekend-to-weekend basis, I'm pretty sure there have been three "Buds" since I've been here.

I know I should get a place, but the finality of it is a little daunting. As though if I sign my name on a lease, I'm committing to a lifetime in Louisville.

This particular morning, I happen to step out to my truck at the same time Bud's sneaking out of Roxanne's room, pulling his navy blue uniform coat over his shoulders. He nods in my direction as I open the truck door, and I do the same in return as he climbs into a relatively new extended cab pickup. It's worth noting that the patch on his coat bears the name Marty.

I wonder what it would feel like to be in a prolonged relationship with a woman who couldn't even be bothered to remember my name.

Or like my dad, to be married to a woman who couldn't be bothered to come home at night.

The little house with the black shutters draws my attention as I near the end of Wonder Lane. Alexis keeps the blinds closed most of the time now, ever since I spotted her having a dance party in the living room. It's just as well, because I'm not crazy about random people knowing she and Bailey live there alone.

I told her last week she should get to know the other people on the street, and she laughed at me. "Yeah, I'm sure the hot-shot reporter wants to hang out with her math teacher neighbor."

My gaze drifts away from the large picture window and instead focuses on the two-story in the cul-de-sac. Pulling up next to the BMW in the driveway, I grab a couple sketches I made last night and roll them up, tucking them under my arm while I begin to walk up the sidewalk. The house is a stunner from the outside, but the inside needs a lot of work.

A *lot* of work.

I've been coming over on the weekends and sometimes after work to do a few touch-ups here and a few repairs there, because Harley and her roommate Annie can't afford to spend a lot on upgrades at the moment. The stairs came first, and then a couple busted-out spots in the upstairs walls.

Last time we met, they asked if I could make some repairs to the kitchen cabinets. Repairs would be easy enough, but I think we can revamp the look of the cabinets for just a little more and make them even better, which is why I made the sketches.

Rapping my knuckles on the door, I bring my fist up to blow some warm air into it while I wait. It's an abnormally frigid day even for January, so working outside is definitely not an option.

The door swings open, and my expectations of being greeted by one of the two lovely ladies are dashed. Instead, I'm met by Harley's six-foot tall wall of a boyfriend. I don't know if it's his black hoodie or the messy mohawk haircut, but something about him always puts me on edge.

Maybe it's the fact that I've noticed his girlfriend is beautiful, and I'm fairly certain he's aware that I've noticed. But he can't fault me for having eyes in my head, and I haven't made a hint of a move on her. Quite honestly, I've been trying to temper myself since Alexis accused me of hitting on everything that moves.

Not that I should care what she thinks.

"Hey, Ryan." The purposeful glance at my tool belt swinging from my waist should mentally get the point across that I'm here to work. And only work. If there's a jealous boyfriend in the picture, I'll be cutting myself out of the frame.

"Hey. You just missed Harley and Annie. They went to go pick up some groceries."

"Oh," I say, shifting the sketches under my arm. "Should I come back later?"

"Naw, man, come on in."

He moves aside and I step into the foyer, shrugging out of my coat. Harley and her boyfriend are a perfect example of an odd couple. I'll be fixing a hole in the wall, and she'll show up after the end of her workday in one of her stick-thin skirts and sky-high heels. The girl always looks camera-ready. Ryan will ride up on his motorcycle a little later, wearing a leather jacket and dirty boots. He always leaves his helmet by the door.

Right now, he has motor oil smeared across his jeans.

He crosses the foyer and moves into the kitchen, so I follow, placing my rolled up drawings on the counter. When he opens the cabinet below the sink and kneels down, I can't help but crane my neck to see what he's doing.

"Annie dropped her ring down the drain." He pauses in his kneeling position to glance back at me. "I asked her if it was some weird mood ring or something she got out of a Cracker Jack box. Of course it has to be some fancy gemstone that her dad gave her for her college graduation. Tanzanite, I think she said?"

"So they up and left you to find it?"

"I'm the guinea pig." He turns a channel lock against the pipe in an effort to remove the trap at the bottom of the sink. "How's your daughter doing? Bailey, right?"

"Yeah, Bailey. I'm surprised you remembered. I'm hanging out with her in a couple of hours, actually."

"Don't be too impressed with my memory." He repositions himself and moves his shoulders farther under the sink. "You seem to be a frequent topic of conversation here."

It's hard not to cringe as I glance back toward the foyer. As hard as I've tried in the past not to put myself into awkward situations, I've taken a few in the jaw over the course of time. Doing so today is not in my plans.

"Annie, I mean." One quick move of his wrist and the trap pops loose, sending water pouring onto the towel he's holding. "Annie's constantly talking about you."

"Oh." Relief washes over me as I lean against the counter and fold my arms across my chest.

"What do you think of Annie?"

"Annie?" Hmm... *Interesting hair choice with one side of her dark curls shorter than the other. Stunning almond skin tone. Nice, airy laugh.* "She seems cool, I guess."

Ryan chuckles as he attempts to move without spilling water everywhere. "Man of few words, and yet you said a mouthful. What's Bailey's mom's name again?"

"Alex," I answer quickly. "Alexis."

"Alexis. See? I really don't have a great memory." He opens one of the cabinets and pulls down a plastic container, placing the trap inside where the dirty water pours out. "Were you together very long?"

"No, not really." It's the only thing I can think to say that doesn't make us both look like idiots. Telling the truth would likely bring on the same questions I've received every single time someone's asked me about Alexis. *You know what causes pregnancy, right? Did you think you were untouchable? I'm surprised you weren't more careful.* And the thought of telling people I was too drunk to know what I was doing? *Sure, Jake can't handle his liquor. The same Jake that's at the bar every Friday night drinking with the rest of us.*

"Man, this hood is strangling me," Ryan states as he jerks the sweatshirt above his head, tossing it into the corner. As he returns to the trap and makes sure it's empty, I can't help but notice the large tattoo visible just under his T-shirt sleeve. Rounded and beveled edges mark the bottom of the design, with some scrolling letters underneath. When he reaches across the sink for his towel, the word becomes clear.

"Saved," I say aloud. Ryan wipes his hands as he gives me a quizzical look. "Sorry, just noticed the tattoo on your arm. My friend Parker back home has one like it. Well, not like it exactly, but a God tattoo."

"So he's a freak, huh?" He smiles before tossing the towel on the floor and pushing it with his boot to wipe up a puddle of water. "You from Kentucky? Indiana?"

"Southwest Tennessee. Small town."

A rank odor fills the room, and Ryan makes a disgusted face, plucking the ring from the container only to have it slip from his fingers. It rattles onto the hardwood where it spins to a halt next to my feet. Stooping, I pick it up and wipe a small smudge from the side with my thumb. Ryan bends to pick up the towel and drapes it over the side of the sink before he steps over and I hand him the ring. He inspects it for a second and then drops it into his pocket, shoving his hand in after it like he's afraid it might escape.

"That's a gross smell," he says with a quick laugh.

"I've done enough plumbing, I guess I'm used to it."

"I've smelled way worse being an EMT, just wasn't prepared for that. So, what brings you to The Bluegrass State?"

He cuts a wide path around me and pulls one of my drawings from the counter, unrolling it for inspection.

"A girl," I admit. "Not the kind I'd usually chase. This one's about three feet tall and can't say my name right. But it turns out we have a connection."

"Yeah, Harley said she's a cute kid. I guess maybe she saw a picture or something?"

Instant deadbeat dad moment as I realize I don't have a picture of Bailey. Why haven't I ever thought of that before?

"No, I think Bailey was outside the day Harley stopped by the house. Alex's house, I mean."

"She probably told me that. Another example of the not so stellar memory." He glances over at me and taps his index finger on the paper in front of him. "You sure you could do all this work for the figure you wrote here? It looks pretty extensive."

"The cabinets really aren't in bad shape. There's the one side piece on the far end that would need to be replaced, but the rest just need to be stripped and sanded. Once they're refinished and have new hardware, they'll look new."

"And all the tile here?" He points to the area behind the stove on the drawing.

"Just a backsplash. Really easy to install and I could do it for next to nothing."

"Very cool." He rolls the paper up once more and slides it to the back of the counter. "Thanks for what you're doing for Harley. I know you could be charging a lot more for the work."

"It's kind of nice to have something to do, honestly. It's been a while since I've been the new guy in town. That's taking some getting used to."

Ryan grabs the trap and heads out of the room, presumably to clean it before he replaces it, so I take the opportunity to glance under the sink at the rest of the plumbing. As old as the house is, it appears to be in pretty good working order.

The house itself is a perfect candidate for a bed and breakfast. Old and stately, like a page right out of a history book. Too bad suburbia built up around it. Like one of those old tobacco plantation houses, except this one is overrun by little ranch-styles from a more recent time. Wonder Lane could easily serve as the backdrop for a Norman Rockwell series. *Leave It to Beaver*, maybe.

"I was just thinking," Ryan says as he returns to the kitchen. "If you want to meet some new people, you're welcome to hang out with us tomorrow."

"Could be fun. What's on the schedule?"

"We usually leave here about 9:30. Worship service starts at ten."

Right. Meeting people, Sunday morning, God tattoo. Probably should have pieced that puzzle together a little faster.

"Thanks. I appreciate the invite."

"But..."

"But I don't really do that God stuff."

Ryan doesn't say anything, but nods as he kneels by the sink again to replace the trap.

"Not that I fault you for doing it," I continue. "It's not my place to judge."

That statement causes him to laugh, which echoes through the room even though his head is under the sink. "What is it about the 'God stuff' that turns you off, just out of curiosity?"

"People trying to be perfect. Just feels like setting yourself up for failure to me. I'm not perfect, and I don't need the hassle."

"Yeah, that doesn't sound like a great proposition to me either." He twists his wrist one more time around the trap and then backs out of the small space. "None of us are perfect. Far from it. Myself especially."

"That doesn't bother you then? Sitting there trying to act like you have it all together?"

"I'm not a good enough actor to pull that off." He turns the faucet on and glances under the sink to make sure nothing's leaking. Grabbing the plastic bottle of dish soap by the sink, he squeezes some into his palm and begins washing his hands. "That sounds like religion to me. I'm not into religion. Messed up people taking time to meet together and find friendship, though? I'm all for that."

"Messed up people," I repeat, not able to keep the skepticism out of my voice. "Sorry, I've just had too many personal experiences with church girls to go for that. They're fine with the messed up person you are on Saturday night while they're sitting on a barstool drinking Jack and Coke. Fine enough with it that they'll take you back to their apartment. The next day, they suddenly get all religious. Think they need to 'fix' you, like they're your personal missionary or something. God sent them to save you. Sleep with you first, of course, but afterward they get the sign from above. Fate, or destiny, or whatever they choose to call it."

The sound of the front door opening causes Ryan's eyebrows to lift as he gives me a dry smile. He's probably glad for the interruption so he doesn't have to address that little rant. Louisville is turning me crazy.

"Did you find it?" Annie wants to know the instant she sees Ryan, her normally bright face looking almost ashen. Without a word, Ryan reaches into his pocket and pulls the ring out, depositing it into her waiting hand. "Oh my word, thank you! I could just kiss you!"

"Don't you dare." Harley gives her a stern but playful look as she brushes past and heads up the stairwell, phone in her hand.

"Harley's on a call with the governor's office," Annie informs Ryan with a smile. "Hey, Jake."

"Annie." I give her an acknowledging nod of my head, and she rewards me with an eager smile.

"Why does my ring smell like poo?" She wrinkles her nose as she turns her attention back to Ryan.

"Not my fault," he says, raising his hands to show his innocence. "You need help bringing things in?"

"Would you mind? I'll go upstairs and wash this ring."

"Just don't drop it down the drain," Ryan teases. She shakes her head, causing her curls to bounce. As soon as she begins her walk up the steps, Ryan grabs his coat from behind the door. Not wanting to remain inside while he gets credit for acting like a gentleman, I grab my coat as well.

"Man, it's cold," Ryan states as he opens the door. "Even a snowman would want a coat today."

I don't bother answering as I follow him down the sidewalk.

"Okay, one more thing and I'll shut up," he continues as he pulls open the back door of Annie's Jeep and grabs a canvas grocery bag. "We take people to the hospital in the ambulance every day, and sometimes that's a life or death situation right there. Things happen in the ambulance that bring people back from the brink. You know what I mean?"

"I think so," I answer hesitantly, taking the bag when he offers it.

"Sunday morning isn't that for me. The turning point, do or die stuff...the ambulance ride, if you will...that was intensely personal. Not made for public consumption."

He hands me one more bag before he grabs two himself, closing the door but not making a move toward the house yet. I feel a morality lecture coming on, which would normally cause me to turn tail and walk away. For some reason, though, I just plant myself on the sidewalk and wait for him to finish. Maybe because he doesn't seem like the traditional preachy type with that mohawk and the giant tattoo. Or maybe simply because the guy is standing out here with his breath forming a cloud in front of his face in the cold air. Gotta respect a guy who's willing to take it that far, enough to hear him out anyway.

"Sunday morning's like a post-overdose support group. The after-the-crash follow up at the doctor's office. A monthly blood pressure check."

"But what's the office fee?"

I admit I put that out there just to see how he'd handle my skepticism, but instead of going for a rebuttal, he laughs as he shakes his head.

"Like I said, shutting up now."

He turns toward the house, and as we walk up the sidewalk, he peeks into one of his grocery bags.

"Green beans," he groans, wrinkling his nose as he glances over at me. "One of these days I'm going to work up the nerve to tell Harley they're not really my thing."

The door opens a couple seconds before we reach it, revealing Harley standing just inside the doorway, wearing jeans, a T-shirt and what have to be the thickest pair of wool socks I've ever seen. The dark-haired beauty is also wearing a smile, but it's not for me.

"Thank you," she says as she stretches up to kiss Ryan when he walks through the door. She gives me one of those "also-participated" smiles that I've become familiar with in the last year. I've gotten plenty of them from Camdyn. The smiles that tell a man she's happy you're there and all, but you're not the guy.

In this case, I'm finding that I'm not bothered by it, which is a relief.

She plucks the goods from my hands and then gives Ryan one more parting grin as she turns to take her groceries to the kitchen. I'm not quick to follow, but wait for Ryan to head in her direction with his own bags. He's not eager to move, instead opting to stand where he is and watch her as she walks away.

I'm almost tempted to laugh before he lets out a low whistle and raises his eyebrows as he turns toward me.

"Definitely not breathing a word about the green beans today," he tells me with a solemn shake of his head.

A couple hours have passed by the time I brace myself against the cold wind as I stand on the porch, knocking on the door. I hear Bailey's bubbly voice almost immediately, but thanks to the locks I installed when we first arrived, she can't manage to open the door. That knowledge admittedly gives me a little surge of pride.

Alexis backs away from the door the instant she has it open, and I hastily step inside and close the door behind me.

"That wind is brutal!" she says as she offers a slight smile. "I hope you haven't been outside today."

"As little as possible." I don't bother taking off my coat, because I know Bailey's not going to let me sit down. The fact that she is dragging her own pink puffy coat with the leopard print hood behind her is enough to tell me that she's been awaiting my arrival.

"Jay's taking Bailey to Donald's," she states matter-of-factly as she stands in front of me like a soldier reporting for duty.

She's so serious, I can't resist teasing her a bit. "He is? Why didn't anyone tell me about this?"

"You know." Bailey crosses her little arms over her chest and turns to face Alexis. "He knows, Mommy."

"Of course he knows. He's just being silly."

"Don't be silly to me," Bailey demands as she pokes her bottom lip out.

"Yes, ma'am." I kneel down to help her into her coat, trying to hide the smile on my face.

"Have you been eating chocolate?"

As I finish buttoning the snap over the top of Bailey's zipper, I wait for her to answer Alexis. When she doesn't bother to give a response, I glance up expecting her mom to be getting a wet wipe or something. Instead, her eyes are focused on me.

"What are you looking at me for?"

Her eyes widen in surprise, and the corner of her lip lifts ever so slightly. "Um, because I asked you a question."

"Me? Have I been eating chocolate?" I can feel my eyebrows drawing together as Bailey grabs onto my hand, clearly not interested in her mom's conversation. "I just had some hot chocolate. Annie made it for me—out of a box. You were right. It wasn't as good as yours." Bailey clamps her entire hand over my index finger and then does the same with the other hand over my pinky, trying to pull me in the direction of the door. "What, are you a chocolate bloodhound or something?"

"This Annie person must not care about you at all."

Bailey's pulling doesn't cease, so I lean down to tickle her until she stops. "I hardly think giving me boxed hot chocolate means she doesn't care about me. Not that she does, either, but the two don't go hand in hand."

Alexis bites her lip to keep from smiling, and I barely even notice Bailey jerking on my arm anymore.

"If she cared about you, she wouldn't let you leave with chocolate on your face."

"I don't have anything on my face," I argue.

"You do. You've got a little…" Taking a step toward me, she rubs her finger along the top of her lip and then points to me. When I shake my head, she balls her hand into a fist and licks her thumb, stretching her hand in my direction. I manage to grab her wrist when it's about two inches from my face.

"Whoa!" My sudden exclamation causes her jaw to drop open, and she would probably attempt to back away if I wasn't holding her wrist. "Did you just try to spit clean me?"

"I don't know what I was doing," she mutters, glancing at her wrist wrapped inside my fingers.

"I'm pretty sure you were about to lick my face."

"I would never." Red splotches spread across her neck as she shakes her head and scrunches her eyes closed. "I'm just so used to being with Bailey. I can't believe I did something so incredibly stupid. So stupid."

The delicate skin of her wrist feels warm under my fingers, and I know I should release her so she can back away, but I can't seem to force myself to do it. Something about her makes me feel a little off balance lately. I'd like to tease her until it makes her half crazy, but not as much as I want to put my arm around her and pull her closer. The arm that's currently occupied as Bailey tugs on my hand yet again.

"So, aren't you going to do something about it?" I let the question hang in the air for a second and wait for her to open her eyes and meet my gaze. When she finally does, there's confusion written all over her face.

"I'm sorry," she manages to breathe.

Her level of sincerity makes me laugh, and as I do so her wrist relaxes a bit in my hand.

"Your apology is nice and all, but it doesn't get the chocolate off my face."

"I can't." She draws her wrist away when I let go, and I tilt my head to the side and give an exaggerated sigh.

"You can."

"Absolutely not."

Her eyes never leave my face, and something inside me just wants to shock her. Fluster her a bit. Get under her skin the way she's getting under mine.

"Here?" I ask, pointing to the area under my nose, knowing full well that she pointed to the left side of my mouth. When she shakes her head, I move my finger farther to the right.

"No," she says, looking a bit conflicted, as though she'd like to help but can't make herself commit.

A smile crosses my face before I drag my tongue along my upper lip, afterwards trying to judge by her reaction whether I was successful. The look on her face tells me otherwise, so before I have time to think about it, or she has time to react, I grab her wrist one more time, raise her hand to my lips, and place the tips of her fingers against my face.

"Jake!"

"Cut a guy a little slack," I insist, knowing that I've teased her enough to make her uneasy.

"Disgusting," she whispers as she presses her thumb against the top of my lip. She stares at my chin, as though she doesn't want to have eye contact and physical contact at the same time. When she pulls her fingers away, it takes a second before I can force myself to swallow.

"Thank you." Those expressive eyes meet mine, trying to tell me a million secrets, but I haven't learned to read them yet. She steps back and drops her gaze to Bailey, so I do the same.

"Come on, Jay," Bailey says as she jerks on my hand again. Pretending I don't know why she's pulling me in the direction of the door, I stop in my tracks and give her a stern look.

"What are we doing again?"

"Is you kidding me?" She presses her lips into a thin line and stares up at me, and I can't keep up the pretense. I'd like to think the two of us are growing on one another, but I'm pretty sure both of us know she is just a heartbeat away from having me wrapped around her little finger.

"Alright, Bailey. We're going to a steakhouse, right?"

"Donald's!"

"Oh, yeah, I forgot. McDonald's."

We walk out the door while Alexis shivers in the door frame as she tells us to have fun, and then I struggle to strap Bailey into my truck after removing that huge fluffy coat from her body. By the time I manage to get her situated and find myself in the driver's seat, Alexis is still waiting in the doorway, determined to watch us until the very last minute. I lift my hand to wave, and the action seems to draw her out of whatever trance she was in. Lifting her fingers for only a second, she backs into the house and closes the door.

It's the first time I've been alone with Bailey since we've been to Louisville.

Although it kind of feels like a monumental accomplishment, a huge part of me wishes there was a slightly difficult brunette in my passenger seat.

# Chapter Nineteen

## Alexis

The cold wind forces the door closed a little faster than I intended, and it makes a slamming noise as it comes to a rest behind me. Not that anyone would notice, since I'm alone in the house for the first time. Covering my face with my hands, I cringe as I think about the past couple minutes.

Treating Jake like a three-year-old, and then his accusation that I wanted to lick his face. So humiliating. And beyond that, when he brought my hand up to his lips...

No matter how many times I manage to convince myself that I have things under control, my body has to betray me and act like I want Jake touching me. He grabs my wrist, and suddenly the blood in my veins feels like it increases in temperature. He shows me that dimpled smile, and my words seem to get stuck in my throat. Moves my fingers to his mouth, and a swarm of angry butterflies fills my stomach.

Of course he knows exactly what he's doing, which is why he always laughs at the effects of his actions. I can't manage to turn it off, either, even as he's telling me he just left some other woman's house.

Annie. I can picture her in my mind: blonde hair cascading down her back, lips always in a semi-pout, lives in an apartment where everything is painted red and she has a heart-shaped bed. Making hot chocolate from a box.

She sounds dreadful.

Groaning noisily, I pick up Hoppy from where Bailey left him on the counter and carry him to her bedroom, berating myself for being so ridiculous. Annie could be nothing like I pictured. She could have black hair, for all I know. Flaming-bright red tresses just like on Bailey's Ariel pajamas that I threw in the dryer earlier.

Imagining a hundred different beautiful women Jake could have been with before he arrived at our house isn't really helpful, and it's a total waste of my free time. Instead, I turn on the TV, settling on a movie from the 1940's. Gene Kelly dances into the frame, and I plop onto the couch and pull my legs up against my chest. The blue plaid furniture beneath me is used, just like our first attempt at furniture, but the owner assured me this couch hadn't been with cats. And it doesn't smell anything like my Great Aunt Betty.

An unexpected knock on the door causes my heart to jump, and I hesitantly rise and head to the front window. Peeking out the blinds, I half expect to see Jake's truck in the driveway. Instead, there's a Jeep. The smidgen of the blue coat I can see from the corner of the window doesn't look familiar, either.

I leave the upper lock fastened so the door will only crack open about an inch. When I peek out through the small space it's only to find a woman about my age, one side of her hair slicked to her head and the other side full of bouncy black curls. Instantly deciding she doesn't look too frightening, I unhook the latch and pull the door open farther.

"Hi," she says, stepping into the house without waiting for an invitation. "Just thought I'd stop by and say hey. Harley and Ryan are having dinner with his sister, and I knew Jake was taking Bailey for a while. Seemed like a perfect opportunity."

Her mention of Bailey causes me to furrow my brow, but she doesn't seem fazed.

"Sorry, guess I should introduce myself. Annie Jessup."

The hand extends in my direction, and I take it even though it makes me a bit uneasy. "Alexis Jennings."

"Hey, what about that! A.J., just like me. I bet you got that a lot growing up."

It takes me a minute to respond, because I'm glancing behind her to see if she's dragging a vacuum. Or cleaning products.

"Nope, not once."

"Oh." She shrugs but doesn't dwell on the idea, and smiles as she pulls off her gloves. "Jake talks about you and Bailey a lot."

The name-dropping of my baby girl again gives me a slight chill, until I start placing two and two together. Hot chocolate Annie?

She begins unbuttoning her coat, which is sky blue and hangs to her knees, and I can't help but notice a sparkle when she pulls the sleeve from her arm. The ring on her right hand contains a stone that is a deeper blue, almost shimmering purple, offset by what look like diamonds. It's probably worth more than my car.

Not exactly what I had pictured, but maybe Jake's looking to improve his lot in life.

"You're the Annie that's dating Jake?"

"Dating Jake?" She drapes the coat over her arm and shakes her curls vigorously. "How funny! I have no idea where you got that idea. Not that I didn't try flirting with him at first, because he's such a doll, but the man is like a wall of steel. Can't break through the fortress."

Jake, a wall of steel? Give me a break.

"How do you know Jake?" It seems like an innocuous question, but the answer may determine whether the hair on the back of my neck continues to stand on end or settles itself down.

"He's been doing work on Harley's house."

Right—beautiful news reporter.

"And," she continues, handing me her coat, "before you ask, he's not dating her either. She has a boyfriend, but even if she didn't, the man won't even smile sideways at us. He's all business."

My eyes focus on the blue fabric in my hands, so soft that I wish I could run my hand across it, but I can't do so in front of my nutty houseguest.

"What are you doing here exactly?"

Probably not the nicest thing I've ever said to a stranger, but she laughs it off as though it doesn't bother her at all.

"Just a friendly neighbor-to-neighbor visit. Since we're going to be running into each other from time to time—presumably, anyway, once the weather's nicer—I thought we should get acquainted. Don't you have southern hospitality and all that jazz down south?"

"Down south?" My voice raises a little at the end of the word, making me sound like I'm almost unhinged. Perhaps she's not the only nutty one in the room. "I don't really think of where we lived as down south."

"Well, south of Louisville is south, as far as I'm concerned."

I sense that she's not leaving anytime soon, so I drape her coat over the back of the couch and lower myself beside it. She doesn't hesitate to cross the room and sit next to me, turning herself slightly so she's facing me. She even folds one of her legs partially under her on the cushion as she gets herself comfortable, causing one of her pink-sequined tennis shoes to sparkle as it dangles above the carpet.

"I would say welcome to Wonder Lane, but technically I became Harley's roommate after you moved in. So you really should welcome me, in that case. I'll let you off the hook, though."

It's like being hit with a runaway conversation train. And I can't figure out how to get off the tracks.

"Thanks, I think."

"What brought you to Louisville? Jake says you moved here for a job?"

Her intense scrutiny makes me wonder if my hair's out of place. After all, I was having a mini tantrum right before she came through the door. "Um, yeah. I teach high school algebra." I slide my hand up to push my hair behind my ear, casually making a momentary ponytail with my hands to make sure I don't have any stragglers.

"So you're practically a rocket scientist," she states, actually looking semi-impressed.

It might have been a silly statement, but it gives me a teensy boost of confidence. Smoothing down my hair, I calmly place my hands in my lap.

"More like a zookeeper, most days."

She widens her eyes a bit as she stares at me. "Wow. Static."

Static? What is that, one of those new cool person catchphrases? And to think I haven't even heard it at school yet.

"Hmm, yeah. Completely static," I say with a nod, hopefully agreeing to something pleasant.

"Girl, I'm serious about the static. It's like full-out science experiment up in here. Balloon to the head static."

"Totally," I breathe right before I sense it. At first it's just a slight tickle against my cheek, but then it turns into a tingling sensation all over my scalp. "It's me, right? I have static?"

"Massive." She giggles as she bends down to dig through her Coach handbag. "I've got the perfect thing, though." Pulling a purple travel-sized bottle to her knee, she suddenly turns serious. "Carrying hair product in your bag is a necessity when you rock a 'do like mine. May I?"

There it is...she's selling hair products.

"Sure."

She wastes no time, spraying some of whatever-it-is into her palms. It only dawns on me as she's rubbing her hand across my head that it might be a little weird for a relative stranger to be practically petting me.

"Are you a hairdresser?" I pose the question more to ease my discomfort than to begin the expected spiel about her wondrous hair products.

"Nope. I own an upscale resale shop, The Revolving Closet. You should come by sometime. I'll hook you up."

Pure instinct forces me to glance down at my department store special jeans, complete with the frayed ends from excessive wear and the occasional trampling by my tennis shoes. Upscale, me? Obviously I don't even pay to have my jeans hemmed.

And I'm sure she's mighty impressed with my Indians T-shirt that boasts the year I graduated from high school. Pure class on display right here.

My phone begins singing "Picture to Burn" by Taylor Swift, and I jerk it off the coffee table wishing I had put it on silent. That fleeting thought is replaced quickly with a sense of dread.

"Sorry, it's Jake," I explain to Annie, drawing it up to my ear.

It took me a while to let my guard down enough to let him take her out of the house, so of course the instant I do, I get the phone call. My heart squeezes a little in my chest as I think about what might have happened.

"Jake? Please tell me Bailey's okay."

"What? Yeah, of course."

"Does she want to come home?"

"I'm going to go out on a limb and say no." He hesitates a second and I can hear screaming in the background. Happy screaming, though…not blood curdling screaming. "She finished her hamburger with nothing on it and would love to join the screeching pack of kids, but she's wearing Cinderella socks."

"Right. She knows she has to wear socks."

"Yep, she's given me the mom lecture already. Kudos for drilling it into her head like that. I guess you want me to buy her some, then?"

"What?" I rise from the couch and begin pacing across the floor, sidestepping Annie's fancy purse in the process.

"I'm assuming you don't want her to get these Cinderella socks dirty. I know how you feel about dirt."

Anxious regret courses through me as I realize he's teasing me for trying to lick his face. We're not in that place, after all. In order for him to be able to joke with me like that, we either have to be friends or casual flirty acquaintances. I'm still contemplating whether I can allow the former, and we're certainly not the latter.

"I actually don't have an aversion to dirt, as it turns out, so feel free to get as much dirt on the socks as you wish."

"Oh. Well, I think it's an overstatement to say that I *wish* her to get dirt on her socks, Cinderella or otherwise."

"She can wear the socks. It's fine."

He laughs on the other end of the line, and I glance over to find Annie watching me curiously. "Go on, Bailey. Your mom says the socks are good-to-go."

"Was that all?"

"I'm not sure. You got anything else?"

It would appear that the wall of steel is collapsing on me. Or, if nothing else, Jake has suddenly decided I'm worthy of flirty banter. This isn't going to wear well on my nerves.

"No. I have absolutely nothing."

"Are you sure? Because it seemed like you might want to do some verbal sparring. If you're game, I'm totally up for it."

Reaching up, I wrap my fingers around my neck, as though it's possible to somehow protect myself from that too-intimate tone in his voice.

"No, thank you. I have a guest."

"You have a guest? I don't believe you. Who is it?"

"Your friend Annie."

"Are you giving it to her about the hot chocolate?" His voice changes to a whisper. "She uses a box, Alex. A box."

"Just watch our daughter," I mutter as I end the call.

The rectangular electronic device in my hand stares back at me, as though it doesn't realize it witnessed the downward spiral of that conversation into a cesspool of smarminess.

"Everything okay?" Annie wants to know.

"Yeah." I attempt a smile as I march back to my spot on the couch, shrugging my shoulders. "He just had a question about socks."

She nods her head as she stands and steps over to the kitchen, where she begins rinsing the hair product off her hands. One glance over her shoulder in my direction, and I feel sure the questions are just beginning.

"So, that's an interesting ringtone."

"Is it?" Before I place my phone back on the coffee table, I make sure it's set to vibrate.

"Yeah." She turns and grabs the towel off the handle of the oven to dry her hands. "Redneck heartbreakers in pickup trucks? Sounds like a Lifetime movie waiting to be told."

"Probably just an unimaginative ringtone chosen on a whim, in all reality."

"You use that ringtone for your mama?"

She settles herself next to me on the couch again, and I shake my head with a sigh.

"No."

"Then it's interesting, that's all. My ringtone for my ex is 'Since You Been Gone' by Kelly Clarkson. Just in case I need a reminder when he calls that I'm better off without him."

Something about that admission causes me to relax a little, and I can't help letting out a small laugh. "You know, I've never even had a picture of Jake to burn. Maybe that would have been therapeutic."

"I have a picture of him on my phone, but you can't burn it. The phone, I mean."

"He sent you a picture of himself?"

"Are you kidding? That would be weird." Annie shakes her curls as though she's ridding herself of that thought, and then turns to stare at the TV. "I took a picture of him while he was nailing a board on the stairs. So I could show Harley the work he was doing, of course. Don't judge me."

I try to hide my smile behind my hand as I focus on the dancing couple on the screen in front of us.

"Mind if I watch the movie with you?" she asks without looking in my direction.

I give the requisite yes without even thinking about it, because of the deeply-ingrained mantras in my mind about being kind, loving my neighbor, and showing courtesy. It's what my mother would do, after all. Invite the neighbors in off the street, make sure they're warm, feed them dinner, and be certain they know they're welcome.

Even though part of me knows I only said yes out of politeness, I can't deny that having another adult sitting next to me on the couch is long overdue.

Around three hours pass before Jake opens the front door, allowing Bailey to barge in overflowing with energy and excitement. Annie's shoes rest near the bottom of the couch, and she has her feet pulled up under her on the cushions. Our Gene Kelly movie ended a bit ago, but an Alfred Hitchcock mystery came on in its place.

As it turns out, Annie and I have a lot in common. Her parents are practically perfect too, and she was trying to fit into that mold for a long time. Until recently, anyway, when she broke away from a rather controlling ex-boyfriend. Now she's embracing her freedom.

It's kind of the same idea I had when I tried to break free from Jake, who is currently standing in my kitchen. Maybe I should have shaved half my head, too.

Bailey wraps her arms around my thighs as I rise from the couch, and I have to grab the armrest to keep from falling over. "Jay chase me up the slide. He's a tiger and him wants to eat me."

"Are you serious?" I shoot a surprised look at Jake for Bailey's benefit before I grab her hand. "Let me make sure you have all your fingers. Let's see…one, two, where's your thumb?" She wiggles it with a big smile. "There it is. I was worried there for a minute."

"I should probably get going," Annie announces as she begins putting her shoes on her feet. "You've entertained the crazy neighbor long enough."

"You don't have to leave," I tell her, wrapping my arm around Bailey's shoulders.

"I need to turn in pretty early tonight. I'm playing bass at church tomorrow morning so I have to be there bright-eyed and bushy-tailed. And you know it takes forever to get this hair looking perfectly random." She winks at Bailey as she stands up, draping her purse over her shoulder. "Jake, you going tomorrow?"

He's still standing by the kitchen and hasn't made a move to take off his coat. It's Saturday night, so he probably wants to bolt. Maybe he'll go employ his flirting on someone at one of the clubs.

"I'll give it some thought," he says noncommittally, offering Annie a rather crooked half grin.

"Well, don't be a stranger. Come over for dinner one night, okay?" Annie pulls her coat from the back of the couch and slides one arm into the sleeve. "All of you. Just let me know ahead of time so I have enough food."

Jake nods as Annie gives me a parting wave, and then she slides out the door, leaving the three of us awkwardly in her wake.

"Jay, want to see my pony?" Bailey tosses her coat toward the wall, leaving it in a heap as she trots down the hall, her fine brown hair flying around her face. Looks like I'm not the only one who has been plagued by the static monster today.

I glance at Jake, but the playfulness he had on the phone is gone. "You probably want me out of your hair," he says.

"Don't worry about it. You won't hurt her feelings if you leave. I'll make sure she understands."

"Okay."

His uncharacteristic hesitance causes me to have all sorts of unwelcome thoughts. Maybe he needs a friend. Maybe those couple hours with Bailey changed things. Maybe the two of us shouldn't be in the same room together, since I obviously have some sort of stomach affliction when he's in the vicinity.

*Seriously, thank you stomach. I get it. Jake's attractive. You don't need to keep assaulting me.*

"Or…"

Bailey bursts back into the room with the horse she got for Christmas, and he bends down to inspect it, looking at it so closely it seems he might want to buy it from her. He's clearly figured out some of this dad business in the past month.

"You could stay," I blurt, the volume of my words a shock even to me. Cringing, I fight to bring my voice down a notch. "If you have nowhere to be, of course. Not that you wouldn't, because you're you and it's Saturday night. And I'm not implying anything unseemly by that, just casually observing the fact that you're charming and rather good looking so you should have no problem finding company on a Saturday night. If you're actively looking for it, which I'm in no way saying you are."

The horse all but forgotten, he looks at me from his position kneeling next to Bailey, brows lifted slightly but no smirk or cocky expression on his face.

"You finished?"

That's it. Am I finished, like I'm officially the lame dorm mom or something. *Oh, look, the weird uptight girl just spewed her word vomit all over me. How peculiar.*

My stomach goes on full-out revolt, like there's an angry battle of Rock 'Em Sock 'Em Robots going on in there.

Am I finished?

"I really hope so," I answer quietly.

He stands up and starts to take off his coat, but pauses with it midway down his back.

"You sure?" he asks.

"Only rarely, and even then it's touch and go."

He smiles as he finishes removing his coat and drapes it over the back of the couch.

"Anybody ever tell you you're funny?"

"Funny ha ha or funny needs psychiatric attention?"

"Take your pick."

"Neither, actually. I was just stalling because something's desperately wrong with my brain."

He laughs as he scoops Bailey up with one arm and deposits her over the side of the couch. "What are you watching? Old movies?"

"Hitchcock. We can change it if you like."

"Don't change anything. I'm good."

The instant he settles onto the couch, Bailey launches herself onto his lap and trots the pony across his chest.

"What's the pony's name?" Jake asks her as he protectively places his hand against her back. Pre-mom Alexis might have missed that, but now I know all the tricks for keeping her from falling off the couch, the bed, or practically any high surface.

"Jay," she states, leaning her head on his arm.

"That's my name." He presses the tips of his fingers against her side until she giggles, and then he relaxes his arms around her. "You don't want your pony to have the same name as me. What should we name it? Is it a girl or a boy?"

Bailey squints and wrinkles her nose to indicate she's deep in thought. "Hmm. I think…a girl."

"You were going to name a girl after me?" He drops his jaw, and Bailey showcases a huge smile.

"No, a gooder name I think. Pickles."

"Pickles." He repeats Bailey's choice without even a hint of emotion.

"Yep."

"Well, it's nice to meet you, Pickles."

She lays her head on his collarbone and gazes at the TV. "Mommy, can Jay watch Belle?"

"I don't know if Jake wants to watch *Beauty and the Beast*. We'll have to ask him."

He relaxes into the couch and pretends that he's just as tired as Bailey. "Can we watch Belle, please?" He rests his chin on the top of her head as he stares at me, and I divert my attention from him by looking for Bailey's DVD. Once I find it, I busy myself with loading it and fast forwarding through the previews so I don't have to look into those blue eyes again. They've been trying to read me too closely lately, and I'm not sure this book wants to be opened.

Once the townsfolk are safely singing "Belle" as the heroine skips around town with her nose in her book, I excuse myself and head to the bathroom to lock myself inside. My sudden emotion is completely ridiculous, and deep inside I'm berating myself for that very thing, but I can't seem to stop the moisture from clouding my eyes.

Just a short time ago, Annie and I were sitting on that couch joking about ringtones for our exes. I was thinking about how I couldn't wait to escape from Jake. Wishing I had the ability to truly start over the way Annie has. Not giving any thought to the way my personal wishes affected my baby girl.

Jake didn't fight me when I took complete custody of Bailey. He signed the paperwork without any argument at all because he wanted nothing to do with her. I said he wouldn't have to pay child support, against the wishes of my lawyer, and he had no hesitation doing whatever I asked. He's barely had any part in her life since that day. All I wanted was to keep it that way.

But my little girl is sitting on her dad's lap right now watching a movie that I'm pretty sure he has no interest in. I would have taken that moment from Bailey. And even if she never gets another one as long as she lives, she'll have this one.

"You're a horrible person," I whisper to my reflection in the mirror, observing my slightly red nose and the tear sliding down my cheek. Sniffling, I grab a tissue and blot at my eyes, leaning my head back to try to staunch the flow of tears.

Jake sitting on the couch holding Bailey—that I wouldn't have expected.

Jake in my house and me locked in the bathroom crying—yeah, sounds about right.

Forcing the biggest breath I can muster, I unlock the bathroom door and make my way down the hall until I can see the couch again, Bailey resting against Jake, her eyes barely propped open as she watches her movie.

"Everything okay?" he asks quietly as I sit about a foot away from them.

Rather than trusting myself to speak just yet, I offer a slight smile as I nod in his direction. He stops looking at me and focuses instead on the Beast on the screen, so I take another quick breath.

"Did you really chase Bailey up the slide?"

"Yep." He nods but doesn't take his eyes off the television. "Up the slide, up the steps, through the rope maze. I even got stuck once and this six-year-old kid named Timmy stomped on my stomach."

"Yikes." I can feel my eyes getting watery, but I try to fight it. "Thank you. I'm sure that meant so much to her."

"Yeah, well, it didn't exactly mean nothing to me either." He glances at me just in time to witness a tear sliding down my cheek. His eyes glass over before he forces them back to the movie, and he clears his throat. "Bailey's a really good kid. One of the parents in McDonald's told me that. 'Takes after her mom,' I said. She laughed like I was joking, but I wasn't. And I should say thank you."

"For what?"

"Giving her a good life."

Seeing as how I'm oddly emotional and don't have an appropriate response to that statement, I choose to focus on the television and say nothing, like a coward.

Jake doesn't engage me anymore, for which I don't blame him. Instead, he holds Bailey as we watch Belle come to the realization that the Beast isn't really so bad. By the time the movie is halfway over, Bailey is fast asleep.

"Do you want me to take her?" I whisper. Jake glances at me and then down at Bailey.

"I kind of want to know what happens to Belle."

I fight the urge to laugh as I rise and reach for Bailey. "Don't worry. I'll let you finish the movie."

"But it makes it kind of weird if there's no kid in the room."

"Yeah, mega weird." My eyes meet his as I scoop Bailey up, and I think I note a hint of mischief in his gaze. I wait until I turn toward the hall with Bailey to allow a smile to cross my face.

She doesn't fight me as I pull the covers over her body and press a kiss to her forehead. That trip to McDonald's must have really worn her out. I sit on the edge of her bed for a couple minutes, simply staring at her face. I breathe a couple of prayers, mostly that I won't totally screw her life up. That I can be the mother she needs. Then I place my first two fingers lightly over her nose and lips, just to feel her breath on my skin.

I've done that every night since the first night I brought her home. Placed my hand just so to make sure she's still breathing. It felt somewhat rational in the beginning, when she would lay eerily still and not make any noise. Now it feels almost nutty, but I can't seem to get out of the habit.

A warm hand on my shoulder causes me to halt with my fingers above Bailey's face.

"I paused the movie. Hope that's okay."

Thank goodness my back is to him, because I can only imagine the look of panic on my face.

"No, you'll have to start it over at the beginning now."

"For real?"

His hand hasn't moved from its spot, and his mere closeness causes me to squeeze my eyes shut and bring my hand up to pinch the bridge of my nose.

"Of course not. I'm just being odd to try to make this less awkward. It's not working."

He takes his hand off my shoulder and sits beside me on the bed, but I don't dare look at him.

"Do you think something happened to her today?"

"No. Should I?" I twist my face in his direction, and he doesn't avert his eyes from mine.

"You were checking to make sure she was breathing."

"How do you know that?"

"I've done it with my dad enough to recognize it."

It's too intense, being this close to Jake and staring into those eyes. Trying to divert his scrutiny, I look at the floor and shove my hair over my shoulder.

"It doesn't mean anything. Just a weird mom thing I've always done."

Not wanting to remain in such close proximity, I stand and move toward the door, only pausing once to make sure he's following. Since he's right behind me, I don't stop at the couch but continue to the kitchen to pour myself a glass of water. Without giving it a lot of thought, I grab a glass for Jake as well.

"Here." I hand him the glass as I place my knee on the couch, sitting cross-legged as far from him as possible. He takes it quietly and holds it against his knee, his fingers barely gripping the side of the glass. He doesn't restart the cartoon, but simply sits there staring at the screen, which has gone blue. Maybe he really doesn't want to watch the movie without Bailey in the room. As if anyone would know besides me, and I seriously doubt he cares what I think.

"I don't know what I'm supposed to do, Alex."

Something tells me this conversation is headed in an uncomfortable direction. Rather than watch its descent, I attempt a smile.

"Well, if you hit the 'play' button on the remote, your movie should come back on."

He shakes his head slowly as a grin plays about his lips. "Cute, but this really isn't funny."

"Okay." I take a drink of my water, more to give myself time than because I'm thirsty.

"It seems like there's some kind of way this should progress, but I just can't make myself do it."

Something in the way he makes that statement instantly puts me back in Jackson on the tailgate of Cody's pickup. *Can't ever follow through with Alexis. Too good.* It's preposterous, though, because Jake and I aren't dating. Surely he doesn't think just because he's here and Bailey's asleep that I would...

"I know there are legal steps I should take and all that, but it seems like if I go down that road it's going to cause a rift between us. And I don't want to do anything that makes you lose time with Bailey, because you don't deserve that. In all honesty, I'm the one who deserves nothing." He begins tapping his finger against the glass almost nervously. "The thing is, I want to be part of her life. Not just a 'pop over once a week' kind of guy, but I want to try to be a real dad. With things the way they are, I just don't know how to make it happen."

I rest my head against the couch and let out a breath of relief, carefully keeping my focus on the blue television screen.

"You don't need to do anything, okay?" Turning my focus to the glass in my hands, I twist it carefully and watch the light coming from overhead dance across the water. "You're Bailey's father, plain and simple. If you want to spend time with her, I won't stop you."

"When, though? I don't want to take anything away from you."

"So don't," I offer simply. He immediately turns to stare at me, so I reluctantly look in his direction. "I owe you an apology."

"Not likely."

"Yes, very likely. Back at Christmas, when we were at my parents' house, I told you we couldn't be friends."

"I recall that."

"Probably not the nicest thing I've ever said."

He laughs as he exhibits one of those rare smiles I only see when flirty Jake pops into play. Dimple pronounced, one side of his lip a little higher than the other, straight white teeth on display. "Don't worry about using good manners on me. I'm cool about it, really."

"I'm not. I know this is going to sound completely crazy, but since I was a kid, I've been extremely aware of when I've done something wrong. It just sits on me like a stench I can't get rid of. Anyway, just know that I'm sorry about saying that. It was unkind."

"So what are you saying? You want to be friends now?"

He doesn't change his expression, and I allow myself to smile back at him even though it feels like a horrible idea. I've seen the way Jake uses his charms to his best advantage. Even though I'm aware of them, I'm not entirely certain I'm immune.

"I guess what I'm saying is that we could give it a try. And you're welcome to come over anytime to see Bailey."

"That's a dangerous statement. What if I show up every night around dinner time?"

"Then I'll figure out pretty quickly that I need to plan on cooking for three."

He nods as his hand extends toward me, across the vacant space in the middle of the couch. Without giving it much thought, I take it in mine.

"Friends?" He poses it as a question, but I'm sure he already knows the answer.

"Friends."

He looks down at our hands, which forces my eyes down to our hands as well. Clasped together in a handshake—nothing odd about it, but he doesn't let go. For some crazy reason, that knowledge makes me reluctant to let go, too. He should be the one to let go, right?

"So what would friends do now?" he asks quietly. "This is kind of new territory for me."

"Most of my friends enjoy repainting my living room or doing my laundry."

"I can do that. Where's the paint?"

Instead of making me feel manipulated or causing my stomach to flip upside down, the easy smile he exhibits this time causes me to relax a little. Only very little, because he is still Jake, after all.

"Or I suppose you could just finish watching the movie. And let go of my hand."

He shrugs as he cocks his head to the side and meets my gaze. "I could." He squeezes my hand lightly before his fingers trail across the inside of my palm, renewing the stomach gymnastics that I erroneously thought I had under control. As his fingertips bump against mine, he pulls his eyes away from me and turns to the TV. It's the only impetus I need to grab the remote and push the play button.

There are not many things I'm sure of at the moment, but I know without a doubt that there needs to be another story playing in this room besides the Alexis and Jake plotline.

# Chapter Twenty

**B**ailey informs me as we're leaving the house that she needs to make a special card for her friend Landan. We have a shoebox full of thirty-something cards that have been filled out meticulously, but those won't do. Landan deserves something unique.

Part of me wants to argue the idea that Landan might not really exist. I certainly didn't see that name on the list of kids when I filled out the Valentine's cards, but Bailey's quite adamant. So I drop my purse on the floor, pull some construction paper out of a kitchen drawer, and draw a giant heart with glue. After dumping a handful of purple glitter on the design, I write the name Landan and tell her it will have to do.

Ten minutes later, I drop Bailey off at day care only to have her run that paper directly to one of the teachers. Lana. Seems like I should have seen that one coming. I'm sure poor Lana will forevermore assume I'm slightly off, since I can't spell her name.

I'm pretty sure that's going to be the worst part of my day, but that turns out to be incorrect. When I come back from the restroom before third period, there is a giant heart-shaped box on my desk that is presumably full of chocolate. Chocolate that is probably delicious and would stop my stomach from growling, since I didn't have time to eat my breakfast. Chocolate from some secret admiring source, because it's Valentine's Day and things don't just happen to appear randomly like that.

My mind rolls through the possibilities. Mr. Jennings, maybe? I mean, we're only friends who happen to share the same moniker, but he might have done it as a gesture of goodwill or something. Coach Andy? We're not exactly close or anything, but he did comment the other day that I had great volleyball player legs. I think it was a compliment. Then again, maybe he was trying to recruit me for some faculty team.

"Hey, Alexis?"

My eyes drift to the doorway, where Mr. Westlake has his hand wrapped around the side of the door and is smiling in my direction. Benjamin. He's kind of attractive, in a Mario Lopez kind of way. If I squint really hard.

"Oh," I mumble as I nearly trip on the foot of the desk. "Hey, Ben. How are things in the English department?" I can't help glancing down at the chocolate. Was it Benjamin?

"Pretty good. Didn't see you this morning. Everything okay?"

He was looking for me. Very interesting.

"Sure, just running a little late. Was there something you needed?"

"Nope. Just wanted to make sure you knew about the staff meeting. Talk to you later." He knocks his knuckles against the door as he steps away, and I drag my fingertips over the heart-shaped box, slightly perplexed.

"I hope you don't mind me sitting that on your desk, Miss Jennings," Rose speaks up from the first row. "Too tempting to have it sitting on my desk through the whole class period."

A couple of the girls next to her snicker, because they know I'm pathetic, thinking I have some random secret admirer. To tell the truth, I'm not sure what's worse: the fact that I have no one who is remotely interested in me, or the fact that I thought someone actually might be.

"Delivery," I hear just behind me, and I turn to see LeeAnn from the front office step up to my desk. She places a dozen white tulips with pink feathery patterns decorating their petals onto my desk, as though she wants to drive a final nail into my coffin.

"Beautiful," I comment rather absently, glancing around the room to try to decide who the lucky recipient might be.

"Yes, they are," LeeAnn confirms. "Variegated tulips are so gorgeous. They mean you have beautiful eyes, you know."

"Well, I'm sure some lucky lady will appreciate them," I tell her with a self-deprecating smile.

She shakes her head as she lifts her eyes skyward. "You should. They're stunning."

For a second my heart skips a beat, but I'm not sure if it's because I'm excited about the flowers, or because I'm worried that it's an elaborate prank. Still, I have to look, don't I?

Sure enough, the card says Alexis Jennings. Plucking it from its perch atop the gorgeous petals, I glance out at the girls in my class. "Well, there you go," I announce as though it was all a big joke. If it were a joke it would definitely be on me, but I do try to maintain some semblance of authority in my classroom. Outwardly, anyway.

I lift the flap on the little cream-colored envelope and pull out the rectangular piece of cardstock that's teeming with hearts of various shades of red and pink. Just four words on the card, but my eyes immediately swim in tears.

*Love you Mommy. Bailey*

One of the male students makes a smart remark about my sappy boyfriend making me cry, and I laugh it off as I tuck the card safely in my top desk drawer. I know they're from my parents, but I simply keep that knowledge to myself, along with the emotion that rises up in my throat.

"Autumn Avenue Medical, Crystal speaking."

"Mom." I finish tidying up my desk, pull my purse out of the bottom drawer, and close it with my foot as I stand. "Happy Valentine's Day."

"Aw, happy Valentine's Day, sweetheart. Did you call just to tell me that? That's really thoughtful." Her voice changes to a whisper. "You're really not supposed to call me at work, you know. Personal calls."

Of course, no breaking of the rules. Ever. But this isn't even breaking, just slightly bending.

"I know, and I won't talk long. I just wanted to say thank you for the flowers."

"What flowers?"

"The flowers I got at school today?" I turn the lights off as I step into the hall, listening to the sound of my feet tap against the cold tile in the deserted corridor. "Never mind, Dad must have sent them."

"I doubt that. We don't have any money to spare right now, and he's been at work all day too."

"Well, then who…"

I don't even bother finishing my thought, because I know Mom's not going to speculate about the source of the flowers on the phone with me. Not on a personal call, anyway.

"Must be a secret admirer," she whispers. "Gotta go, honey. Love you."

"Love you too," I say before she hangs up. Sure, a secret admirer who signs my flowers from my kid. I don't care what planet you're on, that's totally creepy.

I try not to think about it as I drive to Bailey's day care, or when I apologize to Lana for spelling her name wrong (to which she laughs), or as Bailey's pulling out each of her little cards on the way home and fake-reading them to me from the backseat. I even try not to think about it when she asks where I got the flowers. "A little birdie gave them to me," I tell her.

There's a knock at the door around five thirty, and Bailey immediately hops up from the picture she's coloring.

"Jay's here!" she announces, as though she needs to do so. He's become a pretty steady fixture in the evenings, just kind of hanging out with us until Bailey goes to sleep each night.

She twists the door knob, pulls the door open, and lets out a squeal. Jake's face is impossible to see, because he's holding a gray stuffed rabbit that looks to be at least three feet long, along with a host of other things.

"Is Jake hiding under there somewhere?" I ask mischievously. Bailey giggles and places her hands over her mouth.

He pops his head around the rabbit and widens his eyes at Bailey. "I'm here. This guy thought he might be able to be a friend to Hoppy. What do you think?"

"I think him's super big!" Bailey reaches up to take the bunny from his arm, and he immediately steadies the boxes in his other hand.

"Hey," he says as he glances in my direction. "So I thought about taking my girls out tonight, but I figured with it being Valentine's Day and everything, it might be crowded."

"Your girls? Have you decided to adopt me?" I can't help but laugh as I place my hands on my hips.

"Still considering it." He hands me the top box. "Pizza. Half cheese for Bailey, half sausage and mushrooms for you."

Turning my back to him, I place the pizza box on the counter and pause to think for a second. "How did you know I like sausage and mushrooms?" I busy myself with the box, not wanting to see his reaction.

"Just guessed, since you put them in your spaghetti. Seemed logical."

To say that I expected a different explanation would be an understatement, but his response seems pretty genuine.

"Nice flowers," he adds, pointing to the bouquet on the other end of the counter.

"Yeah, got them at school." Spinning to face him, I tilt my head to the side. "What's in the box?"

"Nope. I can't give away all my secrets right off the bat."

He slides the extra box next to the flowers, and I pull out three plates for the pizza. The tiny table in the kitchen is barely big enough for the three of us. At first, when Jake stayed for dinner, it made for some awkward conversations. Now, it just seems like the new normal.

"Did you have a good Valentine's Day?" Jake asks Bailey, picking a mushroom off his pizza. It's probably silly that the sight of it makes my heart swell in my chest, but knowing Jake doesn't like mushrooms makes his gesture of putting them on the pizza a little more heartfelt.

"Uh huh. We eated cookies with sprinkles and I got a big box of suckers."

"You got cards from a bunch of suckers?" He catches my eye and winks.

"No," Bailey says with a hint of exasperation. "Suckers like yummy suckers. The licky kind."

"Oh, gotcha. Get any cards from your boyfriends?"

"Ew." She takes a bite of her pizza and a string of cheese hangs off her chin. "Boys are yucky."

"You do know I'm a boy, right?"

"You're okay. Boys like my size are yucky."

"Good. You stay away from boys. That's a good policy."

He pauses to take a bite of his pizza, and I take the opportunity to insert myself into the conversation.

"So, how about you? Did you have a good Valentine's Day?"

"I worked with Zippy all day, so it wasn't great."

"Zippy?"

"I can't remember the kid's name. They call him Zippy because it takes him so long to do things, and it just kind of stuck, I guess."

"Not your best day ever, then," I say as I lean back slightly in my chair. "Most memorable Valentine's Day. Shoot."

"Wow, let's see..." He glances over at Bailey and uses his napkin to wipe some pizza sauce off her chin. "Besides this one, naturally? I'd have to say third grade."

"That's pretty specific. This must be a mesmerizing story."

"Horrific is more like it. I didn't have any of those little cards to hand out, so the teacher put a piece of tape over the slot in my coffee can."

"A piece of tape?"

"Yeah, so no one could drop their cards in, right? At the end of the day, only one card had made its way inside. Faye. She had to have picked that tape back to get her card inside and then sealed it back up."

"She must have really liked you. I can see why that stands out."

He begins picking at his pizza and looks down at his plate. "Well, it stands out because I was a jerk about it. I didn't want a card from Faye. She was the outcast of the class. Funny hair, always smelled a little weird. I made a big point of giving it back to her in front of everyone. Proving that I didn't need her charity, I guess. She cried."

"That's horrible. If it were possible for me to think less of you as a person, I would."

That comment earns me a rather smug, crooked smile. "Because you already have the lowest possible opinion of me, I guess?"

"Naturally."

"Alright then, little miss perfect. Your most memorable Valentine's Day."

It takes me a few seconds to scan through the days past and pick a stand-out. "Okay, it was my senior year, and there was this guy named—"

"Cody Hewitt. Continue."

My mouth hangs open just a tad as Jake takes a bite of his pizza. "Maybe you should tell the story, since you seem to know so much."

"Does this guy have any clue what an idiot he is?" he asks through a mouthful of pizza, holding his napkin in front of his lips.

"We don't say that word." I glance from him to Bailey and back again, hoping he gets my drift.

"Idiot, no kidding?" I widen my eyes, and he shrugs apologetically as he focuses on Bailey. "Right. Bailey, we don't say that word."

"Jay says it," she states, pulling some cheese from her pizza.

"Clearly I'll have to work on that." He leans back in his chair and places his hands in his lap as he returns his attention to me. "This Cody guy must be a few fries short of a Happy Meal. That's all I'm saying."

"That's easy to say when you don't know him."

"I don't want to know the guy. Anybody who could treat you like that isn't worth the wasted effort."

"Really?" Pizza all but forgotten, I cross my arms against my chest. "It seems to me that it wasn't that long ago that you weren't particularly nice to me, Mr. McAuliffe."

"Solidly before the official 'friend' phase. I can't be held responsible for anything before that point."

"How very convenient for you."

He has a slightly roguish glint in his eyes as he picks up another slice of pizza. "Alright, let's have it. What did Boy Wonder do on Valentine's Day?"

"He showed up after dinner to do his homework and he brought me a pink rose, but he also brought one for my mom."

"Like a Mrs. Robinson thing." He picks a mushroom off his slice and drops it to his plate before taking another bite.

"Of course not. It was really sweet."

"Manipulative," he states around a mouthful of pizza.

"Not in any way."

"How can you not see it?" He lifts his glass of water and takes a drink, drawing his eyebrows closer together before he places the glass on the table again. "It's like that slimy kid on *Leave It to Beaver*, always kissing up to the mom. Can't trust that guy."

"Don't be an idiot," I mutter, returning to my pizza.

"Mommy says it!" Bailey proclaims, clapping her hands. Naturally Jake laughs at my expense.

"For your information, kissing up to my mom isn't really beneficial. I rarely listen to her advice. Look how long she wanted me to talk to you before I finally decided to allow you a smidge of leeway."

"Your mom recognizes me for the rare gem that I am."

"She's half blind, seriously. She needs bifocals."

"Did you know your parents had my dad over for dinner Sunday?"

"What?"

"He told me last night that my girlfriend's parents had him over for dinner. Made him meatloaf and potatoes, and even sent him home with half a chocolate cake."

"Wow."

"He thinks they were buttering him up for something."

"Like the slimy kid on *Leave It to Beaver*," I offer with a hint of a smile.

"Exactly." He drops his napkin on his plate and leans forward on his elbows. "He's been sober for three weeks."

"I can't tell if you're being serious or if you're still teasing me."

"Totally serious."

I reach out and wrap my fingers around his arm, not really sure what to say. His eyes lock on mine, all hints of mischief gone from his face. He brings his hand over to cover mine on his arm, tracing a line horizontally back and forth with his thumb.

"Thanks," he whispers, not breaking his focus.

"I didn't say anything."

"Your eyes did. They're very vocal."

My gaze drops to the table, and I clear my throat. "What did they say?"

"Everything you won't. You have beautiful eyes."

I gently extract my hand from his and rub it self-consciously against my collarbone.

"Bailey play with Zippy now?"

Quite possibly the most welcome interruption I have ever experienced. Looking at Bailey, I force a smile. "Zippy?"

"Jay's bunny." She slides off her chair and joins the rabbit in the living room, where she scoops him up and hauls him in the direction of her bedroom.

"Home run with the rabbit," I tell him as I stand and pick up her plate, placing it on top of mine. Turning to the sink, I begin rinsing the plates as Jake drops his in from my left. Continuing past me, he picks up the white box that he deposited next to the flowers.

"So, I got you a little something," he announces, gesturing toward me with the box. After turning off the faucet, I reach down for the towel and dry my hands before taking a step in his direction.

"What is it?"

He places the box in my hands, but I don't make a move to open it.

"Only one way to find out."

"It's not going to jump out at me, or bite me?"

He raises his eyebrows as he watches me, the hints of brown and gold flecks in his eyes standing out as he tries again to read me. I'm fairly determined not to be so transparent.

Lifting the lid of the box, I stare down at the pattern of blues and reds with the large white T on the logo. "It's a Tennessee Titans jersey," I announce, although why I feel that necessary is beyond me. Jake knows what it is, after all.

"Yeah," he says, plucking it out of the box. "It's your size though, see? The one you have is from high school and big enough to fit a three-hundred pound linebacker."

His statement makes me want to laugh, but I manage to keep it together. "What difference does that make, really?"

"To the guy watching the game with you in the future, it'll make a huge difference."

"How huge?"

"You're covering up a stunning picture with a tent. Why do you have such a big jersey, anyway?" His fist drops to waist level with the jersey still held inside, and he nods almost imperceptibly as he stares down at his fingers. "It was his, right? Cody's? I don't know why that just dawned on me."

"Yeah." I set the box on the counter and reach forward to pull the jersey from Jake's grasp, twisting it until I locate the back. Stretching it up over my head, I slide my arms up and into the sleeves, tugging it down over my T-shirt. "Perfect fit," I add, smoothing it across my abdomen. "Way better than Cody's. Thank you."

He turns and looks at the tulips next to him, tapping his fingers absently against the countertop.

"Before you ask, I have no idea who those are from." I reach for the envelope stuck to the top of the flowers, holding it toward him between my first two fingers.

"They're from Bailey, right? I mean, that's what I assumed."

He rotates a little until he's facing the living room, and then he rests his back pockets against the wall as he crosses his ankles.

"Hmm. Yeah, they're from Bailey. Such a thoughtful kid, right? I guess it's in her genes."

"Must be," he tells me with a shrug of his shoulders.

Stepping in front of him, I pinch him lightly in the stomach. "You're full of surprises, you know that? The fact is… Ugh, I can't believe I'm even going to say this."

"What?" He straightens as he stretches himself a little taller, and I can't help but smile.

"Maybe—in this one specific, teensy little case, as it pertains to you—I should have listened to my mother."

# Chapter Twenty-One

## Jake

Never in my wildest imagination did I think that I'd still be sleeping in the same bed I occupied on my first night in Louisville. Not after four and a half months. For the life of me I can't figure out what's keeping me here. The owners are nice, granted, but shouldn't I want a little sense of permanence? Maybe a neighbor who is not Roxanne?

The sound of my truck door slamming must rouse her from her television viewing, because the door next to mine opens a couple inches as I step onto the breezeway.

"Hey, Roxanne," I say as I shove the key into the lock. She fully opens the door when I acknowledge her presence, wearing pink sweatpants with one leg reaching to her shoe and the other pooled beneath her knee. Even though I have no way to prove it, somehow I know they're the kind that have a word written on the rear end. "Sassy" or "feisty" or any other adjective that shouldn't be on a person's tail.

"Jacob." She attempts to clear her throat, but I know it's not going to help. Her growly voice is pretty permanent, as far as I can tell. Her shoulder-length blonde hair looks like she attempted to curl it, but the back is still stick straight. The pink lipstick she has on has bled into the little feathery wrinkles above her lips, too.

"It's Jake," I tell her for the millionth time.

"Honey, you're not plain enough to be Jake."

"And yet somehow it's still Jake," I add as I open the door. "Be good, Roxanne."

"I'm always good," she states through the door.

The clicking of the door should be enough, but I lock the deadbolt anyway. It's the same exact sound I heard a few minutes ago when I left Wonder Lane. Just like every other night for the past few weeks, I watched Alexis tuck Bailey in, told them good night, and Alexis locked the door behind me when I stepped onto the porch.

I slide my coat off and drop it on the bed, running my hand through my hair. Things are kind of getting out of control. At first, it was fine seeing Bailey on Saturdays. Then I started seeing her a couple times a week, and before I knew it I became an every-night dinner guest. Now I'm there several hours each day, and when Bailey goes to sleep, all I want is to ask Alexis to let me stay a little longer. No part of me wants to leave that house on Wonder Lane.

No better than my dad, in reality. Like an addict craving a fix.

Picking up my phone, I scroll through the contacts and stare at the names for a moment, wondering if I should reach out after so much time. Somewhere deep inside I doubt that it's a good idea, but I'm missing some of the comforts of home. The parts of home that actually felt comforting, anyway.

The ring sounds twice before I consider hanging up, but as soon as I hear the click I know it's too late. I sit up straighter on the bed, absently cracking my knuckles on my free hand while I wait for Parker's voice to sound on the other end of the line.

"Jake?"

"Hey. Hope I'm not intruding on anything."

"Are you kidding? You can call me anytime, you know that."

There it is again—the forgiving nature I don't deserve.

"Sorry to call so late, man. Just thinking about home tonight for some reason."

"I can't blame you there, because I do that myself. Everything okay?"

"Yeah." I pause, readjusting myself to the fact that Cole is speaking to me at all. Part of me still doesn't believe it. "I owe you a huge apology."

"Water under the bridge."

"Maybe for you but not for me. I'm sorry, and I'd tell her too if I thought it was a good idea."

"Listen, we both know you're sorry, okay? Cam was just asking me the other day if I'd heard from you. She was here a couple weeks ago but she's back home now."

"What do you mean, back home? You're not still in Nashville are you?"

He laughs, and I can almost imagine us back at work, lining boards up while we chat.

"It really has been forever since I've talked to you. I'm training in Florida."

"You're yanking my chain."

"It seems crazy, right? Still can't believe it myself sometimes. How's Bailey?"

"She's absolutely the best kid imaginable. I go over there for dinner every night, practically."

"You eat dinner with Alexis every night?"

Now it's my turn to laugh. "Trust me, things are different in Louisville. Don't make a big deal of it, but I can sort of see why a guy might be interested in the whole family bit."

"What was that? I think I'm hearing things."

"Very funny. I'm getting to the point now where I don't even want to leave at night. It's pathetic."

"You're interested in her?"

That's a loaded question.

"Well," I stall, trying to decide how much information I want to divulge. "There would be no point in that because she's too good for me. I've screwed her life up enough as it is."

"What do you mean, too good for you?"

"She's smart, funny, looks good without even trying, absolutely the nicest person I know."

"I agree then. She's too good for you."

My eyes focus on the wall in front of me as I shake my head. "Didn't realize how much I missed that."

"What?" he asks.

"Brutal honesty. You want to know the kicker? She's hung up on some guy she knew from high school that was an absolute jerk to her. And I can't even make that argument because I've been a jerk to her in the past, too."

"Wow. I've never seen this side of you."

"What side is that?"

"Set on a particular girl. How many women do you go out with in a normal month up there?"

"A normal month?" I ask, standing and pacing across the room. "Let's see, if I add two and carry the one… Zero? Yeah, that sounds about right."

"You're not going out with anyone?"

"Nope."

"And you're spending all your free time with Alexis and Bailey?"

"That would be a yes."

"You're practically married already."

"You're a comedian."

"Does she know?"

"That you're a comedian?"

"No, that you're interested in her. What does she think about it?"

Roxanne's cough sounds through the wall, and it makes me wonder if she's got her ear pressed against it. "No way would I tell her that. I did get her flowers for Valentine's Day. Lost my nerve and signed them from Bailey, though. I'd been planning it for a week, too. Even asked the florist what kind of flower would subliminally tell her that I liked her eyes."

It's only after I hear his laughter on the other end of the line that I realize how ridiculous I sound.

"This is why I can't make a move on her," I complain, leaning my back against the wall. "Thank God I haven't said something stupid that made her laugh at me like that."

He clears his throat as he attempts to stem his chuckling. "Since when do you thank God for things? It's like you're living on another planet in Kentucky."

"For your information, I've been to church twice. I've been doing some remodeling for a couple neighbors of Alexis, and they asked me to go with them. It's different."

"Different how? They're not charming snakes or something like that?"

"Nothing weird. For example, one of the group leaders is this guy named Duke who looks like a biker. He had a leather motorcycle vest on last time I saw him. Huge beard. Annie's got half of her head in a buzz cut and the other half has a bunch of wild curls. Ryan has an overgrown mohawk and dresses like a heavy metal guitarist."

"Sounds like an interesting bunch."

"Exactly. Not a group of people trying to look the same and fit in. They just show up the way they are, wearing whatever they want."

He hesitates before he answers, so I sit on the bed and tug at the laces on my boot with my free hand.

"They could be almost convincing," I continue, pushing against the floor in an attempt to kick the boot off. "The social side of things they've got locked up. It's the whole reason to be there in the first place that trips me up, you know?"

"How's that?"

It's to Cole's credit that he's never really pressed me on the religious angle. I know he's into the God stuff, and he's talked about it enough that it's obviously not an act. For whatever reason, it seems to work for him.

"I've been to just enough church to remember the 'do this, don't do that' pointers. Pretty sure there's some sort of limit on rules you can break and still be able to join the club."

"Nope." His quick answer hangs between us as I loosen my other boot.

"What do you mean, nope?"

"Hang on, let me look something up. You have a Bible?"

My eyes dart over to the red volume next to the bed. "Yeah, Gideon on the nightstand."

"Jake...are you in a hotel room?"

"Yeah, I live in a motel."

"You'll do anything not to have to clean up your own messes," he jokes, rustling through some papers. "Alright, here it is. Luke 11. Just read Luke 11, okay? The prodigal son."

"I'll say yes just to get you off my back," I tell him, finally kicking off the second boot.

"Fair enough. You better call me with updates on the Alexis situation. I'm a little in shock over this whole turn of events."

"I can do that." Leaning back on the bed, my mind drifts to meeting Cole in the mornings for work at his Aunt Rosalie's bed and breakfast. "You know what I could go for right about now? Rosalie's peach cobbler."

"No doubt. Crunchy on the edges with a big scoop of homemade ice cream."

"Peaches still warm, right out of the oven."

"That's probably what heaven tastes like," Cole states with a laugh.

"I'll take your word for it." Grabbing the Gideon book from the nightstand, I stare at the gold lettering on the front. "Take care of yourself, man. Maybe we'll get back that way sometime soon."

"You better look us up if you do. And take care of yourself, too. And that little girl."

We say our goodbyes, and I drop the phone onto the bed without setting the book down. The sound of a muted thump coming through the wall causes me to drop the book on my lap and stare at the random prairie landscape photo on the wall.

"What do you think, Roxanne?"

The fact that she immediately clears her throat tells me everything I need to know.

Her voice comes across rather muffled, but I still understand her words.

"I like peach cobbler, honey. And your lady friend doesn't know how lucky she is."

# Chapter Twenty-Two

## Alexis

I've heard it said that March comes in like a lion and goes out like a lamb. There's not enough personal experience in my memory to comment about that one way or the other. Here on Wonder Lane, though, March comes in like a dead woman sprawled across the corner of my yard.

I pull the Mitsubishi up to the house, never taking my eyes off her still form. It's a relatively mild day for this time of year, and she's clad in a pair of black running tights and a bright green fleece jacket.

Bailey takes a couple cautious steps in her direction when I release her from the car, but she won't go any closer. Can't say that I blame her, because I'm not looking forward to it myself. Holding Bailey at arm's length behind me, I inch closer to the woman, until I'm just about a foot from her sneakers with the little green frogs on the side. Using the toe of my boot, I nudge her heel.

Her eyes fly open as she tilts her head up, rising onto her elbows. "Oh! You're not Josh."

"Not the last time I checked," I answer, keeping a wary eye on her and one hand on my daughter.

"You didn't see a physically fit guy run by, did you? Tall, glasses, perfect olive complexion?"

Bailey wraps her arms around my thigh, so I reach down and pick her up. Her puffy coat makes her extra bulky and difficult to hang onto.

"Is there some reason you're taking a nap in my yard?"

"Josh's yard," she says, rolling up to one knee as she struggles to stand, pressing her hand to the ground in the process.

"We were jogging and he wanted to log an extra mile. I figured I'd have a few minutes until he got back."

As she manages to stand in front of us, I notice her face is flushed and her breathing rather labored. "Are you sure you're okay?"

"Josh runs a lot faster than I'm used to, but I didn't want to tell him he was killing me." She sucks in a noisy breath. "You live here? I should know the neighbors, but the past couple months have been a little hectic."

Her hands find their way to her hips for a few seconds before she reaches up to try to straighten her ponytail. Several strands of her auburn hair cling to her forehead, and her effort to move them away only serves to make her look more disheveled.

"You're my neighbor?" I ask, shifting Bailey on my hip.

"Not anymore. I used to live here when I was taking care of Josh's house while he was overseas. But he came home last month and kicked me out because he was in love with me." She shoves her hands into the pockets of her jacket and rocks back on her heels. "It's kind of a long story, really. I'm Maddie, by the way."

"Alexis," I add, trying not to smile. Another jogger rounds the corner, and Maddie immediately begins running in place.

"I was never here," she whispers, offering Bailey a smile before she meets the athletic-looking guy with glasses on the next driveway over. He lifts a hand in greeting when he sees me, and I do the same.

"It's not nice to sleep on the grass," Bailey tells me quietly.

"No, it doesn't seem like a wise choice, does it?"

"Silly."

Bailey trots off toward the front door, and I walk back to the Mitsubishi to grab the little pair of pink fairy wings from the car. It never dawned on me before that Bailey having little friends would result in her being invited to endless birthday parties. Four so far since we've been in Louisville, and all for people we don't know. More specifically, people I don't know. Bailey always informs me that the kid on the random invitation is her friend from daycare, and I always assume she's correct. How would I know the difference, really? The last kid was all of two years old and didn't seem to care that Bailey was present, so I'm fairly certain they aren't hanging out on a daily basis. I didn't think to invite her daycare friends to a party for her back in December. It was just the two of us, celebrating alone.

Tomorrow's party is for Jemma, but this time I got wise and asked Lana whether she's really Bailey's friend. After being told that the two of them play together quite a bit, and Jemma is turning four, we located the nearest dollar store and bought a pair of pink wings. What's a single mom on a tight budget supposed to do, after all?

With a sigh, I lift the key for the door and smile down at Bailey. She doesn't know that birthday parties are a struggle for me. I'm sure they seem magical to her, because she's not sitting in the corner wondering who will finally talk to her, if anyone does. Back home I wouldn't either. If there was a stranger in the room, I'd walk right up and introduce myself.

The problem is, I've never been the stranger myself, and it's starting to wear on me.

"I'm hungry," Bailey announces, just like she does every day when we get home. I'm pretty sure I could set my watch by her stomach rumblings.

"Me too. Jake's going to bring us dinner tonight, remember?"

"Yay!" She puts both feet together and hops through the door that I just pushed open. "Hoppy and Zippy and Bailey."

It's really impossible not to laugh at her over-exuberance. Not only has Hoppy continued to talk using me as his own slightly unhinged, funny voice, but Zippy has decided to join in on the lunacy borrowing a low, husky voice with a slight Australian accent that Jake graciously provides. We really are quite the ridiculous pair together, but Bailey laughs like the two of us are the funniest comedians in the world.

"Jay is my Gump." Bailey drops her coat on the ground, but then looks up at me and picks it up. As she's placing it on the hook behind the door, I draw my eyebrows together.

"Jay's not your Gump, baby. Only Gump is Gump."

"Yes he is. Gump's Mommy's dad, and Jay's my dad."

A couple of the protective layers I've built up around my heart crack and begin to crumble, leaving behind a raw, tender burn. One day soon I planned to explain everything to Bailey. I've spent countless hours searching for just the right words. Looks like I won't need them now.

"Yeah, you're right," I whisper, blinking back irrational tears. "Gump is my dad, and Jake's your dad."

"They's both good ones."

For probably the first time in her four years on the earth, I can answer that statement without telling a guilt-inducing fib. "Yeah, sweetie. I think you're right."

She asks for a cookie and momentarily forgets the trajectory of our conversation, which causes me to breathe a sigh of relief. I was already imagining her asking why Jake doesn't live with us, and I know I'm not prepared for that conversation in any way, shape, or form. I'm barely comfortable explaining that one to myself.

A knock sounds behind me on the door, and Jake steps in, holding a brown bag in his fist with a drink carrier balanced on his arm. He's taken to letting himself in without waiting for me to answer the door, which admittedly doesn't bother me the way it should.

"Jay!" Bailey yells, abandoning her quest for the cookie and going straight for whatever fast food Jake has in the bag. When he sets the food on the table and Bailey recognizes Chinese takeout containers, she wrinkles her nose. "Where's my chicken nuggets?"

The pouty state of her bottom lip is enough to make me unsuccessful in holding in my laughter, but I manage to pull it back in fairly quickly.

"There's chicken," Jake says calmly. "Orange chicken, chicken teriyaki, and chicken fried rice."

"Chicken yucky, chicken nasty, chicken ew."

She crosses her arms over her abdomen, and I shoot Jake an apologetic glance. Not that it does any good, because his attention is focused completely on Bailey.

"Kudos for thinking up so many ways to tell me chicken is gross, but I don't accept complaints about food you haven't tried yet. Maybe you can tell me how much you dislike it again after dinner."

"I not eating that." She sits at the table and plops her chin onto her fist, giving him a pitiful expression. Gump would fold like a giant house of cards, and I'm fearful Jake is a goner this time.

"That's a shame, because only people who eat dinner get to partake in these M&Ms I brought. They're all pink, too, because I know you like pink." He pauses to withdraw a clear bag full of the pink candies he just described, and Bailey cranes her neck to see if he's telling the truth. "Oh well. More for your mom and me, right?"

Without waiting for an answer, he places the candy on the counter behind him and takes three plates out of the cabinet to his left. As he's closing the cabinet door, he focuses on me just long enough to offer a slight smile. "Hey, Alex. Nice wings."

His eyes dart down to my hand by my side, and I realize as I glance down that I'm still holding Jemma's birthday gift. With a shrug, I place them to the back of the counter where they'll be safe. "Birthday gift for one of Bailey's friends," I explain.

"And here I thought you really were an angel after all."

"As if we both don't know that's a joke." Instead of looking at him, I take the plates from his hand. I've decided in the last couple weeks that it's not good policy to openly stare at Jake. At best, he catches me noticing that he's good looking. Not cool. At worst, he tries to read me with that piercing gaze. Too intimate. Somewhere in between we wind up in a kind of awkward state with my body undergoing odd chemical reactions that make me feel all sorts of uncomfortable.

Avoidance of overt eye contact seems to be the best medicine.

"I guess I'll try it," Bailey says almost imperceptibly from the table. Jake lifts his eyebrows at me before he turns to the table and pulls out a chair next to Bailey.

"Thanks munchkin." He winks in my direction, and for a split second, it almost does feel very Gump-like.

"She finally dozed off," I whisper to Jake as I round the corner from the end of the hall, finding him sitting at the edge of the couch with his foot propped up on one knee. Somehow we've made it all the way to "take your shoes off and stay a while territory" without having made any mention of it. Not that I necessarily want to comment about his wearing of shoes or lack thereof, but his level of comfortableness in my home isn't lost on me.

Normally I have time to change before Jake gets here, but since I stopped for the fairy wings tonight, I'm still rocking my sweater dress/tights combo that I wore to school today. Too formal to go plopping myself on the couch all crazy-like, so I try to sit like a lady on the other end of the sofa.

For his part, Jake's not wearing the normal construction company getup that he normally sports after work. He obviously went home and showered, because his light blue polo shirt and dark jeans smell like fabric softener and there's a hint of masculine body wash emanating from his skin. If he were sitting any closer, I might be willing to admit that it's clouding my brain. As it stands now, I'm only in a normal state of befuddled-ness.

"Annie called you while you were with Bailey," he states, draping his arm across the back of the couch. It looks almost enticing enough to slide under, but I remind myself not to scare him away and remain put.

"You answered my phone?"

"No. When you didn't answer, she called me. Wanted to know if you were interested in coming over tomorrow afternoon. Some sort of girl thing."

Annie's kind of like the Cheshire Cat of Wonder Lane. Always popping in when I least expect her, leaving me confused when she leaves. She certainly makes life more interesting, though.

"That's sweet of her, but Bailey has a birthday party tomorrow. The wings, remember?"

He nods as recognition passes over his features. Then he leans his head against the back of the couch as he stares in my direction. "Why don't I take her?"

"You want to take Bailey to a birthday party?"

"Well, when you put it like that, it sounds so appealing." He laughs as he turns his body toward me a little more. "No, I guess I'm not offering to go to a birthday party as much as I'm saying I'd like to give you a chance to have a little fun."

"Why?"

"I don't know…because you deserve it?" He draws his eyes away from me and focuses on the actor being interviewed on the television. "You work incredibly hard and completely focus on Bailey. Even tonight, you were giving her all the chicken off your plate."

"She liked the chicken the best."

"Exactly my point. You didn't even think about keeping it for yourself."

"That's just a mom thing," I argue.

"Really? 'Cause I had a mom, and it wasn't like that." He places his fingertips against my shoulder, just enough contact to make me look at him. "Let me do that for you, please. I want to. Go hang out with Annie for a while and relax."

That charming aura he seems to cloak himself with dances across the sofa and wraps itself around me. Even if I wanted to tell him no, I'm not sure my lips would follow through. The man could probably convince me to give him my car if he doesn't stop that intense eye-studying scrutiny he's been practicing lately.

Not that giving up the car would be a particularly hard sell. I could use an upgrade.

"If you're sure you don't mind."

"I'm looking forward to it," he insists, the corner of his mouth lifting slightly. He doesn't take his eyes off me, and I can't help but notice the gentle pressure of his hand against my shoulder.

"*Almost Midnight with Jamie Price*," I interject, forcing my attention to the television. "It's been a long time since I've seen this show. Normally I'm in bed by now."

"That's a shame."

"What?" My eyes swing in his direction, landing on him just as he drags his hand away from my shoulder.

"Nothing. You deserve the world, that's all. You shouldn't spend your Friday nights alone."

His eyes tell me that he's paying me a compliment, but the fact that I'm not in agreement brings my ego down a notch. Rubbing the hem of my sweater dress between my fingers, I try to play it off as a joke.

"Well, technically I'm not alone, because you're here. Anyway, what would I do with Bailey? Have you watch her while I went out on a date?"

He smiles, but not that charming gesture with the dimples that proves irresistible. This smile doesn't touch his eyes, and he turns away from me to look at the TV.

"Absolutely, if that's what you want. I'd be happy to watch her anytime."

"I'll be sure to alert the hordes of guys breaking down my door," I mutter.

"You can't tell me no one at school ever asks you out."

"Well, that would be illegal."

He laughs as though I just told a grand joke, but the truth is, I'm a bit flustered by his choice of topic and the change in his body language.

"No, no one at school asks me out," I continue. "Honestly, there aren't many single guys there. And the ones who are single probably erroneously assume that I'm involved with Mr. Jennings, since we share the last name, our classrooms touch, and we seem to wind up eating lunch together a lot."

"He's not your type, huh?"

The amount of thought I force myself to go through to ponder his question makes my eyebrows pinch together. "I'm not really sure I have a type, not in that way at least. Beyond the usual nice, smart, and so on."

"That's a cop out answer if I ever heard one."

Is it? Seems to me that it beats desiring someone unkind who lacks of intelligence. Not that I need to share that with Jake, because this is already making me more uncomfortable than I care to admit. Besides, what am I supposed to say? Someone like you, except preferably not a gigolo.

The effects of my internal overthinking threaten to show on my face, so I stare at the blonde woman on the television, watching her perfectly painted lips break into a smile as she laughs at something Jamie said. Something about her seems so familiar...

"Oh my gosh, she looks just like your friend's wife," I blurt, glancing at Jake. He squints as though he's trying to focus before shifting his position on the couch and nodding.

"Yeah, Camdyn. She's on TV with Jamie from time to time."

"She hangs out with Jamie Price," I repeat haltingly.

"Yeah, she writes books. Girly stuff I imagine, but I'm not much of a reader."

Grateful for the distraction, I walk into the kitchen and retrieve my phone from the counter, stopping on my way back to pull up the search engine.

"Camdyn Parker, right?"

My eyes remain on the phone as I sit down, and when I glance up, I realize I've settled myself a little too close to him on the sofa. I'm trying to decide whether it's too awkward to slide away from him when he leans closer and glances at my phone screen, his arm sliding behind my shoulders.

"No, her books aren't Camdyn Parker. Camdyn Taylor, and some other fake name she had before that."

I begin typing her name into the phone's search bar, and the feel of Jake's hand resting on my left shoulder makes my fingers slide awkwardly across the screen. Camdrb winds up being the result of that effort, so I begin erasing as my pulse increases. My second attempt isn't much better, because as soon as I think I have it he says, "You spelled it wrong." The closeness of his voice is expected, but still makes me want to lean away from him. My brain, anyway. My body seems to desire the exact opposite. While I remain perfectly still, willing my mind and body into some sort of truce, Jake uses his right hand to touch the keyboard on my phone, spelling out the name.

The instant he finishes, a wealth of information appears on the screen, beginning with an official website. He touches her name at the top, and when the phone refreshes her face is front and center on the screen. Who Is Camdyn Taylor, About C.W. Oliver, Books, Movie News, etc.

"She makes movies?" My voice has an odd sound, similar to a half Marilyn Monroe-half laryngitis hybrid. I clear my throat hoping Jake won't notice.

"How is the casting going?" Jamie asks on the TV, as though he heard my throaty question.

"You know I can't talk about those types of top-secret things," she tells him, glancing behind her as though she's being watched. She leans a little closer to the camera, and her voice grows quieter. "Honestly, they tell me nothing. Less than nothing. I think they're scared to death I'll screw something up. The only thing I can tell you is that I have it on good authority that yours truly will be in the direct vicinity of George Washington himself."

"They are actually trusting you to stand next to the first president of our country?"

"Definitely a risky move, but in their defense, he's already dead."

Jake chuckles, bringing me back to my present situation and the realization that he still has his arm wrapped around my shoulders. Purely to get closer to the phone, I'm sure.

"Have you talked to him lately?" I ask, trying not to read too much into his actions. "Cole, I mean."

"Yeah, a little bit."

My eyes won't move from her face on the television, where she just said something else that has Jamie laughing.

"What is it about her?" I wonder aloud, leaning back so at least his arm will be against the couch and not solely resting on my shoulders. That way maybe I can begin to tell myself that he's just trying to be comfortable.

"What do you mean?"

"I mean, you cared enough about her that you almost screwed up your friendship over her. What makes her your type? What did you like about her?"

He leans his head back against the couch, merely an inch away from mine, and lets out a sigh before he bothers answering.

"I don't know." He rubs his right hand along his jeans at his thigh, and I drop the phone to my lap. "No, that's not true. Parker and I basically had opposite philosophies the past couple years. He never dated anyone, because he was only interested if he knew she might be the right girl. I thought he was crazy. The way I saw it, he had a list of missed opportunities a mile long. So when Camdyn showed up, my interest in her was the same basic interest I would have had in any pretty girl. It was different for Parker."

"How so?" His arm around my shoulders is so perfectly still, I begin to wonder if he even realizes he left it there.

"He didn't come back to work telling me that he met her, or that he wanted to date her. He started talking about her like he'd just discovered life on another planet. She was fascinating to him."

His hand slides away from my shoulders as he pulls it down and rubs his fingers across his face, almost like he's tired. The immediate lack of his warmth is rather disappointing, but I remind myself that he shouldn't have his arm around me anyway.

"The thing is, he made her sound irresistible to me, too. The more I think about it, I'm pretty sure what I was looking for in that situation wasn't her at all. Just someone or something to feel that way about. Something that matters."

The TV switches to a commercial break, singing something about spicy volcano tacos, and I find myself glancing in Jake's direction.

"Anyway," he continues, "you asked what my type was, right? I'm thinking she has to be brunette."

"I see you as more of a blonde guy."

"There you go stereotyping." He meets my eye and holds his gaze steady. "Definitely brunette, dark eyes. She has to be kind and patient, careful with details, borderline perfectionist. Maybe a little mysterious, and loves kids. That's a must, of course."

"Sounds like you're becoming picky." Although I intend my words as a joke and offer them with a grin, he nods at my statement.

"I am, very picky. What about you? What does your type look like?"

"Probably a billionaire who owns his own yacht and has one of those private islands."

"Very funny," he says with a sigh, crossing his arms over his chest.

"Okay, being totally truthful... I don't know what he looks like. He's smart, definitely quick on his feet. Makes me laugh. Constantly challenges me to do better, be better. And I won't worry about whether he's devoted to me, because he's waited for me for a long time."

"Waited for you," he repeats, tension showing in the movement of his jaw. "I guess you mean like you, before you and I—"

"Yes."

"So you're looking for a guy who's never messed up? Parker told me I should read about the prodigal son, and that guy did some screwed up stuff. His dad still took him back, though."

For a split second, my mind flashes to Heather and her constant teasing about Wonderland. I can hear her joking that I've gone through the rabbit hole. That could provide a logical explanation for why Jake McAuliffe is giving me a Bible lesson.

While we sit on the couch in my house.

In front of the TV where we just saw the married woman he once made a play for.

Who happens to be moderately famous.

"Of course I don't think there's anyone who's never screwed up in their life," I finally say, trying to tamp down the illogical feeling of panic I sense rising inside.

Those blue eyes finally leave my face as he tilts his head to look at the ground. "You think that guy is out there, then?"

"Why shouldn't he be?" My eyes wander to the floor, wondering what he's finding so fascinating there. "I can't afford to give up everything I ever expected my life to be. Things have definitely changed with Bailey, but anything is possible."

"Yeah," he whispers, leaning toward the edge of the couch and placing his hands on his knees.

*Does he think if I find someone that he won't be part of Bailey's life anymore?*

"Jake," I say, reaching out to touch his arm. The simple motion causes him to turn his head toward me again, and I wish I could read his eyes the way he reads mine. There's some sort of storm lurking in their depths, and I can't tell if I need to heed the warning.

"Listen, in no way am I here to make you unhappy. That's the absolute last thing I want."

"I know," I answer automatically, because somewhere deep inside his words resonate.

"Don't settle."

My eyes widen as he turns his entire body in my direction and takes my hands in his. The feeling of my own pulse beating against his fingers turns my stomach in knots, and I fight the urge to pull away. Not because I'm worried about what he might do, but because I'm worried about what I'll do. Maybe it's the constant, every-day contact, or the fact that I don't have any other viable offers on the table, but Jake has been chipping his way into my heart lately. Little by little, one sweet word to Bailey at a time.

I desperately want to keep that thought locked away, because having it out in the open is only going to hurt.

"Don't settle," he repeats. "If that guy shows up, just make sure there's something there besides the fact that he waited. If you want a disciplined guy, that's great, but don't let that be all there is."

"You act like the whole thing is about platitudes and denial." A thick breath catches in my throat, causing my eyes to tear up as Jake leans in more earnestly, making sure I'm focused on him. It's impossible not to be, with his face just inches from mine and his eyes holding me captive.

"No, it's all about right and wrong. You see everything in black and white, Alex. It's probably why you like algebra, because you can't talk your way into a correct answer the way you can in any other class. Ask someone to elaborate on the history behind the Civil War and they can probably go off on a tangent about southern rights and the price of cotton, but it's not like that with algebra. Either x is 4 or it isn't."

"This isn't about math."

"No," he agrees, holding my hands tighter. "It's about you and the fact that nothing's perfect. You've spent your entire life trying to live up to the idea that you can be flawless, but you're not. And the minute you became imperfect wasn't with me, as much as you want to keep punishing yourself for it."

A tear makes its way down my cheek, and I pull my hand out of his so I can brush it away.

"You don't know that much about me, not really."

"You hate not measuring up." Since I've removed my right hand, he wraps both his around my left. "I bet you've been that way since you were a girl, never doing anything wrong. And you don't want to do anything to disappoint your parents, either. You aren't responsible for what happens to them, and you're not responsible for Heather."

A response is probably necessary, but I can't force any coherent thoughts past the obvious roadblock that is Jake's spot-on analysis. It makes me want to pull the neck of my sweater over my head and pretend to disappear rather than to continue staring at that handsome face.

"You're so devoted to making sure Bailey has a good start, but as awesome as that is, don't sacrifice yourself. She comes alive when she sees you shed that faultless image. When you're pretending to be Hoppy, or dancing around the living room, or rewriting her books in your head while you read them. And I have no right to say anything, I know that, but I care about the two of you."

He abruptly releases my hand and stands so he can step around the couch and grab his shoes.

*Tell him not to leave.*

But I can't. Instead, I rise from my spot on the couch and brush at my eyes again before straightening the hem at the bottom of my dress.

"Listen, don't mind me," he mutters as he kneels to tie his shoe. "I'll be around tomorrow sometime before noon so you can go hang out with Annie."

"Are you sure?"

"Yeah." He tilts his head up so he can offer a smile, like he's trying to prove that the conversation that left me shaken rolls right off his back. "I've been thinking through some things, and trying to figure some stuff out. You know what, though? It doesn't matter. I should probably go."

He moves in the direction of the door, and I can't make myself go around the barrier of the couch.

"Thank you," I say, watching him grab his jacket from the back of a kitchen chair.

"For what?"

*Everything,* I want to say. *Holding my hand for five minutes, even if it was just to lecture me. Looking at me like you see me, and I'm important. Making me feel reckless and valued at the same time.*

"Dinner," I lamely offer. "Offering to watch Bailey tomorrow. Just showing up."

He stretches the jacket across his back as he shoves his arm into the sleeve. "You don't have to thank me," he states, pulling the keys to his truck from his jeans pocket. "I'd do pretty much anything you asked, but you've probably figured that out by now."

There's a lengthy pause as he waits by the door, looking in my direction like he has something more to say. Finally, he shrugs his shoulder and makes a step toward the porch. "Good night."

"Good night, Jake," I whisper after he closes the door behind him. Minutes tick by as I continue to stand by the couch, just watching the darkness through the corner of the blinds and keeping an eye on the place where he just walked out. Finally, I resign myself to the fact that the headlights aren't returning and he's not walking back through the door.

Why I would want him to do that in the first place is vaguely confusing. There's absolutely no future in harboring any sort of feelings for Jake. If we didn't have a past together, and he actually had some chance of being the guy, and things were different…

But they can't be. Bailey's sleeping in the back bedroom, I'm still trying to figure out how to live a new normal, and he has a past three miles longer than the average person's grocery list.

# Chapter Twenty-Three

## Alexis

Finding new friends so I can make Louisville home is difficult even on the best days. Usually I make a joke at my own expense to try to brush off my uneasiness and wind up alienating people in the process. Who wants to be friends with a pseudo-intellectual, self-deprecating high school teacher who can't manage to carry on an adult conversation?

The most frustrating thing is the fact that I've never had this problem before. Even though I'm not the most outgoing person in the world, I've never been the one to fade into the wall or try to pretend I wasn't present. But maybe my sense of belonging came from being in the place I called home. From the minute I entered the world until the day I left for Louisville, I'd occupied the same little circle of influence on God's green earth. Maybe fitting in wasn't so much having a group of friends as much as it was simply dwelling in the same rut as everyone else.

Really, how many of my "friends" have contacted me since I moved to Louisville? Only Sadie. Not that I've longed to talk to any of them either.

That thought doesn't help matters as I stand on the porch of the two-story house that sits at the end of Wonder Lane. The stately jewel of the subdivision, without question. Even though Annie invited me over, I can't imagine myself fitting in with Harley Laine. "Louisville's sweetheart," I heard someone call her on the news the other night.

Since Jake arrived at the house and took Bailey to the park, there's no way for me to fake some excuse for not attending. No doubt Annie would mention it to Jake later, and he would wonder what exactly I was doing when he watched Bailey, and why I lied to him. Not a conversation I want to have.

Pressing my finger against the doorbell, I shift the cookies I made toward the crook of my arm. Even though Jake didn't leave until later than normal last night, I set my alarm and woke up early so I could prepare something to bring along on my visit. Probably a leftover gesture I picked up from my mother—never arrive at someone's house empty-handed.

Annie flings open the door and her eyes widen as she takes in the plate of cookies.

"Alexis is here!" she calls over her shoulder. "She brought snacks." She smiles as she steps aside to let me in. "I knew I liked you."

*Maybe I should take snacks with me everywhere. Hi, I'm Alexis, have a cookie.*

"I hope I'm not late," I offer, which I recognize as pathetic as soon as the words pass my lips. It's not like I'm meeting the Pope for breakfast or something. My neighbor invited me over to hang out.

She leads me through the foyer into a dining room that looks like it belongs in an episode of a show on PBS. Far too classy for this little subdivision. It looks like it should be in the residence of a wealthy family in the south; one who has all the cousins over for holidays.

I'm hearing southern twang ringing out with choruses of "welcome home, honey" in my mind when we cross into the living room, which has a cozy looking couch but otherwise is pretty drab. In fact, there's a large water spot along the wall where there's obviously been a leak at one time. No wonder Jake's been over here doing some remodeling.

"You barely missed seeing Harley with bed head. She was at Tiny's with Ryan last night and somehow they ended up working in the kitchen."

"Tiny's?" I ask hesitantly. Harley looks up at me from her place on the couch. At least I think it's Harley. She's wearing faded jeans with a huge hole in the knee and a plain white T-shirt that looks like it came out of one of those department store packages of undershirts. With her face free from makeup and her hair in a twisted knot near the top of her head, she looks significantly younger than she does on TV.

"It's a little greasy spoon diner that Harley hangs out at all the time," Annie explains. "She met Ryan there too. *Aww, isn't that sweet.* Let's just get it out there and over with, so we don't have to draw out the mushy stuff."

The girl just to the right of Harley on the couch chuckles at Annie's statement.

"Have you met Maddie?" Annie wants to know. She strips me of the cookies and places them on the coffee table.

"Yeah, she nearly died in my yard," I say, offering a forced smile. "It's nice to see you again."

"You too," Maddie says, reaching out to take one of the peanut butter cookies. "I really think I was in Josh's yard, though. But I could be wrong, since I was suffering a lack of oxygen at the time."

Annie plops onto a beanbag in the corner, leaving room for me on the sofa. "Harley and Maddie know each other through work. Not that they work together, but Harley's interviewed her."

"Oh," I answer, glancing between Harley and Maddie. "Did someone call the cops when you took a nap in their yard?"

Harley laughs as she carefully inspects the cookies, choosing one of the smallest. "Not exactly, although that sounds like something they would send me to cover. Maddie's the corporate spokesperson for Kent Cooper."

The three of them smile as they look at one another, leaving me totally in the dark. "Sorry, Louisville newbie here. Who exactly is Kent Cooper?"

"He owns Cooper Corporate Financial," Annie quickly states. "His wife, Faith, comes in my shop all the time with her clothes. Harley is her biggest fan."

"She's actually my fan," Harley tells her with a wink. "The truth is, Faith and I are about the same size. I get a lot of her hand-me-downs. That goes no farther than this room." She pointedly stares at Maddie, who holds her hands up in mock surrender.

"You think I'm about to tell the Coopers that kind of information? I have a strict avoidance policy, thank you very much. All except for their daughter, who is semi-normal. I happened to walk in Cooper's office last week when he was mid-breakfast, more aptly known as drinking raw eggs to the average person. I dry-heaved twice in his office and couldn't manage to get myself under control. He had to come downstairs to visit me about twenty minutes later, and I still gagged while he was mid-explanation about his feelings on an ad campaign. It's not appropriate office etiquette, in my opinion." She pauses to cross her arms over her abdomen. "Drinking raw eggs, I mean. There are just certain things you shouldn't eat at the office. Raw eggs, stinky fish, any kind of cabbage, cheesy poofs…"

Annie giggles, and I find it impossible not to laugh myself.

"What's your story?" Maddie asks me, helping herself to another cookie. "These are dangerous. I'll have to run an extra mile today, and you're to blame."

"Thanks, I think." After adjusting myself awkwardly on the couch, I clear my throat. "Well, my daughter and I moved here a few months ago from Tennessee. Bailey—that's my daughter's name—is four years old. It's my first year teaching high school algebra. I suppose that pretty much sums everything up."

"I call foul," Maddie immediately states. "Sorry, I don't know where that came from. I guess I've been hanging out with Josh too much lately and I've picked up some of his lingo."

"Well, if you're going to call foul you have to state your reason clearly," Annie retorts, her smile telling me that she's clearly amused by Maddie's outburst.

"She's leaving out a big part of the story," Maddie continues, glancing at me rather apologetically. "I saw the good looking guy helping you move in. Josh's mom and I were getting in the car that night. Sorry, I shouldn't have even brought it up."

"No, it's okay." Really, it's more uncomfortable than *okay*, but what am I supposed to say? "You're talking about Jake. He's Bailey's dad."

"Jake's a pretty cool guy," Annie adds. "He's been doing the remodeling for Harley."

"So you two are..." Maddie frames her drop-off statement as a question pointed at me, and I feel my eyes widen involuntarily.

"Nothing," I blurt, rethinking the word the instant it crosses my lips. "Friends, I guess. He spends a lot of time at the house. But it's not like that. Last night he gave me a brotherly lecture about who I should date."

"Yikes." Annie rises from the beanbag, which makes a swooshing noise at her exit. She grabs three cookies before fluffing the beanbag so she can sit cross-legged atop it again. "He doesn't like who you're planning to date?"

"Planning to date," I reply with a laugh. "I'm not planning to date. He seems to think I'm kind of old-fashioned. A prude, quite frankly. Anyway, I don't exactly have a line of guys waiting for the chance, so the point is moot."

The whole room falls silent, like I've sucked the very life from it. Rather than sit here watching them feel sorry for me, I reach out to grab a cookie for myself.

"We should find Alexis a man," Annie announces.

"How fun," Maddie agrees.

"Annie too," Harley adds. "She needs some kind of distraction so she'll stop bugging me."

"I never bug anyone. Besides, I may possibly be seeing someone. Just once now so I don't want to jinx it, but we are going out again tonight."

"Annie!" Harley pulls her feet up to the couch, her gigantic navy blue wool socks coming to rest close to my leg. "I can't believe you went out with someone and didn't tell me."

"You were busy with Ryan's family. Anyway, it's no big deal. On to Alexis, though. Who are we thinking?"

Harley draws her eyes away from Annie so slowly, I'm fairly certain the two of them will have a conversation about this later.

"I could probably come up with some good names if I put some thought into it," Maddie says. "Maybe look through the employee listing at work."

"What about Denton?" Harley adds. "You've probably seen him on the Channel Six news…Denton Price? He's quite the catch, and a nice guy to boot."

"Denton's probably not the guy for her," Annie counters.

Harley furrows her brow as she returns her eyes to Annie. "Why not? What's wrong with Denton?"

"I just have it on good authority that he's already seeing someone."

"Good authority? How do you know more about Denton than I do? I see the guy every day." Harley leans her head back against the sofa and lets her feet slide back to the floor. "Wait a second—you and Denton? Annie?"

Annie's mouth twitches a little as she stares at Harley. "Don't make a thing of it. We got to talking last week when he called for you, and then he asked me to go to dinner with him. It might amount to nothing, and I don't want things to be awkward, okay?"

"Okay," Harley adds quietly. "How can my best friend date my coworker and not bother to tell me? No matter, let's move on. Alexis?"

"I think I liked it better when we were focusing on Annie," I can't help saying. "I'm really not looking to date anyone right now, so it's all good."

"How disappointing," Maddie states as she sighs loudly.

"Listen, why don't we devote our time to something more noble than our love lives?" Annie suggests. "No offense, Alexis."

"None taken."

"I'm all for noble." Maddie adjusts her voluminous auburn hair over her shoulder. "We've got a full crew, too. The perfect opportunity to get something done if we put our minds to it."

"What do you mean, a full crew?" Harley adjusts her own hair in its topknot, almost as though Maddie's action was contagious.

"I'm in marketing, Alexis is the numbers lady, you're the one who gets us into the right circles, and Annie can dress us to the nines. We can't possibly lose."

"She sounds like she's plotting a crime," Annie deadpans from her slowly sinking beanbag. She's now sitting about two inches lower on the right side.

"No, I get what she's saying," Harley says, looking at me like she's searching for agreement. "We could form a group and do cool things, like volunteer at the homeless shelter."

"Sure," Maddie adds. "And when we're not helping people, we could do something between ourselves. Just meet and chat and have coffee and snacks. Oh, like one of those book clubs! Except I don't like coffee, and I don't really read."

I'm the first to giggle, but I attempt to stifle it by placing my hand over my mouth. It's no use, because the laughter is contagious and Annie and Harley join in almost immediately.

"I've been really busy," Maddie attempts to explain. "It's not like I'm illiterate or something. Come to think of it, I did read three Camdyn Taylor books over the winter, but that was before Josh was back."

"Camdyn Taylor," Harley says with a sigh. "I can only imagine what that woman thinks of me after I tried to go undercover in her dressing room."

"That's so funny." I relax a bit, allowing myself to ease into the conversation. "Did you know she's married to Jake's best friend?"

"He's very attractive," Maddie states. The rest of us look in her direction, and she shrugs as she grabs another cookie. "What? It's a fact."

Harley nods in my direction, and we share a conspiratorial grin. I remember well running into him at the drug store. Attractive is an apt description.

"Ladies, before the chair eats me alive, I propose a toast." Annie pushes forward from her beanbag once more, and the motion deposits her on the hardwood on her knees.

Maddie narrows her eyes as she focuses her gaze at Annie on the floor. "We don't have glasses."

"We have cookies," Annie counters.

"I think I've already had six."

Maddie's words cause me to laugh again, but Annie clears her throat and reaches out for a cookie off the tray.

"A toast, then," Annie begins, causing the rest of us to reach forward and grab our own cookies to hold aloft. "May our doors ever be open to one another as long as we all shall live."

"Or at least while we're all on Wonder Lane," Maddie adds.

That sentiment causes Harley to smile. "To the girls of Wonder Lane."

"The girls of Wonder Lane," we echo, tapping our cookies together in midair.

The four of us chat and laugh for nearly three hours before I decide I should probably go. When I walk back up the street, I feel almost foolish for dreading the visit earlier. For better or for worse, I'm pretty sure I now have a unique group of friends I can call on when I need something. Since I started the morning with no one to rely on here except Jake, that matters more than it normally would.

The red truck isn't in the driveway when I get back to the house, so it seems like this would be a good time to pick up some milk and bread from the grocery store. Of course milk and bread never wind up being the only purchases, so while I'm in the store I wind up spending a bit too much time staring at a display of lip gloss. Once I've been standing in that spot long enough to have one of the stockers ask me if I need help—twice—I pick the tubes of gloss up one by one and hold them against my wrist.

Thinking about dating someone new shouldn't be so terrifying, should it? The girls convinced me that I could take some small steps into the fray and get myself out there, and it sounded great while we were together in our group of empowerment, but now that I'm standing in front of the lip gloss rack...

It doesn't help that the stocker looks like a teenager and seems way more self-confident than I am at the moment.

While I'm talking to the cashier and mentally chiding myself for spending money on two tubes of lip gloss and a concealer stick (solely picked up for the way I looked in my rearview mirror earlier), Jake calls. Wants to make sure I'm not out somewhere looking for the two of them. Just checking in, he insists. Take my time, and he'll keep watching Bailey as long as I need him to.

Perhaps irrationally, it instantly makes me feel like a bad mother. Jake is watching my daughter, and I'm plotting ways to make myself attractive to the opposite sex.

That's my mindset as I pull the Mitsubishi out of the grocery store parking lot, and it keeps tugging at the back of my subconscious while I speed down the street and eventually hit I-65. The thought refuses to relent, right up until the point where I hear the wailing sound behind me and look up to see the flashing lights in my mirror.

*Never pull over by yourself on a secluded highway.*
*Keep your hands where they can be seen.*
*Be honest and forthright, and show respect.*

My heart beats erratically as I sit in the driver's seat of the car, seat belt rather constrictive against my chest, willing my breathing to calm down as I wait for the officer. Why my dad's words are ringing through my brain is a mystery. It was the lecture he gave when I turned sixteen and got my license—the same lecture he gave Heather a year later. That advice has never come in handy for me before now.

I roll my window down as a car zips by me on the left, a little too close for comfort, and I pray no one I know from school sees me. My concern quickly shifts, however, when I see the gray uniform coming toward me in the side mirror.

"Good afternoon," the baritone voice says at the window.

I can't even muster up the nerve to look at him. "I guess you want my license and registration? Should I get them now?"

"Do you know why I pulled you over today?"

*Because I thought I could buy lip gloss, that's why.* Slowly I reach toward the glove box and lift the handle, making the move to retrieve my documentation.

"Yes, sir. I was speeding, and I'm sorry. Too much on my mind."

He takes the information from my hand and tells me he'll be a moment, and then leaves me with the misery of knowing I'm going to have to pay for a ticket now. That lip gloss didn't look quite as expensive just a couple moments ago.

In all my dad's advice, he never mentioned the fact that the minutes seem to turn into hours as the car sits on the side of the highway, the flashing lights like a beacon to every passing vehicle. *Look at the rule-breaker.* And they each gawk at me in turn as they drive by, witnessing my humiliation.

The sound of a car door closing behind me causes me to glance at my side mirror again, and I avert my eyes as I see him approaching. He clears his throat when he reaches the door, and I turn but keep my focus on his hands holding my driver's license.

"I'm not quite sure what to do with you, young lady. I'm a little surprised to see you."

That phrase causes me to raise my eyes a bit, and they travel up his trim midsection to his chest and rest on his last name. HEWITT.

My eyes immediately dart to his face, partially shaded under the hat but still recognizable in an instant. His hair isn't falling over his collar anymore, but those eyes are the same.

"Cody?"

"You're a ways from home, aren't you Alexis?" He peers at me, his eyes sweeping the interior of my car. I can't help but notice that they come to rest on Bailey's place in the back seat.

"Just a mile or two," I say, watching as his eyes slowly move back to me. "I live here now."

"I think I knew that," he casually comments, his forearm resting against the top of the door. "Your sister told some of the guys back home."

That simple statement makes me wonder exactly how much Cody knows.

"So, you have a kid?" he asks, gesturing to the car seat behind me. Absolutely no beating around the bush, but I guess it's better to throw it all out in the open anyway.

"Yes, a daughter. She's four."

"And you're not married?" He straightens a bit after asking the question, clearing his throat. "I didn't see a ring. And your last name's the same."

Instinct causes me to glance at my left hand, even though I already know there's absolutely no jewelry there.

"Not married," I confirm.

"Divorced?"

"No."

My face heats a little. A complete and utter betrayal by my nervous system.

"Huh." He trains those hazel eyes on me, barely staying in the shadows of his hat, and I force myself to look at him. "Guess things change, don't they?"

"Yes, they do," I answer without skipping a beat. "Who would have thought you'd become a law enforcement officer? You never could pass a test without help."

He smiles, and I'm hopeful that it's just enough of a push to get past the uncomfortable topic of a few seconds ago.

"Still willing to point out that you're smarter than me," he jokes, tapping his fist on the top of the car. His laugh isn't as easy as I remember, but it still sounds familiar. As he pauses to take a breath, he sobers a little. "What happened that night? You were supposed to wait for me."

Unconsciously, I focus on the cars whizzing by. Red, white, another white.

"What do you mean?"

"I told you to wait for me and I'd be right back. I had to take Mindy to her brother's house because she didn't have another ride. By the time I got there, you were gone."

"You came back?"

"You honestly thought I wouldn't?" He glances back at the road behind him, as though he's realizing there are still cars speeding past us. "No sense wasting time, right? You seeing anybody?"

It's just a normal breath entering my throat, but the impact of his words makes me choke on it. I cough three times, and he actually sticks his hand in the car and pats me on the back. So abjectly humiliating.

"Are you okay?" he asks, his hand settling on my left shoulder and sitting there, impossible to ignore even though I force myself to pretend that I don't notice.

"Sure, I'm okay. And no, not seeing anybody."

He pulls a pen from his pocket and makes a show of clicking it in front of my face before he holds it out to me. "Here. I just need you to autograph this. And make sure you write your phone number."

"Are you giving me a ticket?"

"Do you want me to?" He offers that familiar crooked grin, and I feel a small smile tugging at my own lips.

"Of course not." Placing the pen against the pad of paper he handed me, I hold the tip to the page and can't seem to make my fingers move. Sadie's voice rings in my ears. *Don't be plumb stupid, Alexis.*

But she doesn't know what I know, right? He just admitted that he didn't leave with Mindy after all. He came back, but I was already gone because I'd jumped to conclusions. I was with Jake. It was me. *I* was the one who didn't wait.

*Except it's not even about that,* Sadie's voice taunts. *He already proved he wasn't worthy of you, remember?*

The pen sits stone-still on the paper, my mind warring as Cody waits. It tastes of revenge, making Cody wait a little. The vindictive part of me wants to tell him that he had his chance a long time ago. The self-preserving part of me tells me that I should hand the pen back and tell him politely to have a nice life. But there's still that teenage girl living somewhere inside who prayed so hard for Cody. Maybe it's not a coincidence that he pulled me over today, when the girls of Wonder Lane just convinced me that I might be able to see myself dating someone. Maybe this is the answer to my prayer, just a decade too late.

Better late than never, right?

*The good looking ones don't ask twice,* Heather's voice sounds in my head.

So the pen starts moving, even while I have trouble deciding, and I find myself handing my number to the hope of a second chance.

# Chapter Twenty-Four

## Jake

The wide open room is fairly empty this early in the morning, which I sort of expected. Normally I show up with Annie, Harley and Ryan, but this morning I needed to be alone. I sit three rows from the back, not in a pew like the church my granny used to attend, but in a gray metal folding chair. It's not particularly comfortable, but I didn't come here because I'm looking for comfort. There's really no good explanation for why I'm here, at least that I can think of at the moment.

Alexis came back from spending time with Annie and her friends yesterday, and I could tell something changed. Bailey rattled on about what we did at the park, and something about her mom's face told me that she was a little distracted. She was in some sort of mood, but not a happy or sad mood. Just off.

Last night, after we ate dinner and Bailey fell asleep, I was hoping to spend some time with Alexis. Maybe even get into some tough subjects and sort out how she felt about certain things. Then the phone rang, and everything changed.

She has a date with Cody next Friday night.

Alexis has a date with Cody, and I said of course I could watch Bailey. I usually come over anyway, right?

Not what I wanted to say. My instinct was to question his motives, worry about her judgment in going out with the guy, and tell her he shouldn't get a second chance. How could I say that, though? Sure, the guy treated her like dirt in the past, but no worse than I have. Since I don't want to condemn myself, I try to remind myself not to be too harsh on him.

Still, I can't stand that guy.

Leaning forward, I place my elbows against my knees and drop my head to my hands. It shouldn't come as such a surprise, really. Things were going too well. Somehow I convinced myself that it didn't matter if Alexis is too good for me. As long as she didn't realize it, I could live with that. But she's too good for Cody, too, and that fact is going to drive me flat crazy.

A hand touches my shoulder, and I twist my head to the right, glancing up to see Duke. His graying beard stretches a good six inches past the neck of his T-shirt, and as I look back down I notice dust on the toes of his chunky black boots.

I move over to the next seat, making room for him beside me. While he plants himself next to me, I cross my leg and place my right foot on my left knee, trying to appear a little nonchalant. Probably too late, since he felt the need to single me out.

"How's Jake today?" he asks, bringing a small smile to my lips.

"I'm good. You?"

"Right as rain, but I don't believe you. Usually guys who are having good days don't crash church early just to hang out alone."

"That obvious?"

He chuckles as he crosses his arms over his midsection. "I could guess the main offenders, I suppose." He grabs the end of his beard like it's going to help his train of thought. "Money trouble, work problems, or the most likely culprit, which is a doozy."

His guessing game strikes me as funny. "What's that?"

"A woman."

It's impossible to stop the laugh from echoing across the room as I shake my head. I glance around, just to make sure no one's tuned into our conversation. "Just for argument's sake, let's say there's a girl."

He nods slowly but doesn't look in my direction. "Okay. What's she like?"

"She's one of those who never does anything wrong. Probably been reciting Bible verses since she was 'knee high to a grasshopper', as my granny used to say. Beautiful, inside and out." I pause as something starts to click inside my head, and I feel the guilt clutch at my chest.

"She has no idea," I mutter, trying to process the thoughts rolling through my mind. "She doesn't realize how fantastic she is, and it's my fault." Duke looks over like he's going to correct me, but I continue before he has a chance. "That's why her going out with Cody bugs me, right? Because he reminds me of myself? I want to protect her from a guy like me?"

"Are you really so bad?"

A simple question, which my ego silently answers with a resounding "no." My conscience isn't quite so hasty to answer.

"It seemed like we were talking about something similar last week, weren't we?" Duke clamps his hand on my shoulder so he can obtain my full attention. He's just intimidating enough that he earns it. "Mistakes and failures and flat-out wrong choices. The cross was the punishment for all of it. Well, except that one thing. What was it again? That thing it didn't cover?"

It's impossible not to recognize his trick question, since I well remember last week. The topic resonated with me enough that Ryan and I had a two-hour conversation when it was finished, after which I called Cole to get his take on the subject. I ended the day reading that Gideon Bible in my hotel room until my eyes wouldn't focus.

"It covered everything," I tell him quietly. "All of it."

He squeezes my shoulder before removing his hand. "Yeah, that's right. Seems to me, in that case, it would make more sense to thank Him than to try to work off debts that are already paid."

Rather than driving his point home, he stands and gives a simple nod of his head as he walks away.

A couple scoots into the row of chairs in front of me, talking to one another, and music begins playing from the speakers in front.

Something makes me think about my granny again. I can almost picture her face while I tell her that I've been reading the "good book," as she called it. Embracing the cross and everything it represents.

*Honey, my heart's done tickled pink*, I hear her voice in my head.

It's enough to keep me sitting here silently as people mill about me. A few of them pause to tell me hi, and I return their smiles and then go back to my thoughts. Eventually Annie taps me on the shoulder, and as I rise to prepare to greet Harley and Ryan, instead I stop in my tracks.

"Alex," I say, taking in the sight of her glowing skin and her hair falling softly over her shoulders. She looks light and happy, a fact that both encourages and disheartens me at the same time.

"Jake? I'm surprised to see you here."

"Jake's been coming with us for a while," Annie pipes up, moving over to make space for Alexis. She moves past me and sits in the chair next to mine, balancing Bailey on her knee.

"The two people church doesn't like," Alexis says, offering a rather shy smile from mere inches away. It would be easy to wrap my arm around the back of her chair. Maybe rest my fingers on her shoulder.

"Don't be nutty," Annie tells her, poking her in the arm. "We love you guys."

Bailey lowers herself to the floor and climbs up onto my lap, smoothing her blue dress over her knees. "Can you take me to someplace fun soon?"

"Sure," I say as she wraps her arms around my neck. "How about Friday night? I'll take you somewhere nice. Maybe you can wear one of your dresses."

"Really?" The top of her head rests just under my chin, and I hold her a little tighter. "Thank you, Daddy."

My throat constricts, and I focus on the stage, knowing I can't look at Alexis. Bailey's words caused instant emotion, and I'm afraid to see her reaction.

I know my own, though. Instinctively I look upward, knowing I have much more to thank God for than I ever thought possible.

# Chapter Twenty-Five

## Alexis

She looks far more prepared for this than I am. Makeup expertly applied, with the liner extending just to the corner of her eyes and her lashes curling up to make dark frames. Glowing skin with a delicate blush to her cheeks and a touch of crimson on her lips. Navy blue dress with a scoop neck and sequin detailing at both the hem and the bottoms of the sheer sleeves. No, never mind. There go the goose bumps over her arms. Now spreading to her bare legs. I watch as she bends to rub her shins, trying to force the telltale signs of nervousness to abate.

"Mommy?"

Averting my gaze from the mirror, I hastily stop rubbing my leg and rise to my full height.

"Bailey. You need help?"

"Uh huh." She turns around so I can button the back of her Cinderella-style light blue dress, and as I lower myself carefully so I don't twist my ankle in my strappy gold high-heeled sandals, I feel the familiar prick of tears stinging the inside corners of my eyes. I've been battling them all week, it seems. Every time I think about Bailey crawling onto Jake's lap in church and calling him Daddy.

The timing of that was almost unfair. Each night since then I've caught myself staring at him, wondering how me trying to move on with my life is going to affect his relationship with Bailey. If I do start seriously dating someone, he's going to come out on the short end. How can I have him over here all the time?

Then I remind myself that I could allow Bailey to spend time with him separately from me, and my heart constricts. Losing even five minutes of my precious time each night with Bailey seems like a terrible option. If it came down to that, I'd have to sacrifice my love life for my daughter. Not even a question.

As I struggle to rise on my heels, I begin wondering all over again why I'm going through this charade.

"Pretty pretty?" Bailey asks, spinning in a circle.

I sniff as I shake my head to try to bring myself back to the present. "The most beautiful girl I've ever seen."

"Where's Daddy taking me?"

There it is again, an exclamation point on all my insecurities.

"He said it was a surprise," I choke out, forcing a deep breath into my lungs. So deep, I can actually feel the fabric of the fitted dress compressing my chest. Why did I let Annie talk me into this outfit? Just because I have a friend with access to fashionable clothes doesn't mean I have to wear them. And a good three inches above my knees, practically alerting Cody to the fact that I'm trying desperately to get his attention.

"I like prizes," Bailey tells me matter-of-factly, oblivious to the fact that I'm having a mini-meltdown. Inwardly, anyway.

A knock on the door sends my attention scurrying back to the mirror. Why did I let Annie put those strategically-placed-to-look-random waves in my hair? They're so predictably ridiculous. I might as well announce to the world that I'm trying to be one of those chair occupiers for the Oscars. Oh, Julia Roberts needs to use the restroom? Bring in the girl who's overdressed for no practical reason.

The knock sounds again, sending me into a new level of panic. Jake doesn't stand out there and knock like that. He knocks twice, fairly loudly, and then lets himself in. It has to be Cody.

My knees feel like they're disconnected as I make my way to the door, moving slowly in the heels. With my legs slightly wobbly, I run the risk of breaking an ankle. That thought and the sheer hesitation I feel toward greeting Cody war within me as I think about letting him in. But I have to, don't I? I turn my back to the door and raise my shoulders as I take a calming breath, twisting the doorknob before I lose my nerve. Slowly facing the door, I halt as I see a huge bouquet of pink daisies, and then my eyes move higher to lock not on those hazel eyes I remember from math class, but on the blue eyes I've become familiar with lately. The ones that fade from aquamarine in the center to cobalt blue on the edges, hedged in by that brown border that sprinkles into the blue here and there.

The flowers move down to his side, and something within me shrinks. It's awkward meeting him like this, and his silence is telling.

"I know," I offer preemptively. "Annie helped me get ready, and I look——"

"Beautiful," he finishes, surprisingly sober. No hint of a smirk or that flirtatious tone. It's just enough to halt my justification, and to cause me to fully see him instead of worrying about myself.

Jake McAuliffe, standing on my doorstep wearing a fitted black suit with a tie. Looking irresistibly perfect, with the exception of his tie being a little crooked. My fingers reach out to straighten it before I manage to order them to stop. The slow smile that creeps onto his face is all I need to set me at ease.

"I'm impressed," I say quietly, finishing with the tie and running my palm against it to smooth it out. "Do you always start your dates this way? In a suit and bringing flowers?"

"Never. But I am pretty crazy about this girl."

He offers a wink right before Bailey squeals behind me. I move out of the way so she can see him, and he steps inside to offer her the flowers. The way her face beams, I'm not sure I can take much more without starting over on my makeup.

"Mommy, can my flowers get a drink?" She cradles them in her arms as she carries them to the kitchen, so I follow her to grab a tall glass to place the stems inside. We don't have any vases in the house. I've never had a use for one before.

"Bailey Nicole, I don't think I've ever seen a prettier girl in all my life," Jake states from somewhere behind me. She responds by carrying her shiny black shoes over to where he's standing, and he kneels so he can help her slide them on. I can't seem to make myself move from the kitchen, simply watching the two of them bond without me. The thought is such a sweet ache that it has me shaking my head again to try to avoid crying before my date even starts.

Within a few seconds she's ready to go, and Jake pauses by the door just long enough to allow me to make my way to them. When I reach Bailey, she slides her hand into his, and I smooth my hand over her silky brown hair.

"I'm going to take her to dinner and a movie," he softly states, "but I'll have my cell on me the whole time. If you need anything, call me. I'm serious."

The thought of Jake going all big-brother on me again immediately makes me self-conscious. "Is it that bad, really? I can change."

His eyes sweep over my dress before he focuses on my face again. "You're kidding me, right? No way did you look in the mirror and think for one second that you're not absolutely gorgeous. And just in case he doesn't tell you that, I'm just going to put this out there so it pops into your head later: He's an idiot. There, I said it."

"Jake," I mutter, looking down at my hands. He doesn't have to tell me he doesn't like Cody. I can tell, and I'm sure it's because he sees his time with Bailey dwindling. But it's just one date, and it probably means nothing.

"Tell your mom bye." He presses Bailey forward, and she wraps her arms around my thighs, squeezing tight enough that I almost lose my balance.

"Bye Mommy."

And just like that, Prince Charming and Cinderella walk out of my life, leaving me here like a discarded pumpkin, overdressed and with a noticeable absence of singing mice to lift my spirits.

Cody presses his hand to the small of my back as we make our way to the table, following a waiter who has three pieces of jewelry studding his eyebrow. If I didn't feel overdressed before, when Cody showed up at the house wearing dark-washed jeans and a blue T-shirt with three buttons at the collar, I do now. The instant he pulled up in front of the casual chain restaurant, my heart sank. If we were hanging out like old times and sharing mozzarella sticks and nachos in front of a big screen watching football, this would be perfect. But this is supposed to be a date, right?

Not that I'm trying to be a snob, even if I have a designer label on my dress that I never would have looked at before today. But I haven't seen Cody in years, and if we're trying to catch up and see where things stand, it would seem there would be a more ideal location where people wouldn't be screaming at the television screen. Or pounding back shots of tequila. Or having the birthday song sung by six waitresses while they tie balloons on the patron's chair.

Those arguments don't cross my lips, though, as we reach our table. It's right in the middle of all the commotion, where I awkwardly sidestep a tray of food that's being maneuvered around a high chair.

Our table would seat four, but rather than sit across from me, Cody settles himself by my side. After the waiter takes our drink orders, I busy myself looking at the menu, but when I glance up, Cody's staring at me.

"What?"

He offers that familiar crooked smile while he shrugs his shoulders. "Nothing, you just look better every time I see you."

"Thank you." I quickly settle on an entrée in my mind and place my menu on the table, folding my hands together in my lap. "So, what made you decide to go into law enforcement?"

The waiter delivers our drinks, so the conversation is put on hold while we order our food. As soon as he disappears with the menus, though, Cody places his elbows on the table and looks over at me.

"Just kind of fell into it, I guess. Dad's always been a cop."

Somewhere deep inside I probably knew that. He lived with his mother in Tennessee, and his father was in Michigan. But he didn't like to talk about his dad back then, and he certainly never mentioned following in his footsteps.

"What about you?" he asks, taking a sip of his soft drink. "What are you doing with yourself, besides being a mom?"

A slight smile tugs at the corner of my mouth. "I teach high school algebra."

"Shut up, you do not."

"I do, actually. I figured if I could get you through four years of math, I could teach just about anybody."

"There's probably a lot of truth to that." He turns slightly so he's facing me, draping his arm over the back of his chair. "And here I thought you took all those math classes just to be close to me."

"Hardly," I counter, swirling my straw around the bottom of my glass.

"Yeah, I guess that was the other way around." When I look up to search for a teasing grin, I find it right where I expected it. "It's a good thing we had Mr. Samuels for math. If we had a math teacher that looked anything like you, I might have failed big time. Or I might have become a mathematician. I certainly would have been inspired."

"Very funny."

"I gotta tell you, I never was much interested in math. Except for maybe one plus one, where you were concerned."

The slender fingers of his right hand curl around his glass, and I watch them fastidiously, thinking of a way to divert to a new topic of conversation. I'm not ready to talk about us yet.

"I'm a little surprised you're not seeing someone," I say, searching for new ways to steer the conversation. It's a valid topic. An attractive man who wears a uniform every day is likely to invite female attention.

"Oh, I had a girlfriend for a while. A little over a year, but it didn't work out. We broke up last month. Turns out that's perfect timing, though, because I never expected to run into you."

"Well, hopefully we won't have to meet that way again. I've been watching my speed very carefully."

He laughs as he brings his hand over to place it on my shoulder, rubbing his thumb across the sheer fabric on my arm. The goose bumps break out in full force again, which doesn't surprise me. Cody's touch has always caused a reaction.

"Is it cold in here?" I ask, trying to evade the obvious by rubbing my hands down my arms.

"Not really." He pulls his hand back, settling it on the table. "What is it with girls always being cold?" I simply shrug my shoulders as he takes another drink of his soda. "Oh, there's a club up the road I thought we could hit after dinner. They have a live band on Saturday nights, but it's not that bad on Fridays. Mostly heavy metal music, but I know you love that."

Eh, Cody loved that. We always had the radio tuned to the local metal station because it's what he wanted. I kind of like a country song myself. Or a symphony orchestra. The occasional screaming guitar, but it has to be well crafted.

I'd like to protest that I'd rather go somewhere quiet and talk, but I find my lips saying, "Sure." Complete and utter betrayal of my inner feelings. I vow to bring them into submission for the rest of the evening.

"Do you remember when I caught that pass in the fourth quarter when we played the Bulldogs? Senior year?"

I nod my head, because I do. It was a spectacular catch, and I screamed so loudly I had a hard time using my voice the next day.

Even Cody couldn't believe he still had the ball when he came up off the ground after hitting so hard. He practically soared through the air to make that happen, and it was visually beautiful.

"You know Sean had a video of that?" He laughs as he raises his eyebrows. "He had no idea, but his dad had it with a bunch of stuff he recorded when they installed their pool. Just a bunch of Sean's dad walking around talking about a big hole in the ground, and then, boom! There's twenty minutes or so of the game, then right back to his grandma talking about her cat during Christmas or something. It was hilarious, but he recorded it for me. I have it at home if you want to see it sometime."

I manage to smile enthusiastically, despite the fact that I don't care about Sean's pool or his grandma's cat. I don't even have a desire to see Cody's catch again, to be honest. Most things that I have built up in my mind as spectacular wind up not being quite so great, when inspected in the light of day. I'm afraid that wonderful catch might rank as one of those.

The waiter saves me from answering by placing our food on the table. I unroll my paper napkin from around my silverware and pick up my fork, glancing at Cody to find him gazing at me. Without bothering to ask anything, I simply stare back at him.

"Man, Alexis, you were pretty in high school but you're a whole new level now." He offers one more lopsided smile before he picks up his own fork. "I'm thinking it's a good thing we didn't hook up back then. You're worth the wait."

Two hours of music so loud I could feel the beat pounding through my chest, not to mention standing on my feet in these new shoes, and I'm so finished. Cody doesn't even have to ask me twice if I'm ready to go. I was ready within two minutes of arriving in the place, when Cody excused himself to go to the restroom and a man with a skull tattoo across his neck decided it was appropriate to feel the sequins at the hem of my dress. It took a second of him rubbing his hand across my thigh for my brain to even register enough to push him back, and he simply laughed. Said something crude that I didn't repeat to Cody, and I won't detail for anyone else.

There was no mistaking the fact that I was overdressed, and I'm not sure how Cody missed it.

Well, I take that back. There was one woman wearing a shimmery gold dress that had a neckline that plunged to her belly button and a slit that reached clear up her thigh to where her underwear should have been, had she been wearing any. But I don't think she was there for the music. I'm pretty sure she was looking for customers.

By the time we're safely tucked in Cody's SUV and heading back toward Wonder Lane, I'm emotionally and physically drained. My feet hurt, and the effort of trying not to stand on certain points of my feet caused my ankles and shins to hurt. Add to that the fact that my ears are ringing and the smell of smoke is wafting around me, and I feel pretty unattractive. So unattractive, in fact, that I made a point of pulling my lip gloss out and touching it to my lips again before we got back in the vehicle.

He doesn't talk for a couple minutes, but when he reaches over and takes my hand, it doesn't make my pulse race like it might have a couple hours before. That fact keeps me rather pensive, and although he brings up a couple light topics of conversation, I don't offer much more than simple answers the rest of the way to my house.

The SUV pulls up next to Jake's truck, and I automatically reach for the door handle.

"I guess that's her dad's truck?" Cody asks, pointing out his window.

"Yeah," I say, hesitating while I wait for him to say goodbye. Instead, he leans toward me, placing both his hands on my left arm.

"Listen, he's not going anywhere, right? You've got a captive babysitter, and you don't even have to pay the guy. Why don't we go back to my place?"

My heart sinks a little, because instantly I know the answer to the question I've had in my mind the last few years: What if it had been Cody instead of Jake? And the truth is, it would have been no different. Just messier.

"No thanks," I whisper, giving him a sad smile.

His eyebrows draw closer together, and he drags his finger down my arm, trying to cause a reaction. For the first time since I can remember, it's not working.

"It's inevitable," he adds in a husky voice. "Come on, Alexis. You know we've wanted to be together for a long time. Now's the chance, and there's no reason to wait."

Those words provide the motivation I need to pull against the door handle and step one of those heeled sandals out onto the pavement.

"That's the problem," I tell him, gently pulling my arm away. "Despite appearances, I'm still waiting for the guy. And you're not him." Sliding my other leg out, I stand on my aching feet and bend over so I can see him, where he's still leaning over toward the passenger side. "Good night, Cody."

The sound of the door closing behind me is a sweet release, and as I pause right there in front of his SUV in the driveway to slide my shoes off, I can't help but smile. The sound of his engine is like background music signaling that I'm finally moving on with my life.

The door to the house creaks as I push it open, but Jake and Bailey aren't anywhere to be seen. At eleven o'clock I expected that Bailey might have crashed, but I thought Jake would be watching TV. His shoes are next to the couch and his suit jacket is draped over the back, but the house is quiet. After depositing my purse on the kitchen counter and tossing those offending shoes on the floor, I creep down the hallway until I can peek in Bailey's room.

My hand moves over my heart as I take in the scene, Jake's back propped against the headboard with his arm around Bailey, his head resting on top of hers, his top button undone and his tie loosened. Her face is pressed against his chest, and I can hear the sound of her breathing. As I move closer, I expect to hear a similar sound from Jake, but I don't. Not a whisper of anything. Reaching out, I place my hand against his, feeling a familiar jolt run through my veins.

I pull my hand away, watching as his eyes flutter open. As he begins to register the scene in his mind, glancing up at me and then down at Bailey, my heart begins to beat erratically. It's Jake, isn't it? My heart's traded Cody for Jake? One obviously wrong guy for another?

"Hey," he says with a grin, gently extracting Bailey from his embrace and placing her pillow under her head. He draws the covers up over her shoulders, bending to place a kiss on her forehead. I take a couple steps back, unsure what to do with my new revelation. How can I want Jake, whose very presence every day is almost destined to make me abjectly miserable?

"Date didn't go so well?" he asks quietly, standing in front of me. His hair is slightly disheveled, and the sight of that on top of his askew tie and unbuttoned collar makes him look like one of the guys in those magazine perfume ads. The ones that invite you to mess them up a little.

"Why would you ask that?" The words come out too defensively, but he doesn't seem to care. His smile is easy, almost lazy. Unassuming, like he has no clue about the knots that are tying up my stomach at the moment.

"You have lip gloss on, so I'm guessing he didn't kiss you good night." He quickly shrugs and places his hands in his pockets. "Not that you have to do that on a date, at all. Sorry. It's none of my business."

I force my attention to Bailey so I don't have to answer immediately, putting a little distance between us. Since he just pointed out the lip gloss, I simply sweep my hand across her hair instead of kissing her cheek, whispering good night. Turning, I see him still standing there, hands in his pockets.

"No," I tell him. "No, it didn't go well. Sometimes the past should be left in the past."

"Good," he says, accompanied by a rush of breath. "I mean, not good that it didn't go well, but good that you aren't upset about it."

"Good," I repeat, moving in the direction of Bailey's bedroom door. "I want to say thank you, by the way. For watching Bailey, but not just that. Thanks for taking her out tonight. For making her feel like a princess. For bringing her flowers."

"It's not a problem," he whispers, glancing at her sleeping form.

"You're a good dad."

His eyes cloud up and he clears his throat, and I know I've said too much. *Just smile and leave the room, Alexis. Quick smile…take an exit.*

I start to walk past him, but stop short, raising to my toes to quickly kiss him on the cheek. He moves though, right as I'm leaning into him, and my lips land on the corner of his mouth. My eyes widen as I pull away, but the damage is done.

Why was I kissing him on the cheek in the first place? And of course he was going to look to see what I was doing! Any sane person would!

"Sorry," I mutter. "I'm sorry, Jake."

He nods in my direction before he turns to head down the hall. Doesn't even say a word, but walks to the living room to slide on his shoes, while I remain just a couple steps behind, mentally beating myself up and cringing over my stupidity. So much for being cool. Three minutes in his presence and I'm practically falling all over him.

When he grabs his suit jacket in his fist and looks at the floor, I fight the urge to apologize again. He didn't respond the first time, so I know he doesn't want to hear it. That doesn't stop the desperate wish that I could go back to the way things were a minute ago, though.

*So stupid.*

His eyes come up to meet mine, and I can't read his expression. He's not playing it off as a joke, which is what I'd normally imagine him doing. Instead, he takes a couple steps toward me, where I stand awkwardly by the wall, waiting for his reaction. He doesn't stop until he's close enough that I can't move without bumping him, and I train my eyes on his, still waiting.

The sensation of his suit jacket dropping onto my bare feet causes me to draw in a breath. He exhales against my cheek, his fingertips lightly touching my hair and then the top of my ear, skimming over my cheek.

"Jake," I whisper, and he shakes his head, his nose barely missing the tip of mine as he places a finger over my lips. Looking at him while he stands so close is too intense, so I close my eyes, leaning my head back just enough to feel the sensation of my hair touching the wall. His finger leaves my lips, and instead I feel his thumb tracing along the bottom of my jaw.

I was wrong to think I traded Cody for Jake. Cody didn't affect me this way, where I wanted to run but didn't want to miss a second of what might happen. But Cody had been a boy, and Jake is...

My eyes refocus on him as I think about his motive. Huge mistake, because I've never seen this amount of passion in his gaze. Maybe once or twice while we were arguing, but definitely not while standing this close.

"Jake," I try again, but this time he silences me with his lips, kissing the corner of my mouth like I'd accidentally done to him. When I gasp, he draws back only enough to move his kiss to my bottom lip, barely touching me before he backs away, glancing down to my hands.

He traces a line across the back of my hand before entwining his fingers with mine, raising our hands together to his chest. His eyes don't leave mine as he presses his lips to the tips of my fingers, afterwards settling them in front of his chest again as a pained expression crosses his face.

"Say the word, and I'll walk away," he breathes against my lips. When I don't make a move, he covers my mouth with his, slowly drawing me in, one hand holding tightly to mine while the other finds my waist and pulls me closer. Nothing within me resists as I bring my free hand up to wrap it around his arm, mesmerized by the tenderness of his kiss. It's everything I always imagined a first kiss should feel like. Tentative, but filled with longing. Absolutely unselfish, like he's inviting me to share with him rather than taking from me.

I unwrap my fingers from his and lift my arms to his shoulders, locking my hands behind his neck. He keeps his hand at my waist, but the other weaves into the back of my hair, pressing me closer. My back is still touching the wall, but rather than succumb to my attempts to pull him against me, Jake removes his hand from my hair and spreads it against the wall near my head, holding himself back.

Whatever story his body language tells, though, his kiss doesn't hold back. It grows deeper as the seconds pass, and I could be content standing here as long as my legs hold up beneath me, tired feet all but forgotten. He breaks the connection between us, drawing back and breathing heavily as he stares into my eyes.

It's not enough. I lean into him, almost desperate to taste his lips again. He indulges me for a few seconds, but then groans as he pushes me back.

"Alex."

I never thought I'd like the sound of that word, but hearing it from Jake's lips after he's kissed me makes it sound like a love song.

He traces the line of my jaw again and I don't move, instead searching his eyes, trying to see into their depths. The colors in them are fascinating, and I could study them for hours, if it weren't for the fact that he'd be studying me right back. Reading things inside that I didn't even know I'd written.

One more time he moves in and presses his lips to mine, only for a few seconds before slowly drawing back, stepping away from me and bending to retrieve his jacket. I can't make myself leave that spot by the wall, partly because I don't want to lose the feeling of what we just had, but also because I don't want him to say anything. Not that he got carried away, or that I kissed him first, or that it didn't mean anything and I should forget it. I don't want him to say anything, because I want to hold on to it just a little bit longer.

He steps across the room and puts his hand on the doorknob, and my eyes follow him, begging him to walk away. Willing him to open the door and step out into the night.

It almost happens. He twists the door knob and pulls it toward him, but as he's stepping onto the porch, his face turns back and he focuses his eyes on me. One last moment of connection, just a shared look.

"I'm not sorry," he says, pulling the door closed behind him.

# Chapter Twenty-Six

## Alexis

Maddie rises to her feet and stares out the window again, watching Josh throw a ball to Bailey in the yard. He's wearing a navy blue sweatshirt and a stocking cap that covers his forehead all the way to the top of his glasses, but I bundled Bailey into her coat like she's headed to the North Pole. No wonder she's having trouble catching.

"He'll make a great dad someday," Maddie states with a sigh, tracing a little heart on the window with her finger.

"Forget that," Annie tells her, retrieving her hot cocoa from the kitchen before plopping onto my couch. "Get in here and take your coat off. We've been waiting for you so we can get the dish on the date."

Maddie slides her coat off her arms, stepping away from the window to place it over the back of a kitchen chair. When she steps to the stove to ladle out some cocoa, Annie clears her throat.

"Come on, will you? Every time I say the word 'date' Alexis turns beet red. I'm dying to hear this."

"While we're waiting, why don't you regale us with details about your date with Denton last night?" Harley suggests, giving Annie a sly grin.

"What makes you think I went out with Denton last night?"

Harley simply raises her eyebrows, calling Annie out nonverbally.

"Ready," Maddie states, settling between Harley and myself on the couch. Annie's sitting across from us in a kitchen chair. I offered to take that place, but she insisted she would be fine.

"Okay, so I was with Denton last night," Annie admits, narrowing her eyes at Harley. "There's nothing to tell. He's nice. I like him."

"Boring," Maddie mutters, taking a sip of her cocoa.

Annie huffs and her arms fold across her chest, causing the curls atop her head to shake with the movement. "What do you want me to say? Sure, he's attractive on TV, but you should see him when he's at home trying to make sure there's not an animal in his crawlspace. Wearing his jeans that have paint on them from when he first moved into his place. Asking me to hold the flashlight, so of course I flick it off and he screams like a girl."

"Oh, Annie," Harley says with a laugh.

"But the best is on Sunday afternoons when he hasn't shaved in a couple days. He'll put on a flannel shirt, and then he looks like a real lumberjack. Of course when he kisses me it does scratch my face, but then it will be gone Monday because he has to be clean shaven for TV."

"Too much information," Harley states, placing her hands over her ears. "I do have to see Denton every day, remember?"

"And I see Ryan every day, Green Beans," Annie counters. "You two make me sick, but I don't plug my ears because of it. At least I have some common courtesy."

"This is quite entertaining," Maddie says, offering a shrug as she looks in my direction. "Alexis and I could watch this all day."

"Absolutely," I agree with a smile. It might have been best to stay quiet, because Annie turns her attention to me.

"So...give us some details. I can tell something happened last night. It's written all over your face."

A slight sense of dread comes over me as I glance back at the door. "Okay, but this stays between us, right?"

"Of course!" Annie states emphatically. "Girls of Wonder Lane information does not leave this room. Right?" She glances at Maddie, whose eyes widen in shock.

"Why are you looking at me? I'm virtually a steel trap."

"A steel trap," Harley repeats, giving me a small smile.

It doesn't make me feel much better about sharing any information, but I'm dying to tell someone.

"He kissed me."

Annie lets out a whistle while Maddie laughs, and I nervously grab a piece of my hair and begin twisting it around my finger.

"So the date went well, I take it?" Annie prods, a mischievous smile on her face.

"No…Jake kissed me."

Three mugs of cocoa make their way to the coffee table at the same time, the bottoms clinking against it like a choreographed movement.

"Hold the phone," Annie says, leaning forward. "When did this happen? I mean, it's pretty obvious you two have feelings for each other, but I thought you were dead set against being in a relationship with him."

"Obvious?" I ask, feeling heat creep into my face.

"Well, he watches every move you make, like he can't keep his eyes off you. You stare at him a lot, too, but you try to hide it so no one will notice."

"Just because he looks at me doesn't mean he has feelings for me."

"Did you go on the date at all?" Maddie wants to know, her back flush against the couch so I can see Harley too.

"Yes. Jake picked Bailey up before we left. He was wearing a suit and he brought her flowers."

"Wow," Harley states, wide-eyed. "I think I would have kissed him too."

"It wasn't like that," I add, growing more self-conscious. "Going out with Cody was just like being with some random guy that I didn't know, rather than someone I shared a deep history with. When he brought me home, he didn't want the date to be over, but I told him good night. And then when I came inside, Jake was there, where he'd fallen asleep next to Bailey."

"So did you two talk about this?" Annie places her elbows on her knees as she props her chin on her hand.

"Not really. It just happened, and then he left."

"Was it awkward?" Harley asks.

Awkward? I suppose *I* was awkward, but...

"It was perfect," I whisper. "About as close to perfect as possible, anyway."

"Wow."

The final word was said quietly enough that I have no idea who uttered it, but it doesn't matter. We sit in silence for a few seconds, and then the front door opens.

"Hey," Josh says, poking his head inside. "Jake's here so he's playing with Bailey. Mad, were you still riding over to Mom and Dad's with me?"

"Yeah." She rises from her seat and carries her mug to the sink. "Sorry I've got to run, ladies. You can give me the dirt later." She winks at me as she grabs her coat and steps toward the door.

"See you!" Josh calls as they exit, and I take my focus off him in time to see Harley standing up as well.

"Annie, don't we have something to do?" she asks, a hint of a smile touching her face.

"Huh? Oh! Yes, most definitely. Something to do." Annie stands up and carries her chair back to the kitchen. "I want more details at church tomorrow."

As they walk out the door, I'm left alone sitting on the couch, nervous energy filling every part of my body. Jake's outside with Bailey, and I have no idea what to do. What to say. How to feel.

My indecision doesn't last long, though, before Bailey bursts through the door.

"That's that!" she announces, heading straight down the hall to her bedroom. Jake enters the house a few seconds later with a smile on his face.

"The ball landed in the mud," he explains, crossing to the sink where he turns on the faucet. I could sit here and wait for him to turn around, but instead I follow Bailey down the hall, making a pretense of taking off her coat. She throws it on the floor nearly every time we walk through the front door, so I'm quite sure she can take it off by herself.

"Hey," I say when I see her sitting on her bed and pulling off her shoes. "Did you have fun?"

"Yep. Josh wants to see me tonight."

"Oh?" I bite my lip to keep from laughing. "What makes you think that?"

"'Cause he told me. I can play with him and Mad."

She jumps up from the bed and heads toward the living room again, so I remain in her room a minute and try to collect my thoughts. It's so much easier to decide to put one foot in front of the other when I feel like I have some sort of control over my destination.

"There you are," Jake says, drawing my attention to the door. "Can we talk for a minute?"

The same thoughts that flooded my mind last night take residence again. *Mistake. Spur of the moment. Forget about it.* But he takes my hand in his, thumb slowly drifting across my knuckles one by one, and my mind goes completely blank.

"I have a problem." He tilts my chin up, forcing me to look into his eyes. "I keep thinking about the way you looked last night, and it's bothering me."

There it is. He's going to tell me I've done something wrong.

"Why?" I manage to ask.

The corner of his mouth tilts up just enough to force his dimple into existence. "Because I know it was for Cody, and I wish it was for me." He wraps our free hands together, holding both of my hands in front of him as he continues to gaze at me. "You deserve to be with someone who knows how incredible you are. Someone who has no other motive than simply being with you." His grip on my hands tightens. "Let me take you out tonight. Josh and Maddie offered to watch Bailey."

"You want to take me out."

He gives a nearly irresistible sheepish grin while he nods his head. "I know it's a few years too late, but... Alexis Jennings, please date me."

A small laugh escapes before I can manage my answer. "Are you going to wear a suit?"

He releases my hands and pulls me into his arms, my cheek resting against his maroon shirt. I bring my finger up to trace the pattern that's on the shirt, one line after another.

"If I do, will you wear a dress?"

"Maybe."

One quick kiss on my forehead and he releases me, backing away. He makes it all the way to the door before he turns back with a slightly perplexed look on his face.

"You did say yes, right?"

I can't fight the smile that crosses my face.

"Yes."

"Daddy, there's a flower in my pocket. It's for you." Bailey steps into my view just past the doorway and extends her hand to Jake, holding out what appears to be a weed. He scoops her up into his arms, giving her a big kiss on the cheek, complete with a smacking sound.

"Thanks, kiddo. I have to run, but I'll see you in a bit, okay?" He deposits Bailey on the floor, and then looks at me again. "Six o'clock?"

I nod, but as I watch him walk away, something inside me begins to sound an alarm. Jake's not the kind of guy I'm looking for, and even though it's hard to deny that I feel something for him, it's beginning to resemble playing with fire.

Two weeks ago I couldn't imagine myself going on a date, and now I'm preparing for the second in two nights. Almost like

Heather, juggling boys until she finds one that might make it a couple weeks. My eyes drift to Bailey, where she sits on my bedroom floor, pulling a new dress onto her Barbie. As I glance down at my own dress, I close my eyes and say a quick prayer that I'm not making a huge mistake. Bailey and I went shopping after Jake left, and I located this light gray sheath dress with an embroidered lace overlay and a pleated hem at the bottom that ties it all together. I still feel guilty for buying it. It's not like Bailey and I are destitute, but I am trying to keep our heads above water, and there's always that nagging thought at the back of my mind that my car could be headed for the graveyard at any given moment.

Watching Bailey push against the Velcro on Barbie's dress, I grab my cell phone and head into the hall, dialing as I walk.

The ringing stops, and I hear the click before I hear a voice. "Sadie's House of Ill Repute. Lorna Jean speaking."

Even though I fight the urge to roll my eyes, I can't help but grin.

"Very funny, Heather. Where's Sadie?"

"She had to run to town with Brent, so Jonah and I are hanging out. She forgot her phone. You want me to have her call you?"

I lean against the wall in the hallway, breathing out a sigh. "No, I'll be gone by then."

"Well, whatcha want? Maybe I can assist you."

Heaven help us all if I actually could be assisted by Heather. "I need help."

"Should I call 9-1-1?"

"No, not that kind of help. Advice."

"Oh, I am a wealth of that, sis."

I shake my head and focus my gaze on the ceiling. "Promise not to yell at me."

"This is gonna be good."

"Promise," I repeat.

"Okay, okay. Promise. Why do I want to yell at you?"

I wrinkle my forehead and grit my teeth, preparing for the onslaught of swearing. "I went out with Cody Hewitt last night."

Silence.

"Did you hear me, Heather?"

"Yes, but I made a promise." She pauses, but before I can get a word in, she begins again. "I got nothin', Alex. That's pretty dumb. I never figured you to do something so stupid."

"I know, I know. It was totally stupid. But I have now solidified the fact in my mind that Cody's not right for me."

"Hallelujah." I hear a heavy breath make its way into the phone. "You ain't regretting something you did last night, I hope?"

"Heather!"

"Sorry," she blurts. "You're the one asking for advice here. So if you figured out he's a bum, what's the problem?"

I march a few paces down the hall, farther away from Bailey. "The problem is, when I got home last night, Jake kissed me."

"Now you're talking!" she states, a bit of excitement in her voice. "I can totally get behind this."

"We're going out tonight."

"Sweet sister Susie, I'm totally jealous of you."

"Am I making a huge mistake?"

The question hangs between us, like it got tangled up in cell phone air space somewhere, smashed between a cloud and a satellite radio signal.

"The totally hot father of your kid wants to date you. Kind of seems like a no-brainer."

"Is it?" I mumble, right before a knock sounds on the door. "I think he's here."

"Go get your man," Heather orders, hanging up the phone.

Bailey darts toward the door while I head to the bedroom to get my shoes. I've just emerged from the closet when I hear Bailey yell that Jake's taking her next door. Normally I'd insist on telling her goodbye and taking her there myself, but I'm actually relieved for an extra moment to get myself together.

Once I have my shoes on, I glance in the mirror, relieved that I look a little more like myself this time around. A dressed up version of myself, but still Alexis.

Grabbing the phone again, I can't resist texting Heather. *Guess it's not Boringland around here today.*

She answers almost immediately. *Boringland? Alex, your life is far from boring. Have fun for me!*

This time when the knock sounds on the door, I actually think I'm ready. Stepping across the living room, I open it with a smile, not dreading it like last night. He's standing there in his suit, looking absolutely perfect with the exception of that silly tie, which has to be a full inch off-center.

"You seem to have a tie problem," I tell him as I reach up to fix it for the second time in as many days.

"Do I? Or did I just like you fixing it so much yesterday that I messed it up again on purpose?" He grins as he pulls a bouquet of flowers from behind his back. Gorgeous lilacs spill from the sides of the vase, with white roses tucked into the center.

"Jake!" I place my hand over my mouth, but quickly pull it away so I can take the flowers from his hand. "You didn't have to do that." I step back, wrapping both my hands around the vase. "Are you coming in?"

"I'll wait right here."

It doesn't take me long to situate the flowers in the kitchen next to Bailey's, and then I return to my date, closing the door behind me. He holds out his arm, and I can't help but think that this must be odd for him. Jake has never struck me as the traditional, romantic type.

"Where are we going?" I ask, tucking my hand inside the crook of his arm. He simply smiles.

Dinner at a quiet restaurant with real tablecloths, a walk by the river so we can look at the reflection of building lights against the night sky floating in the water, and eventually Jake and I find ourselves at one of Harley and Ryan's favorite haunts, a little restaurant named Tiny's. We order blackberry cobbler from the very large, sweet gentleman with the shaved head who owns the place, and then we settle in at a corner table.

"What's your absolute favorite food?" Jake asks, placing his hand over mine on the table.

That question doesn't take much thought. "My mom's spaghetti and meatballs. How about you?"

He pauses to look around like he's thinking it over. "Shrimp. My granny made it once when I lived with her, and there was just something about the way she did it. It was so good."

"How long were you with her?"

He turns my hand over and begins tracing his finger across the lines, like he's inspecting them, but I have a feeling he's just stalling.

"You don't have to talk about it," I add.

He glances up, meeting my eyes for only a second before he looks at my hand again. "About a year. Mom was there for maybe three months, and then she moved in with Randy. He took her to Florida, and that was that. I was with Granny until she got sick, and then Dad had to come get me. 'All the way to South Carolina, what a waste of gas.' I know he didn't mean it against me, but just the situation in general. She shouldn't have taken me there in the first place."

"And your grandmother?"

He shakes his head but doesn't shift his focus from my hand. "Died three weeks later. Mom didn't tell me until the next year."

"I'm sorry," I whisper. Tiny places the cobbler on the table, and I smile up at him only to get a nod in return. It's likely that he realizes we're deep in conversation.

"No," Jake says, folding his hand over mine once again and drawing his gaze up to focus on me. "Don't be sorry. I don't regret a single thing that happened in my life, because if one thing was different, I might not be here with you."

"Not one regret?" I sink my spoon into the cobbler, pausing with it on the edge of the bowl. "Not a single mistake you wish you could fix?"

He stares at me, and I know he's trying to read behind my eyes. Whether he can do it or not is still a bit of a mystery, but a sad smile crosses his face, almost like he knows I would try to go back and fix my mistakes. Not to do so goes against my very nature.

"No," he finally says. "Some mistakes aren't nearly as important as we think they are, Alex."

Somehow the conversation turns back to the light topics of earlier in the date, and we finish our shared bowl of cobbler and head back to Jake's truck. He opens the door for me, and as soon as he's on the driver's side, he reaches over to take my hand again. It's been a constant the entire evening, the physical contact. The knots in my stomach have been fairly consistent, too, because my feelings for this man are pretty overwhelming. That might not be a bad thing, if I thought we had a future together. I'm still not sure it's possible.

He makes me forget when he looks over at me, though, with the complete openness of his expression. The smile tugging at his lips. My knowledge that he's gone above and beyond in his effort to show me how important I am to him tonight.

By the time we pull onto Wonder Lane, I'm almost sad. We'll take Bailey home, and then Jake will leave, and it's going to be hours before I see him again. It's an unhealthy attachment I'm forming in my heart.

"Thank you for tonight," I tell him as he turns off the truck's engine.

"No, let me help you get Bailey before you tell me good night. Please?"

I can't deny him that, and he walks next door and knocks, waiting until Josh appears at the door, a sleeping Bailey in his arms. He hands her over to Jake, who crosses the space between our houses while I hold the door open. Instead of following him back to the bedroom, I wait by the front door, not wanting to intrude on his time with her. It will be easy enough for me to check in on her when he leaves.

He reappears from the hallway, sniffing a little. "Man, that kid tugs on my heart," he says, reaching up to rub his nose. "This is always the worst part of my day."

"Why is that?"

He stops in front of me, wrapping his arms around my waist. "I hate leaving this house. My girls. I'm pretty sure part of me stays behind until I come back the next day."

"Are we your girls?" I ask with a smile.

He removes his hand from my waist to brush my hair back from my cheek, and then he simply shrugs. "God willing. I know I ask Him every day."

I wrap my arms around him, feeling the curves of his back beneath his dress shirt. He leans in just enough to brush my lips with his, similar to last night, as though he's trying us out to see if we fit. It's not enough. A little of Jake is never enough. Instead of waiting, I kiss him the way I want Jake to kiss me. The same sort of kiss I would have expected Jake to offer—bold, passionate, fiery, and aggressive.

He responds for a minute, but then pulls back, dragging his mouth away and taking in a shuddering breath. The break of the bond between us almost makes me gasp. "Wait," he says, backing away a step.

My heart sinks, because while I'm certainly not adept at dating, that seemed like a pretty fantastic date to me. The best one I've ever been on. Naturally I can't help messing things up afterwards. "What's wrong?"

"Nothing." He backs a couple feet to the arm of the couch, taking a seat on it as he holds my hands. "Before this goes any farther, I need to make sure we're on the same page."

The impact of his words makes me want to sit down, but I remain where I am, unmoving.

"Any farther?"

"Where do you see this going?" He pulls one of his hands from mine and runs it through his hair, causing almost an exact repeat of his disheveled state from last night. "You're not really someone I can date without consequences, you know. It feels like it has to be serious or nothing."

"And serious isn't your normal course of action," I conclude, feeling the dejection wash over me.

He squints his eyes a bit, like I just hit him with a left hook. It wasn't my intention. Just stating the facts.

"Not in the past, which is why I have to square it up with you. This is serious to me."

"It's serious to me too," I answer defensively. "Everything is because of Bailey."

He reaches up to jerk his tie loose, like it's suddenly suffocating him. "Then fast forward a year from now. Do you see us together?"

Sliding my hand out of his, I step past him and sit on the couch, where I begin nervously toying with the stitching at the hem of my dress. "You want me to predict the future?"

He sighs as he drops onto the couch cushion from the arm, slouching next to me with our arms touching. He doesn't reach for my hand this time, and that realization makes my heart hurt even more. "Knowing your own heart and mind has nothing to do with predicting the future." He leans his head back against the cushion, staring straight ahead at the black TV screen. "Just be honest with me. That's all I'm asking."

I draw the corner of my bottom lip between my teeth, wondering just how honest I can be. Whatever I say, the easy mood from before has disappeared, gone without a trace.

"I haven't changed, Jake. Not really. All my life I've been waiting, with one single exception, and I haven't lost belief that there's someone waiting for me too. It probably sounds naïve and childish to you, but I want to be someone's first and last. The only one."

"And you can't have that with me," he finishes. "That's what you're saying."

"Jake—"

"That's your deal breaker?"

293

What am I supposed to say? No? I'm willing to give it all up simply for a slight chance?

"Shouldn't it be?" I answer quietly.

"You know what? It's not your fault. I convinced myself that you might want..." He clears his throat and stands up. "It doesn't matter. You were honest, and that's what I asked for. Thank you."

"Please," I whisper as he moves past me.

"Good night."

There's no need to turn around to see that he's gone. When I hear the door close, I know. Dropping my head into my hands, I let a tear slide down my cheek and drip onto my knee, my fears about a relationship with Jake feeling like they played out before my eyes. How will I face him tomorrow when he wants to see Bailey? Will he even come over, after what I said?

Pushing myself up from the couch, I cross into the kitchen and touch my fingertips to the lilacs, inhaling their delicate scent. Bailey. I need to see Bailey.

She's breathing heavily when I step into the room, covers pulled up to her chin and Hoppy cradled in her arm. Jake must have done that. Fresh tears build up in my eyes at that thought, and I place my hand on her rib cage, following the gentle rise and fall as she breathes. I'll never get tired of watching the simple act of her breathing. Bending, I place a kiss on her forehead, careful not to wake her. The last thing I need is to startle her awake to the sight of me crying.

I should go straight into my bedroom, change into some pajamas, and crawl into bed. My body doesn't want to cooperate, though. It wants to reinforce the idea that Jake is gone. The fact that I ran him away. My legs carry me back to the living room, to the window at the front of the house, and my hand reaches up to lift the blinds ever so slightly, just so I can peek out. When my eyes focus on the red pickup still sitting in my driveway, everything freezes.

The sudden knock on the door startles me enough that I almost scream as I drop the blinds, but instead I just remain there a couple seconds, willing my heart rate to return to normal. Hastily brushing at my cheeks to remove any stray tears that might have left their evidence, I turn to the door and pull it open ever so slightly. The sight of Jake just beyond the door with his hands in his pockets and his eyes rimmed with red causes me to open it wider, leaning against it as I wait.

"You're wrong," he says. "I know I should just leave it alone, but I can't, because you have it all wrong."

My heart threatens to break into a thousand pieces at the realization that he cares enough to fight tears over me. Over us.

"How?" It's all I can choke out before emotion steals my voice.

"You say that you want to be someone's first, and I know you look at me and that's probably a big joke," he begins, rubbing his nose while he sniffs. "You are the first, don't you see that? Last night, when we kissed, that was the first time I've ever kissed someone I love. Tonight was my first date with a woman I love. First shared blackberry cobbler. First time I've handed the love of my life flowers. The first time I've looked into someone's eyes and seen myself being content even one year from now, let alone five or ten years. But I see that with you. Decades of firsts, and every one of my lasts."

The dress is wrapped so tightly around me, it's cutting off my lung capacity. Or maybe it's just my emotion. I drag in a painful breath, watching him pace the porch.

"And all I want is this," he continues, gesturing at the house. "Every time I leave at night I lose precious time that I could be spending with my family, because that's how I see you. So if I don't fit into your plans, it's not because you wouldn't be first with me. You're already first, you and Bailey, and you always will be, no matter who shares your life with you."

I know I should say something, but I can't. The words are stuck in my chest, burning with a slow ache.

"I gotta go." He shakes his head as he turns to walk away, squinting his eyes closed like he's mentally reprimanding himself, but he doesn't dawdle as he walks to his truck. The second he's inside, the engine comes to life and he backs out of the driveway, headed into the night.

I close the door behind me, locking the deadbolt and then the lock Jake put at the top of the door to protect Bailey. My fingers linger on it for a second, and then I slide to the floor, letting my tears pour out over another failed second chance.

# Chapter Twenty-Seven

## Alexis

The alarm clock on my nightstand tells me it's four a.m., but it's really irrelevant. After being up all night, the actual time doesn't matter. I've cried and prayed and cried and prayed, and I know what my heart wants, but I can't find peace about anything. Haven't for so long, I can't remember what it feels like.

Taking my cell phone from its resting place next to the bed, I bring the screen to life, where it confirms to me once again that it's no time to be contemplating life decisions. Jake still hasn't called. Not that I expected him to, but part of me keeps hoping.

I touch the contact number before I even think, almost panicking when I hear the phone ringing. *Hang up*, my brain orders, but at the same time it pleads not to do that. If I wake him, he'll think something's wrong.

"Hello?" the voice sounds on the other end of the phone, gravelly and half-asleep. "Alexis? What happened?"

"Nothing, Dad," I say, fighting tears. "I just…need you."

"Is it Bailey? What's wrong? Let me get the car and I'll be there as soon as I can."

"No." I sit up in bed, clutching a fistful of blankets in my left hand. "Nothing's wrong. I shouldn't have startled you. I wasn't thinking."

"What's wrong?" Mom asks in the background.

"Nothing, just go back to bed," he tells her. The sound of him groaning alerts me that he's up, moving about the house. Probably in the hopes that Mom can go back to sleep, even though

I'm sure she's wide awake. "Now, tell me what's going on, sweetheart."

A fresh round of tears pricks at my eyes, and it almost makes me angry. My chest already feels as though I've had a weeklong racking cough.

"It's Jake," I manage to tell him. "He took me on a date tonight."

"Oh?"

It occurs to me that it might be strange to talk to my dad about my love life, but it's too late.

"He says he loves me."

There's hesitation on the other side of the phone, and I wonder if I've shocked him.

"And what about you? Do you love him?"

Even the question makes my chest ache like it's anticipating more tears.

"I do. I love Jake."

*How could I not see it before?*

"That's fantastic, honey. Of course we like Jake, and we want you to be happy."

"And I want to be happy, but every time I think about moving on with a new life, I can't get past it. Everything that happened. The things you went through because of me."

*The stupid mistakes I made, and the fact that I might want something totally different now. Isn't that a cop out? Alexis messed her life up, so she has to change all her dreams?*

"No," he states forcefully. "Don't you dare make the same mistakes I made, do you hear me?"

"What?" I whisper, staring at the window and the tiny sliver of light coming through the blinds. A streetlight, not the break of day.

"I had to leave the place I was called to be because I couldn't forgive, honey. That's a miserable place to find yourself."

I shake my head, knowing that he's wrong. They were at fault. I heard them with my own ears.

"They did horrible things, Dad."

"We all do, but it wasn't them I couldn't forgive."

Rising from bed, I wander back to the kitchen, letting my eyes linger on the flowers Jake brought, both mine and Bailey's.

"I don't understand."

His sigh is loud enough to make me stand perfectly still. "The anger I felt was very vivid, sweetheart. In the end, most of them apologized to me and I forgave them, but I couldn't seem to forget about the venom I'd held inside my heart. It plagued me. Enough so that I couldn't be their pastor, because I felt like a failure."

That admission causes even more pain in my chest, so I press my palm to my heart. "I didn't know."

"I didn't want you to. Didn't want anyone to, but I see you walking down the same path. You've always been such a good girl, Alexis, that you take any deviation personally. But some mistakes aren't as important as we make them."

My fingertip grazes the petals of one of the white roses. "Jake said almost that same thing at dinner."

"Maybe Jake was supposed to be in your life. Beauty from ashes, if you accept the grace given and extend a little to yourself."

"Yeah?" I whisper, taking in his words.

"That's the trouble with trying to be perfect. The closer we think we're coming to it, the harder we're going to crash when we don't measure up. And we can't, no matter how hard we try." He pauses for a minute, and I walk back to the blinds at the front of the house, peeking into the darkness, wishing the red truck would reappear in the driveway. "The drive to do the right thing is good, but it can't save you. Only grace can do that, but you have to let it in."

"I know." A small smile crosses my lips—the first in hours. "Thank you, Dad."

"I love you, sweetheart."

An even bigger smile breaks onto my face, light as the laugh bubbling up from deep within.

"I love you, too. Better go back to bed and tell Mom we're fine."

"Good night."

Dad's words follow me back down the hall and into the bathroom, where I pause at the sink to splash water on my face. My eyes rise to the mirror, watching the water drip from my chin. The right side of the mirror. I've been there all along, but I was too jaded by my own conscience to be able to see it.

*Thank you for my blessed life, and I'm sorry. Sorry for thinking I could somehow earn favor. For taking Your gift for granted. I won't anymore, not a second of it.*

I almost convince myself to return to my bed and try to sleep, but I can't quite commit. Adrenaline is coursing through my veins, because suddenly everything makes sense...the reason I took this job, that Jake decided to follow us, that I rented the house on Wonder Lane. It's all mapped out before me like a beautiful portrait that I couldn't see, all because I'd made myself small enough to be stuck inside it like a maze.

Mirrors don't tell lies, but they can't see past the surface either. My mascara is smeared under my eye and across the top of my cheek, just like the red lipstick I tried to hide when I was still a girl. Nothing's changed except the knowledge that I'm loved despite my imperfections.

It's kind of like that lipstick itself, really. It has all the potential to be a complete mess if it isn't in capable hands, but in the right hands the red can be made truly beautiful.

# Chapter Twenty-Eight

## Jake

The road welcomed me until I nearly ran out of gas, even though I had no idea where I was headed. At first I traveled in the direction of the motel, only to arrive at the parking lot and turn around, determined to go back to Wonder Lane and plead my case again. By the time I'd returned, though, I convinced myself that it didn't matter. So I just drove, nowhere in particular, for hours.

Returning "home" wasn't much better, because I've not been able to relax at all. Instead I've been sitting here, still wearing every stitch of clothes I wore for the date, minus my jacket. And it's no good. If I can't get it together in a few hours, I'm going to have a hard time showing up for Bailey, sitting next to Alexis in church.

The most pressing thought that keeps thundering through my brain is that this changes nothing. So Alexis doesn't want me. Yeah, it stings way more than I thought it would, but it's not going to alter the way I feel. It doesn't mean I'm any less Bailey's dad now than I was a few hours ago, so I have to pretend like nothing happened. Like I'm fine being a part-time family member.

My brain won't calm down because I have no idea if I can put on that sort of show.

I can't seem to stop my hand from shaking as I rub it across my cheek, feeling the roughness that alerts me that I'm due for a shave. I'll need a lot more than that before I go out in public. Some kind of eye drops to combat the redness. A couple pots of coffee. Maybe something to fight deliria. I'd almost swear I just heard Alexis say my name.

A soft knock sounds in the room, followed by the sound again. Just my name, spoken gently. Picking up my phone, I bring the screen to life, seeing that it's five o'clock in the morning. No wonder I'm imagining things. I'm probably exhausted.

That thought doesn't keep me from rising out of the chair across from the bed. Not even from crossing to the door, and although I shake my head as I release the locks, it doesn't stop me from opening it and peering out into the night. Finding my eyes on a white Mitsubishi.

"Where's Bailey?"

Sure, it's rude, but it's the only thing the surprise and panic in my brain can come up with.

"She's sleeping in her car seat," Alexis says, glancing back at the car. "I needed to see you, and it couldn't wait."

A breath of relief escapes as I press the palm of my hand to my temple. The woman has no idea how she affects me, even now, her face free from makeup and wearing her pajamas. They're at least two sizes too big, hanging from her frame. I'd like nothing more than to scoop her up in my arms and kiss her.

*Get it under control.*

"It's pretty early," I tell her, leaning against the door frame.

She nods, looking almost apologetic. "I couldn't sleep. You're still wearing your tie."

Even though I know she's right, I still look down out of instinct, as though I need proof.

"Couldn't sleep," I say simply.

That seems to loosen her up, and she takes a step in my direction, wrapping her arms around her midsection.

"You're cold. Do you want to come in?"

She glances back at the car. "No, I don't want to bother Bailey."

Retreating into the room, I reach for my suit jacket, wincing when the door closes behind me. As I pull it back open, she's standing stone-still in front of me, eyes wide. That's enough to make me smile as I wrap the jacket around her shoulders. She blinks up at me through those long eyelashes, and it nearly undoes me.

"Listen, forget about all that earlier," I say, straightening the jacket around her neck. "It's unfair of me to try to give you an ultimatum. It's not like I can't control myself, because I can. And I don't need to rush anything or push you. There's no reason to put a label on us, because the fact is, this is whatever you want it to be."

She grabs the side of my jacket, holding it closer. "You promise? Whatever I want?"

My heart wants to protest, but I know I can't. A sigh slips out before I can say yes, but I nod my head anyway.

She moves closer and presses her hand to my chest, on top of my crooked tie and directly over my heart. "I want you."

The deliria again. No other explanation.

"Come again," I manage to mutter.

"It's so simple I couldn't see it, but it's been in front of my face the whole time." She smiles that irresistible smile she possesses, and I can't help but reach up and wrap my hand around hers on my chest. "I'm so glad you followed us to Louisville. You've become the most important part of our lives."

"Really?"

"Really. Do you remember earlier when we were talking about things we regret?"

"Of course I do."

"I've been thinking about that all night. I had a ton of regrets, you know. So many different things that I couldn't seem to forget, but now I only have one big one. Well, two, actually."

My eyes dart to Bailey in the back seat of the car, her head tilted to the side as she sleeps. Who'd have ever thought the mere sight of my daughter could make me forget everything else I worried about before?

"Do I want to know your regrets?" I ask with a bit of hesitance.

"Yes," she tells me with a smile. "My number one regret is that I didn't realize I loved you until tonight. I could have been kissing you for weeks."

It's impossible not to laugh when I let that one sink in. My fingers tighten around her hand at my chest, but I don't say anything, just letting her words sound in my mind a few times. *Didn't realize I loved you...*

"The second thing," she continues, "is that I want Bailey to have your name. She's your daughter, and I want everyone to know she belongs to you."

"My name?" I whisper.

"And maybe someday I can convince you to give me your name, too. I already belong to you, Jake." Pulling my hand back, she presses our fingers to her heart instead of mine. "You wanted to know if I could see you in my future. The answer is, I don't see a future without you."

There's nothing else I need to hear. I lean forward to kiss her, tasting a hint of peppermint lip balm as I draw her to me. She melts into my arms, and I can't help but smile against her mouth as I hold her, just as I'd imagined doing earlier. Instead of protesting, she throws her arms around my neck and kisses me again. The peppermint takes on a salty taste, and I pull back, noticing the tears sliding down her face.

"What's wrong?" Using my knuckles, I brush a tear from her cheek.

"I can't seem to stop crying tonight," she tells me, sliding her head down to my shoulder. "Just a side effect of loving you, I guess."

That's enough to render me speechless for a minute, so I simply hold her, careful not to release her from my arms. She doesn't seem eager to leave either, snuggling against my chest.

"I hope the crying is short-lived," I finally say. "I'd rather you smile when you think of me."

"I already do."

"And I should probably stop calling you Alex. I know it drives you crazy."

"No." She pulls back, staring up at me. "Please don't stop calling me Alex. It sounds beautiful to me now."

"Beautiful," I repeat, studying her eyes. Fascinating, the way they don't hold anything back. The way they tell me everything I want to know. "I love you."

She laughs, hugging me tightly once more. "I love you back. I can't even imagine what my life would look like right now if I hadn't been that stupid girl chasing the wrong guy. Finding the right guy in the process."

"The right guy," I repeat, resting my chin against the top of her head. "I like the sound of that."

"The only guy," she clarifies. "Thinking God wasn't answering my prayers, when He was really telling me I had it all wrong. What if I had met you back then?"

That question sinks deep as I shake my head. "You'd have met a messed up kid who wouldn't have realized how much he'd one day love you."

She steps back and smiles. "I should probably take Bailey back home. Definitely not a mom of the year moment, but I don't think she would mind me making sure you don't miss any more time with her."

"Or time with you," I add, returning her grin. "Just let me get my keys." Her eyes widen in surprise, and I quickly hold up my hands. "To follow you home, that's all. Make sure you get home okay. You are my girls, remember?"

She pulls open the door to her Mitsubishi. "Of course I remember. I'll never forget."

# Chapter Twenty-Nine

## Alexis

It's a funny thing, starting over. Forging a new identity. Embarking on a new adventure. It's what I expected all along, from the moment I accepted the job in Louisville. When I first toured the little house on Wonder Lane. When I considered stepping out on my own for the first time.

My eyes drift to the rearview mirror, spying Bailey sleeping in the back seat. The same as the day we first pulled onto Wonder Lane, and if I thought she filled my heart then, that feeling's even deeper now.

I can't help but smile when I think about that day last fall, every part of my heart filled with dread, simply because that red pickup truck was behind me. Simply because my past was following me out of town.

It's the same view this morning, with the night trying to fade into the day, that red pickup still in my rearview. Curiouser and more perfect than I ever could have imagined.

My future, following me home.

# Epilogue

Annie straightens the tulle at the end of one of the folding chairs on the lawn, peering ahead at the large oak tree. The whole thing is simple. Simple enough that her parents would probably balk at the presentation, but it's what the bride wanted.

"What do you think, wedding planner?" She turns and locks eyes with Maddie, who places one hand on her hip.

"Seriously, stop calling me that." Maddie straightens her violet dress and glances around at the few people milling about the yard. "I don't want to take any responsibility if this whole thing falls apart, especially since they didn't want a rehearsal last night. Who does that? But I suppose it's just as well, since Harley and Ryan have vanished into thin air."

Annie drops her arm casually over Maddie's shoulders, the long side of her asymmetrical haircut hitting Maddie on the right arm. "They'll be here, okay? Don't worry so much."

Maddie sighs and glances at her friend, giving a half-hearted smile. "I like your hair like that. It suits you."

"Thanks, me too," Annie says, moving to adjust the tulle on another chair. "So does Denton, which is an added bonus. Where did Josh run off to?"

"You're kidding, right?" Maddie's eyes drift to the house, where more people are moving in and out. "He's inside resigning himself to being the third string best man."

Annie simply laughs and heads in the direction of the house, with Maddie following on her heels. The crowd on Wonder Lane certainly isn't large. Some people from church and a few family members, but nothing like the crowd her parents would invite if she ever got married.

As they reach the front porch, they're almost bowled over by the young woman charging outside, who quickly straightens when she sees them, one hand clenching the top of her light blue dress.

"Hey! One of you gals have a safety pin? Wouldn't want to go busting out of my dress, and I seem to have a strap problem."

Maddie lifts her eyebrows at Annie, who gives a simple "yes" and heads inside and up the stairs. Heather turns and marches back inside and into the dining room, where Alexis is standing along the wall as she places a jeweled headband on Bailey's head. Maddie follows, her eyes darting between the two sisters, who definitely look like they're related. Heather's hair is falling over her shoulder in curls, while Alexis has her hair in an updo.

"Mad!" Bailey announces, turning to look at the newcomer. "Am I pretty?"

"Do you even have to ask?"

"She does," Heather states. "She asks every single person who comes into the room, because she's trying to hog all the attention." Heather winks at her niece, who sticks out her tongue in response. "Holy whiskers, you're just like your mother. Cheeky little thing."

Bailey retreats to her grandmother, reaching up to take her hand.

"If she's hogging attention, she's taking after you," Alexis adds, smiling at her sister. "Do I look okay?"

"Way better than okay," Heather tells her, taking her hand.

"Safety pin!" Annie announces, stepping into the room. Heather pulls her hand back and allows Annie to grab the top of her dress.

"Let the record state that I was about to get all sentimental and mushy and stuff, but your handsy friend is being borderline inappropriate with me so it'll have to wait."

"Careful, or I'll stab you," Annie warns, mischievously smiling to herself.

"When Sadie Lou gets back from getting Jonah his potato chips she'll cry all over you, I'm sure," Heather adds. "I'll wait to do my crying until after I see if Jake has any good looking friends."

"For goodness sake, Heather," Bailey's grandmother says, lifting the girl to her arms.

"Oh, Mom. You know I'm only kidding. I've already staked the place for good looking friends, but they're all taken. You don't see me crying, do ya?" She cranes her neck a little to peek out the window. "Never mind, who's the motorcycle guy? I haven't seen him yet."

"Taken," Annie states, seemingly deriving a bit of cheer from Heather's misfortune.

"Sorry!" Harley yells as she steps through the doorway. "Got held up at the airport." She barely pauses as she begins a sprint up the stairs.

Ryan comes in right behind her, placing his helmet by the door before running his hand through his hair. "Annie, you care if I wash my hair in the sink?"

"Yes I care! That's disgusting and there's food in there."

He cringes but then points upstairs, a small smile creeping onto his face. "I can just go up there. We're married."

Annie rolls her eyes as he begins to march up the stairs. "Stay out of my bedroom, and hurry up would you!" She drops her head into her hands as she groans. "I'm going to have to move out. I can't take the two of them."

"What was that about?" Maddie asks, eyes wide as she stares at Annie.

"Ryan and Harley went to Vegas to get married. I was sworn to secrecy. If they would have come back when they were supposed to, no one would have even known they were gone."

"I can't believe it." Maddie settles herself into a chair. "It's like this whole neighborhood has gone totally nutty. You got any other surprises up your sleeve, girls?"

Annie glances at Alexis, but the two of them just laugh as Bailey's grandma places her on the ground, where she spins to make her dress float out around her.

"Looks like the right place," Cole says, opening the door of the rental car.

Camdyn smiles at him over the roof after she steps out onto the pavement. "It looks a lot like Rosalie's house. Different vibe being at the end of the subdivision instead of nestled along the river, but I like it." She stands perfectly still, staring at the home in front of her, lost in thought until Cole steps up to place an arm around her.

"Hmm, it might take a lot of convincing."

She glances over at her husband, raising her eyebrows. "What exactly are you talking about?"

"I'm sure this would be a great setting to write, and since you're not far from Sybil Brantley and all your old family records…"

"Because I randomly crash houses of people I don't know so I can use them to write my books? Be reasonable." She pauses to give him a sheepish grin. "Rosalie's place doesn't count. She runs a B&B, so she welcomes strangers into her home. Besides, when do I have time to write? I'm always following you around making sure you don't need pointers on your batting stance."

"Oh, please."

"Don't you think you'd better find Jake? We're pretty late, after all. I can go inside and try to find him if you like."

"Absolutely relentless," he says with a laugh, kissing her cheek. "Go ahead inside and snoop, if you're so determined. I'll just wait out here."

She blows him a kiss as she glances back, tossing her blonde curls over her shoulder before she begins up the steps, admiring the Corinthian columns on the porch. She stands before the double doors for a moment, letting her eyes sweep over the house before she knocks and pushes the right door open.

Nothing antique rests inside, which immediately gives her a sense of disappointment. With the commotion of people moving every which way, though, it's short-lived. Immediately to her left is the dining room, where she spies the woman of the hour. Although they've only met once before, at the drug store on Christmas Eve, the sight of her makes Camdyn smile. Anyone who could make Jake settle down must be an incredible person, after all.

She steps up to the doorway, but doesn't say anything for a moment while she looks at Alexis. Camdyn recognizes the dress immediately. Vera Wang. It's one of the pictures her friend Lily has been showing her for the past month or so. *Textured organza with a draped bodice and split-front overlay,* Lily's words ring through her mind. *Don't you just love the rose detailing at the waist?*

"Hello," Camdyn states timidly, moving just inside the door. The large group of ladies is slightly intimidating, but she just has one question to ask and she can be on her way.

"Camdyn Taylor," squeaks the auburn-haired woman sitting in front of her, catching herself as she begins to slide backwards from her chair.

Maybe not as incognito as she'd hoped. Camdyn returns her focus back to Alexis with an apologetic smile. "I'm sorry for interrupting. Cole's looking for Jake."

"I'll take him!" The one who recognized her rises from her seat, shrugging her shoulders. "I mean, I need to look for Josh anyway, right?"

"Totally nutty," another woman with a dark, asymmetrical haircut whispers to Alexis, causing both of them to laugh.

The eager one steps up to Camdyn, smiling as she waits for her to exit the doorway, but Camdyn pauses, carefully studying her face. She squints just a bit, and then tilts her head with a curious gaze.

"We've met before…" Camdyn states, letting the end of the sentence trail up so it sounds more like a question, posed to convince the young woman to offer her name. Mission accomplished when her eyes light up.

"Maddie," she offers. "Yes, we have. Louisville, last October. I was at your conference. You wrote something in my book about Josh, only we weren't together yet. I was totally freaking out about it, but it's all good now because we're engaged."

She holds up her left hand, showcasing her ring as though that's going to jog Camdyn's memory.

Camdyn tries to stifle a laugh as she begins to remember their first meeting. "The girl with the mother."

"Yes, I have a mother!" Maddie exclaims. "I mean, of course I have a mother. I can't believe we're having this conversation again." She shrugs and takes another step into the hall. "Shall we find Cole? I feel like I know him, since you talked about him a lot that night at the conference."

"I do have a habit of talking about Cole," Camdyn states with a laugh, giving Alexis a parting wave. "And I think you talk a lot when you're nervous."

"So embarrassing," Maddie mutters as Camdyn follows her back out the front door.

Jake lets out a deep breath as he stares out the back window. They dusted the room the best they could, but the old glass still seems a little foggy. The bookcases lining each wall don't help the room seem brighter, either. Someday Harley might want him to help remodel this room too, but a library probably doesn't sit at the top of the to-do list.

"Hanging in there?"

He turns at the voice to see his future father-in-law standing at the doorway in a suit and tie.

"Absolutely. I'm a little more worried about you. Haven't tried to shove your family in the car and take them back to Jackson yet, have you?"

Jake takes a couple steps toward Nick, who reaches out to pat him on the back. "No, as tempting as it is, I can't make the math work."

"Please, not math," Jake says, shaking his head. "I get enough of that from Alexis."

"It's simple math," Nick insists, holding his hand up. "Five seats in the car. Two for myself and Crystal." He folds down his pinky and thumb. "One seat for Heather. That makes three." His ring finger goes down, leaving only two. "Of course I'd take Bailey. You understand."

"Sure," Jake mutters with a smile.

"So it leaves just one seat for my daughter *and* my son. That's not good math."

Jake doesn't know what to say to that, so he's relieved when the man pats him on the shoulder again and turns to head toward the door.

"Hey, Nick, have you seen my dad?"

Nick turns and pushes his glasses up on his nose. "Yeah, he's outside talking to your friend Duke. Fascinating guy, that one. I can't believe he held the patents on those motorcycle parts. Must have made a killing when he sold them."

Jake's brow wrinkles as he considers those words, but he doesn't have long to think before Ryan bursts through the door.

"So sorry, man. We got delayed at the airport."

"It's about time you got here," Josh states, rising from a folding chair near the door. "Everybody's walking around calling me second runner up best man, and what are you doing messing around at the airport today anyway?" He steps toward Ryan and reaches out to touch his hair, which is standing straight up in the middle like a black mountain peak, glossy as though it's still wet.

"First off, don't touch my hair. I had to use Harley's hairspray and I'm not real sure it's gonna hold up." He smiles, standing a little taller as he straightens his suit jacket. "We might have been in Vegas, and I'll spare you the details, but let's just say that she's officially stuck with me now. And you knew I'd show up. I take my runner up best man detail very seriously."

"Nice," Jake tells Ryan, holding out his hand. "Congrats, bud."

"Thanks." Ryan takes his hand, giving it a quick shake before he glances around the room. "So, what's the story? We just waiting now?"

Josh pulls back the sleeve of his jacket and glances at his watch. "Ten more minutes. And nobody knows what's going to happen, because they didn't have a rehearsal. Maddie wasn't very happy about that, because she's taking this wedding way more seriously than Jake and Alexis are." He turns his attention to Jake. "Maybe you should have run off like Ryan and Harley."

"Are you kidding? She would have never gone for that! Too easy." Jake shakes his head at Josh. "In all seriousness, though, we wanted our friends and family around. And that includes you knuckleheads." The three guys laugh as they turn to look out the window to see people beginning to sit on the chairs outside.

"Got room for one more?"

Jake turns in the direction of the door and freezes in place at the sight of his old friend standing in the doorway. "I thought you had a game tonight."

"I had to pull a few strings, and I have to catch a plane as soon as the wedding's over."

"Looks like you're out of the wedding party." Josh offers a shrug of his shoulders to Ryan.

Jake steps up to the newcomer as they shake hands and then pull one another into a hug.

"Guys, this is Cole Parker." He stands next to Cole and nods at the others. "Josh, Ryan." Taking a step back, he focuses on Cole once more. "Man, I'm surprised to see you."

"You honestly think I would miss this? If I don't see it with my own eyes, I might not believe it happened. I did have it on good authority that you were never, ever getting married."

"I think I did say that," Jake states with a smile, shoving his hands in his pockets. "When was that, your wedding day?"

"Bachelor party," Cole answers. "But I won't tell Alexis."

"No doubt I said it to her at one time, too," Jake answers. "Good thing she rarely takes me seriously."

"Ready, sweetheart?"

Alexis turns from her spot alone on the porch to find her dad, arm extended, waiting to take her to her groom. She smiles as she watches Heather and Bailey step around the side of the house, hand in hand.

"Just a minute, Dad. One more thing."

She disappears into the house for a few seconds and then emerges through the doorway, holding a pair of red suede pumps with round toes and two-inch heels.

"Are you borrowing Heather's shoes?" he asks as she steadies herself by holding his arm, balancing on one foot while she tries to slide her foot into the shoe. It tips on its side, so she shoves the layers of her dress aside, trying again.

"Nope, my shoes." Letting out a sigh, she lifts the front of the dress again, trying to see her feet. "If I wore Heather's sky-high shoes, I'd be taller than Jake."

"Here, let me help." Her father lowers himself to the step beneath her, kneeling as he retrieves the first shoe to slide it on her foot. She touches her fingers to his shoulder to keep herself upright.

When he's finished, he rises to his feet and she shakes the layers of her dress, fluffing them out again.

"You sure you want to wear those? They don't seem like something you'd normally wear." He extends his arm again and waits for her to take it. This time, she latches onto it with a smile.

"No," she says simply as they begin down the steps. "They're not me. They're gaudy and frilly and they make me feel sort of clumsy, but I need them today."

He stops walking at the bottom of the porch steps, turning his focus to his daughter.

"Why is that, sweetie?"

She looks straight ahead, to where Heather and Bailey stand in the yard chatting.

"Is this not the most beautiful dress you've ever seen? Really?"

He laughs as he nods his head. "Of course. It's very pretty."

"It's all about the way a person sees things," she says as she smiles at her dad. "There's some red underneath, but if it wasn't there, I'd have no idea how beautiful the white really is."

A hand touches her right elbow, and she turns to see Jake standing beside her. Jake, who should be waiting for her with the preacher.

She withdraws her hand from her dad's arm and clutches her tulips in front of her. "What's wrong? You're not supposed to see me."

He laughs as he fights a smile, forcing a dimple into existence on his cheek. "I'm pretty sure we've done everything backwards from the beginning. I'm not worried about bucking tradition here. Can I talk to you for a minute?"

Alexis gives her dad an apologetic smile, and he simply gives the two of them a look of confusion before he retreats around the side of the house. She then turns her nervous attention to Jake, who actually has his tie on straight for a change.

"Your timing is a little off," she says as she removes one hand from her flowers, placing it on top of his. "We sort of have pressing plans at the moment."

"Yeah, I've already been scolded by the preacher for abandoning my post," Jake tells her, twisting his fingers through hers. "The thing is, I've been thinking about the vows. He's probably going to say for better or worse, richer or poorer, and all that."

"Most likely. Standard procedure."

"Well, it's good, but… I feel like we've done better or worse, you know? That's too easy a promise."

She adjusts her stance on those red heels, determined not to twist her ankle. "So as long as we both shall live is too simple for you? Please continue. I can't wait to hear this."

He gives a rather sideways smile as he glances in the direction of their guests. "Really, I haven't given it *that* much thought. It was more of a passing flicker of a thought." He pauses and looks down at their intertwined fingers. "The last wedding I went to, they wrote their own vows. I just don't want you to think I don't mean them if I didn't write them. Does that make sense?"

She looks down at her tulips, remembering the last time she saw that particular variety of flower. Valentine's Day, at school. The card read from Bailey. It's nearly impossible to hide her smile as she returns her gaze to his face, but she forces it into submission.

"Okay, so you specifically mentioned richer or poorer. Is this some kind of stumbling block?"

"What? No, I've been sleeping in a motel and you were going to use your great aunt's cat couch. I'm pretty sure we've crossed that hurdle."

"But what if I told you I've just come upon a sum of money?"

"You'd have to turn it in to the police, because your conscience wouldn't let you keep it."

"Touché. So I'm just going to go out on a limb here and guess that you're regretting the fact that you don't get to profess your love for me in front of an audience?"

Somehow he manages to raise his eyebrows and squint his eyes partly closed at the same time.

"I thought showing up and wearing the suit was a pretty big statement."

She laughs as she tilts her head to the side, pulling her hand from his just long enough to pretend to straighten his tie.

"Maybe we should have practiced," he continues, glancing in the direction of their guests again. "Why didn't we do that again?"

"Because it's a big enough accomplishment to get you to come to one wedding. I didn't want to risk it twice."

"This is a valid point." He leans in closer, and Alexis responds by inching back.

"Ahem…pressing business, remember?"

"Right," he agrees with a nod of his head.

She straightens her shoulders and attempts an intimidating glare. "Mr. McAuliffe, do you want to marry me or not?"

He lets his gaze sweep over her dress, finally meeting her eyes. "I thought you couldn't get any more beautiful, but here you go and surprise me. You look amazing, Alex."

She squeezes his fingers, refusing to grin. "You didn't answer me. Do you want to marry me or not?"

"You know I do." He releases her hand, taking a step back as he goes through the motions of straightening his tie again. "Now stop delaying things. This is a day of firsts for me and I'm ready to get it started."

He winks as he turns to saunter around the side of the house, and she laughs as she looks in the other direction to see her dad peeking around the opposite corner.

"You can come out now," she tells him, watching as he takes the few strides to return to her side. While she's tucking her hand into his arm, his glasses slide down on his nose just enough that he can look over them.

"I have to say, I've performed many weddings, but that's the first time I've ever seen a groom leave his place like that."

"Really?" she asks, moving in the direction of the wedding guests. "Well, you might as well get used to that kind of thing with Jake around. He's anything but predictable. In fact, if there's one thing I've learned by now, it's that there's a first time for everything." She stops in her tracks and looks up at her dad. "Do you know what I just realized?"

"Tell me," he says, urging her forward.

She begins walking again, seeing Jake standing ahead at his proper place by the preacher. "Things aren't going exactly like I pictured, but I'm pretty okay with that." She smiles as she watches the grin cross Jake's face while he bends to say something to Bailey. "Actually, I'm more than okay with things being slightly backwards, and that's a first."

# A few years later

## Wonder Lane

Annie settles onto the sofa, wedging herself between Harley and Alexis.

"You guys have to get a bigger couch if we're going to keep meeting like this," she mutters, peeking past Alexis to see Maddie squeezed near the arm of the sofa, looking completely uncomfortable.

"That better not have been a fat joke," Maddie complains, placing her hand on her abdomen. "One more month and I'm planning to lose a ton of weight."

"You'll still be carrying the weight around, just in your arms instead of your stomach. Have a name yet?"

"We're still debating." Maddie cranes her neck to look at Josh in the kitchen. "Scratch that. I'm suggesting and Josh shoots each name down like he's sitting there locked and loaded, ready to fire at will."

"Not true," Josh protests from his chair at the kitchen table. "I was perfectly fine with Natalie."

"Oh, how could I forget?" Maddie says, rolling her eyes. "He's perfectly in agreement with me about a girl's name, which would be super convenient if we were having a girl, wouldn't it?"

"Hope is down for the count," Jake states, stepping into the room from the hallway. He continues to the kitchen, where he drops an almost-empty bottle into the sink. "Or at least for a couple hours, anyway. You need anything, babe?"

Alexis shakes her head as she catches his eye, giving him a smile. She'd nearly forgotten what it was like having a newborn in the house, but Jake had been a trooper. She was able to relax way more this time around than she had when her parents helped with Bailey, and she was fairly convinced that it was because Jake didn't want to miss a minute. She couldn't fault him for that, and it made her love him even more.

"He's too sweet," Annie adds. "Harley's even crying."

"Oh, knock it off," Harley tells her, smacking her playfully in the arm as she rises from the couch and heads down the hall, brushing at her eyes.

"Give her a break." Ryan plops himself into Harley's empty spot, taking up even more of the couch than Harley had. "My sister Kelsey left on her first mission trip this morning, and Harley's not handling it well. The two of them are practically inseparable, you know."

"No fair!" Bailey folds her arms over the side of the couch next to Ryan, making an exaggerated pouty face. "Who's gonna play Scrabble with me now?"

"Uncle Ryan," he says, reaching out to tickle her.

She laughs and takes a step back. "Only if you want me to b-e-a-t you. Because I w-i-l-l."

"Trust me, I k-n-o-w." He shakes his head as she takes a seat on the arm of the couch, leaning against his shoulder. "How did you get so smart, anyway?"

"My mom. And Mrs. Randall, and first grade."

"I can't believe Mrs. Randall is still teaching," Maddie says. "I had her for first grade."

"In that case, I can't believe she's still teaching either," Annie teases. "I also can't believe I'm sitting here with all you old married people on a Friday night. I must be completely lame."

"Or you have no better offers," Harley adds as she steps back into the room, eyeing Ryan on the couch. "You seat thieves. Bailey, when are you coming over to try on my shoes again?"

"Mom?"

Alexis pulls the hem of her T-shirt down to camouflage the remnants of her baby weight as she places her feet on the coffee table in front of her. "Any time Harley wants you to try on shoes, go for it. Maybe she has other things she'd want you to do, though. Learn how to load the dishwasher? Mop the floor?"

"Yuck." Harley wrinkles her nose as she looks at Bailey. "Why would I teach you to do those things? Disgusting." She winks before sitting down on the edge of the coffee table, facing Ryan, who reaches out to take her hand.

"I could braid Ryan's hair!" Bailey squeals. Harley places her fingers against her lips to hide her laugh, but Ryan looks up at Bailey and shrugs.

"Why not? You know I like to change it up. Go for it, kiddo."

She wastes no time, gathering his hair away from his shoulders into her fist and combing through it with her fingers.

"Where is that pizza delivery?" Maddie asks. "Not that I'm starving or anything, but I *am* eating for two."

"Should be here any minute," Jake tosses over his shoulder as he rinses bottles in the sink.

"Harley's news is on!" Bailey announces, causing the room's attention to swing to the television.

Alexis uses the lull in the conversation to glance around at her friends. She couldn't have imagined finding a more unlikely group of confidants when she moved to Louisville, but now she wouldn't trade them for the world.

"I'm Summer Davis, and Denton Price is off for the evening," the woman on the screen states.

"What's up with that?" Annie asks as she glances at Harley. "Denton took a day off and didn't tell me?"

"I'm not his babysitter. Maybe he needed a day away from you."

"Ouch." Annie rises from the couch and pokes her finger in Harley's side. "You can have your seat back, Benedict Arnold. Watch out for her, Alexis. She's evil."

Harley winks at Alexis as she settles into Annie's vacant spot, pressing her side against Ryan. Alexis simply gives her a mischievous smile.

"Worn out yet?" Annie asks Jake as she takes a glass from the cupboard.

His natural reaction is to look in the direction of Alexis, keeping his ever-watchful eye on her from his vantage point in the kitchen. "No. Of course it's tiring for both of us, but so worth it. I kick myself every day for missing this with Bailey."

She presses the glass against the refrigerator to fill it with filtered water, and then stands beside him, placing her hand on his forearm. "Good job, Dad."

"Thanks," he mutters, clearing his throat. He lowers himself in a chair next to Josh and peeks over his arm at his phone. "Baby names? Give me the short list, maybe I can help."

"That's Maddie's thing, really," he states, darkening the phone screen.

"If it was Maddie's thing, you wouldn't be staring at names on your phone."

Josh sighs and pulls his glasses away from his face, placing them on the table. "The thing is, I'd like to name him after one of the guys I enlisted with, to honor them. One of the ones who didn't come home. I can't seem to agree on anything else."

"That seems like an awesome thing to do." Jake crosses his arms against the table. "What are their names?"

"Terence and Andrew. That's my problem. How do I choose? It seems wrong to leave one of them out."

"You could have two boys," Jake suggests.

Josh grins and glances at Maddie. "Not sure how Mad would feel about that, and since there's no guarantee that they *would* be boys, that's a risky game to play."

"Andrew Terence Mason. Doesn't sound so bad, does it?" Jake smiles as a knock sounds on the door.

"Pizza!" Instead of rising from the table, Jake and Josh turn their attention to Annie standing behind them.

"Seriously? You two lazy boys expect me to answer the door?" She sets her glass on the counter and begins shaking her head, swinging her glossy black hair over her shoulder. "I'm not footing the bill for the pizza." She jerks the door open and takes a step back when the guy standing behind the door isn't wearing the standard delivery uniform.

"Hey." He steps inside and places a stack of pizza boxes on the table, then turns to brush off his shirt before facing Annie again. "I brought pizza."

"Denton, what are you doing here? You took the day off to deliver pizza?"

He regards her with a hint of a smile on his face, but manages to remain fairly stoic as he rearranges the boxes. "I had other business today, that's all."

"And somehow the rest of these yahoos knew to have you bring them pizza?" She turns her attention to the living room and places her hands on the waistband of her leopard-print skinny jeans. "Harley? Why do I feel like you're behind this?"

"As though I have any control over what Denton does or doesn't do. But I did know he was going to be off work today. We all did."

"Even Alexis?" Annie readjusts herself, crossing her arms over her abdomen. "That girl can't lie."

"Technically, you didn't ask me," Alexis states, slowly pushing herself up from the couch. She makes her way into the kitchen, standing behind Jake and placing her hand on his shoulder. He reaches up and wraps his hand over hers, but Annie stops focusing on them and instead looks at Denton.

He doesn't make a move to explain, but allows her eyes to graze over him. They move across his shoulders and his fitted white T-shirt, and then to his slightly disheveled sandy blond hair, and finally to his green eyes. When their eyes meet, he offers one of his perfect newsman smiles.

"What are you up to, Denton Price?"

"Somewhere near five-eleven, last I checked."

"Hilarious." She steps closer, gathering his shirt in her fists near his waist. "Spill the beans."

He leans down to press a quick kiss to her lips before answering. "Just had a little real estate transaction to take care of, that's all."

"Real estate?"

"Yeah, I bought a house."

"What? Where?"

"Suburbs, nice neighborhood." He turns to take a glass from Alexis, thanking her before filling it with water.

"Are you kidding me? I didn't even know you wanted to move to the suburbs."

He shrugs and leans against the refrigerator. "Couldn't beat the neighbors." He gets a mischievous glint to his eyes as he looks down at Annie. "I'm sure you've seen the house. Weeping willow trees in the yard, wooden bench on the porch, flowers on top of the mailbox."

"That house is on Wonder Lane," Annie answers, twisting her mouth to the side. "Belongs to the Martins."

"Not anymore. It belongs to me, and maybe someday my wife." He quickly pulls his drink out of the way as she wraps her arms around him.

"You're not allowed to propose to me on television," she tells him, causing him to laugh.

"Thank you for telling me that…again. Point taken, I assure you."

Harley rises from the couch and grabs Maddie's hand, pulling her up as well. They share a smile as they walk into the kitchen, because everyone but Annie knows that Denton has a ring in his pocket. That he's planning to propose tonight.

Maddie grabs a plate for her pizza, but pauses to look at Annie and Denton, embracing one another by the refrigerator. Glancing at Harley, she holds up her right hand, extending her pinky.

"To the girls of Wonder Lane," she whispers.

Harley nods as she smiles, glancing from Maddie to Alexis. "The girls of Wonder Lane," she agrees, linking her pinky with Maddie's.

Alexis steps up to them, wrapping an arm around each of their shoulders. Before she has a chance to say anything, Bailey is in the midst of them, placing her tiny hand atop the other girls' pinky fingers. "If you're gonna have a secret club, you need a handshake. You learn that pretty much the start of first grade, at recess."

"Is that so?" Harley asks, removing her hand from the pile. "Show me what you have in mind."

"Hmm..." Bailey squints her eyes and wrinkles her nose as though she's giving it intense thought, and then she broadens her stance to give herself more stability. "Got it. Snap, clap, snap, fist bump, wiggle!"

"Wiggle?" Maddie asks, placing her palm flat against the top of her baby bump.

"Maybe we'll skip the wiggle," Alexis answers with a chuckle, playfully sweeping the end of Bailey's braid along the side of her cheek. Bailey places her hands on either side of Maddie's abdomen, waiting for the baby to kick.

"He'll do the wiggling," Maddie mutters to Alexis, giving her a self-deprecating smile. Alexis simply shrugs as she stares at the little group in her house. Definitely not the life she pictured when she left Tennessee. The journey that started all wrong had become so much more than she hoped or imagined.

Her mind drifts back to that first night, alone in her new home with Bailey, the two of them resting against the mattress on the floor. She can almost picture Bailey asking her to read, cuddling Hoppy against her chest as Alexis detailed the exploits of Alice while she was in Wonderland. Bailey cried for home, and she couldn't shake the silent fear that she was doing the wrong thing after all. That maybe she had followed the white rabbit a little too far herself.

She even remembers what she was reading that night, the part where the caterpillar questions Alice with all the nonsense.

The way he leaves her a little confused about whether she's right or wrong. She felt a little that way herself, that first night.

It gives her a surge of happiness to realize she doesn't feel that way anymore. She knows precisely who she is, and where she belongs.

Alexis McAuliffe.

Resident of Wonder Lane.

Exactly where she's meant to be.

# About the Author

Christina Coryell is the Amazon bestselling author of The Camdyn Series and the Girls of Wonder Lane series. A resident of small-town southwest Missouri, where she lives with her husband and two children, she does most of her writing in unorthodox places and with lots of noise in the background. She hasn't ever chased a white rabbit down a hole, but strangely enough the rabbit is her favorite animal. You know, fuzzy tail and what not. She also has pretty stellar parents, and two sisters who luckily have never thought her boring. (Or have they?)

She loves to hear from her readers and welcomes interaction on Facebook, Twitter, and by email at her website, www.christinacoryell.com.

Independent authors rely on your support. If you enjoyed Curiouser, please consider telling a friend and writing a review.

# A Few Words

When a new book package arrives on my doorstep, my kids always pop it open to the exact same page. This one. Wanting to know what I said about them. My husband does the same thing, although he tries to be incognito. It's true, just like it was last time: I love all three of you.

To my parents, and my sisters, and the early readers who help me iron out the story, thank you for everything you do. To my street team — you all are awesome. Thank you so much for your support. And to Linda, for fielding odd questions and always being honest and mildly sarcastic. I appreciate you more than you know.

Special thanks to Kassi Hillhouse, who photographed all the models for Wonder Lane, and a huge thank you to Mallary for giving Alexis a face. It was a true pleasure working with you both.

Sometimes I have a pretty solid idea in my head of how a scene is going to go, and something completely unexpected pops up. Something that causes me to stop in my tracks and wonder if there's more to the story than even I know. I'm so very grateful and humbled by those moments, and I thank God for them.

During this series, the concept of Christians hurting Christians popped up more than once. Can I be honest with you? The people who have loved me the most in this world are Christians. The people who have hurt me the most in this world are Christians, too.

I could provide you with a laundry list of bullet-pointed examples, but the fact is they don't matter. What matters is this: I have plenty of ugly moments. I'm not talking about when I wake up with a head cold and forget to brush my hair. I'm talking temper gets the better of me, my pride gets hurt, "woe is me" ugly moments. Moments when I'm not the person God called me to be. Moments when I'm fallen and human and broken.

Guys, owning the ugly is one hundred percent terrifying. But without the ugly, we can't showcase the beauty of grace. If you've read my books, you already know a whole lot about my ugly. Thank you for taking this journey with me, and I hope we can fully embrace the beauty together.

*Christina Coryell*

# Available Now
## Girls of Wonder Lane

### Book 1
#### Simply Mad
Madeline Heard wants what many girls want—a little respect, a boost in her career, and to find a guy to share happily ever after. Can she find a way to have everything she wants, or should she be careful what she wishes for?

### Book 2
#### Crowned
Louisville's hottest reporter appears to have it all—a perfect job, great car, beautiful house, and designer clothes. She's poised to set herself up as the woman at the top, until a gruff old biker, a teenage girl, and the absolute wrong guy threaten to derail her plans.

### Book 3
#### Curiouser
Alexis has spent the past few years living someone else's life, but she's finally ready to make a fresh start. Outrunning her past might prove difficult, however, when Jake McAuliffe decides to follow her out of town.

# And Don't Miss The Camdyn Series

Available Now:


A Reason to Run
A Reason to Be Alone
A Reason to Forget
For No Reason
Unwrapped


Camdyn Taylor is a bestselling author hiding a bit of a secret—her identity. The victim of viral video proposal infamy, she heads out of town in the name of book research seeking a little anonymity. She never expects that a wrong turn could wind up not only changing her perspective, but possibly her entire life.

Equal parts romance, chick-lit, and women's fiction with a little history thrown in for good measure.

Printed in Great Britain
by Amazon

58672652R00192